D1603787

DEVIANT OR DIVINE

HUNTER KAY

NEW OLYMPUS BOOK 1

DEVIANT OR DIVINE

NEW OLYMPUS BOOK 1

HUNTER KAY

 NAZAR PUBLISHING CO.

Nazar Publishing Co.

Deviant or Divine, New Olympus Book 1

This book is a work of fiction. All characters, locations, events, names, and incidents are products of author's imagination. Any resemblance to names, places, events, persons— living or dead— is entirely coincidental.

ISBN: 978-1-7379896-0-8

Deviant or Divine

Editing by Madeleine Thornburg
Cover Design by Roya Hejazi

to my younger self, who strung myths together in her head
like constellations

Table of Contents

The push and pull of fate is like the wave that carves the coast.

SUMMER

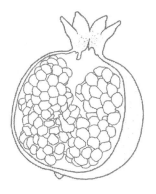

LEILA

Leila grasped at her bedding, her eyes flying open when her flingers twisted blades of grass instead of cotton sheets. All she could see was endless blue--it hurt to look at, it was so bright. The more she blinked, the less she could picture her bedroom.

She put a hand over her eyes to block out the sun's rays. A breeze blew by and tickled her stomach and her hand flew from her face to the bare skin of her midriff.

Frowning, she realized two things simultaneously: the first was that she didn't have a stitch of clothing on her. The second was that she didn't remember anything before waking up.

These realizations, she knew, should terrify her. She waited a few seconds for the fear and panic to come but they didn't.

She didn't feel scared. Confused? *Very*.

Leila sat up and covered herself as best as she could with her arms and legs folded around her. Her long, dark hair curled down her back and the sides of her arms. She raked the long locks out of her face.

Why am I here? Why aren't I at home, in my bed? She thought. Then, *where* is *home?*

Home for Leila felt like a blank space in her mind. She didn't even feel homesickness but then she didn't think she could feel homesick for something she didn't know she had.

Leila felt the breeze whisper down her body, goosebumps erupting down the back of her arms and legs. Taking a look around, she noticed she was in a clearing full of white flowers and deep green grass surrounded on all sides by towering pine trees. Her eyes traced over the jagged silhouettes the tall trees cut out of the sky, the names of each tree bubbling to her lips.

"*Pseudotsuga menziesii*—Douglas Fir. *Pinus ponderosa*—Ponderosa Pine. *Cedrus*—Cedar." Leila's voice was so quiet, she barely heard herself speak.

She had never been somewhere so beautiful, so...*peaceful*. Well, she couldn't remember but she was pretty sure. The white flowers were bell shaped and looked like sugar dusting the grass. She gingerly reached out to feel the petals.

"*Convallaria Majalis*," she murmured. *Lily of the Valley*. How she knew the flower's name, she wasn't sure. Maybe she was a gardener? Or worked in a flower shop? Maybe she was well read?

Maybe I'm a botanist, and I hit my head while collecting samples...while naked.

All of Leila's possible lives bounced around in her head but she couldn't see herself as living any of them. She was an open-ended question she couldn't begin to fathom how to ask.

A warm breeze, smelling sweet like pomegranate, caressed her face and she turned her head to one side of the meadow where she spotted a break in the dense tree line.

There might be a path to get me out of here, she thought. Then she frowned. *And lead me to where?*

But she figured she couldn't stay in the clearing much longer, especially without clothes. She stood, her long dark hair brushed her arms as it swished behind her with each step she took.

As she reached the edge of the clearing she looked over her shoulder. She didn't want to leave without taking one of the delicate, bell-shaped flowers with her. Crouching, she grabbed onto one of the stalks. A warm, tingling energy bloomed through her hand. This didn't startle her either, in fact the warm energy was almost familiar, like a memory .

The breeze picked up and she heard, no, *felt* a woman's voice.

Of course it feels right, Leila-joon. The voice was soothing, though she couldn't place where it was coming from. It was like she could hear it in the wind and in her head all at once.

Another question to add to the list: *Who is the lady in my head?*

Holding the flowers in her hands she could feel the energy growing stronger. It stretched from her fingertips to her chest like a live wire. She didn't have any pockets so as she walked she gathered some of her hair and tried to tuck the flowers in as best as she could behind her ear. The energy traveled from her hands to the lilies, she felt each part of the flower from the stem to the leaves to each petal— and though she couldn't see them, she could feel the flowers growing, threading their way through her hair. Her hands shook as she put them back by her sides—from the mysterious energy or from the knowledge she grew a flower crown, she couldn't tell.

One thing she was sure of—she didn't have that ability before today.

The forest floor felt soft under her feet. The earth was cool but not damp, and the canopy of trees provided relief from the bright sun. It was quiet except for the occasional light rustle of wind and birdsong. The path went on for a couple of minutes before the trees thinned out and she came upon a road. The forest continued on the other side of the asphalt, and the road curved away out of sight on both sides.

Leila gave a soft groan. *Now what?*

Which way was she supposed to go? The sun was blocked by the rise of evergreens and the breeze much cooler than in the clearing. She gave an involuntary shiver and was reminded she was naked out in the open.

Naked, no memory, and most likely not from around here— she was a perfect victim for any serial killers that happened to be driving around. Not to mention the dip of the sun behind the trees meant night was fast approaching. She crossed her arms. Now was the time to panic.

Leila considered turning around and heading back to the clearing—the only place she knew she was safe—when a motion down the road startled her. She froze as a white car came around the curve of the road and stopped in front of her.

The driver turned off the car, the low hum of the electric car silenced. The driver's door opened and a beautiful woman got out, her heels clicking on the asphalt as she came around the car to Leila. The woman wore a white, flowing pantsuit, the bodice's gold embroidery made to look like wheat stalks. The gold she wore matched her wavy, blonde hair.

The woman stopped, her hand raising up to slide off the large tortoise shell glasses from her face, revealing gold eyes. They caught on Leila, taking in every detail of her. She only paused a moment before she took the remaining strides to Leila and pulled her into a tight embrace. Leila only briefly registered the fact this strange woman was holding her as she was still fully naked before the woman pulled back to look at her. She smelled like freshly cut grass and something wild, something earthier.

"I'm so glad you're here. I didn't actually think..." She spoke with a posh British accent, trailing off to wipe a manicured finger gently below her eyes. After a breath to compose herself, she gave Leila a brilliant smile. "You must be freezing! I have just the thing."

Leila's skin cooled quickly in the spots where her hands were. She went back to the car and grabbed a bundle of white, neatly folded clothes in her arms and came back and handed them to Leila.

"There, honey, get dressed and then we can get going. I've never done a pickup before but they were accurate. Of course they would be, but still, I'm impressed. Down to the time and mile marker and everything," she said over her shoulder as she turned away for Leila to change. Leila wasn't sure why the woman turned away from her to give her privacy to change when she'd already seen everything, but she still felt grateful.

After Leila put her underwear on, she was careful lowering the delicate dress over her head, so as not to ruin the arrangement of flowers in her hair.

"I—I'm sorry, I can't seem to remember, but who are you?" There was a moment where Leila forgot she didn't have a memory—she forgot she forgot, which was getting too confusing.

The dress she wore was a white chiffon shift with bell sleeves that hit at her mid thigh. When she had finished buckling in the straps of her platform sandals, she stood to find the woman had turned around and was watching Leila with a look of quiet awe on her face. The woman absentmindedly stroked the chunky gold bangles at her wrists.

She straightened the jacket hanging off her shoulders and cleared her throat. "Sorry, I know this must all be confusing to you, but it will all make sense soon...more or less. My name is Camille, I'm your...mother."

My mother? Leila thought.

Camille couldn't be older than thirty *at most*, and Leila was...seventeen. She knew that, at least. Plus, the fact Camille had light blonde hair and cream colored skin, and Leila's hair was the darkest brown and her skin was olive and tan. Leila didn't see a resemblance even recognized Camille's face. Leila must have looked as shocked as she felt because Camille let out a laugh.

"I'm not really, only technically—sorry, I'm rubbish at explaining all of this." Camille took a deep breath before continuing. "I'm the mortal Vessel of Demeter, the Goddess of Harvest, Agriculture, and a myriad of other things.And you...what is your mortal name, honey?"

"Leila," she breathed. *Mortal name? Vessel? Goddess?* Camille's answers only stirred up more questions for Leila, and she was starting to feel like the world she woke up in wasn't one she knew anything about.

"Leila," Camille said her name slowly, like she was testing out the flavor of it. "Leila, you are the Vessel for Persephone, the Goddess of Spring and Fertility. And the daughter of Demeter. Your Goddess is my Goddess's daughter—so by that account, you're my daughter!"

Leila-joon. The same woman's voice from earlier laughed through the trees around her and the leaves swirled in little spirals of wind. Camille didn't seem to notice.

Persephone, Leila thought, calling out to the voice she'd heard. It had to be Persephone. The warm feeling in Leila's chest returned along with a momentary pounding in her ears, out of sync with her own erratic heartbeat.

Camille reached for Leila's hand. "I know it's confusing, but we can't be late. I promise everything will make sense soon, *Leila*."

Camille squeezed Leila's hand reassuringly. She let go and started to walk around the car.

"Where are we going?" Leila asked.

"We're going to the grand temple of Zeus, in New Olympus."

"New Olympus?" The name was too familiar, like the woman in her head. Why did she feel like she'd been there but only in a dream?

Camille opened the driver door to her car and looked back to Leila, small smile spread on her lips like she was sharing a secret with her, one she'd been waiting to share for a long time.

"New Olympus: the home of the Gods," Camille said before getting in the car.

Leila took one look back over her shoulder at the path between the trees, the panic she felt dissolving into excitement. Before she got into the car, she saw herself in the passenger window—the reflection was dark and her features mostly obscured, except the outline of her hair and the halo of white buds that crowned her head. She opened the car door and got in.

To New Olympus.

BLAKE

Blake sat on the steps of Zeus' temple, his back to the setting sun.

He was near one of the white marble columns, thicker than tree trunks and taller than the old evergreens blanketing the mountains around the city. He sat still enough that he could have been mistaken for one of the statues lining the perimeter of the grand temple. Even if he positioned himself down the steps in the growing crowd of Vessels, satyrs, dryads, and naiads mingling, he knew he wouldn't be welcome. He wasn't exactly a mingler, either.

He could just imagine the unease rolling off the other Vessels as they regarded him, trying to figure out what Blake would do.

I'm not like that—like him, Blake argued.

He sat, his head resting on his clasped hands portraying a look of false serenity, his dark hair falling into his forehead. Like he was praying and not nursing a wicked hangover. Blake had mastered this stillness from years of toeing the line between outcast and loner. He figured it was easier for everyone if the young Vessel of Hades wasn't that visible —it wasn't fun to be constantly reminded of one's mortality. He learned to absorb noise and release nothing, even in the last couple of months when his circle of friends finally started to grow.

He always felt like a boulder in a room of earthquakes. A room of noise and excitement echoed and multiplied until it was unbearable —until he cracked.

Kat understood this a bit—and drinking always helped ease that destructive teetering he felt in big groups. Without a drink in his hand he took what precautions he could—isolation and a dark pair of sunglasses would get him through today's Induction. Blake's permanent purple under eyes the only color staining his pale skin.

He was always losing his footing.

Not anymore, he promised himself.

Blake could hear Danny's quick footsteps before he sat down. Danny wasn't exactly what he would call *subtle*, his long limbs and curly russet hair making him stick out. Where Blake wasn't generous with his movement, Danny was teetering with energy; his gawky body vibrating with the need to stay in motion.

"Hey!" Danny said, grinning. Unlike Blake, Danny was quick to smile in all situations. "Have you heard who they think is coming? I saw that Ares kid with the shaved head taking bets. I didn't—obviously—but my money's on another Zeus. If the crowd is anything to go by, it has to be either Zeus or even Apollo. They don't announce open attendance for just anybody."

Danny had a way of steamrolling through a conversation without noticing he was doing it. It suited Blake fine because it meant he didn't have to contribute often. Even now, one of the few times he'd seen his friend this summer, he couldn't dampen Danny's energy. Blake's head and jaw ached, and talking was an effort.

"I have no idea." *And I don't care.*

But he had to admit Danny was right. Usually only the mayor and the most powerful Vessels get to witness an Induction and welcome a new arrival to New Olympus. Which, unfortunately for Blake, meant him. As the Vessel of Hades, god of the Underworld, he had a standing invitation to every important ritual in New Olympus—whether he or anyone else wanted him to attend.

And since he had been to every Induction since he was Inducted himself at age four, he knew which Vessels were represented. Almost everyone, if he remembered correctly.

Blake's stomach did a queasy flip-flop.

Almost. He tried to push the thought out of his mind.

"You're probably right," Blake said. "Not that we need another Zeus running around."

"True. I just hope the Gift is a good one," Danny continued, "Elliot's was the worst, remember? I smelled like fish for a week."

Every Vessel was given a 'Gift' at their Induction: a show of power. Their classmate was a Vessel of Poseidon— the god had to have a twisted sense of humor to flood the temple with seawater and seaweed. Blake could remember the fishy reek it left in his clothes through multiple washes. He had to throw out his favorite hoodie.

"That was bad," Blake said, lifting his head. He finally swept his gaze across the temple, taking in the crowd.

He could spot Harvey in the middle like he was already mayor, all smiles firm handshakes. The sleet colored suit he wore was fitted to his tall frame, making him seem older than seventeen, and his silver lightning bolt cufflinks flashed against the dark brown skin of his hands. Their elections were more ceremonial—no one cared to go against a Vessel of Zeus for mayor, but Harvey had a sharp smile on his face like he was campaigning anyway.

Even though Harvey was in the thick of the crowd talking to some older Vessels, Harvey's friends weren't too far away. Blake spotted Bianca's periwinkle curls easily. She was near the middle of the crowd as she laughed at something her best friend Min-Seo said. Min-Seo tilted her head up to Bianca, and if anyone didn't know her they would think she was angry, her mouth set and her eyebrows furrowed. But her Bianca had to cover her face with her hand in order to control her laughter. She even clapped a hand onto Mason's shoulder, his golden glow rising off his skin as he too laughed at whatever Min-Seo said to them.

They turned their heads as the final member of their group, Elliot, called to them. He pushed his way through the crowd, dark spots forming on his cream sweater where his wet hair curled onto the fabric on his shoulders.

Years of being stuck in class with this group gave Blake an odd feeling when he watched them. He wasn't their friend but he knew them well. He guessed it was like watching a character on a television show grow up. Blake peeked at Danny from the corner of his eye and saw how he tried to look like he was scanning the room too but his eyes kept catching on Bianca. Blake looked away to hide his smirk.

I guess childhood crushes don't die down so easily.

Blake's gaze caught on Alicia in the corner smoking by a pillar, a blush blooming up his cheeks. He didn't know much about women's clothes but he guessed the gauzy pink ostrich feather gown she was wearing wasn't exactly day wear. He absentmindedly wondered where her Hephaestus was, or her Ares for that matter.

Farther away, Martin surveyed the crowd like a general surveyed a battleground. Their eyes locked for a second before the mayor looked away. Blake could have sworn the sides of Martin's mouth quirked up a hair.

It reminded Blake of the part he had to play, the ever present shadow they lived in. Not so much the shadow of the gods they served—but the myth of the gods themselves. Being in such a large gathering of Vessels felt like echoes of all of the past Vessels were there as well, taking up the precious air in the temple and leaving Blake to choke.

In other words, his hangover had not gone away.

"It's nearly sunset," Danny said without looking at the sun behind him. He was hyperaware of time, sometimes to the second, even though he didn't wear a watch. Blake could see the burnt orange tint the light cast through the gaps in the columns. The new Vessel should be here any moment.

Danny drummed his hands on his thighs. He coughed. "So, do you think there's going to be a party at Prep Housing? You know we could just check it out, for like five seconds, it's probably not our scene anyway but—"

Danny's voice died down, or rather, Blake stopped being able to hear him as his entire being zeroed in on the far side of the temple. The crowd silenced and parted for the figure walking to the middle of marble space. Blake could only see the top of her head—could barely register the thick dark curls crowned in sugar-white flowers—because he felt like he was sinking underwater, everything felt cold and numb and alive all at the same time.

Every hair on his body raised, and he knew a god's presence had joined the Vessels: the Induction was beginning. The crowd felt it as well, looking around as the air became heavier. Blake didn't bother looking around—gods didn't take corporeal forms at Inductions. If Blake was the praying type, he would have prayed to Hades in the moment that his guess was wrong, that the girl in the center of the temple *wasn't* the Vessel for—

Any other god. Please, Blake pleaded. He wasn't directing his thoughts to Hades now but *any* god who would listen. *Fates defy me, please!*

Time slowed down, or maybe everything was normal and it was his pulse jackhammering so fast time couldn't keep up. He was surprised the foundation didn't shake as his heart tried to beat its way out of his chest.

Everyone was kneeling, their arms outstretched to the new Vessel. She had turned around, confusion written on her face. A distant part of Blake's brain notice she looked like she was the same age as Blake.

His mouth was dry and his breath uneven. He felt like he was unraveling.

Get a grip! He clenched his hands into fists until he was sure he broke skin.

He could barely feel Danny's hand clasping his shoulder and heard him whispering, asking what was wrong. Blake couldn't answer—he didn't trust his words. No one but Danny noticed Blake's distress.

Martin was almost done with the ceremonial greeting, his voice booming out, "—and in our fortune, we have found a new Vessel. One who will uphold the wills of the gods, and grant them the power they deserve. Your fate has been carved into Mount Olympus itself."

He smiled, and Blake gritted his teeth like he was preparing for impact. This was it. This could be the moment that changed everything. Blake willed himself not to lose his footing, like he promised.

"Leila, you are to receive your gift as the new Vessel of Persephone. *Power to the gods.*" Gasps echoed through the atrium like a flock of birds taking flight and then cries of shock as a rumbling sound erupted through the temple.

The ground and the columns shook and the marble tiles cracked around them as thorny vines broke from the floor and snaked their way up the columns. The vines were as thick as ropes with thorns like shark fins. As the vines made their way up, buds grew and bloomed into ruby roses. The rumbling continued and a mountain of dirt burst through the floor. A sapling broke through the dirt and quickly grew up into a full sized tree. Vessels struggled to get out of the way to avoid the ever-growing roots snaking across the floor. It was like watching a time lapse of the life of a tree. The vines had stopped growing and the heady scent of nectar hung in the air.

Leaves sprouted from the reaching branches and a sea of red flowers bloomed its way around the tree. Then just as quickly, the flowers swelled and darkened into fruit. The tree shuddered the scent of flowers was replaced by the sweet and tart scent of pomegranates.

Pomegranates. Of fucking course.

The crowd fell silent once again and Blake swore he could hear *Hades'* laughter all the way from the Underworld. The last of the sunset was fading and an orange panel of light fell on the girl. Her eyes were wide and the light made her brown eyes practically molten. The white bell flowers tangled in her wild hair like a crown. She was the only person still standing in the entire space. The Gift was given, but the crowd knew what the pomegranate tree meant: the reminder the myth was never too far away. Her arm extended up to the lowest branch, her fingers reaching for one of the ripe red pomegranates.

Blake couldn't take it. The smell of the fruit turned his stomach. He stood up suddenly and made his way out of the temple, down the steps leading to the winding road down the mountain. He knew he wouldn't be missed and he refused to let the other Vessels see his face. They'd make their assumptions about how he reacted, spinning a look into a thousand rumors. He pounded down the steps as applause and cheering sounded from behind him.

He didn't want to be there, he didn't want to see how it ended, how the floor was crumbling underneath him despite his best efforts. He felt it again, the teetering feeling like he was walking on a tightrope with no safety net. Gripping the keys to his car tightly, he leaned into the feeling, ducking his head as the last of the sunlight winked out behind the trees.

He headed into the night.

I don't have to keep finding my footing if I'm in free fall.

ALICIA

Alicia watched Camille as she guided Leila down the steps. Her best friend was beaming, proud as any mother for their daughter as people came to them and gave them different blessings. It was interesting to see all the fanfare a Vessel of Persephone got—she didn't even get this crowd and she was the Vessel of *Aphrodite*, for goddess' sake —but then again, she couldn't remember a time when Persephone has ever been represented in New Olympus. She admitted there was *some* merit to the shock and awe.

Especially that tree, she smiled. *Subtle.*

Vessels representing abstract concepts like dreams or love, had some flexibility in how the Gift manifested itself during their Inductions. Alicia recalled the cool kiss the silk ribbons left on her skin from Aphrodite's Gift.

She took a drag of her cigarette and watched Leila and Camille get in Camille's car. Camille's eyes were fixed on Leila like she was a vase near tipping. Her smile was genuine, a contrast to her usual near-robotic poise. Alicia approved. Cami only ever mentioned feeling the ache of sadness of missing her mythic daughter only a handful of times, but Alicia never knew how deep that ache went. Alicia could talk to her another day, she figured Cami must be overwhelmed.

Her driver pulled up and got out, opening Alicia's door for her. She crushed her cigarette under her baby pink heel. She wanted to let herself smoke in her car but she didn't want the smell settling in her long, red hair. Plus, she learned the hard way that ostrich feathers were *very* flammable.

Her driver closed the car door behind her. The sounds of the crowd muffled, leaving her to her thoughts in the sleek, cool interior. She leaned back on the soft leather and closed her eyes. It wouldn't take long to get to her apartment since she lived so close to the mountain. The sweat cooled on Alicia's forehead, and she let out a long sigh. An Induction during the dog days of summer wasn't something she had looked forward to going to with her fair complexion.

Alicia let her thoughts drift in the dim backseat of the car. The thorns, the vines, the roses, the tree. She tried to not notice the absence of a certain Vessel in the crowd. Alicia had become proficient at being able to see if *he* was there. Every event she accepted an invite to received a last minute decline from him, leaving a space in the crowd making up his shape. Not that she'd seen him in a year and knew what he looked like presently—her Hephaestus.

Her Arnie.

He wasn't mine, never mine. I was only his, she reminded herself. *And even then, not even his.*

Her gut twisted, and she felt the familiar sensation of heaviness that left her mouth dry whenever her thoughts circled back to him. Her eyebrows creased and she focused back on the Induction and the roses blooming up the marble, trying not to count the minutes until she would be back in her apartment with her hands around a drink.

Her body felt it first.

The hum of the AC faded as she felt a sudden unfurling in her core pull an invisible line taut through her middle, making her open her eyes in shock. She gasped. The feeling, her powers. She didn't notice before in the crowd or in the haze of cigarette smoke. It was overpowered by noise and the magic of the Induction. Her powers were...not what they used to be. If any of the other Vessels knew how weakened her powers were—she couldn't stand the pity. Her powers weren't extinguished, exactly.

But they were close.

She didn't need anyone knowing how weak she was, how she felt like she was trying to light a candle in the middle of the ocean. How she was running out of air.

Her body burned with a feeling she thought was lost. Power flared in her core like her own personal sun, extending its warmth through her limbs. Aphrodite's magic was regarded as easy to understand; everyone could picture little arrows flying through the air shot by cute, chubby babies. The other Vessels were wary of how love could be conjured with the pinch of an arrowhead. What they didn't know was what they couldn't see. Alicia and her sister Vessels didn't just give out love, they could *sense* it.

And this sense...this sense was filling Alicia. Before, she had only used this extrasensory gift when she was bored—like skipping through channels on the tv, she would pluck at the love from the Vessels around her. She grabbed onto this feeling and didn't let go. She gulped down air, trying to make space in between her lungs where she hadn't felt anything in such a long time.

As the feeling passed through her, she let her eyes flutter closed.

This was not lust or infatuation or any of the other fleeting flavors she had tasted many times before. This was something *older.* Alicia couldn't understand what it was but she knew it was important. She yanked her delicate, jewel-encrusted clutch apart to get to her cell phone. Her hands shook in the aftermath of using her powers—well, her powers used *her,* but she wasn't complaining.

With shaking fingers, she opened her phone and had almost all of the numbers dialed until she realized whose number it was. Old habits die hard, even her embarrassing need to reach for Arnie to steady her. The passing skyscrapers of downtown New Olympus became a blur of grey.

LEILA

Leila rested her head on the glass of the car window. Other Vessels had rushed to her after the Induction, introducing themselves and giving blessings. They talked at her and all she could do was smile.

Leila's cheeks hurt.

She stared out the window at the passing city landscape. The night had fallen slowly, even for late August, and now the city lights illuminated their drive.

She squeezed her hands around the softball-sized pomegranate in her lap. Her mind caught on the moment she plucked the fruit from the tree that had erupted from the floor of the temple like a snag in a sweater. She didn't know why she instinctively reached up for the fruit, why or even kept it with her. She didn't know if she even liked pomegranates.

"Is the floor ruined? At the temple?" she asked to break the silence. It was the easiest question to ask, closest to sane.

Did I really see people with horns growing out of their heads? Some of them had tree bark for skin or fins for hands!

Camille's gold bangles glinted in the dark car. She glanced over to Leila with a warm smile.

"Oh, no, don't worry, the magic of the temple will undo any damage done to it. Though I do hope they go with a different pattern on the floor this time. Could do with some updating." She laughed. "Martin —the mayor—his Induction blew the roof off the temple. Literally."

Leila didn't respond, but knowing she wasn't the only one to inflict property damage at their Induction made her feel fractionally better.

They drove past the city buildings, the glass skyscrapers reached into the night and the bright restaurants and shops brimmed with people. Camille gave a commentary about various businesses, people, and her own stories of growing up in New Olympus. Leila noticed Camille didn't need prompting, so she just listened and looked out the window. It was comforting to sit and see a magical city.

She didn't understand a lot about the city she woke up in, but she could understand its beauty. The large art galleries on every corner, white and expansive like a fresh canvas; the efficient glass and black marble skyscrapers, sturdy enough to hold up the sky; the cozy coffee shops, and the lavish boutiques, each begging you to lose an afternoon in. And from what she could see, there were restaurants and food trucks from every part of the world. Camille promised they would eat soon, and as she talked about her favorite Persian restaurant, Leila's stomach growled.

Leila and Camille locked eyes and shared a surprised laugh.

"I know this is a whirlwind of a day," Camille said. "I have dinner waiting."

The city skyline soon faded to a suburban landscape. There was a river hugging the outskirts of the city. Leila craned her neck when they went over a bridge separating the city and suburbia. The river was black in the night but she felt like she could see the currents glittering and rushing past their car in ribbons of onyx.

"The river Styx," Camille clarified. "The original river is the boundary between here and the Underworld. This one isn't the same—I took a yacht down it at the summer solstice, so much fun."

Leila let the conversation fade. She didn't exactly know where she stood with Camille, not that she knew where Camille stood with her either. Camille was chatty and friendly—more older sister than mother. Leila wasn't that bubbly of a person, so she had just let Camille do all the talking at the temple. She was also the person Leila knew the best in her new life. Leila wondered if there was something Camille wanted out of her, or if she was doing this out of a favor to this Myth everyone talked about.

She couldn't help herself from staring at each house, as they felt like they were plucked from different neighborhoods in space and time. The only things they had in common were they were all large, breathtaking, and expensive looking.

"A lot of Vessels of the same god grow up together in the same house. As you can see, some Vessels keep the original architecture," Camille pointed to a gloomy Victorian bulging with five or six chimneys and towers, "or they can start fresh."

"Is that where we're going? Persephone's—er, my house?" Leila asked.

Camille didn't answer right away. "Well, no. You see...you're the first Vessel of Persephone in a long time. There wasn't time to prepare anything before your Induction. We may have god-like powers, but we have our limits."

Camille let go of the steering wheel with one hand and squeezed Leila's. Her hand felt like summer sunshine. Leila squeezed back and gave Camille a smile, all the while wondering why there hadn't been a Vessel of Persephone.

And how long, exactly, is a "long time"?

"So, where am I going to live?" Leila asked after a minute.

Camille didn't respond; instead, she swung the wheel abruptly to the right, moving the car to the side of the road.

She looked past Leila and pointed. "Here."

Gold and glass and glittering—the mansion shone like the sun. Every light was on to greet the two of them. Leila had to look away it was so bright.

"Welcome home!" Camille beamed. They both got out of the car, and she grabbed Leila's hand and led her up the long driveway. Camille's grip was stronger than she let on, and Leila was starting to think Camille was a force in heels.

The inside of the house was simple: white arches and white marble with white furniture and gold accents. Large glass vases housed stalks of wheat Leila suspected were made out of real gold. Camille fit in perfectly.

Leila noticed as Camille showed her the house, from her carefully arranged centerpieces—curving, crystal horns overflowing with gold fruit and flowers—to her framed pictures of faraway farmland, how her face shone with pride. And something else, an eagerness on Camille's waiting face. She wanted Leila to love her home as much as she did and it made Leila's heart swell.

They ended up in front of a set of French doors. She regarded Camille's manicured hands, folded neatly in front of her, eyes slightly creased—Leila's only indication at the undercurrent of emotion, the stress and worry. She remembered how Camille's eyes hadn't left Leila all through the ceremony and after, hovering close if Leila ever faltered.

She felt her throat close at the thought someone was here to look out for her in this new world. This new *life*.

She coughed. "Your house is beautiful," she said. She curled her fingers to hide the crescents of dirt under her nails.

Camille clapped her hands together, a coy smile on her lips. "Before we have dinner, I thought I would show you my greenhouse."

Leila could feel it now. *Warmth.*

Light cut through the glass, splashing prisms across the white walls. The warmth of heat, yes, but also the warmth of *magic*, nurturing and sweet. Calling to her own. Her magic was the only thing familiar to her, though Leila could not imagine magic being anything near familiar.

They approached, and Camille threw a smile over her shoulder, matching the beautiful warmth and lacking any of the hesitation from before.

She grabbed the doorknobs with both hands and pushed.

A wave of heat gently caressed Leila's face. The smell of earth and plants wafted out, floral and wet.

Camille strode in, a torch among the green. Leila followed, her steps more careful.

All she could see at first was blooming shades of green. There were trees and flowers and bushes and fruits and *life*. This place was alive, thrumming with a sweet heartbeat beckoning Leila to step farther into the greenhouse. Her steps grew confident over the mosaic walkway, her curiosity outshining any last reserves of hesitancy.

The white iron and glass structure swirled up above her, the windows fogged from the heat. Spiral staircases jutted up to balconies where even more plants were housed.

The latin names tumbled around her head.

Nymphaea thermarum, Pseudanthodendron, Leptosporangium

Cyatheaceae, Solanum lycopersicum, Mangifera indica

She didn't realize she had grabbed onto a plant, an icy green bush, her fingers brushing over the velvet leaves.

"*Stachys byzantina*," she murmured.

"Interesting. See, I had to learn all of the scientific names," Camille said behind her, startling Leila. "Sorry, I know this can be a little overwhelming, come this way."

Camille beckoned Leila to the center of the greenhouse, where the mosaic stone path led to a circular opening. A ring of young trees lined the perimeter, and benches were scattered around. Leila could hear a fountain gurgling softly nearby.

Camille stood in the middle beside a large clay pot filled with earth. She placed her hands on the lip of the vase as if to steady herself, and took a big breath.

"I've grown every plant, tree, shrub, and flower in here. I want you to add yours. I have seeds you can choose from..." she gestured to a stone bench at the edge of the circle where a briefcase lay open, full of corked vials of seeds.

Leila broke into a grin as she practically ran to the briefcase. She gingerly started to pick up each vial, her hands shaking with excitement. They were unmarked but Leila found she didn't need a label to get a feeling for what the seeds could be. Glimpses of petals and branches, fruits and seasons filled her mind with the touch of each vial.

Her heart fluttered.

Potential.

That's what she was holding.

Ever since she felt the first flurry of power spring from her hands, she had been wanting to try her powers out again, in private. Without the spectacle of ceremony.

A couple of minutes passed while Leila picked her way through the trove of seeds. No doubt Camille had many more stored somewhere in her large mansion. Leila finally plucked a corked vial filled with dark red seeds. She frowned, looking around at the conservatory, the uniform arrangement.

It's neat.

This won't fit in one bit.

Clutching the vial, she turned and walked back to where Camille stood at the clay gardening pot. Leila pulled the cork and shook out some of the seeds onto her open palm. Holding the seeds gave her a surge of energy, and heat traveled through her body. She figured she could probably bloom the flowers in her palm but she tried to remain calm. Her hands shook in anticipation.

She looked back up to Camille and she nodded to her encouragingly.

With her other hand, she scooped a small hole and placed the seeds inside, then covered them back up with the soil. She felt the soil, cool and moist, as she placed her palm on it.

Leila took a breath and fluttered her eyes closed. She allowed the heat building in her limbs, her cheeks, her heart, to flow down through her left hand and drain into the seeds.

For a few moments, the sounds of the greenhouse fell away as her heart hammered in her ears.

Then her power flared, and she opened her eyes and gasped.

Six green tendrils sprouted from the soil around her hand. She raised her hand slowly, coaxing the plants to grow. She wasn't sure how but she could feel each step like a recipe she was remembering. It grew taller, and leaves shot out and reached outward. When they had grown about a foot, buds appeared at the crest of the plant.

Blackest violet petals unfurled, shining velvet in the bright light of the greenhouse. Six obsidian *iris germanica* in full bloom, like six black holes in contrast to the harmonious colors of the rest of the plants. The magic left her lightheaded and trembling, but the residual curls of magic in her veins yearned for more.

Leila couldn't help herself—she laughed. A bubbling giggle as she touched the soft flowers, *her doing*. This realization rooted her in her place.

The crown of white flowers, the tree at the Induction, now the flowers here.

Mine. From my *magic.*

She had power, *real* power. As natural as the sun and as inevitable as rain. This was all hers, her duty and her blessing.

She sniffed.

"I–" she started before her voice caught and two tears escaped down her cheeks.

Camille's own eyes were rimmed with tears.

"I cried, too," she said before enveloping Leila in a crushing hug.

Leila scarfed down the vegan *cacio e pepe* within seconds. Cami—Leila'd been reminded she could call her that—ate her pasta with more care, using both her fork and her knife with a pause between each bite to take a sip of her white wine.

They talked about the Induction and laughed over Cami's descriptions of the other Vessels. Leila felt relieved at the normalcy of the meal after the greenhouse.

Cami swallowed the last of her second glass. "Yes, yes, the redhead's my best, *best* friend. You two're going to get along so well."

Leila snickered into her own water glass. Cami was much more lively when tipsy—if that was even possible. Her accent started to sound less refined.

"I hope so," Leila said. She vaguely remembered seeing the red-haired woman, and she didn't look too happy to be at the Induction. Though, she did dress for a party.

"Hmm, who else?" Cami asked. "You'll meet the rest of the Junior Council in a couple of days, so I'll skip them...You already met Martin..."

Camille got up from the kitchen island where they sat and went to the fridge to get another bottle of wine. Leila played with the last pasta noodles on her plate, the only survivors of her massacre.

She tried to remember the faces of the crowd at the temple, the other Vessels, but it was hard. There was so much going on, and every Vessel paled in the presence of an actual goddess. Leila had focused on the soft murmurings of Persephone, the unseen hand giving Leila her Gift and completed the ritual at her Induction.

She remembered the hypnotic floral scent, the charged air, heavy and metallic. She remembered the molten orange glow of the setting sun slicing through the columns and the dark silhouette of the figure retreating—

"Cami, do you know the Vessel, um," Leila paused to try and

remember more, "I think I saw a Vessel but I don't think I saw his face."
She didn't know for sure if the figure was a *he* but she remembered the
broad shoulders filling out a hoodie, their arms stuffed into the pockets
as they walked away. The sun's rays cast them in a weird light, Leila
swore to herself she saw a black glow around their head.

Like a dark crown. She shook her head. *Wow, I'm tired.*

"But he had a nice body?" Cami waggled her eyebrows as she
poured herself another glass.

Leila burst into surprised laughter and raised her hands in
defense. "I can't say. I only noticed him when he left the temple in the
middle of the Induction, so maybe? Do you know who that is?"

Cami froze, mid-pour. Leila noticed her frown into her wine
glass.

Cami brightened. "Who knows? You know, I don't even know
every Vessel, there's *so* many of us. Should I call Alicia to schedule
dinner later this week?"

The uncomfortable silence dragged on for only a moment but
Leila bristled.

Cami is lying, she realized. This settled heavily in her stomach.

She opened her mouth to ask Cami why she lied when a trilling
bell sounded from somewhere else in the house. A doorbell.

Leila looked at Cami in surprise and found the same look
mirrored back at her.

LEILA

Leila sat at the edge of a twin bed in a messy room while Bianca and Min-Seo grabbed her a drink. They'd shown up to Camille's house and whisked her off to the New Olympus Preparatory Academy housing for a Junior Council Welcome Meeting. With barely a word of approval from Camille they rushed off, the tires of the sky-blue Jeep squealing.

Leila tilted her head back; there was a tightness starting to build behind her eyes threatening a headache. The last time Leila checked the time was the brief glance to Camille's oven. She tried to ignore the music blasting from Bianca's speakers and concentrated on the feeling of the soft glow of the dozens of Edison bulbs hanging down from Bianca's room.

A thud and a high laugh brought her back to the room.

"OK, so I don't know how you feel about vodka, so I only put a couple of shots in it." Bianca said.

Leila looked down the red coffee mug of pink liquid and then up to Bianca's smiling face. Bianca held up her own mug with *But First, Coffee* written on it. "Sorry, all my other cups are dirty. *Someone* didn't do their chores this week."

Leila gave a soft smile back and clinked her mug with Bianca's then took a sip. First she tasted sweet pink lemonade and then a chemical-like burning taste.

"Ugh," she grimaced, making Bianca laugh and the blue

corkscrew curls fall into her face. Leila never tasted something so awful, and she could still feel the liquid going down and coiling in her stomach.

Min-Seo walked into the room from their shared kitchen area holding a bottle of vodka by the neck. She winced at Leila in sympathy.

"Yeah, I wasn't a fan when I first tried it either." She took a pull of the bottle and wiped her mouth with her hoodie sleeve and coughed.

"Oh god, Minnie, no," Bianca shuddered away, still laughing. "We're not at the party yet!"

"I'm trying to get in all the partying I can before school starts, leave me alone," Minnie replied as she went to Bianca's desk and changed the song on the speakers. A bass guitar bubbled out and a female voice started to croon.

"I see, so you're trying to top Midsummer or...?" Bianca asked, one eyebrow raised.

Min-Seo replied with a thumbs up as she took another swig. Even Leila laughed then.

"Let me guess, there isn't a 'welcome meeting', is there?" Leila asked.

"Sorry," Bianca winced. "We had to think of some way to get you out of there so we could meet you!"

"And what's more boring- and safe-sounding than a welcome meeting?"

Leila looked between the two, recalling how she had looked between the tall Bianca and the small Min-Seo as they introduced themselves to her and Camille.

"Hi! I'm Bianca," she threw a skinny arm around the short girl next to her, all smiles and pep. "This is my best friend, Min-Seo." The shorter girl gave a nod, her sharp olive green eyes and a ghost of a smile on her lips made Leila feel like she was being sized up.

Best friend.

Leila felt a pang of jealousy, seeing the two roommates so close —though she didn't understand how they fit together since they seemed like two pieces from different puzzles. Bianca wore gold and silver jewelry, her makeup perfect. Her lacy white blouse and high-waisted jeans set off her gold-brown skin, making her glow. She wore red strappy heels. In the car, she was animated and talked nonstop—about everything and nothing—over Min-Seo's head-banging loud music.

Min-Seo occasionally stopped drumming on the dashboard to contribute to the conversation, shaking her cropped onyx hair around to the music.

Min-Seo now twirled around, her feet half out of her loafers and her brown plaid slacks billowing with the movement. Her tight crop top showed off a twinkle of a belly button piercing. If Bianca was a head cheerleader, Min-Seo wasn't even at the game.

For lack of anything else to do, Leila took another drink, the burn not as bad as the first time. In fact, it warmed her. She took another small sip.

"Do you think you'll come to New Olympus Prep when school starts next week?" Bianca asked.

Leila took another sip as she thought about it. She grimaced at the taste again.

"I don't even know what I'm doing tomorrow, so I guess we'll see?" She heard Min-Seo chuckle.

"I haven't heard of anyone becoming a Vessel older than ten, let alone seventeen!" Bianca exclaimed. "No offense, but it's highly unusual."

"Really?" Min-Seo interjected. "One of the other Athenas said she remembered hearing someone being Inducted at twenty-two, which I doubt, but——"

"Yeah, OK, so you heard *someone* say maybe they knew *someone*? I was Inducted when I was four," Bianca interrupted.

"I was an early bird: two," Min-Seo said.

"So...you've lived *here* ever since?" Leila asked, taken aback. Looking around the dorm room, she couldn't quite imagine a four-year-old could live here alone and was even more confused by the laws of this city than before.

"No, we didn't move in until ninth grade! You have to live with your other Vessels when you're younger. But it's just more fun to live in Prep Housing now."

"Yeah, and Bianca doesn't have a stick up her ass, unlike all the Athena's I've lived with."

Right, Min-Seo is a Vessel for Athena, and Bianca is a Vessel for Iris, she remembered they had said on the doorstep of Camille's house.

"Athena...wisdom, right?" Leila said to Min-Seo.

"Yeah, and a whole handful of other stuff."

Leila turned to Bianca.

"And Iris is...sight?" She guessed.

Bianca gave a chuckle. "Not quite."

She tipped her head back and raised her hands. The large bulbs that hung from the ceiling like clusters of grapes flared, gold light turning white and brightening every corner of the room. The light got brighter and brighter, causing Leila to squint, but suddenly the white light was gone, replaced by arcs of rainbows, drenching the room in a kaleidoscope of color. Leila gasped.

"Wow," she breathed.

Bianca opened her eyes and as soon as she did the lights dimmed back down to its foggy yellow. Leila could still see the rainbows, like a dying echo.

"This is crazy. I'm still not used to..." she wanted to say the word *magic* but she felt silly. The two girls looked at her expectantly. "This is all so much to process."

She frowned down at her near empty mug. She felt a warm hand on her shoulder and looked at Bianca.

"I get it—we get it." Her smile was softer, like the comforting glow of the bulbs ahead. "This is weird and hard to get your head around. Believe me, I'm still surprised by the Gift, the Myth. But as much as it's weird, it's also wonderful."

She felt the bed sink slightly on her other side and Min-Seo looked at her with her unnaturally bright green eyes. "And besides, I know a part of you feels so right in the middle of all of this."

Leila couldn't help but smile in agreement because a part of her —a growing, climbing, blooming part of her—did feel right in all of this.

This magic.

After getting ready, they left for the party. As they walked, Leila bit her lip in nervousness, immediately regretting it as she momentarily forgot she was wearing red lipstick. Bianca had offered it, and catching a glimpse of herself in the mirror, she was surprised by how much she loved how the color brought out the warmth of her tan skin. The fiery color made her feel ready to face her new classmates.

That and the second mug of vodka and lemonade.

The dormitories were separated by grades, as Bianca explained on the way up, with the upperclassmen housed in the building they were in.

"I think the underclassmen are going to try to sneak in anyway," Min-Seo added.

They took the stairs rather than the elevator to try and avoid the crowd. The closer they got to the common area—an entire floor according to Bianca—the louder the music became. At first it was a hum, and then she could feel the faint pounding of the beat through the walls. There were people in the brightly lit stairwell, small groups chatting—until they saw her and then Leila's skin crawled at their stares. Except one couple too busy making out, leaning against the railing without a care who saw. Three girls looked at each other and cracked up. Her stomach was full of butterflies and she didn't know if it was from the alcohol or the nerves. As they rounded the final steps of stairs, her nerves fully kicked in. Her butterflies became full pterodactyls, clawing at her insides.

I can't do this, she wanted to say. She slowed her steps but it was too late; Bianca grabbed the fire escape door and opened it.

The common room was dark, but soon Leila's eyes adjusted and she could make out crowds of people dancing and tables set up with food and drinks. She could spot couches farther off and even people playing games of pool and beer pong.

"Let's get a drink," Bianca half-yelled over the music. Leila nodded eagerly.

Multi-colored fairy lights were strung up on the walls, but only added a little light to the dim room as they made their way to the drinks. A boy with sun-blond hair was getting himself a drink out of a bowl of red punch. He looked up at the girls with a wide grin in recognition. He looked like he was in full sun for a moment, as if a light shone on his form alone.

"Mason! Is that for luck?" Min-Seo pointed up to the white sweatband around his head. Bianca went ahead and started making them drinks.

He touched it. "No, I don't need any luck, I'm on a winning streak today." His eyes flickered to Leila, who stood silently next to them, and his grin widened. "Persephone! Gotta say, the Induction was top notch."

"It's Leila, Mason," Bianca chided while handing Leila a drink.

"Right, right, my bad," Mason raised his hands in apology and Leila noticed the freckles scattered on the bridge of his nose also ran down his arms.

"No worries, I'm getting used to it myself," she replied with a smile. She took a sip and coughed. "Bianca, this is..."

"Strong?"

"I was going to say *foul*, but yeah, that works."

Mason cracked up as Bianca blinked at her innocently.

"Mason, are you scaring off the new Vessel already?" A deep voice called behind them, the lilt of an Australian accent tinging his words. She turned around to see the source of the voice, but not before seeing Bianca roll her eyes.

Interesting, she noted.

They turned to see a boy walking up to them, his smirk making a dimple pop on his cheek . His shoulder length brown hair was secured in a backwards baseball cap. Though he was tan and muscular like Mason, his muscles weren't as bulky, but lean like cords of rope. He was also taller than Mason—taller than all of them—and he walked with an almost imperceptible hitch to his step. She looked closer and saw had a metal prosthesis on his left leg that went up to his thigh. He came around the table and slapped Mason's arm.

"Tell me he isn't giving you any trouble, darl," he said with a wink to Leila, making her cheeks flush. She was so unused to the feeling she looked down into her drink.

"Seriously, Elliot? Can you keep it in your pants for one second?" Min-Seo reached over the table to swat Elliot but he dodged her hand neatly.

"Can you?" He retorted then looked at Leila with brows furrowed. "Sorry, I'm Elliot. Sometimes I forget my manners in front of such a pretty gal."

"Does that line work?" Leila blurted.

Bianca turned to Leila. "No, it doesn't, and he doesn't have any manners in any situation."

"Bianca, you hurt me so." He feigned being struck in the chest, which she stuck her tongue out at. Even Leila rolled her eyes. "Mason, are we playing or what?"

"As a matter of fact, Elliot, I was just about to ask Leila to play."

"Ah, she has a name!"

"She does," Leila stepped up to the drink table. "And what are you playing?"

Mason and Elliot looked at each other with eyebrows raised.

"Have you heard of a game called King's Cup?"

Leila had not heard about King's Cup, but she doubted she'd remember the rules anyway—they were all designed to get her to drink. They gathered around a table full of discarded playing cards, with others joining them. She recognized the lanky Vessel for Zeus, Harvey from the Induction. The soft glow of the string lights reflecting off his deep skin and his easy smile—especially when a boy showed up halfway through, his dark lashes and thick Spanish accent were a huge contributing factor to Harvey's losing streak from then on.

She couldn't figure out if they were good friends or boyfriends for most of the game until Harvey got to dare the quiet boy. Harvey was so tall he stood over him, a big smile on his face.

"Oscar, I dare you to kiss me," he said before the boy captured his mouth in a long, involved kiss.

Well, that settles the question.

"Yes, we get it, you guys are cute," Min-Seo was impatient. "Can we get back to the game?" She didn't get an answer from the two boys, who had discarded their cups for each other's hair.

"I guess we can call it a draw," Elliot said, slapping his cards down. "Looks like I'm the reigning champ, Minnie."

"Bite me," Min-Seo said, slapping her own cards down.

"Oh believe me, I would, but I respect that you don't swing that way."

Mason leaned close to Leila. "They're both *very* competitive and sore losers."

"You think?" she replied and they both laughed. She was starting to feel weightless and restless, the edges of everything were soft and blurry.

I think I might need a break from drinking.

The DJ on the far side of the room changed the song and Leila couldn't help but sway. She looked back at the crowd of people dancing on the far side of the room.

"We should go dance," Leila said to the group.

"I have been waiting for someone to say that all night," Bianca agreed and started finishing her drink.

"Can't we play another round?" Elliot asked.

Oscar broke off his kiss to look at Leila. "I'm coming with. I love dancing."

"You lovebirds are ruining my winning streak," Elliot said, waving at Harvey and Oscar, who both impressively flipped him off at the same time.

"C'mon, let's go," Bianca said, slapping her cup down and grabbing Leila's hand. The rest of the group started to move away from the table, leaving half-empty cups and cards scattered about.

"I guess I'll beat you at dancing, like I do everything else." Min-Seo called over her shoulder. Elliot rolled his eyes and jogged to catch up with them.

After that, Leila lost track of time. She didn't technically know any of the songs, but they all had a fast beat and an easy chorus everyone shouted to. As they all jumped around, she noticed everyone had their own distinct style. Elliot was more of a nodding, off-beat kind of dancer while Mason liked to jump and fist pump; Min-Seo twirled around, letting her hair fall in her face, and Bianca was the most social, grabbing hands and singing into faces. And Leila was doing all she could to try to keep up.

When everyone got refills, Leila disentangled herself from the group to find the bathroom. She needed a moment of peace from the Vessels all around her.

"Are you sure you don't want me to come with?" Bianca asked.

"I'm fine," Leila replied. But after leaving the common area, Bianca's directions left her head just as quick. The dorm hallways blended into each other, only illuminated by the red glow of the exit sign. Finally, she found an empty bathroom, giving herself time to splash some water on the back of her neck. Exiting the bathroom was disorienting—the bleached bathroom light turning back into the red darkness made her pause and try to quell the fuzziness surrounding her alcohol-soaked brain. The distant sound of a door opening didn't make her freeze but the feeling of being watched did.

It was like someone blew a breath on the back of her neck. She turned around to see a boy walking down the hallway and she knew she was the direction he was headed in. He was taller than her, with inky, black curls that fell messily on his forehead, his thick eyebrows furrowed. He had deep purple bags under his eyes—

She caught her breath.

His eyes were grey—so dark they could be black. He kept his distance but his eyes stayed on hers. She didn't know how long they stared at each other; her heartbeat was hammering too fast in her ears to hear anything else. She opened her mouth to say something— *anything*.

"You," she exhaled. At the Induction, she'd only caught his silhouette for a moment, but her brain had memorized his shape: *he* was the figure she'd seen, a shadow against the setting sun. And now he was here, looking at her with enough intensity to pin her in place.

"You." His voice was thick with venom, surprising her.

In a blur, he approached her—so fast all she could do was back up into the wall. "Are you following me?" He asked, his voice low and every word measured.

"No?" It sounded like a question coming out. He invaded her space, splaying his hands on either side of her face. He was so close to Leila she could feel his honey breath. "I don't even know who you are."

He scoffed, unbelieving. "You're not going to ruin my life again."

"Again?" She breathed, frowning. His eyes flicked to her red mouth for only a second but her whole body buzzed under his stare.

I just got here, how could I have ruined his life?

If her magic felt warm, looking into his eyes *burned*. A cold fire, like a biting wind in winter.

"Blakey," a sing-song voice crooned from behind him. It broke whatever tension had built up between Leila and the boy. He blinked, dropping his hands and stepping back like he was in a daze.

The girl who'd called to the boy snaked her pale arms around him, turning him to her. She had near-white blonde hair and wine-red lips in a smile that made Leila's skin crawl.

The girl looked at Leila, her stare unnerving.

"Is this supposed to be the new Vessel of Persephone?"

The motion of the girl had torn her eyes from the boy, but she looked back at him—his eyes had never left hers. She distantly noted she was holding her breath.

He was silent for another long moment, still looking at her. Then, he tilted his head, as if appraising her. Leila felt bare.

"Apparently."

BIANCA

When Bianca planned an impromptu party for the new Vessel, she didn't expect any trouble. Then again, trouble didn't factor into her meticulously color-coded planner.

"I can't believe you lost the new Vessel," Minnie snorted as they made their way through the dormitory's long halls.

"I didn't lose her," Bianca retorted. *Not yet.*

"Slow down, B, I don't have long legs like you." Minnie huffed. Bianca dutifully slowed, though the panic she felt kept rising at a steady pace. Then they rounded the next corner and found Leila—and *him.*

And her, Bianca corrected herself when she saw Blake's girlfriend Kat looming behind him. She didn't go to New Prep, but Bianca had seen her around the dorm this summer to recognize the Vessel of Hecate.

"Apparently," Blake said, his head tilted towards the Vessel of Persephone.

Bianca shot Minnie a look, conveying what she couldn't say out loud with one glance. She knew Minnie long enough she could read her facial expressions like a book. Minnie's jade eyes were streaming as many expletives as she was thinking herself.

His eyes never left Leila, making Bianca's skin crawl.

She wasn't psychic—her powers were physical, corporeal and blessedly uncomplicated for her—but when she saw the look on Kat's face as she regarded Leila, it gave Bianca a sense of wrongness so strong it couldn't be misinterpreted. *Danger.*

She cleared her throat to speak up, putting on her best and brightest smile.

"There you are. Thank you *so* much for finding our friend," she put extra warmth in her words as if she could make them more believable even to her.

"Oh, of *course*," Kat mimicked Bianca's tone, but with none of the sincerity. Kat's pale fingers were entwined in Blake's curls in a way she supposed were meant to look playful and lazy but were as possessive as if her hand were curled around a leash.

What is going on? Does this have anything to do with the Myth? she thought, then wanted to kick herself. *What in this city* doesn't *have anything to do with Myths and Fate?*

Finally Blake looked away from Leila, dragging his eyes to his girlfriend.

Then Leila spoke, murmuring something just out of Bianca's earshot. Blake's focus snapped right back to Leila, something startling him enough to break through his stony mask.
Kat scoffed, her dark mouth breaking into a smile.

"Oh my goddess, no one's told her. That's so cute, she has no idea!"

"No idea about what?" Leila sounded irritated.

Bianca caught Blake's eyebrows as they shot up, looking genuinely surprised. It reminded her of when they were little: before he donned a permanent scowl, before he ever fell in with Kat and that whole crowd. It reminded her of his big grey eyes and his messy black hair, when Blake and Danny were inseparable.

The moment passed and his mouth quirked to the side, cruelly.

"You may be the Vessel of Persephone," Blake snarled. He took a step closer to Leila and the air felt colder in his presence—the eye of a storm. "You may have some part to play in the Myth, but I want you to stay the hell away from me."

Bianca tried to catch Leila's eyes.

"Are you done?" Minnie reproached. "You've made your point."

Bianca wished Harvey was here, with his rigid posture and commanding voice he'd crafted after years of leadership. He'd know what to say to diffuse the situation. Frowning, she knew she wasn't one of the more powerful Vessels, so her word carried no weight. She hated the hierarchy that was given to them by Fate. Even though most of her friends never made her feel inferior, she couldn't help but find herself powerless in situations like this.

She felt Elliot's presence before he spoke, his broad warmth right behind her. She smelled his ever-present salty, clean ocean water scent mixed with whatever bougie hair conditioner he was loving at the moment.

"*Ladies!*" he sang, his voice dying as Blake looked down the hall to where the Vessel of Poseidon had sauntered over.

Another match to the powder keg. One downside of being mortal with immortal powers, it was too easy to get out of control.

"Fucking pricks," Elliot swore and Bianca resisted the urge to hit him. "Why are these freaks here?"

Blake stilled, the air around him rippling.

Even though Blake and Bianca had grown up going to the same school, seen each other suffer through puberty and pimples and awkward braces, there was so much she didn't know about him.

And when Blake looked back at Elliot, his eyes black from one corner of his eye to the other, when swirls of black smoke lifted from his dark suit, and his lopsided smirk revealed too-sharp canines—Bianca couldn't think of one thing she knew about Blake.

Because he was not the same person she'd been around most of her life.

"Prick? Elliot, you know, pricks in glass houses shouldn't be throwing stones," he dropped his smile and the hallway was soon crowded in shadows, oppressively dark yet infinite.

Then he passed by them, and the familiar red light of the exit sign returned. Minnie grabbed Bianca's hand in the dark, and as soon as they could see their feet on the floor, they raced to Leila who blinked as if in a daze. Elliot scratched the back of his neck, trying not to look as scared as they all felt.

Thank the gods that's over.

Where was Blake going? She wondered what path he was heading down, the one so different than the rest of them. It'd been so long since she'd seen him with his only friend, and she couldn't remember the last time she'd seen the Vessel of Hermes.

I need to remind myself to say hi to Danny later, she resolved.

"Who was that?" Leila asked.

"Blake," Bianca answered after a long pause. "Vessel of Hades, god of the Underworld."

ELLIOT

"What just happened?" Leila asked again as they rejoined the party. She had to think she was hallucinating.

I know I did, he thought as he remembered his own first night in New Olympus.

Elliot pushed the double doors to the balcony with all the frustration he felt. That whole pack of weirdos put him on edge. He didn't like how they got under his skin so easily, especially Blake. Someone was already out on the balcony, their back to Elliot and his friends. A curl of smoke came from the lit cigarette dangling from their hand.

"Hey, do you mind if we hang here for a minute?" Elliot said to the person on the balcony. "Alone?"

The figure turned and Elliot swallowed a groan.

Bart. The leather jacket and the flash of his lip ring gave him away. He'd shaved his mohawk since the last time Elliot saw him.

"Do *you* mind?" Bart said with a thick English accent. He talked as if he was one move away from losing it, a smirk on his face and a blade in his palm. Bart liked being trouble, and apparently he hadn't yet learned the Vessels of Ares only *instigated* it. Before Elliot could roll his eyes, Bart took one last drag of his cigarette, crushed it under his boot, gave a final mock salute and stalked back into the party.

"Does he even go here?" Mason asked, slipping through the

same door Bart had left, his cheery voice cutting across the balcony.

The cool air helped clear the feeling of tension, and he inhaled deeply through his nose, letting his senses find the river Styx in the night. His eyes fluttered closed as he let the movement of the river wash away his anger—at least some of it. This was one of the few useful tricks he'd learned from the older Vessels of Poseidon. And how to tie nautical knots while three sheets to the wind.

He turned back to his group—which was minus Harvey who hung back to keep an authoritarian eye on the party—and leaned against the railing. Minnie and Bianca had basically formed a secret service-style ring around Leila. They walked her forward with their arms raised, in case someone got too close. Her eyes were wide but not frightened, more like she was making sure she was able to take everything in.

She's doing better than most, he noticed. His own encounters with the darker parts of New Olympus had left him more shaken than he'd like to admit.

Elliot shifted his weight to his right leg, easing up slowly off his prosthesis.

"That was Chaos," Mason said, scratching his headband. He was the satellite orbiting the three girls.

"Yeah, no, that was pretty crazy," Leila agreed.

Elliot looked at Bianca, and she gave him a look he could hear in her most annoying voice: *I'm going to tell her, stop asking me about it.*

Bianca turned to Leila and sighed.

"Those people you just met, Blake and Kat?" She hesitated slightly saying Blake's name, searching Leila's face for anything.

Recognition? Or something else?

"That was Chaos. Mason literally meant the group was Chaos incarnate," she looked up, her light blue curls giving off a soft glow against the dark of the night. "There are Vessels of every god and goddess in the Greek Pantheon. There are different ways to group ourselves—"

"Major and Minor," Mason said. "Corporeal or Ethereal—"

"Hot or Not," Elliot risked a sharp glare from both Minnie and Bianca.

"—Chaos and Order. It's not strict, of course. You can hang with whoever. But sometimes, you feel the difference—some more than others, and they group up. Sometimes."

"OK.. So we're all sorted into magical cliques?" Leila pursed her red lips in thought.

Elliot smiled to himself.

"Basically," Minnie muttered. "Chaos Vessels are more trouble together anyways. But in the last couple of months that group has been *trouble.*"

Elliot tapped his prosthesis on the railing, making a nice clinking noise. Sometimes he didn't realize he was doing it, but the rhythm calmed him down when his other methods failed. And when his cup was failingly empty.

"New Olympus is supposed to be balanced, that's the whole point. They have Blake now, so there's starting to be this power shift," Bianca said. Elliot clinked the railing faster.

"Why? Is Hades Chaos or something?" Leila asked.

clink, clink, clink, clink, clink

Bianca looked at Elliot again, this time her eyes were softer. She looked away to Leila.

"No, Leila, but you are."

LEILA

"Well," Bianca bit her lip, struggling to explain while the city lights behind them haloed her blue hair. "What I meant is that you *could* be Chaos but nobody knows."

"There hasn't been a Persephone in decades, right?" Mason asked.

"Centuries," Minnie corrected. "This is the first time in a long time we've had so many Vessels present for every god."

Leila looked at all of them gathered on the dark balcony but they were only partly making eye contact back. She was ten steps behind what they were telling her, and she didn't know how to catch up.

"So I *could* be Chaos—what does that have to do with Blake, if he's Order?" she looked at them again. The wind rustled around them; the summer night had started to cool.

"Spit it out," Leila said. "I can handle whatever else it is, really."

"Because of the Myth," Mason started. "Between you and Blake—"

"Between *Persephone and Hades*," Bianca interrupted, "it's the— how do I say this—it's the influence of Hades over Persephone."

"Influence?" Min-Seo scoffed. "Is that what you call it?"

"Look, we're taught everything about the Pantheon as soon as we get here so we know everyone's Myth," Elliot said. "There's a pull, as Vessels."

"A compulsion to fulfill the Myth," Min-Seo said, tilting her head to the side. "Along with our powers given to us by our god, we follow their path."

The muffled beat of the bass behind Leila was like an erratic heartbeat.

"What's my Myth? What does it have to do with Hades, er, Blake?"

Does it have to do with the fact that I couldn't look away from him? A blush bloomed up Leila's neck, like a reflex. "*Do I know you?*" The words had tumbled out in the space between her and Blake. He hadn't liked that question, and now she knew why. Leila wanted to kick herself.

"You basically make winter happen," Mason offered. Leila noticed that even in the dark, she could see every inch of him, like he was standing in an invisible sun.

"I *make* winter happen?" Leila repeated. "That's it?"

"That's the gist of it. I'm sure you'll be briefed about it when we get to school."

So there's more? Leila resisted a groan. There's always more.

"So in the meantime, what do I do? Just avoid him?" Leila deadpanned. She liked these people but she was starting to feel coddled and caged.

And I don't like being caged. That was a resolution she could feel swirling dark in her heart.

"For now, yeah. I don't know why you would want to hang out with him anyway," Elliot said, raking a hand through his long hair. "Death Vessel and all."

Bianca rolled her eyes and looked at Leila; even Min-Seo's lips gave a small quirk.

"Right, I'll keep that in mind. Any chance I can get another drink?" Leila said, rubbing her arms together, she could feel goosebumps traveling up her skin. "I can't be the only one who needs one."

Min-Seo laughed and put her hand on her chest. "A girl after my own heart."

ALICIA

It was very, very late.

Or very, very early, depending on the person.

Her condo, the back corner suite of one of New Olympus' luxury high rises, felt bigger than it usually did. And no amount of wine could make her feel warm like the flare in her power had at the Induction.

The floor-to-ceiling windows reflected her dimmed interior back at her. Instead of overlooking the sprawling city, Alicia's apartment had views of the untamed mountains ranges bordering New Olympus. It was breathtaking to anyone who came to visit, but Alicia was certain it was a strategic placement Arnie probably paid extra for.

Like I'd ever want to see you and your pathetic warehouse again, she'd said to him. Alicia hadn't known that would actually *be* one of the last times she would see Arnie.

She tipped the bottle back, only a couple of drops falling into her parted lips. She'd have to break into the reds soon.

When Arnie was done with someone, he was entirely and irrevocably done. If only I had that resolve.

Alicia hadn't bothered to change out of her ostrich feather robe — she had the forethought to kick off her strappy heels, though.

On a lonely night like this—when she was young and living across the river in her New Olympus Prep dorm—she would sit at the window, sneaking cigarettes and listening to sickly sweet music while giving herself over fully to her powers. The bitter smoke kept her tethered to the world as the rest of her tasted everyone's love in the building, the block, even the city. She tasted the sweet, the sour, the rotten. She took it all in.

Buzzed on love.

This was when Alicia's powers were accessible, without thought. A part of her as vital as her lungs.

She felt the absence of her powers in every breath.

A soft crooning voice started to sing and that's when she noticed her record player was on, playing an old soundtrack from an Italian movie that Arnie made her watch when she was sick.

My sentimentalism is going to kill me before liver failure does.

She groaned at the same time as the front door buzzer went off.

bzzz....bzzz, bzzz...bzzzzzzzzz

Alicia sat up, too quickly, and the room spun momentarily. The buzzer went off again and again until she hoisted herself up off the couch and made her way to the small screen that was mounted on the wall.

She touched the screen to talk to whoever was down at the front doors. Her doorman had long since clocked off.

"Hello?" She said, her voice a little hoarse from disuse.

"You called me?" The voice said.

For a moment, her stomach flipped, as she could only remember one person she'd called that evening. The hope that swelled in her crashed hard as she recognized the voice. The thick Cockney accent that carried a smirk all the way through the intercom could only belong to one man.

Bartie, Ares, eighteen. And a big mistake, she chided herself.

"Did I?" She didn't have it in her to fake politeness.

"Aw, c'mon love, let me up. I'm freezing down 'ere! Came all the way from the 'burbs for ya," Bart pleaded. He was still young enough—or, she hoped, one of the few good Vessels of Ares—not to realize the full authority he had over Vessels of Aphrodite. He was genuine in asking for permission to enter her apartment.

Without thinking too hard about it, she touched the screen again, unlocking the door.

As she waited for the young Vessel of Ares to make his way up to her place, she smoothed her long auburn hair in the mirror, wiping away her smudged mascara. After she was relatively happy with how she looked, she scrolled through her call log to find how many embarrassing third-maybe-fourth-glass-of-wine phone calls she made. Five to Bartie and two to Cami. She didn't even want to look at her texts.

I need to have this phone taken away from me, she chuckled under her breath.

A quick knock brought her back and she opened the door to the punk Vessel of Ares on her doorstep. He kissed her on her cheek with disarming softness compared to his studded, smoke-scented exterior—she barely felt the cool metal of his lip ring. Bartie was pale like moonlight with a shadow-colored buzz cut. The first time she saw him, she noticed how every piece of him seemed sharp—from his cheekbones to his steel toed boots—and even the sweet parts of his possessed a kick. He walked past her straight into the living room.

She followed him, noting the way his shoulders filled out his leather jacket, how the long fingers of his right hand kept twitching near a spot by his jacket where he most likely kept a blade or some other weapon—an Ares instinct, she'd noticed—and the peek of a rather naughty neck tattoo she still hadn't asked him about.

Not that they had done a lot of talking the last time he was there.

"Do you want something to drink?"

He flicked his eyes around the room, probably eyeing all entrances and objects that could double as weapons.

She walked into the spacious kitchen and opened her freezer for the bottle of expensive Russian vodka she kept for special guests of the Ares variety. One of the only things she kept in the freezer other than her eye mask.

Why cook when there's takeout?

She poured him two fingers.

He drummed his fingers on the marble island between them.

"What trouble were you up to tonight in the '*burbs*?"

He smirked, the lip ring popping. "No trouble."

"No trouble?"

Bartie balked. "Well, a little gathering at the Prep Housing."

"Mm-hmm," she said, running her hands across the cool marble.

"What?" He laughed.

"Nothing, nothing. I didn't realize you were one of those *well-behaved* Ares."

Bartie took a sip of his drink, the muscle in his jaw jumping.

"I'm not."

And there it is.

The flare of anger, of jealousy, the Ares streak; bullet fast and very hot. Alicia liked testing him—for some sick sense of power, to remind him of his youth but also to know how short the fuse was.

"You do like to follow orders, you have to admit."

The tension in his jaw left as soon as it appeared, back to his cheeky grin, low light kept glinting off his lip ring not unlike a lighthouse guiding a careening ship to shore.

"You're funny when you're drunk."

"You haven't seen me sober," Alicia matched his side smirk. She reached out, teasing a finger down his cheek, feeling the sharp planes of his face. He held his breath as she reached the side of his mouth.

"I saw the new Vessel tonight," he offered, sliding to his elbows and catching her hand in his. They were surprisingly warm, his long finger traced patterns at her wrist.

"Oh?" Her curiosity was genuinely piqued and she leaned in closer. "Partying?"

Was Camille there? I don't remember her telling me anything about it. And I didn't think she would let Leila out of her sight.

"Yeah, with those pricks who think they run the school. Harvey, Elliot, Bianca, that whole crew."

"Zeus and Poseidon, what's new?"

"Right? They kicked me out of the balcony to take care of that Persephone chick."

"Leila," Alicia corrected. "Why? What happened?"

"Something with Blake, or Kat, or both. Hell if I know."

"Aren't they the leaders of your little pack?" She almost felt embarrassed that she was so eager to gossip about people from her old school when she'd graduated a few years back. Without her powers it was like being cut off from every one of her favorite shows.

"I'm not interested in their weird drama. Seems kind of juvenile of Kat."

"What is? Juvenile, I mean?"

Bartie bit his lip. "Acting all jealous of that Leila girl, thinkin' 'er and Blake are going to break up."

"Because of the Myth?" Alicia asked, trying to put the pieces together.

Was what I felt after the Induction related to Leila and Blake? How could that be?

"It's stupid, Leila's been here for all of three seconds. And from what I saw, her new friends aren't going to let her anywhere near us. Typical Order."

Alicia reached for the glass in Bart's hand, finishing the rest of the vodka with a smile. She set the expensive crystal down and made her way to the couch. Her mind was spinning with questions, and the glimmer of something else she didn't know how to vocalize. The couch seeped cold to her bare thighs through the thin chiffon of her robe. She suppressed a shiver.

"So it goes. Order likes collecting little pet projects," she sighed. Order had a way of making everything so...*sterile*. "They better watch out, they have their hands full with this one."

Bart sat on the couch with all the grace of a bomb. He extended an arm behind her, casually, but didn't touch her.

"Really? She didn't look like much when I saw her. I mean, it's plants."

"It's always the ones you don't expect, Bartie."

"You know, you and Cris are the only ones I let call me that," he said, leaning his head back, thoughtfully.

The mention of Cris' name was enough to turn Alicia's stomach. She shifted her robe.

"Cris misses you, you know." His voice was soft. She'd rather take his anger, cauterize her heart with it. Or pity. But this, this was...sympathy.

That was enough to nearly kill her buzz.

She cleared her throat.

"Cris knows where I am, I'm sure, so," she trailed off.

They sat in silence for a minute. Alicia knew Cris would come up; she met Bartie when he was first working security. Cris was the Ares-shaped elephant in the room. Alicia had first met Bartie when he was working the gang's security. Bartie was young, a foot soldier to whatever Cris needed—Alicia didn't care about what Cris' business was, and now she never will have the chance to ask.

Cris was her past, just like Arnie. Cris and Arnie were more similar than they'd like to admit—both weren't big on sharing—the difference being that Cris had a habit of leaving people in pieces.

The wailing notes of the accordion warbled out of the record player, old record fizzed and popped.

"Please tell me you didn't spend the whole night sitting here all alone, torturing yourself with this," he waved an arm at the wall where the record player sat next to a lonely fig plant.

"And what if I did?"

"You're better than a buggerin' accordion, love," he said with a sudden seriousness.

"I am?"

He gave Alicia a look, ran a frustrated hand over his buzzed head, then got up. He walked over the record player, lifting the needle out, leaving them in sudden silence. He fiddled with the wires a bit.

She turned her body to him.

"I hope you aren't breaking my baby," she called to him.

He flicked his gaze back to her for a moment, mischief in his eyes. Then he pulled out his phone and connected it to the set of speakers that surrounded the player. A kick drum then a frenzy of guitars joined in. The male singer joined in, his voice deep and sure.

"I was going to play a symphony or some other bullshit, but I, uh, only have this," he winced, embarrassed.

Alicia laughed, and it surprised her.

"What?" He grinned and it made her stomach flip flop and she wanted to kick herself. This shyness and hesitation was new, but she didn't know why.

"Nothing," she said. "I like it."

She looked at him, matching his grin, staring at his eyes she now realized were a light blue.

He leaned in, capturing her smile with lips. It wasn't a soft kiss— it was tentative, seeking permission. She deepened the kiss, running her tongue on the steel of his lip ring. He placed his hand around her jaw, and she could feel his power at her pulse point. Something reactive unspooled at her core and she gave in to the feeling, pulling him down with her.

Alicia opened her eyes for a moment and saw herself reflected in the windows of her apartment, the spun copper of her hair spilling off the couch in a reckless waterfall, her soft pink legs wrapped around Bartie's gunmetal grey form. Her face was blurred and distorted but Alicia could pretend she was happy.

She wasn't sure how long she could keep pretending. Distractions helped.

LEILA

The sun was blinding, sharp, and slowly stabbing Leila through her head.

Leila groaned.

She turned over, hand flinging up to shield her eyes, and grasped at the sheets under her.

"Finally, our Spring Goddess has awoken," Bianca's voice was close to her. Leila moved her arm a fraction to see Bianca sitting at her desk—fresh-faced, legs crossed prettily, not a periwinkle hair out of place as she typed away on her computer.

"My mouth tastes like death," Leila croaked.

She heard Minnie's laugh echo from the other room.

"Aww, here," Bianca extended a cold mug of water to her.

Any response she had was soon swallowed with the blissfully cold water. She finished it in three gulps and handed the mug back.

"More please," she rasped.

Bianca laughed.

"Ha, no. You need to get out of bed. Camille has been insistent on getting you back to her," she grabbed her phone and showed Leila the screen, scrolling through message after message from Camille, each one less prim and polite than the last. "I don't even know how she got my number."

"So do you call her 'mom', or is that too weird?" Minnie popped her head into the room. Leila looked up at her face and something registered, a broken image spliced between all the mashed up memories of the night before.

Fingers in hair and lips all tangled together.

Minnie flopped down on a beanbag chair across the room.

"I—uh, no, I don't," she turned her eyes from Minnie back to Bianca. "That's too weird—on top of everything else, you know?"

Bianca snorted and was about to respond when a knock interrupted them.

"Odds that's Camille on the other side of that door," Bianca said as she got up and walked out of the room.

It was quiet for a moment as Leila tried to figure out how to approach her memory of Minnie—at least, she thought it was a memory.

"So..." Leila trailed, looking at the trim of Bianca's bedspread, the Edison lights above her, anywhere other than Minnie. She let the silence grow between them.

"Yes," Minnie said.

"Huh?"

"Yes, we did kiss," Minnie finished. "I'm assuming that's what you're trying to ask."

"I—yes... sorry," Leila stuttered, "I just can't really, um, remember?"

Minnie smiled, one corner of her mouth curling up. "You're a good kisser, if that's what you wanted to know."

Leila's face bloomed with heat, and she buried her head in her hands to Minnie's delighted laugh.

"That was a good dare, wasn't it?" Elliot's deep-voiced drawl entered the room before he did. Leila looked up to see the Vessel of Poseidon as he held a drink carrier with three iced coffees balanced in one hand and palmed the fourth. He raised the plastic cup to his lips and took a slow sip from the straw while making eye contact with Leila.

He winked.

Leila rolled her eyes. "So I have you to thank?"

"Yup," he passed out the iced coffees to Bianca and Minnie, handing one to Leila before easing into the chair Bianca had just occupied. An imperceptible wince crossed his face and Leila wondered briefly if it had to do with his prosthesis, but a lazy smile appeared on his face like it never left. "Though if it weren't for you two I would've won that game of Truth or Dare."

Suddenly Leila remembered how much her face was overheating and was grateful for the cold drink slowly condensating between her hands. She took a sip and frowned before taking another couple of sips, not wanting to be rude.

Coffee is gross, I guess.

"Like daring yourself to hook up with that naiad was going to win," Bianca said, crossing her arms.

"No one was daring me to do it, so I had to take it upon myself!"

"You can't 'dare' yourself in Truth or Dare! That's not how it works!" Bianca threw up her hands.

As Elliot retorted, Leila looked over to Minnie and they made eye contact. Minnie mimicked shooting herself, making Leila laugh.

Maybe they're exes? Leila guessed, looking between Elliot and Bianca.

"Some of us are too hungover to stand your arguing," Minnie said over the pair's persistent bickering.

Bianca blushed a little bit but Elliot held his smirk.

"Is Persephone's Vessel feeling a bit wilted?" Elliot turned to Leila.

"Actually, yeah. I don't know about you, but yesterday was a lot."

"Agreed," Minnie chimed in.

"I'd like to say it gets easier from here, but I'd be lying," Elliot took another sip of his coffee.

"It's not that bad, there's rituals and meetings and parties—fun parties!" Bianca emphasized. Leila was grateful for Bianca, relieved there was someone so reassuring on her side.

"Wait," Bianca perked up, "where's Harvey? I need to talk to him about the school's dance budget."

"He was with me! Then he got a call from the mayor's office and had to come in for something or whatever—I wasn't listening." Elliot said.

"I can't believe he's still bothering with that internship, it's not like there's any actual requirement to become the mayor—other than being a Vessel of Zeus, of course," Minnie said.

"Harvey wouldn't take the job without earning it. But yeah, Harvey could run through the Marble District in nothing but his Jordans and he would still win unanimously." Elliot replied.

Leila snorted.

"Yeah but work on the weekend? Absolute torture," Minnie flopped back onto her bean bag chair. She hadn't changed out of her outfit from last night, instead adding a sweatshirt and fuzzy socks to the culottes.

"Funny for a Vessel of Athena to complain about working on the weekend," Elliot asked. "What are you going to do when school starts in a couple of days?"

"How sweet, you think I don't get everything done before the weekend comes. Work smarter, not harder, Elly."

"So that means you have more time to do my homework, then?"

All Elliot got in response was Minnie's tongue sticking out.

Bianca's phone buzzed a couple of times. She picked it up and scrolled for a second before giving a quick laugh.

"Camille's at it again. I guess that's our cue. I'm gonna take Leila back, you guys can come if you want, or stay. Next time we need to go to brunch or something!" Bianca started gathering her keys and Leila got out of bed.

She noticed she was in a random band tee and athletic shorts, though she could only barely remember changing into them.

I hope no one wants these right now. She didn't want to see what the night did to her white dress. Bianca tossed her some flip flops.

"If only my baby wasn't docked up north, I could've given you a ride," Elliot said.

"I love you Elliot, but no one wants to ride in that rust bucket excuse of a boat. Not all of us can breathe underwater," Bianca replied.

"Aw, B, you love me?" Elliot clapped his hands to his chest.

Bianca flipped him off before leaving the room.

Leila followed but not before turning and saying goodbye.

"See you at school!" Elliot called after her. "Senior year! Whoo!"

Leila's stomach rumbled and hoped there was something to eat at home—or, rather, Camille's.

Was it home? She didn't know and was too hungover to dwell on it.

But that question in the back of her mind still lingered:

Will this ever be home?

LEILA

The projector whirred to life, filling the white board with moving pictures. Music soon followed, an old orchestral song that sounded like it was being played from a far off gramophone. The cartoon was black and white, the title card reading *"Welcome to New Olympus!"* in swirly cursive font.

Her eyes flicked to Camille who was sitting next to her primly in a white ruched skirt with blue birds on it and white blouse that was way too perfect for the plastic desk she sat in. Camille had insisted she drive Leila to her first day at New Olympus Preparatory School for Young Vessels, and insisted on staying for the welcome with the principal and the guidance counselor.

She's really leaning in to the whole mom thing, huh? Leila thought—not ungratefully. When they had pulled up the school's main building, a sea of marble and brick loomed over her, ready to swallow her up. Leila bit her lip, ready to say goodbye when Camille had killed the engine, grabbing her things to join her. They sat in an empty classroom, watching the welcome video the principal had said was "less of a protocol, and more of a tradition".

She turned her eyes back to the cartoon. The black and white images depicted marble statues and marble buildings—ancient Greece. Cartoon people wearing togas bounced happily to the beat of the music as they went about their day. Everything seemed to be bouncing with the music: the clouds, the flowers, the sheep, and the fish.

"Long ago," the narrator said in a cheery voice, "the gods and goddesses of Olympus ruled over the humans, and in turn, the humans gave them their power. Through the human's sacrifice and love, the Olympians were powerful and Greece was the center of the universe.

"But as time went on, the humans lost their way, and they stopped giving the gods their power and the world fell to ruin—wars raged and disease swept through the land."

The cartoon showed the mountain of Olympus erupting as people fought and cowered. Arrows volleyed and swords clanged together as armored men battled. Goats and sheep and trees fell to the ground, little X's covered their eyes.

Dead.

"Before all hope was lost, Zeus called his pantheon of gods and they put their magic together to create a utopia where chosen mortals could live and the gods could thrive."

The scene quickly shifted, whirling as cartoon Zeus struck his lightning bolt into a map and the words "New Olympus" flashed. Clouds parted and Leila recognized the long stretch of coastline and spine of mountains that protected the city she now lived in.

"In New Olympus, you get to live in a city of magic and divinity, blessed as a Vessel. In return, your life gives your god—or goddess!—a part of their magic."

The map zoomed into downtown New Olympus at a busy intersection where mortals bounced happily to the music. In the clouds above, gods and goddesses looked on serenely.

"Now remember, young Vessels," the narrator chimed, "*power to the gods!*"

Then the narrator said something in ancient Greek and the cartoon ended. Leila turned to see the principal shuffle to replace the reel. Principal Thistlewhait was short and round with a clipped British accent, long pink fingernails and a matching beaded chain on her glasses. On her chest she had two gaudy jeweled brooches: an owl and a figure that was half-man and half-horse.

"All right dear, we have one more video before you can join the rest of the students in class," she grunted as she pushed the reel into place. She guided the film from the spool and into the machine.

She turned the projector on and it whirred back to life without a hitch.

"Ha! Still got it!" The principal clapped her hands together and turned to Leila. "Are you ready to learn about the myth of Persephone my dear?"

There was no video for the myth of Persephone—not specifically.

Principal Thistlewhait apologized to Leila as the credits rolled: "My Goddess and Me: Demeter".

"Don't be sorry," Camille waved her off politely, answering for Leila.

Leila managed a smile in the principal's direction. Her new shoes squeaked on the hardwood floor. The black patent leather oxfords needed to be broken in and her over-the-knee socks offered little protection from the stiff leather already digging into her ankles.

The rest of her New Olympus Prep uniform was comfortable: from her pleated plaid dress in the school's colors of navy and burgundy, to the chiffon bow tied on top her hair to keep her curls out of her face, to the silky navy cashmere sweater with the New Olympus crest stitched into its left breast.

This cartoon was in that same bouncy, happy style as the other video except this was set in a beautiful garden of dancing flowers and trees.

In the middle of the garden was a beautiful woman in a toga. She batted her eyelashes.

"Gosh golly, I'm Demeter! And you must be my Vessels, nice to meet you! I'm here to tell you my story!" Her voice was high and sing-songy as she continued talking about the Vessel's role in New Olympus.

I wonder if I'll have any classes with Minnie or Bianca? Leila hadn't heard from them since she left their dorm a few days ago, but she didn't have a phone yet, so she didn't expect them to send a carrier pigeon or something.

Unless that's a normal thing around here. She wouldn't put it past them.

Her gaze wandered to the large set of windows, the sun out in full. The classroom had a view of the school's rec fields and the sparkling sea beyond it. She was thinking of the Vessels who were now officially her classmates: Mason's sun-blond hair, Harvey's tall form—when the cartoon said a name that snapped her gaze back to the projector's light.

"—and Persephone was my most favorite and cherished daughter," the goddess was brushing the hair of another, younger-looking woman who had to be Persephone. She had long flowing curls and a gown made out of petals.

Leila looked over to smile at Camille, but she was staring at the cartoon completely stone-faced.

Weird.

"We lived in eternal happiness, where flowers always bloomed and fruits were always ripe." The mother and daughter laughed with each other in the middle of the meadow.

The music turned sinister, and behind the two goddesses, a shadowy figure lurked. "But it wouldn't last, because the greedy god of death Hades stole Persephone for himself!"

The shadowy figure emerged, a tall god with fiery eyes and a crown of skulls, scaring the small Persephone. She tried to run but Hades slung a bag over her and dragged her out of the garden. "He made her his bride, but I vowed to get my daughter back, even if the world had to starve!" The goddess turned angry, the beautiful meadow wilting until there was nothing left but dirt.

Leila shifted in the hard plastic of her seat. There was dread coiling in her stomach.

"Finally, Zeus granted my wish, and commanded Hades to give Persephone back—only if she didn't eat any food from the Underworld. Of course, Hades had another trick up his sleeve, making sure I never truly got my daughter back."

The scene shifted to the Underworld, where Hades laughed and laughed in front of table laden with pomegranates as Persephone sulked. Her stomach rumbled and she looked around desperately, sneaking a pomegranate seed into her mouth.

"When Persephone came back to me, we celebrated with life coming back to the earth. What mortals call Spring." The meadow came back to life as the two goddesses embraced. "But since Persephone ate food in the Underworld, she has to go back and be the bride of Hades for half of the year, and the world goes through Fall and Winter. As a Vessel of Demeter, you—"

The audio cut off as Principal Thistlewhait fiddled with the equipment.

"I think that was all of the mentions of Persephone in this one, would you like to see a part of the Hades video?"

"No, I don't believe I'd like to see whatever justification for kidnapping is in that video, thank you," Camille clipped.

Thistlewhait blinked behind her large glasses. Leila could feel the anger roiling off the Vessel of Demeter, which was something she hadn't seen before. Camille looked at Leila and her eyes softened. "I'm sorry, I meant to say that I think you've got the gist of your Myth, and you don't need a rehash—right, love?"

"Right," she said slowly.

"You're right," Principal Thistlewhait agreed, then went on to talk about student conduct and scheduling.

Leila vaguely nodded at her, but she couldn't help but think about what she saw—the abduction, the flowers dying, and Hades laughing.

Not Hades—Blake. His smirk, his fiery grey eyes.

Dread coiled in her stomach.

The bell rang, startling Leila out of her thoughts. The bustle of students outside the classroom door grew louder.

"Well, I think you've had enough introduction!" Principal Thistlewhait clapped her hands together. "That's the lunch bell. Leila, why don't you go join the other students?"

BIANCA

Bianca and Minnie waited for Leila outside the classroom door where she was talking with Camille and Principal Thistlewhait.

"Hey!" Bianca said, surprising her friend as she exited the classroom.

Leila seemed less surprised and more completely freaked out as she flinched at Bianca's greeting. She stumbled back into the door frame.

"Oh my gods, I'm so sorry, I didn't mean to scare you!" The Vessel of Iris looked over Leila, trying to figure out what was wrong.

"Yeah, we thought that we'd escort you to lunch, since you probably have no idea where the cafeteria is," Minnie added.

Leila relaxed into a grateful smile, brushing her long, dark curls behind her.

"No, no it's fine, I had to watch a weird cartoon. How did you know I'd be in here?"

"We have an in with the secretary," Bianca said lightly as she linked her arms with Leila's. They started down the hall.

"More like Bianca practically lives in the administration's office because of how many extracurriculars she's involved in," Minnie added..

Their skirts swished together as they navigated New Olympus Prep—Bianca's legs were the longest and left her skirt shorter than the others while Min-Seo preferred to wear hers at midi-length, leaving Leila in the middle with her skirt brushing the tops of her knees.

"So you watched the welcome video?" Minnie asked. "Pretty spooky, huh?"

"Yeah," Leila's eyebrows scrunched together. "I watched two. One about New Olympus, and the other was about Persephone."

Uh-oh. Bianca's eyes met her best friend's.

Every Vessel knew how it felt to watch your god's Myth for the first time, to see a glimpse into how Fate would bless you in your life. Or curse.

Bianca remembered the way she felt, watching a cartoon of Iris fly around, delivering messages on an arc of a rainbow and filling everyone's cups like she was someone's assistant.

I'm not meant to be filling someone else's cup.

She shook her head at the memory.

"We hoped you wouldn't have to watch it since you're not a kid like most new Vessels," Bianca sympathized.

"It wasn't what I was expecting, but it's not like Blake can come and kidnap me right?" Leila laughed.

"Right?" Minnie agreed. "Plus we've had winter every year even without your influence, unfortunately."

That sparked something in Bianca—a half-remembered conversation from the Induction, but she didn't want to voice it until she was absolutely sure.

He can try, Bianca thought angrily.

Bianca led them to the cafeteria, fragments of light sparking on her heels.

MIN-SEO

Min-Seo couldn't help but smile when they walked through the doors of the cafeteria. Her jade eyes glittered at the wave of heads that tried and failed to subtly catch a glimpse of the Vessel of Persephone. The food line moved at a snail's pace from all the gawking.

Minnie wondered if Leila felt all the eyes on her, but the video she watched with Principal Thistlewhait must have gotten under her skin because she didn't seem to notice. Looking across the cafeteria, she saw a pair of glowing hands waving at her. Sitting around Mason were the rest of her friends: Elliot, Harvey, Oscar.

My boys.

Bianca only got stopped a couple of times on the way to their table with questions about club meetings or general fawning. Minnie tried not to let the feeling of jealousy burn a hole through her each time they stopped. "Exactly how many extracurriculars is Bianca a part of?" Leila murmured to Minnie.

"Too many."

"Sounds exhausting."

"Yeah, it is," Minnie muttered.

Sharing is caring, Minnie reminded herself. But she never really liked sharing. When she lived with the other Vessels of Athena, she had to share computer time and math workbooks and studio space. Being friends with Bianca had always been a competition for her time—and that competition only got more and more fierce as they got older.

Bianca's ever-growing need to prove herself to everyone made her the busiest teenager she knew. Except for Harvey of course.

Bianca doesn't have to prove herself to me, she frowned.

She smoothed out the frown on her face.

"I don't have to join any, right?" Leila said with a smirk.

"No, thank the gods," Minnie replied with a laugh.

Bianca finished her conversation, and they sat down at the table with their friends. Minnie let a smug smile show.

She may lead your club, but she's best friends with me.

"Leila, how does it feel to be an official New Olympus Prep student?" Oscar asked as they sat down. His Spanish accent made his voice even smoother and more velvety soft.

"Undecided," Leila replied, french fry mid-air. "When I get through a class I'll let you know."

"Honestly, same. We've been in an assembly this whole time, so boring," Mason rolled his eyes.

"Wait, I was leading that assembly," Harvey side-eyed the golden-haired boy.

All four boys sat across from them, looking like the de-evolution of the school uniform: from Harvey's starched shirt and ruler-straight tie, to Elliot, who sat across from Minnie, uniform in practiced disheveledness. His long brown hair already looked like a couple of hands had run through it. He stole a fry from Minnie's tray before she could slap him away. The buzz of the cafeteria made Minnie feel like they were in a glass bubble all their own.

Elliot slammed his palms on the table with a loud smack. "Everyone whip 'em out, all right?"

"Don't be gross," Bianca glared.

Elliot gave her a cheeky smile.

"Get your head out of the gutter, darl, I'm talking about class schedules," he stood, hands reaching for his slacks. "Unless you mean..?"

The rest of the table yelled at him to sit down.

"Can we please not traumatize Leila on her first day?" Harvey said. He rubbed one of his temples, his other arm slung over Oscar's shoulders. "OK, I'll go first. Who has Advanced Ethics with me third period?"

There was a pause as they all shuffled through their book-bags and pockets for the pink slip of paper with their schedules printed on it. Minnie used the assembly time to organize her school binder, her schedule written out on the cover.

"I do," her eyes met Zeus' Vessel. She was excited to see what kind of debate they'd get into.

They all continued on, going through their schedules and finding out where they intersected. She loved the first day of the school year; the potential in the air carried her through the halls.

"Min-Seo, what does that big block on your schedule mean?" Leila held her schedule up to Minnie's.

"Studio time, for sculpting," she explained. "I petitioned for the administration to give me studio time so I could focus on art."

Her green eyes flashed, the excitement rushing her words. She'd been working on getting this studio time for so long—and now she was a senior didn't take no for an answer.

I can make anything.

"Dude, why aren't you in my fencing class with me? I thought we were going to do this together," Elliot muttered to Mason.

Mason dimmed, looking down. "I, uh, switched out," he said dismissively.

"Why? What are you taking instead?" Elliot stretched over Mason's shoulder to read his schedule. "Archery? Really? Didn't you once tell me you had the aim of a drunk rhinoceros?"

"That's why I'm taking the class," Mason moved his schedule away.

"I have fencing that period!" Leila reached over the table to meet Elliot's high five.

"We don't have any classes together," Harvey frowned at his boyfriend. "I thought you were the Vessel of good luck."

"*Caerus* is the god of opportunity actually," Oscar's eyes left his schedule to rest on his boyfriend. "So make this an opportunity to cherish the time we're together, *mi amor*." He landed a quick peck on Harvey's mouth and Harvey rolled his eyes.

Minnie didn't see Danny until his hand was on Harvey's shoulder. The rest of the group stopped talking at the flutter of Danny's arrival. The Vessel of Hermes' spoke to Harvey, his voice only audible to its recipient. His russet curls hung down in front of his face as if to shield him from the rest of them. Harvey nodded and thanked Danny. Danny looked at them and waved shyly before setting off again. Minnie could see the creep of red embarrassment making its way up his neck.

"Bye Danny!" Bianca called after the boy. Danny turned abruptly to wave and then ran into a table of students. Trays clattered to the ground.

"Ouch," Minnie winced.

"Double ouch," Elliot laughed, earning a glare from Bianca.

Harvey turned back to his boyfriend.

"You're lucky you're so cute," Harvey said as he checked the watch on his wrist. "I gotta jet, there's still some JC stuff I have to get done."

Minnie watched Harvey hurry out to whatever meeting was next on his schedule. Oscar looked with fingers twirling his dark curls. Minnie felt a twinge of longing seeing that look, but immediately dismissed it.

What does it even mean to have a significant other anyway? Minnie took a big bite of her burger. She'd never had a girlfriend—even though she'd been out since she was a freshman—and so she didn't even know what she was missing. If she was missing anything.

She could feel the urge to sculpt coming on—to throw clay and scrape pieces away, to feel the sediment under her fingers. That was the most familiar want she had and she was excited to start her studio time after lunch.

"So JC is the Junior Council for young Vessels?" Leila asked. A forkful of salad was poised in front of her mouth.

"Yeah, it's so all Vessels under eighteen can come together and meet without the need to 'bother' all the adults or whatever," Mason explained.

"And it brings together all the Vessels who don't see each other if they go to different schools," Bianca added.

"Wait, there's more than one school?" Leila asked.

"Well, some Vessels believe they need to learn with Vessels of their own god. And there are so many Vessels that we can't have just one school to house us all," Mason said.

"New Olympus Prep is the most elite, then there's New Olympus Secondary School, West New Olympus High School, North New Olympus High School, and then some temple schools for the really devout Vessels," Oscar finished.

Leila scrunched her full eyebrows together, a crease appearing in between. She was no doubt getting overwhelmed again—there was so much to learn about this magical place that even Minnie forgot about it sometimes.

Thank Athena I pulled ahead of every other Vessel to get into Prep, Minnie thought. Every Vessel of Athena wants to get into New Olympus Preparatory but only a certain percentage of one god or goddess can be accepted. She made the cut, and never looked back.

"Our school has an entrance exam and an interview process, but there's special cases, like being the only Vessel of your kind. Like you, Leila," Minnie said. "And other creatures: talented water nymphs and naiads, you'll probably see some dryad professors, and even satyrs have a place here."

"Right," Mason mused. "We're the school with the most powerful magic."

"And the most powerful—*hey!*" Elliot balked. Minnie had thrown a fry the moment Elliot decided to chime in, hitting him in the eye. "You didn't even know what I was going to say."

"I can't believe this is the most elite school," Leila started. "Since I'm sitting across from three of the biggest clowns I know."

Minnie's table burst into scoffs and laughter, and she thanked Athena again for her friends—new and old.

HARVEY

Harvey made sure to change into a different outfit before the Junior Council meeting. He wanted all of the Vessels to feel like they're on equal ground and he couldn't do that in a New Olympus Prep blazer.

We're all Vessels of the Olympians, no need to make it more complicated than that.

He changed in the marbled bathrooms of Athena's temple. It was a good neutral ground for all the young Vessels to meet, and it was located in the relative middle of the city—way more accessible than Zeus' temple in the winding mountains.

He adjusted his tie and looked in the mirror. His brown tweed bomber jacket was a couple of shades lighter than his skin, contrasted by his navy button down that was patterned in little lightning bolts.

He smiled in the mirror and ran a hand to the side of his freshly cut hair. He exited the bathroom to the expansive hall.

"I know you're trying to look like the people's Vessel, but there is an advantage to reminding everyone where you're from," a voice behind him said.

Martin. Harvey closed his eyes and took a breath before turning to face the other Vessel of Zeus and the mayor of New Olympus. The mayor was leaning against the wall, and if he wasn't in his usual three piece suit, he would look every bit like a general of ancient epics.

"You're right, sir, but for the first meeting of the school year I thought it'd be best to play neutral," he lied. Martin had an "old-school" approach to leading Vessels: everyone had their place whether it was Chaos or Order, Major or Minor.

Martin approached him. He was shorter than Harvey, but broader, the fabric of his shirt stretched over his muscular chest. He had slick, lightning-blond hair and eyes like storm clouds.

"Good," the older Vessel smiled. "You're becoming a fine leader, and I'm sure you have everything all thought out."

He reached out his hands and adjusted Harvey's tie.

"Thank you, sir," Harvey muttered to him.

"Remember I chose you over a number of Zeus' Vessels because the legacy of leadership must stay in our hands," Martin's fingers ghosted Harvey's throat "Don't make me regret my decision. Order above Chaos, understand?"

Harvey felt his heart hammer. He didn't always agree with the mayor's rulings, but Harvey couldn't help but respect him—at least he would until his reign was finally over.

"Of course, sir. Order above Chaos," he sputtered out, looking down.

The older Vessel's shoes echoed off the marble as he walked away, the only sound other than Harvey's erratic heartbeat.

The meeting was going well, despite Harvey's nerves being on high. As soon as he stepped in front of the crowd of younger Vessels, the addictive power of Zeus electrified his veins, and he stepped into his role as Junior Council Leader like the role was forged for him alone.

Athena's temple was as much a tribute to the goddess as it was to architecture itself; impossible curves of marble and glass panes formed into an expansive atrium that rose and dipped like sand dunes. A mosaic of owls and olive leaves in contrasting stones swirled on the floor and up the walls. Marble benches lined the atrium, filled with the younger Vessels. Despite Harvey's best efforts, the meeting still felt very...territorial. From the navy and burgundy sea of the New Olympus Prep students, to the leather clad and studded Chaos Vessels, to the pure white of the Acolytes—those who study and pledge themselves to a temple—they were all grouped up. Even the public school kids were grouped up, and they didn't wear uniforms. Harvey swept his eyes over the seated mass of teenagers.

It's a start. He tried to keep a positive outlook on it.

"Fate smiles upon us this year," he spoke to the crowd.

"Whoo!" Elliot yelled and a giggle spread across the crowd. He cut his gaze to his friends who sat together in the middle of the New Olympus Prep crowd. He smiled and waved his hand up, commanding them to silence. He noticed all Vessels naturally listened when he spoke. Well, most Vessels.

"Thank you for coming today, and thank you to Athena for letting us meet in her temple, there's snacks and drinks for everyone in the hall. I'll be staying after to address any queries or concerns anyone has. *δύναμη στους θεούς!*"

"*δύναμη στους θεούς!*" The young Vessels repeated.

Power to the gods. Often repeated at meetings or rituals or even on the street in passing. After they spoke the saying back to him, the room filled with noise and movement. He was immediately bombarded with a polite line of Vessels in need of his council.

He was in the middle of talking with a young acolyte of Aeolus and his questions about the borders of New Olympus when Bianca came over to him, meeting his eyes with hers. She hurried over, her eyebrows knitted together in worry.

"Excuse me," he said to the young boy and turned to his friend. Bianca tucked her blue curls behind her left ear in a nervous habit he'd seen her do before every test in school as long as he could remember.

"What's wrong?" He asked.

She looked at him nervously. "I can't find Leila."

LEILA

Leila knew it was Blake in the crowd.

She didn't know what she was going to do but when she saw him —his tall, lanky form moving like smoke through the Vessels—she had to say something.

One minute she was listening to Elliot and Minnie debate whose god had the best temple when she saw him—or rather, *felt* his presence, like he was a magnet for her to get stuck on. If he felt the same, he didn't make it known.

Maybe I get my own built-in kidnap alert system, she thought.

Her mouth straightened to a line, determined. She followed him.

His inky, black hair curled around the collar of his navy blazer— and it only registered distantly to Leila that it was a match to the school uniforms all of her guy friends were wearing. He didn't acknowledge anyone though people made room for him. He walked facing straight ahead, seemingly unbothered by the way that the other Vessels regarded him. Younger Vessels gaped, others stole fearful glances, and some outright sneered.

He didn't waver.

Leila was too preoccupied with keeping up with him without completely eating shit on the smooth marble floor her oxfords kept slipping on, she didn't notice when the crowd thinned to nothing. That they were deeper in the temple. *Alone.*

He stopped walking and turned around suddenly, causing Leila to half-skid to a stop. His grey eyes caught her brown ones, something mischievous brewing . He was smiling, she realized, before he wiped a hand over his face and went back to his stony composure.

He knew I was following him.

"Why are you stalking me?" he asked.

"I'm not! I, uh," she blinked. "I needed to talk to you," she tried not to make it sound like it was a question.

He extended his hands, an impatient gesture at her continued silence.They were about ten feet apart, the stark white of the marble around them made her feel even more isolated.

Why am I so stupid, she chastised herself. But then she looked at his face, the condescending turn of his lips, and stood a little straighter.

"OK? Talk," he stuck his hands in the navy trousers of his uniform.

"Look," she took a breath. "I know about the Myth."

He stilled, looking at Leila warily.

"I get it—why you want nothing to do with me," she said.

Her heart was pounding but she had to get the words out. From the moment they met, he had an effect on her, and now she knew why. She had felt powerless watching the goddess Persephone being ripped from her home. Leila was a mortal but she had to gain her power back.

A way to rewrite my Myth, or Fate, or something!

Leila felt like ever since she woke up in that field, everything in her life had been non-stop, and she was starting to lose her footing. And Blake—from the Myth they shared to Cami's and her friends' reactions to him—was bad news. She wasn't going to be a part of the group of Vessels who aligned themselves with Chaos, like her friends were worried about. Not that Chaos wanted Leila anyway, as Blake's girlfriend Kat didn't seem to take too kindly to Leila.

"I wanted to say I agree with you. Let's stay away from each other from now on," she finished. She waited for him to meet her eyes again or to say something, but he didn't. She turned to walk back the way she came.

I thought I would feel better, lighter. Why do I feel hollow?

"I don't think you do," he said softly.

She turned. "What?"

"I don't think you 'get it'," he ground out, the muscles in his jaw jumping at each word. "Do you know how I've been treated since I was a child because of that Myth? Because of a crime I wasn't even alive to commit?"

"I didn't mean——"

"Vessels like to think a Myth has a hold of us, controlling our actions." He sighed, his shoulders falling. "There are names I've been called from the time I got to New Olympus, you have no idea."

"I'm sorry," she was taken aback. "I didn't know."

"How would you? You get to come to New Olympus as a star ——'*the rarest and most precious Vessel*'. Why would you want to have anything to do with the only bad part of it all?"

That struck a nerve. This conversation was slipping out of her control, Blake seeing right through any pretense of hers without a problem. Leila's chest felt tight, the cashmere sweater clinging to her throat.

"Is that so bad," she countered, "I want to separate myself from anything that could ruin any happiness I have here?"

"No, but it's entirely predictable. If you think you can change your Myth, you're even more stupid than I thought."

Anger coursed through her and she stepped towards him, her shoes echoing on the stone.

"You know, I've only talked to you twice, but maybe the way people treat you isn't because of your Myth, maybe it's because you're an asshole!"

He took a step towards her, staring her down.

"And all I've seen of you is you're a coward who hides behind your friends."

"They aren't here now, are they?"

"Just wait," he deadpanned, "your friends are probably organizing a search party for you."

"And where are yours?" She forced as much ice into her words, despite the heat of anger blazing through every part of her. "Vessel of Hades can't conjure a ghost to be his friend?"

She could see the dark grey of his eyes churning to black.
Good.

"You're exactly like them," he seethed. She could feel his breath on her face, cool and minty. "Why Persephone would choose you as a Vessel is beyond me."

"You don't know what I'm capable of," she bit back.

Do I even know what I'm capable of? He didn't need to know.

"I wish I—"

"*Leila!*" Bianca's voice cut through his words.

She turned to see Bianca, Minnie, and Harvey walking towards them. Leila felt the lift of relief and also a surprising burn of shame because Blake was right—they'd come looking for her.

Leila turned back to Blake and noticed how close they were, how hard they were both breathing. She could clearly see the tired purple under his eyes and the shadow of stubble at his jaw. His lips had curled back at the words that died on his mouth. She'd gotten too close to the Vessel of Hades.

She stepped away quickly.

"What's going on?" Harvey asked. His tone was a practiced friendliness, clear and sunny skies. He and the girls stood a couple of feet away from Leila and Blake.

"Nothing bad, swear to gods," he said with his hand up in the air, the other on his heart. "You can collect your lost Vessel now."

She crossed her arms to stop herself from flipping him off. He looked so calm, unlike Leila.

I'm so angry my hair is frizzing. Her heartbeat was a mess and she felt sweaty all over. She walked to her friends.

As she was rounding the corner, she thought she heard Blake mutter something that made her ears burn. She kept walking in her group as they made their way back to where all the other Vessels gathered, but the word wound its way around her heart and with each heartbeat she could hear his deep, smoky whisper over and over again.

Coward.

Coward. Coward. Coward. Coward. Coward. Coward. Coward.

BLAKE

He left the temple shaking.

It was a good thing his car had keyless entry, his fingerprints attuned to the McLaren GT haphazardly parked on the side-street, or else he didn't think he could have managed to unlock his own car. The driver's side door lifted up like a hand wave as he got closer.

He sat in the car, waiting for the door to shut with a quiet hiss. He pressed his hands to the steering wheel, watched how his long, pale fingers shook and willed them to stop. He had to control himself at least until he was out of sight. He'd learned Vessels of Hades weren't allowed the same margin of error as the other Vessels. He had to be immaculate —at least in public.

One press of a button and his engine roared to life, the power vibrating under his shoes. He didn't waste any time looking at his phone —knowing how Kat had a tendency to send long threads of texts. She could handle a couple hours to herself while he wrested control over his emotions.

He gave a cursory glance to his rear view as he pulled out of the temple parking spot, the orange blaze of sunset casting everyone outside in bronze. Hitting the accelerator and turning the corner to avoid even a glimpse of Leila, he drove deeper into the heart of New Olympus.

Even though she'd left first, a small part of him nagged that *he* was the one running away.

Who cares? He gripped the steering wheel, trying to concentrate on the rush hour traffic.

"Who cares?" He growled out as the light turned green and he shifted into gear with more force than necessary. He turned east, away from New Olympus Prep. He needed to be alone for a while. Blake raked back his hair. Leila couldn't just *agree* with him, she had to make it look like *she* was the one who wanted nothing to do with *him*.

How gracious.

He let out a frustrated sigh as he got caught at another light. Quickly, he backed up and shot down an alley, zigzagging through smaller streets until he broke free from the city. He was at the seat of the mountain ranges that circled like a crescent around New Olympus.

Most of the mountains were left wild, save for some hidden-away cabins—and the Hades estate he'd been sequestered to every winter since he could remember.

He hit his accelerator, the engine responding with ferocity.

"Vessel of Hades can't conjure a ghost to be his friend?" He could see Leila's awful smirk in his memory, taunting him.

A whisper of the same smile was on Blake's face as he wondered if Leila's nice *Order* friends knew the cruelty hiding under her big brown eyes.

Like Leila even knows herself, he mused.

All good feelings soured as he remembered everything else—the fear, the disgust, the distrust in the other Vessels' faces. This had always been the case; his childhood was cold and distant, as if a friendship with him carried a death sentence. It didn't matter if he'd never hurt anyone, people held his Myth over him like a gallows' noose.

Leila shouldn't be the one to get away with being loved and revered for doing nothing, just like he shouldn't be shunned for simply existing.

He hit the gas, watching as the speedometer ticked up, the tall evergreens blurring into green smears.

Stop feeling sorry for yourself. Blake turned on his speakers, suddenly sick of the silence. He wanted to drown out his thoughts.

The bass vibrated through the car, propelling him forward up the zigzag of a road. The sun had finally set, the mountains washed in blues and greens. His headlights were his only guide as he made his way up the mountain. He could feel his power making his fingers itch, his eyes going black from corner to corner. Large shapes moved in the forest—creatures of myth held dominion over the wild, stirred by a Vessel of Hades out of control.

With every razor turn he took, every uncontrolled drift of his wheels made him wonder what was the point of regaining control when he would eventually lose it again?

For a second he could see the sick twist of the wheel as he jerked it to the side suddenly, his car taking flight, flipping over the guardrail, crumpling as it crashed down onto the slope.

His stomach flip-flopped at the thought but he continued his ascent with full control. He thought of how Leila's friends came to rescue her back at the temple when she'd gone after Blake in the first place. They thought he was a monster—they wouldn't hear any different.

Drops of rain pelted the windshield slowly, then with enough intensity Blake had to slow down, but he had reached the peak. The road turned to gravel, then dirt.

He left his car running and leapt out. He was surrounded by walls of trees, the hard deluge of rain soaking through his blazer, running down his scalp to his temples.

Here he could release all of the pent up rage he was feeling—the rage tied with the stress and anxiety—he couldn't keep it inside any longer.

If they think I'm a monster, then I'm a fucking *monster.*

Blake roared out all of his feelings, every ugly thought raked out of his throat. His power surged out of him and a dark shroud covered every living thing within a hundred feet.

He dropped to his knees, exhausted. When he looked up he was in a field of ash, all the life drained out of the greenery.

The rain kept falling, but he couldn't feel it. He looked at the lights of the city below visible with the trees crumbled away.

The side of his mouth quirked into a smile.

I'm the monster.

CAMILLE

The cafe was at the bottom of one of the tallest skyscrapers in uptown New Olympus. It was her favorite because of the way the climbing roses weaving their way through the low fence surrounding the cafe bloomed in beautiful white bundles.

It was Alicia's favorite because the outdoor seating gave her the perfect view to people-watch during the sunny Saturday afternoon. Camille watched her friend's eyes follow the crowd as she sipped her cappuccino.

Camille took a sip of her own flat white with a smile. Even being in the presence of her friend was enough to mellow her out—something only Alicia could do.

"So, Cami, have you brought the boyfriend home yet?'

Cami put her cup down delicately before answering. Alicia didn't like to waste time with shallow questions.

"I don't have a boyfriend, you know better than anyone," Cami placed her manicured hands on her lap.

Alicia arched an eyebrow.

"I don't! You know Martin doesn't like labels—and neither do I."

"Yeah I'm sure his wife doesn't either," Alicia said, low enough only Cami heard her.

If Cami was the kind of person to smack her friend she would have in that moment.

"Don't talk to me about love triangles, Miss Aphrodite," Cami retorted, not unkindly. "Besides, it comes with the territory—we all have parts of the Myth we don't like."

Alicia gave her a good-natured eye roll. Cami knew she was the only one who'd seen the ugliest parts of Alicia's past—she'd picked her up from her heartbreak, seen her through the darkest of nights. And Alicia had been there for her ten times over.

That's what best friends were for.

But, even though it was nearly a year ago, Alicia still looked so pale, so fragile.

"So has your *not-boyfriend* helped you with your little problem yet?"

Cami frowned. "Not quite."

"What do you mean? He's the mayor, he should be able to do what he wants."

"He says the situation is more *delicate* than he thought," Cami's accent clipped every word. She hated how powerless she felt—she *just* got Leila.

I can't lose her.

"So what? Because we haven't had any Vessels of Persephone in centuries doesn't mean we have to observe her Myth to its letter."

"I agree," Cami sighed.

"'*Delicate*', my ass. You don't deserve this," Alicia huffed.

"The things I've heard about the Vessels of Hades," Cami was losing her cool. "Leila and that Hades boy have to be exiled for *six* months! It's bullshit!"

"It can't be that bad—"

"It *can*. Leila all alone in the mountains with that Vessel of Hades —no friends, no family, no protection. It's going to be a nightmare."

Alicia's eyes widened—she wasn't looking at Cami but behind her.

Cami turned to see Leila and her two friends Min-Seo and Bianca, their arms full of shopping bags. Their matching shocked expressions made her heart sink, this wasn't how she wanted her Leila to find out.

Leila rushed out, her friends following her.

Cami called after her without avail; she could feel a wrinkle forming between her brows.

  "Motherhood, am I right?" Alicia said, pulling out a flask from the breast pocket of her camel trench coat. She poured some of the amber liquid into Cami's mug before taking a swig of her own.

LEILA

Leila sped along the wide sidewalk next to Bianca and Minnie, their shopping bags bumping into each other. Finally at an intersection, Leila stopped.

It was a beautiful day, the sun glinting off the tall skyscrapers and shooting yellow rays of sunlight everywhere. The weekend crowd bustled around them, weaving around the three girls standing at the edge of the sidewalk. Leila didn't feel any of it—all the happiness of a day spent with friends gone down the newly opened pit of dread in her stomach.

"Are you OK, Leila?" Bianca asked.

Leila looked up at her friend, her periwinkle hair glowing in the sun. She struggled to find the words, her powers itching to bridge the gap.

What would that help? Camille had warned her about reigning in her magic, especially in a crowd—even if she felt like she was going to burst.

"I don't understand," Leila said. "I just got here." Every step felt so precarious.

"It has to be part of your Myth; all Vessels have to do certain things because of it," Minnie explained.

"It's part of the magic that binds us," Bianca said gently.

"And it fucking sucks," Minnie spat.

"Like what?" Leila asked.

"Like..." Minnie frowned. "Like, Vessels of Zeus have been mayor since New Olympus was founded, because Zeus is the king of the gods in the Myth. Stuff like that. Since this is the first time we've had Persephone and Hades represented, they might not do anything."

Leila looked up at the sky, letting the sun fall on her face. With effort, she took a long breath.

How many sunny days do I have left?

"I'm going to make sure nothing happens," she said as she stalked ahead, weeds bursting through the cracks of the sidewalk with each step.

ELLIOT

His friends were nothing but trouble.

First he had his boys, Mason and Harvey. Mason was harmless, in the same way C-4 was harmless. And Harvey was too strait-laced for his own good, and because of his sparkling reputation he could get away with anything.

Then there was Minnie and Bianca. Minnie might be a tad more competitive than him and she *hated* to lose. Bianca was the worst of them all—her standards were so high all the time, it drove him to be the worst version of himself to spite her.

He could see her blue eyes rolling at him. That made Elliot smile.

He was swinging on the hammock he'd tied between rails at the bow of his boat, the late summer sun warming his tanned skin.

And then there was Leila.

Just because she might be a Vessel of Chaos didn't mean she didn't deserve his friendship. If he believed all the unity shit Harvey liked to talk about, it meant she deserved it even more. So far she'd been cool—and then there were flashes of fire that made him trip up. The way her brown eyes swirled molten, he wasn't sure what to make of it.

"Elliot!" Minnie's clear voice shouted at him, startling him out of his thoughts. "*Hello!!*"

He scrambled out of his hammock—careful not to knock his metal prosthesis—to see Minnie, Bianca, and Leila boarding his boat, each with their own army of shopping bags.

"Welcome aboard, ladies," he fished his cream henley shirt off the railing and pulled it on.

"Wow, Elliot, hoard much?" Minnie looked around at his deck.

"Hey, don't insult *Bernice*."

"Your boat's name is *Bernice*?" Leila said incredulously.

"It means 'she who brings victory', OK? *Bernice* is my baby," Elliot patted the side of the cabin roof and tried not to look displeased when chips of paint peeled off. His boat was a retired fishing vessel, barely big enough to tackle ocean waves. It was older than Elliot but it ran like a dream. Even if he did leave his fishing gear around, dry his laundry wherever the sun hit his deck, and leave all his rope unspooled —that's what gave Bernice her *charm*. And her *eclectic* appearance pissed off all of the yacht owners and luxury sailors neighboring him, which was always a bonus.

I should've gone to see the Twins, he thought. He called the other two Vessels of Poseidon—Aron and Merch—*'twins'* because they were both old as shit, grumpy as shit, and liked to bark orders at him when he visited them at sea. He loved them, even if they never stepped foot on land. He could feel the current of the Styx, slow and mercurial, and wished he was in the roaring tide of the ocean. A trill of fear ran down his left side but he ignored it.

"We need your help," Leila said. She had that look again. He snuck a look at Bianca to see if it was legit but her face matched Leila's.

It's either go along with whatever plan these girls have cooked up or get stuck playing bartender for two talking barnacles, he thought of the Twins.

"What do you need?"

BLAKE

The weekend was a blur and Monday was the halting spotlight threatening to burn a hole into his skull. Maybe showing up visibly hungover would finally get him expelled from New Olympus Prep, but he knew better than to hope—the school hoarded the rarer Vessels more fiercely than a dragon hoards jewels.

And he was the only Vessel of Hades in New Olympus—very rare indeed.

Would public school be any better? Blake rested his head on his hand, his other hand copying the notes on the board without thought. He'd taken ancient Greek since he could hold a pencil; the language came to him easily, so he'd made sure he had this class first thing in the morning to give himself a break.

Most of his friends went to West New Olympus High School, while the rest went to North New Olympus High School. Even if he went to North New or West New he knew he still wouldn't fit in: most of the Minor Vessels went there and he couldn't stand being that big of a fish in such a small pond.

Then there were the Acolytes, those Vessels who devoted their time to their god or goddess. They were schooled in their own temples, wore white, and only interacted with Vessels of their own kind. They were weird as all get-out, but they had a tight community that made Blake jealous. Even if Blake had a choice, he couldn't imagine living in

Hades' temple by himself—just him and the cobwebs.

He lifted the wayfarer sunglasses he was wearing to rub his temples, trying to ease the pain throbbing just underneath the surface. After the Junior Council meeting and his drive up into the mountains, he had drowned all of his awful feelings in partying and had barely emerged long enough to stop by his dorm to grab a fresh uniform before school. He wasn't sure when he'd slept, but according to his headache, he hadn't gotten nearly enough of it.

No, the problem isn't with what school I go to, he mused.

The teacher asked him a question in ancient Greek, the attention bringing him back to the language classroom. Her eyes rested somewhere above his head as she called on him—she never asked him to take off his sunglasses even though it was strictly against the school's dress code, not that she would even know since she never looked him in the eye.

The question was on some part of the reading Blake should've done over the weekend. He almost felt guilty, a part of him remembering how it felt to put all of his effort into school, the excitement of doing well. That part of him felt a world away.

He answered in a bored tone, adding a flourish of the optative and subjunctive in his reply with the hope she would be impressed by the advanced verb tenses and not pick up he didn't know what the actual answer was.

Right or wrong, she seemed satisfied and left him alone for the rest of the class.

The bell rang and he gathered his things to head to his next class: cartography. Even though the whole concept of the class was a huge joke to him—no matter how many maps he made he'd never get to use them; only few ever got to travel outside of New Olympus into the mortal world—he'd still scheduled it in because it was better than continue in ethics or debate.

I'd have to have every god smiling on me to even get the chance to leave New Olympus.

The halls of New Prep were spacious—wide hallways and vaulted carved-stone ceilings—making every sound of students' footsteps and laughter echo into a cacophony. Blake kept his head down and wished for the headphones he'd forgotten in his dorm. He kept close to the side of the hallway as students greeted friends gathered in groups.

As Blake passed an open door, a pair of hands grabbed his shoulder and yanked him into the dark classroom.

The door closed behind him.

Blake didn't need to take off his sunglasses to help him see in the dark, but he did it anyway to show his pupils had blown to cover his eyes in black pools, as they did anytime his powers flared.

"Hey! Look, I'm not trying to jump you," Elliot had his hands up, the sleeves of his uniform jacket straining.

"What do you want?" Blake asked, straightening his blazer.

"We need your help," a voice from behind Elliot said.

Leila stepped around her friend so she was face to face with him. He hadn't seen her since the Junior Council meeting, and the waves of anger threatened to crash back down on him. His eyes darted around the classroom. Just Min-Seo, perched on a chair, her black hair cutting across her jaw, and Bianca, who always looked like she'd stepped out of a New Prep brochure, skirt ironed with a ruler and sweater free of pills.

His eyes slid back to Leila, feeling like he was shifting back into her orbit. Even without the Myth he *knew* pulled them together, she was striking: a head full of long, dark curls laced with red blooming flowers framed her tanned face. Her full lips were pulled in a taut, determined line, and even her brown eyes sparked with a single-minded focus.

I can't be the only one who feels this way, he thought as he watched her friends so fiercely surround her.

"Look, I know we didn't really leave on the best of terms, but," she started, biting her lip. Blake could tell she was working her way to an apology and put his hands up to stop her.

"Is this why you pulled me in here, to make nice?" He didn't want her pity, it made him feel slimy.

Elliot scoffed, but Leila ignored it.

"Do you know what's happening in three weeks?"

"Let me guess, group orgy?"

"On the fall equinox?" Leila pressed.

Blake's smirk dropped. It hadn't crossed his mind how having Leila here could change his current *arrangement* of being shipped into the mountains every fall and winter. He rubbed his eyes, feeling his headache starting to build anew.

"Don't tell me, the kidnapping of Persephone reenacted?" He didn't want to look at her; she was turning into his nightmare.

She probably thinks the same of me, he realized. He'd lived with the shame and guilt of the Myth for all his life, and it was starting to catch up to him. The room felt oppressively dark and crowded.

"We want to stop it," Min-Seo said to him, with kindness. Out of all the Order, he disliked her the least. Maybe because they were in a lot of the same classes—when Blake showed up to them—or maybe because there was something in her he recognized. Something a little lost.

"Stop the Myth? You know that's not the way New Olympus works," Blake replied.

"But it doesn't have to be," Leila stepped forward. "Fall and winter don't hinge on us being together—living together—" she stammered. "Our Myth can go on without us."

Blake thought it over. "So why do you need me at all?"

"United front," Bianca chimed. "How can we contest your Myth without you?"

"Indeed," he mused. "But I want something in return."

"Of course," Elliot rolled his eyes. "Of course he wants something. We're trying to help you, mate."

Min-Seo and Bianca glared at their friend but Elliot didn't seem to notice.

"What do you want?" Bianca asked.

Blake let out a breath, hesitant to even ask for what he wanted out loud.

"If she doesn't have to go to the winter estate, then neither do I. I want to stay at my dorm, here at New Prep." He spoke quickly, desperately. He cleared his throat then added, "the commute is a nightmare."

Before anyone could protest, Leila agreed.

"Done," she said. Then she pushed a folded piece of paper into his hand; the heat of her hand had warmed the paper. "Meet us here so we can talk details."

He pocketed the paper, then slid his glasses back on.

"So mysterious. Can't wait. Is that all?"

"Yes," Leila said.

She didn't bother saying goodbye, or he didn't wait to hear it. The hallway was unbearably bright, the rush of sound nearly bowled him over. His headache was starting to ebb away, but he suddenly felt achy and nauseous. Blake was getting everything he wanted, and yet he couldn't feel worse.

He slid his hand into his pockets, feeling the crisp piece of paper, but the warmth had already slipped away.

CAMILLE

"I don't approve of what you're doing, you know," Camille said without looking up. She was deadheading a very rare strain of golden roses, bred over centuries of Demeter's Vessels. They were special to the Vessels—not because of their gold petals or their blooms the size of cabbage heads—but for their need for care. For the lonely Vessels of Demeter, the frail golden roses needed their constant attention to survive.

Now that Leila had arrived, some of the blooms had wilted due to Camille's neglect. She did feel guilty as she snipped the browning flowers, but she had her flesh and blood daughter next to her.

I'm sure the acolytes at Demeter's temple could come around to help, she thought—though letting someone else take care of her plants made her eye twitch, even if they shared the same goddess.

"I don't think you'll like what'll happen if we fail," Leila said. She was running her fingers over the bark of a Meyer lemon tree, little trills of energy flowing through the wood. Camille considered asking her to revive the gold roses, but thought better of it.

"Well, I can still disapprove. Going against the Myth, it's just not done."

"There's a first for everything; besides, didn't you want me to get involved in something?"

Camille laughed. "I meant drama club or ballet—I loved ballet."

"I'll try both, Cami, but I need to make sure I'm not imprisoned or whatever first." Leila's phone buzzed. "Bianca and Minnie are here."

She left the greenhouse; the plants seemed to visibly sag at her departure. Camille sighed and went back to sniping off the dead flower heads and spotted leaves until it looked perfect. Then she misted the blooms and adjusted the timer on the sprinklers. After, she cleaned the area so there wasn't a single leaf out of place. Only when she was satisfied did she come out of the atrium and take off her gardening gloves. She stopped outside Leila's room, listening as the friends giggled and plotted before walking to the kitchen where her favorite wine was chilling.

Ten years ago, Camille had been able to leave New Olympus to travel to a small vineyard in Italy to research their topsoil. Now she was their best customer.

As she sipped the wine, she spotted a pair of headlights turn into her driveway.

Leila didn't tell me who else was coming, she furrowed her brows, *and Martin knows not to come here unannounced.*

Camille set down her glass, smoothing out her white blouse before going to the window. It was too dark to see, and the glare of the kitchen lights didn't help.

The doorbell rang and Camille went to the front door and swung it open, the last of the summer heat blowing through her foyer. She could feel the flyaways around her face but stopped herself short when she saw who had rung the doorbell.

She couldn't help the frown of disgust staining her face as Blake, Vessel of Hades, stood on her front porch. She'd never seen him up close —she'd managed to avoid anything to do with the god of death—but he didn't impress upon her inspection. The dark purple under his eyes set off the sickly paleness of his skin. He was taller than her, so she straightened to look up at him.

He opened his mouth to say something, but Camille didn't let him speak.

"Get off of my property. *Now.*"

LEILA

Leila hopped down the stairs, careful not to slip on the marble in her fuzzy socks as she made her way to the front door. It was almost seven and Blake should be arriving any minute.

If he even shows up.

"Get off of my property. *Now.*" She heard the rage in Camille's voice before she rounded the corner.

Shit.

"Camille, it's OK!" Leila tried to make her voice as soothing as possible. Camille spun to face her and she realized comfort was futile.

"It's not OK, this—this *monster* is on our front porch! *He's not going to get away with hurting us again!*"

Leila cheeks flamed in embarrassment at her behavior. This was the most frazzled she'd ever seen her surrogate mother—it was still murky what they were to each other, and she couldn't untangle all of the feelings she had since Camille had asserted herself as Leila's mom.

Why did I think it would work? New Olympus still didn't make any sense to her, but surely asking a boy over shouldn't kick off World War III?

"Camille, he's going to help us, I swear!" Leila could hear how her own voice rose to match Camille's. She spared a glance at Blake, who, to his credit, leaned against the doorway while scrolling on his phone, a blank mask of boredom smoothing his features. Only the muscles jumping at his jawline let Leila know anything was amiss.

Does he get this all the time?

"Why can't you do this without him, don't you see he's going to use you?" Camille suddenly pleaded. "Why can't you find a way that doesn't involve him? I don't want to see you hurt, love."

It was awkward enough the person they were talking about was *right there*, but also she now realized she was living with someone who dictated who she could and couldn't see.

"It's the only way. We *need* him," Leila said, exasperated.

"I will not let that *thing* into my home," Leila's eyes went wide at the hostility of Camille's tone. There was more than rage and malice there—this was an open wound.

Blake cleared his throat. "I don't want to cause any trouble," though the crook of a smile suggested something different. He looked at Leila and gave her a nod. "It's obvious I'm not welcome, I'll get going."

He turned, stuffing his hands into his suit pockets, his inky hair curling at the collar of his blazer. With the headlights of his car shining on him, Leila suddenly remembered the figure she saw at her Induction: tall, broad-shouldered and illuminated in the last of the sun's rays.

The image overlapped with Blake's as he stepped off their front porch and onto the driveway to his car.

"*Wait!*" The word burst out of her and soon her body followed. She ran to catch up with him, her fuzzy socks catching on the scratchy cement.

He turned over his shoulder, eyebrows raised, but said nothing as he pressed a button on his car key and the passenger side door opened up like a flag raised to attention.

Leila got in, ignoring Camille's cries, her friends, and even her own protesting thoughts as the doors closed, the engine roared, and they sped off into the night.

ELLIOT

They started the night studying.

At least, that's what he'd tell the Prep Housing monitors when they were caught out of their dorms after curfew.

They were in Harvey's room—a single wedged into the south corner of the upperclassmen floor—the last of the lazy summer sun had set, and Elliot and Harvey shared his small futon with dinner on their laps.

"You cannot tell me you think Taco Tuesday trumps gyro night. You're delusional," Harvey protested between bites of lasagna. Elliot could see Harvey finally starting to relax; he always noticed whenever Harvey was in his own space, the tie loosened.

If only a little bit.

"I haven't missed a Taco Tuesday *once,*" Elliot retorted. "I have given that gods' feast more commitment than I've given to anything. I mean, you've had the chorizo nachos, right?"

"Have to agree with him, Harv," Mason piped up from the floor, scattered flashcards rippling around him on the carpet. "Elliot has never committed to anything."

"Get stuffed, Mase," Elliot laughed.

To Mason's credit, he was the only one anywhere remotely near studying—though Elliot could not figure out why he seemed to be focusing on his archery class, copying down different bow types and arrowhead materials out of a textbook—his own tray left abandoned next to him. Elliot might need to peruse his physics textbook at some point between now and tomorrow if he wanted a fighting chance at his first quiz but it didn't seem too pertinent. The only reason he needed to ace his class was to go to the University but he was a senior who didn't want to go to college—or maybe he did, he hadn't decided. Four more years of coursework made him exhausted thinking about it.

The Twins would love it if I went, he thought of his pushy old friends.

"So, where's the BF, Harv?" Elliot asked as he got up with his empty tray. He made sure to lean on his good leg as he got up.

"Drama club," Harvey extended his own tray to Elliot without getting up. "Thanks."

"Welcs," Elliot left the dorm and took the trays outside into the upperclassmen floor. It was quiet, the echo of the trays clattering loudly as he dumped them onto the tray cart the school kept on each floor.

Elliot closed the door quietly when he got back.

"I thought this was supposed to be senior year," Elliot announced.

"It is, you dingus," Mason said, shuffling his flashcards. Harvey snorted a little laugh but didn't bother looking up from the book he was copying notes out of.

Elliot's arms fell flat.

"I mean," he humphed, "I just went out there and it was *dead*. The entire floor silent, like a freaking morgue. It's our senior year, why are we stuck here studying when we should be living it up, enjoying our youth, partying the night away!"

The boys looked at him.

"First of all Elliot, it's Monday. I'm not sure what kind of party there's supposed to be happening," Mason said. "Second of all, I have a tactical quiz on all of my archery gear I have to ace to keep the class."

Harvey nodded. "Yeah, and I have a debate tomorrow against Minnie and she's going to obliterate me. How can I be a politician if I can't even win high school debate?"

Elliot sighed. "Look, Mason, the pointy end goes into the target and don't shoot the teacher, got it? And Harvey: let Minnie win this one, she could debate both sides on her own."

"I'd pay to see that," Mason agreed. "Why don't we call the

girls?"

"They're busy," Elliot hedged. *They girls wouldn't like it if I told anyone about their plans—even their best friends.* "Besides, we don't need them to have fun!"

"Elliot," Harvey started, but Elliot interrupted him.

"How about we stop into that new bar Drachma for *one* pint and call it a night?"

"I'll pretend I didn't hear you say the name…"

"I did. And we should go. We can't get into a real bar—like Mason said, it's a Monday so no one will be expecting us."

"They're speakeasies, El," Harvey was not-so-subtly rubbing his temple in irritation. Drachma was run by one of the gangs, a bar tucked away in some basement or warehouse where the *nomos* couldn't find them. The *nomos* enforced the laws of New Olympus and didn't take too kindly to those who drank underage. Elliot didn't know much about the seedy parts of New Olympus, but it didn't mean he couldn't use them for a good night out.

"And? We're Vessels of *gods*. I think we forget that sometimes."

"I'm going to be mayor someday, *provided* I don't ruin my reputation."

"In what way? Because I'd love to have a mayor that was actually cool."

They stared at each other, willing the other to give up.

"Ah, fuck it," Mason said, throwing his cards down and breaking the tension. He pushed himself off the floor. "If Helios doesn't want me in archery class, he'll let me know."

"Really?" Harvey deadpanned, but started closing his books anyway. "One drink. I mean it. *One.*"

Elliot tried not to look too smug as he pulled his bomber jacket on.

"You think they'll be cool with my uniform, right?" Mason said, eyeing the navy and maroon of his blazer.

"No!" Elliot and Harvey cried at the same time. They wouldn't card at an illegal bar but there was an implication everyone was over drinking age, and a New Prep uniform would kill the illusion. After Mason changed, the three young Vessels left the sanctuary of New Prep to cross the river Styx into the city.

The air was warm and crackled with excitement. They left the campus on foot—it was more innocuous than hailing a cab—striding quickly, the sense of urgency at getting away pushed them forward. This wasn't their first jailbreak, but it was the first of the school year.

They stopped at the foot of Aetos Bridge—everyone called it Eagle Bridge—the stone bridge closest to campus. It was adorned with great eagle statues in mid-flight, their talons firmly dug into the sides of the bridge as if they were the only thing holding it up. It was nearly a thousand feet long, the metropolis lights twinkling on the other side. It felt like there was an invisible boundary holding them back, none of them wanting to cross it first.

Harvey sighed, rolling his sleeves up. "See you on the other side, boys."

Before the other two could ask what he meant, Harvey backed up, took two strides and leapt across the bridge in one lightning-fueled jump. The crack of lightning split open the sky, diverting off Harvey and bouncing onto the eagle statues. Elliot stuck a finger in his ears to relieve the tension building there in the spike of barometric pressure. One of these days he was going to burst an eardrum.

Harvey looked back at them from across the long expanse of the Aetos Bridge, blue-white electricity crawling all over him. He flashed a rare, non-canditatory smile. Thunder rumbled distantly as the clouds cleared.

Elliot and Mason shared a look. The gauntlet had been thrown. *We can't run across now, can we?*

Mason shrugged and looked up to the heavens. The night was cloudless, each star another point in a constellation. Elliot wondered how the sky looked through Mason's eyes. Helios rode a chariot across the sky, dragging the Sun behind it, bringing the world into light.

Mason looked back at Elliot, but his eyes were ablaze, his hair alight. Then did Elliot realize he wasn't looking *at* Elliot, he was looking *through* Elliot.

Nearly too late he jumped out of the way as a golden chariot raced past him. The heat of the burning chariot nearly singed Elliot's eyebrows off. Mason ran to meet it, taking three scorching steps before lunging into the chariot as it launched off the river's edge. It had no horses to guide it but bucked wildly as if it did. The wheels of fire spun over air like it was on a road. Elliot had to shield his eyes from the light of it. It arced over the river's black waters and skidded to a halt on the other side before disappearing, leaving Mason in a cloud of smoke.

"Did I burn you?" He yelled across the river.

"Not quite," Elliot yelled back.

It was his turn. He stood up straight, even though he had to blink away the afterimage of the chariot burned into his vision. He stepped to the edge of the road, where the river flowed below. The Styx that bisected New Olympus wasn't the same one encircling Hades—it lacked powers of healing and the souls of the wrathful dead. It was wide enough for pleasure barges, commendable yachts, and ferries to move through without issue. When he looked over to his friends across the churning black water that ran cold all year, he could barely make out their features.

He climbed the stone railing of the bridge, standing on it and giving his friends a salute. The wind billowed his jacket back, his hair tickling his face as it whipped around.

He stepped off the bridge. He dropped like a stone and sunk to the silty bottom. The current curled around him but he planted his feet firmly, facing the other side of the river. Even though the Styx was ice cold, he felt comfortable. Being in the water for Elliot was like finally being able to take a full breath of air. Elliot slid his feet farther apart so he was taking a wide stance.

Don't want to mess that up again, the thought of his aim being off made him wince.

He concentrated, feeling every molecule of water, every part of the river from its source high in the mountains to where the mouth of the river met the ocean. He could feel every bend and runoff, every part the Styx touched.

Then he stopped the current.

In the back of his mind he wondered what his friends saw: him jumping off the bridge into the river. Then the river going still. The silence that followed.

Elliot crashed out of the river, propelled by a breaking wave, astride a horse made of the Styx's churning black water. The horse let out a wild bray spitting foam as its hooves clattered over the water. Elliot had a hold of his mane, wrapping around the slimy seaweed in an effort to control the animal. The waves rose and crashed around them, echoes of hooves and whinnies mixed with the roar of the rushing water. Elliot's steed stomped down the waves, driving itself faster and faster to the other side of the river. Elliot could only hold on as his horse galloped across the water. When he got closer to his friends he jerked on the mane, signaling to his steed to slow down. The fervor of the waves slowed, rising only to give the horse a path to land. The horse slowed to a walk on the concrete and stopped in front of his friends.

"You had to go and make a horse," Harvey had his hands on his hips, but he wasn't mad. He was impressed. Little crackles of lightning still crawled over him, and he took a step back from the puddle that dripped from the horse's mane.

Elliot dismounted his steed, drying himself of the river's water. The horse was becoming less and less river and more flesh and blood by the second. His coat was still the dark blue-black of the Styx, his mane long strands of seaweed. He snorted and stamped his hoof on the ground as if to test his own realness.

Elliot held the horse's face in his hands, instructing it by thought where friendly stables were in the city.

Whether the horse listens and goes there, that's up to him.

The horse cantered away, keeping close to the river's edge.

Elliot turned, straightening the dark green bomber jacket and winked at his friends. The three of them burst out laughing, the residual powers burning through them making them giddy. This was why they were chosen to go to New Prep. There were other Vessels of Helios, of Poseidon, even of Zeus walking around the city, even going to other high schools, and running around the temples. But Harvey was the only one who could *make* lighting as well as wield it; Mason the only one to summon Helios' chariot and not burst into flames on contact; and Elliot the only one who could create horses of water. They were the closest to their gods in gifts, closer to gods than mortals.

It's nice to be reminded of it, even if I'm reminding myself.

"Shall we?" he said and clapped his friends on their shoulders. They started off in the direction of the warehouse district. The only evidence of their display was some scorch marks and a puddle drying on the sidewalk.

The warehouse district was near the industrial docks. Elliot had overheard snippets of conversation from some of the dockworkers near his boat. He didn't want his friends to know his invite was more of a hunch.

"Where is it again?" Mason asked. The light from his golden hair was starting to dim. "I think we've been walking all night."

"Mase, we've been walking for an hour, tops," Harvey replied, then turned to Elliot. "But please tell me we're getting close."

"Yeah, yeah, we're close," Elliot dismissed. "I'm looking for a sign."

"Aren't we all."

"A real sign, mate," Elliot ground out. "Five red arrows above the door."

At least, that's what he hoped he heard. The streets were quiet and dark, especially in between the looming warehouses. Summer was gone, the hot night air was replaced with a chill breeze following them down the street.

They walked a couple more blocks, picking up their conversation from the dorm.

"I just think they need to bring back spring roll night, that's all I'm saying," Mason said.

"Spring roll night was the *worst*. It was all spring rolls, Mason!" Harvey shot back. "I can't survive only on spring rolls."

"Harv, it's about the dipping sauces," Mason said with uncharacteristic seriousness. "If you don't know how to utilize the sauces then you're doing it all wrong."

"I feel like we're going in circles," Elliot murmured.

"Thank you El," Harvey exclaimed. "Mason thinks the *best* meal at New Prep is one item with twenty dipping sauces—"

"No, Harv, we're going in circles, like *right now*." Elliot stopped walking and turned right. "This way."

They sped down the block silently until Mason couldn't hold it in any longer.

"OK, but do you agree?"

"Mason, if you think I—" But the answer died in his throat at the sounds of scuffling reached their ears. They gave each other one look before charging around the corner to whatever awful scene they'd overheard.

Four men were kicking and punching at a form crumpled on the ground.

"Hey!" Harvey yelled as he ran across the street. Elliot couldn't help feeling like they were being led into battle. "Stop!"

They tore the men off the person, pushing them out onto the street. They stepped onto the sidewalk making a barrier.

"Walk away," the broadest of the men said. "And we'll forget you interrupted us so rudely." The other men fidgeted, just waiting for the order to lunge at them.

"Not possible," Harvey said. His hands were up in front of him to keep the men back. They would have looked like businessmen in their suits, but there was something distinctly crooked about them; their bloody knuckles and the way they stood made them look like Elliot had stepped into a boxing ring and not a secluded street.

The person on the ground shuddered, sobbing, startling all of them. Elliot looked behind as the person rolled onto his back. He wasn't sobbing, but wheezing out a strangled laugh, his face a broken mess. He looked up at the boys and Elliot recognized him: Bart, Vessel of Ares.

Bart struggled to stand, grasping at the building's wall to get up, leaving a smear of blood. He smiled, split lip and nose gushing blood making his smile gleam red.

"I told them it was hardly a fair fight," he said looking at Elliot and his friends. "'Ello boys."

"We're not letting you off so easy," the leader said, pulling out a switchblade. "Your friends get the same treatment, unless they take their leave and keep their mouths shut." The others followed, brandishing their own blades and bats.

Mason, Elliot, and Harvey looked at each other uncertainly.

"I'm sure we can come to an agreement," Elliot forced as much casualness he could into his voice. "Why don't you let us all go?"

Bart leaned his shaved head on the wall looking up and let out a small sigh.

"No," his voice was thick with blood. "Those aren't the orders."

"And you would know about orders, huh?" the stringy one in front of Mason spat.

Bart looked at him, his eyes flashing red.

"Well, mates, there's no use debating 'em." He spit red. "Let's get this over with."

"Let's," the leader said and Bart lunged.

Time slowed down as a hot breeze swept around the boys. Elliot heard Bart laugh again: a low, despicable chuckle. He could feel his heart start to race, every part of his body aflame with anger—red-hot, righteous *fury*.

Elliot's world narrowed to the man in front of him. He took a step off the sidewalk, the asphalt cracking under him. The man jabbed at him with his hunting knife but Elliot caught his hand first, twisting it until the knife dropped and the man yelped in pain. The man kicked at Elliot's left knee, knocking into his metal prosthesis and bringing Elliot down to one knee. Usually if he got hit hard in his prosthetic leg, the blow would send a painful vibration up his whole leg, but he didn't feel it, only the hammering of his heart repeating the word *kill kill kill kill.*

The man landed another blow to Elliot's jaw, throwing stars into his vision. The cracks in the concrete filled with water that Elliot summoned and punched the man's jaw in one lunge, a jet of water propelling the man into the air and landing hard across the street. He didn't get back up.

The anger coursing through Elliot drained out of him, leaving him cold. He looked around to his friends who stood looking as dazed as he felt and the thugs who lay in different states of pain. Then he looked to Bart, whose eyes dimmed from red to normal. The only color on his body was the blood dripping from his cuts onto his white shirt, slicking his leather jacket, staining his knuckles. He looked too pale and turned to them before stumbling down.

Mason got there first, stopping him from hitting his head on the concrete. Elliot grabbed his other arm and lifted him up. Bart's head lolled forward.

Harvey spun around, rubbing his hands on his head in panic.

"What have we done?" His eyes were wide, making him look young. There was a spray of blood on his chin catching the light.

"They were going to make sure you stayed quiet," Bart gasped out. "You had to fight like you were gonna die—else you weren't gonna leave this street."

How many of Ares' Vessels can control people like that? Elliot wondered to himself.

"I—" Harvey stopped, composed himself. Then chuckled. "Of course this would happen. Of *course*. The Fates must hate me."

"I think Harv finally snapped," Mason muttered to Elliot.

The groans of the men on the ground startled them.

"Hey, we need to go, like *now*," Elliot said.

Harvey snapped his fingers. "Yes, the *nomos* can help us, we'll tell them it was self—"

"Fuck the *nomos*," Bart straightened suddenly, throwing all three of them out of balance. "Don't you know what we do to snitches, future mayor or not."

"You're *hurt*," Harvey pleaded. "Let us take you to an infirmary, or Hepius' temple." Hepius was the god of medicine and his temples acted as small hospitals. Elliot agreed with Harvey—they were quick to help, no matter the time of night.

Bart gave a sad smile. "Hepius only takes heroes and innocents. I'm none of those things."

So it's true, he thought, *the gangs can't get help.*

"There might be another place I can go," Bart said. "The only place I can go now."

"No way," Harvey shot back. "I am *not* going anywhere but back to New Prep. We're going to get written up for sneaking out; I'm not going to be an accessory to *murder.*"

Elliot groaned as he regained his balance. A throbbing pain coming from the place where the end of his thigh met his prosthesis made him wince.

Harvey was pacing around and when he got close enough Elliot pulled on his sleeve, getting his attention. "Harv, we're not caught yet. But we will be if we try to sneak back into the dorm with a half-dead criminal—no offense."

"None taken," Bart shrugged.

Elliot could see the tension in his friend's shoulders, the arguments churning up in his mind but Harvey huffed at him. "Fine.

But if he dies it's on you."

"Cheers," Bart said, spitting blood. "Can we get out of here?"

"Please," Mason hastily agreed.

Harvey sighed and took hold of Bart and all four of them shuffled down the street. Elliot felt the river and led them to it to follow north, moving in silence with an unspoken urgency. The cold of the night creeped in like a leak, reminding him of what had just happened and where the night had gone so wrong.

LEILA

The car sped through the suburbs, houses and street lights blurring past Leila as she stared out the window. They didn't say anything to each other for a while, the only sound was the hum of the car.

How can he be on our side now? Leila's stomach was a pit of guilt and embarrassment. Every time she remembered Camille's face and words as she replayed what she said to Blake and her in their foyer.

This monster
What he did to us?
This monster
I will not let that thing into my home.
This monster

Every time Camille's face morphed angrier and angrier until she was a pillar of blonde hair and red rage. Leila rubbed her eyes, the sudden urge to cry almost overwhelming.

Blake cleared his throat but didn't speak for a moment.

"Where are we going?" Leila asked, voice thick.

I've made a mistake.

"I'm not kidnapping you if that's what you're worried about," he replied. "I'm not *that* transparent."

"I didn't—" She resisted a groan, only because she could allow him *one* jab after what happened back at her house.

Back at Camille's house, not your *house, don't forget,* a little voice whispered in the back of her mind. Instead, she sat back in her seat and stared out the window harder.

"Are you hungry?" he said after a long pause. He spoke slowly, as if trying not to startle Leila—like how one would approach a wild animal.

Leila's first instinct was to say *no* but her growling stomach betrayed her in the quiet of the car.

"I haven't had dinner yet," she admitted. She almost said Camille had ordered food—her version of cooking for every meal they'd had—but she thought better than to bring up her surrogate mother's name just yet.

She snuck a glance to the Vessel of Hades, he nodded to her quickly before turning the wheel and changing directions. Leila had briefly looked at his car before getting in but she felt like she was in a spaceship, the sleek red interior and the twinkle of the dashboard reflected on Blake's pale skin. Half of his face was in shadow, the lamplights outside rolling over his jaw, his neck, dark collar of his shirt, his grey eyes fixed on the road. She wondered why he wore suits outside of their school's Prep school uniform. He looked comfortable in them but it struck her as odd, like he wasn't able to enjoy being a teenager. She suddenly felt miserably underdressed.

"Oh, wait," she said as the thought occurred to her. "I don't have shoes on! I can't go to dinner." She was wearing a pair of mom jeans and a loose shirt Camille had given her with the logo of a planting project in pastel bubble letters. And then her fuzzy socks.

"Don't worry about it," he said. His tone didn't invite a rebuttal and she didn't feel like arguing. Not about her lack of footwear.

They pulled into the parking lot of a small twenty-four-hour diner. The diner had red vinyl booths and a checkered floor, with Buddy Guy playing softly on the jukebox at the front of the restaurant. An older satyr waitress came over to them as they got settled into a booth, her hooves clicking on the linoleum floor. The waitress's goat legs protruded from her powder blue uniform and grey horns stuck straight back from the crown of her head. She poured Blake a cup of coffee with one hand and dropped menus off with the other, then turned and helped a man at the counter. Leila noticed the name tag *Bess* was stitched into her uniform.

Leila immediately tucked her socked feet under herself and studied the menu. They sat in silence until Bess came back to take their orders. She looked at Leila with her pad ready.

"Can I get the vegan mac and cheese, please?" she asked as she handed back her menu.

"Sure thing, sugar," Bess turned to Blake and took his menu. "Don't worry, hun, I already know what you like," she winked at Blake before hurrying off to the kitchen. Blake gave the waitress a shy smile, his eyes crinkling with a warmth that was so unguarded Leila had to look away.

She fiddled with the jade plant accenting the table, rubbing its little velvet leaves. Warmth spread from her fingertips to the plant, filling her with some comfort. With the menus taken away, there was nothing else to distract her from the boy in front of her.

The last time I was alone with him we almost killed each other...

"You're vegan?"

Leila looked up at him, his voice quiet. The warmth was gone—nothing unkind replaced it, still waters.

She cleared her throat. "Yeah, when I came here I wasn't sure what I liked or didn't like, but it feels more like me," she finished.

He nodded like he understood but she couldn't tell if he actually did.

I'm as much of a stranger to myself as to anyone else, she couldn't possibly try to explain it to someone who she needed to convince she knew what she was doing.

"So, without Minnie and Bianca I can't fully explain—only because they know New Olympus better than me—"

Blake raised his hand to stop her. "Do you believe this can work?"

"Yes," she said with indignance.

"That's all I need. Tell me what you can now and fill in the rest later."

"Why is that all you need?"

His eyes met hers, his light grey like an overcast sky. "Because you're a game changer. Maybe the reason Persephone's Vessel makes an appearance is because you're here to throw the whole Myth out. At least I truly hope so."

Before she could ask him what he meant by that, Bess came back with their food, putting a heaping bowl of mac and cheese in front of Leila and an omelette and pancakes in front of Blake. Her question was abandoned when the smell of the food hit her nostrils. They both tucked in.

After a couple of minutes of eating, Leila remembered why they were here.

"How did you find this place?" She said. This was the best mac and cheese she'd ever had.

"Danny and I came here a lot in middle school," he was pouring a liberal amount of syrup on as he spoke, the golden hue catching the light, "it's near my old house. We could only scrounge together enough money for pancakes and free coffee. We would get wired on sugar and caffeine—and Danny is already always wired."

Danny, she racked her brains, *is the same Danny from New Prep?*

"So you're on the Vessel Senators Council right?" she asked, changing the subject, feeling uncomfortable with how familiar they were being.

He was gulping down his coffee between bites. He swallowed and answered, "Technically, yes." Then he put down his empty mug at the edge of the table.

"I'm not eighteen yet, so my involvement is only on a 'ceremonial' level. I have to sit in at the meetings, but I don't get to vote or propose any laws."

"Then why have you at all?"

"Because every Vessel must be represented for it to be fair. With me representing Hades, I complete the Senators Council. I get my best sleep there actually."

Leila pondered for a moment, picking at her noodles. Bess came and refilled his cup of coffee.

"So there aren't any other Vessels of Hades? You're the only one?" *Like me?*

Blake gave a short, hollow laugh. There was something in the way he looked down at the coffee he cradled, the placating smile that stayed on his face even as his eyebrows bunched together hinting at some deeper meaning. "I'm the only one for now, and they need me. Why?"

"I've been called to sit on the Council as well, the next meeting is this Friday."

"That's when you want to make your move." Blake raised his eyebrows, impressed.

Leila filled him in on the details—what she could—over the rest of their food and three more cups of coffee on Blake's part. Leila stroked the jade plant as she spoke, not realizing how it kept growing until it was wrapped around her hand.

"Oops," she said, trying to untangle herself before resuming their discussion. Only after their plates were cleared was Blake satisfied in their plan. He opened his mouth to say something but was interrupted as his phone buzzed. He retrieved it from his breast pocket and looked at whatever message he got, then put it back in his pocket.

"Girlfriend," he said as explanation, though that made a thousand questions crop up in its place. Was the girl Kat from the party his girlfriend, or was it someone else entirely?

Why do you even care, you're trying to get as far away from him as possible, a small voice inside her chided. It was like she was on the edge of the deep end and she didn't know what the next step would bring.

"Thanks," he said to Bess as he pulled out his wallet to pay.

"Wait, you don't have to—" but she stopped herself as she realized she didn't have her wallet on her. She sighed. "Can I pay you back tomorrow?"

"Sure," he said, but in a way indicating he didn't believe she would.

They left, Leila thanking Bess for the good food and Bess gave her a mischievous smile when she said goodnight to both of them. Her ears burned and she prayed Blake didn't understand that their waitress thought they were on a date.

"Where to?" He asked as they got back to his car.

"Back to Camille's," she said quickly. *Why am I being so skittish all of the sudden?* "I have to face the wrath."

He gave a light snort. "If she hasn't already called the *nomos* on me."

I wouldn't put it past her. The drive back was quiet, Leila's stomach churning with anxiety. She was half expecting the red and blue lights of the *nomos'* cars to illuminate her street but it was quiet. She looked back at Blake before getting out of the car.

"Thanks." *Thanks for listening, for dinner, for taking me seriously.* She didn't say any of those things but got out of the car. She felt rude, but the night was wearing on her. It felt like ages had passed since the last time she'd been back to her house, but it'd only been a few hours. She shut the door and walked down her driveway. She heard the window roll down and turned. Blake was leaning across the seat to look at her, his inky hair falling in his face.

"Have your friends find me with the rest of the details," he called. "See you tomorrow— if she ever lets you out of the house again."

She shot him a weak thumbs up. He sped into the night and, if she was correct, not in the direction of Prep Housing. She turned to face her house, the lights a warm yellow.

But all she could think about was grey.

HARVEY

Just breathe, Harvey reminded himself as he kept his head up, trying to will the dawn's light into the dark alley he was hiding in. Twenty minutes ago, Mason and Elliot had gone ahead to make sure the coast was clear and to give Bart a break from running.

"Have you decided yet?" the voice came from behind him, startling him out of his thoughts. He whipped his head to Bart in the shadows, perched on the edge of a stack of pallets, looking like a bird of prey watching for his next meal. The watery light hit his face, clammy and grey from injury. A little plume of smoke rose from a cigarette he had tucked between his fingers and he took a slow drag from it; the way his cheeks sunk into the motion and the sharpness of his cheekbones down to his silver lip ring made Harvey's mouth very dry.

Though Harvey doubted Oscar would disagree on how dangerously good-looking Bart was. *I'm not doing anything wrong by looking.*

Harvey frowned. "Have I decided what, exactly?"

"If you're going to turn me in."

The question was light enough, but an undercurrent of fear ran through his words. Harvey had spent the night half furious and the other half sick with anxiety as they made a slow escape through the city. He was worried for Bart's life, but—shame roiling in him as he admitted it—he was also worried for himself. All his work, extracurriculars and clubs and jobs and internships, the sleepless nights and taking the mayor's shit day in and day out *ruined* after one night gone wrong—he couldn't stop his thoughts from going to the worst conclusion. Bart was right: if anyone would turn him in it would be Harvey.

"No," Harvey said finally. "It wouldn't be wise—for any of us."

Bart turned his eyes on Harvey. Even though his face was a canvas of badly healing bruises and dried blood, there was something untouched and soft in his eyes. The last refuge, uncorrupted.

"Thanks, mate, really."

I don't deserve it, Harvey thought miserably, but he nodded his welcome anyway.

"You can tell me one thing though," Harvey said, stepping closer, making sure to avoid the debris of the alley. His ego couldn't take tripping in front of this boy.

"Shoot."

"Why didn't you go to New Olympus Prep?"

Bart scoffed. "What? And dress up in a bloody uniform? No, it's not for me."

"How many other Vessels of Ares can influence people like that?"

"What do you mean?" Bart's eyebrows knitted together, this had got his attention.

"You made Elliot, Mason, and I all fight to *kill*. I've never heard of any other Vessel ever being able to wield Ares' warlust like that." Harvey had never wanted to kill *anyone*, yet tonight he felt like his anger wouldn't ever be satisfied. Bart had been near passing out, yet he got the three of them to want to fight to the death; he couldn't imagine the power he must have at full strength. And not to mention Bart's healing from his battle wounds.

"I don't think I'm the only one," Bart said softly, his voice betraying the dismissal of his words. Harvey spoke a truth he could guess Bart didn't want said aloud—there was only one solution when a lackey was stronger than his superior and it wasn't pretty. Harvey guessed the only people who knew what Bart could really do were Harvey, Mason, and Elliot. Bart took a shaky breath, looking past Harvey and out to the empty street.

"It's not over, you can get out, I—"

Bart put a hand up. "Look, I can't turn my back on my family—even if they want to kill me."

He said it with his knife smile, the light glinting off his lip ring. Harvey believed him. The Vessels of Ares always had their own strange ways of doing things, partly because of how divided they were. Most of the *nomos* were made up of Ares' Vessels, along with most of the gang's crew members. Both recruited young, and New Olympus didn't regulate the care for kids like Harvey thought they should. Bart was his age, yet there was a chasm between them Harvey didn't know how to get across.

"So, what now?"

"I get punished until I learn my lesson," Bart said.

"Have you?"

Bart smirked, then winced, a hand drifting to some wound near his stomach. He wore so much black it was hard to see if his wounds had opened up again.

Harvey switched his tactics.

"But you didn't take your punishment tonight." *Quite the opposite.* He hoped those henchmen could also heal themselves. Bart's face paled. He didn't say anything, just ran a hand over his shaved head.

Let me make this up, he pleaded. Harvey knew one kindness couldn't erase a whole system's failure—a lifetime of wrongs that almost got him killed tonight. He had no real authority, not yet, but it didn't mean he couldn't try.

Bart offered him a drag of his cigarette and Harvey took it, the smoke working around them. The cigarette was bitter and awful but made him feel warm. Until it raked his throat raw and he wanted to die before coughing in front of the beat-up boy next to him. Harvey coughed. Then coughed a couple more times.

Fuck.

"Thank you," Bart said behind him. Harvey looked at the Vessel of Ares, through the spikes and leather and blood to his bright eyes, sincere.

"C'mon," Mason hissed, sticking his head out from around the corner of the building, saving Harvey from mumbling out a reply. Guilt gnawed at him.

Don't thank me yet.

ALICIA

The knocking had to be a part of her dream—her nightmare. It was the same dream she'd had for months, torturing her with her worst memory: the day she broke Arnie's heart. In her nightmares the memory had mutated, taking on a grotesque light. Every face twisted into inhuman grimaces, shadows ready to grab her if she tried to run. She tried to focus on Arnie's face but somehow his features slipped from her sight like insects scuttling from the light. Except his eyes—the same phrase stuck in the air as he saw her.

How could you?
How could you
How
Could
You?

The knocking sound happened again, booming through her dream making her heart hammer. Then the knocking grew more fervent, shaking the foundation of her dream, throwing her out of her nightmare and back into her bedroom in a violent thrash. Her silk sheets became hard hands wrapped around her, tying her to the bed. The air was hot with regret and unshed tears, her mouth a hard scowl. She wiped her face with shaking hands.

Then she heard the knocking on her door and she sat bolt

upright. She checked the diamond-studded watch she left on her bedside table.

6:24. What the hell? The blackout curtains were firmly closed in her bedroom, but she was sure the sun was cresting over the mountains. *Ugh.*

Sleep still had its tendrils in her, and the echoes of her nightmare lingered in the air.

Some company might help, no matter who it is. Ever since she lost her powers last year she felt an aching loneliness, a chill where her power used to be that never warmed.

Alicia grabbed a silk robe off the floor and put it on, covering her shoulders. Her sweat had cooled and she rubbed her arms together. Besides, she didn't know who had made it past her doorman to bang on her apartment door, and Alicia didn't think the rose velvet bralette and shorts were exactly the right attire to greet strangers.

She flung open her front door to find four teenage boys on her front step. One of whom was cut and bruised, a mess of a face but she knew him.

"*Bartie!*" Alicia exclaimed, her hands fluttering around him, not sure where to start. His shirt was soaked in blood and he leaned heavily on the door frame. She got close to his face; he smelled of hydrogen peroxide and smoke. Her heart surged in concern.

"I'm ok, love," his voice was gravelly and he mustered a wink with the last of his strength.

"What the hell is going on?" Alicia hissed and glared at the other boys surrounding him. She was surprised how scared all three of them looked. With a quick nod she motioned all four of them inside, leaving them to carry Bartie in and onto the couch.

She stood in front of them, arms crossed. She had one mind to tap her bare foot on the carpet to get her point across.

"Well? What do you have to say for yourselves?"

Bartie hid a smirk behind his fist, but she looked between him and the other boys stuffed onto her sofa. *They thought they could drop him off without explanation?* "Hmm? Harvey? What's going on?"

"How do you know who I am?" Harvey asked. He was tall and lanky, made taller and lankier by his posture. She felt bad for him, looking into his big brown eyes.

"Because you're Martin's protégé, am I right?" She heard a snicker from one of the other two and turned to them. "And you're his prep school friend, the one with the ugly-ass boat? Elliot?"

"At your service, darl." Elliot was reclined, even in the small space he had, looking at her with a smile like she was putting on a show. Like he was counting every freckle on her legs.

"I'm Mason, by the way," the blond one on the end perked up, looking a lot like a Labrador puppy.

Teenage boys.

"I'm waiting," she said to the boys.

"They saved me," Bartie spoke up. "I was in a bit of a bind and they helped out. They think I need a place to lie low for a while, while things cool off." Alicia could immediately tell Bartie was lying, even through his thick Cockney accent. He was putting on a bit of bravado for the boys sharing the couch with him, but his teeth were gritted, his fingers gripping the couch's arm like a life raft.

"And they know who we are, since you guessed right away," Harvey spoke up. He was the only one who seemed to look her in the eyes. *Good boy.*

"Not necessarily," she pondered. "It'll buy time, trying to find you. And when they do, well, no one is going to mess with some kids from New Prep."

Harvey seemed to sink an inch with relief. If what Bartie said was true, these boys were risking their hides to help Bartie out and she had to give them credit.

"Speaking of New Prep, I think the first bell is going to ring soon. I'd get going if I were you," she purred to the three boys. They shot up; she was sure they were glad to be released back to their old lives.

They said their goodbyes to Bartie, each a little awkward, a murmur of well wishes and a squeeze on the shoulders. Elliot whispered something in Bartie's ear Alicia thought might be about how lucky Bartie was to be with her. It got him a goodhearted shove.

"Sod off," Bartie growled, but she was sure underneath his bruises a blush would appear. A smile creeped on Alicia's lips as she walked them out.

Harvey turned, his voice low. "If there's anything I can do, please let me know."

  She gave him a nod of thanks and closed the door, not bothering to let him know he couldn't help Bartie or her—not really.

  "Alicia," Bartie's low voice behind her made her turn. It was unmasked of all bravery, raw fear colored his voice. "Cris knows about us."

BIANCA

Bianca had been to the Council building once on a field trip in primary school. The building was all glass and sweeping silver metal, imposing over the law district of West New Olympus. She remembered how small she felt in the atrium, looking up at the murals depicting the Pantheon of gods. Even smaller when she saw the painting of Iris in the corner of the ceiling, kneeling on a rainbow and holding a pitcher up over her head.

And today might be the last time she was ever allowed back.

Too bad I wanted to work here, she thought as she crossed the large space to where her friends were gathered. Bianca had pushed herself in school but whenever she looked out into the future, past New Prep, it was all vague notions of success. Every club and committee, charity, and social event tugged at her attention in the present; she never thought further than graduation. She pinned the visitor's badge onto her blazer and joined Minnie, Leila, and Elliot on one of the benches.

"Cool, we match," Elliot flexed his badge with an easy grin. He wore a suit and tie of dark navy—he even went to the trouble of tying his hair back. Bianca tried not to show how impressed she was; his head was big enough as it is. She wondered if he was also referring to the fact they both wore blue, but she doubted he'd noticed anything past his own reflection.

She fingered the hem of her light blue tweed skirt suit, suddenly feeling the start of anxiety ball up in her stomach. She tapped her heel to dispel some of the energy but she knew she needed to go on a run after this just to be able to sleep tonight.

"How do we know baby Hades is here?" Minnie said, referring to Blake. Bianca was amazed how relaxed she and Elliot seemed to look. Minnie kicked up her sneakers onto the next bench and was using her blazer as a pillow—like she went to sit on Council every day.

"He'll be here," Leila quipped.

A loud bell rang out, echoing through the atrium, signaling the top of the hour and startling everyone out of their thoughts. *The Senators Council is about to meet.*

"OK, now we take our positions," Bianca said. Minnie and Elliot stood up but Leila stayed sitting, chewing her lip. She'd been quiet the whole way here. *Uh-oh. What if she did a runner again?* Leila had explained everything that happened with her and Blake when she left and went to dinner with him, but Bianca couldn't get the image of seeing Camille so devastated at Leila's departure out of her head. Leila's way of thinking was outside anything Bianca would do. It almost made Leila seem a little…

Chaotic? A voice asked. She squashed the thought. Labels separated the citizens of New Olympus. *I'm not close-minded like that.*

Leila looked up at her and her friends. Her curly hair was pulled back into a bun but some curls had escaped around her face.

"You can't go through with this," she said. "I'm sorry I brought you all out here but I can't have you do this with me."

Bianca's eyes widened.

"We're not doing it?" Bianca said at the same time Minnie exclaimed, "It's off?"

"No. I'm still going through with this," Leila sighed and stood up. "But you aren't coming inside with me. I don't know how this is going to go, and I wouldn't be a good friend if I let anything happen to you. *Please.*"

"But we want to be there for you," Minnie replied.

"You are here for me—since my first night here. You've been here for me." Leila's bottom lip wobbled treacherously which threatened to set off Bianca's own sympathetic crying.

"Aww!" Bianca threw her arms around her friend, grabbing Minnie to join the hug in the process. "You're our friend, of course we're going to support you!"

"We're going to win, Leila, why are you so worried?" Minnie's voice was muffled through the clothing.

"You don't know that, you don't know that!" Leila lamented.

The three girls broke apart, cool air rushing in the spaces where they'd hugged each other. Leila stepped back and dabbed her eyes. She was wearing a pomegranate colored suit, the fit loose and billowy. A tear stained her right shoulder which made Bianca's heart lurch.

"I've made up my mind," Leila mumbled. "I'm going in by myself, please don't follow me."

"You're going to kill it, darl," Elliot patted her on the shoulder awkwardly.

He's probably not used to girls showing any emotion besides swooning over him.

"You got this," Bianca said.

"Get it," Minnie chimed.

Leila gave them a small smile and turned to walk to the tall wooden doors of the Senate Chamber.

You got this, Bianca prayed, looking up to the corner mural where Iris' rainbow refracted, trying not to feel so small.

The doors shut on the chambers and the atrium was silent once more, Leila on the other side.

"We have to wait and see now, I guess." Bianca said.

"Come on," Minnie said and walked along the benches, away from the chamber's entrance. Bianca's eyes met Elliot's in question. He shrugged in return and followed the Vessel of Athena. They walked in a line around the atrium, Bianca trying not to look around too much or raise suspicion—though it was hard when three teenagers walked around in a single file line at one of the highest offices of the city.

Minnie seemed to be searching for something along the path, a clue of some sort, pausing every few feet to look at the tile on the floor, her black bob swishing around her. Then she stopped and abruptly started walking quickly to her left across the atrium floor. Minnie walked fast, but Bianca was able to catch up quickly because of her long legs.

With anyone else, Bianca might've had them stop and tell her what was happening, but Bianca had no doubt Minnie was guiding them to the right place.

Wherever that might be.

They came upon a little corridor cordoned off by velvet ropes hidden by the mural depicting the roiling darkness of Hades. Minnie slipped through without pause and disappeared into the darkness. Elliot followed suit without even looking to see if there were guards around. They were on the far side of the atrium, no one Bianca could see, but she still paused.

Elliot popped his head back and extended his hands over the velvet ropes.

"Nothing to be scared about," he said with a wink.

Bianca ignored his hand and ducked under the ropes as smoothly as she could in a skirt.

"I'm not scared," she replied, though it came out much more childish than she'd hoped.

They continued on down the maintenance corridor, veering off a couple of times before Minnie stopped and entered an alcove. Elliot and Bianca followed. When they entered inside, a rush of sound came at them like they were on the chamber's floor.

A horizontal slice of light nearly blinded Bianca from being in the dark but her eyes adjusted, and soon she could see they were underneath the seats of some Senators and were looking down at the mayor.

"How?" Bianca whispered.

"One of the Athena Vessels I grew up with was obsessed with this building—had the blueprints pasted to her wall. This is called the Janitor's View; I won't bore you with the details." She turned back to look out to the chamber floor and Bianca studied her face for a moment. Minnie never had much to say about growing up in a house full of Athena's Vessels, other than everyone driving her up the wall in one way or another. At least it came in handy today.

"Miss Leila, this is highly unusual—I thought your position was explained to you? You're not here in any *official* capacity, just ceremonial," the mayor said jovially from his position in the middle of the floor. He sat behind a large wooden judge's bench and waved his gavel around. A rumble of laughter filled the room, and Bianca gritted her teeth.

Laugh all you want.

"There she is!" Elliot hissed, pointing at the pomegranate-suited girl on the other side. Leila was standing, her arms at her sides.

"I understand my position," Leila said, cutting through the laughter. "And I reject it."

The floor quieted.

"What exactly are you rejecting, miss?" The mayor had his head resting in one hand to turn to her, the swaths of his dark robes pooling around him. He seemed completely disinterested.

"I am rejecting my Myth," she said, then turned to her right. "We both are."

Blake stood up a couple of rows away. From their position, Bianca could see he was in his usual black suit, but today it looked as if it absorbed the light, his hair was out of his eyes and he stared straight through the mayor.

Murmurs scattered through the crowd. The people above Bianca muttered some mixture of prayer or curse.

"Oh? And what do you reject?"

"Winter will come whether Leila and I are living together or not —spring will come too," Blake's voice carried out over the crowd.

"As our Myth doesn't affect anyone else, we're going to abstain from it and continue going to school and living our lives," Leila finished. They glanced at each other and Bianca wasn't sure what passed between them. "Thank you."

"Thank *you*," the mayor said and sat back in his chair.

Yes, Bianca wanted to scream with joy. She looked at Elliot and Minnie and felt her happiness reflected in their faces.

Leila and Blake sat down.

"Thank you," the mayor repeated. "Thank you for letting me know there have been some lessons we have forgotten."

A small chill ran down Bianca's spine, taking the smile she wore with it. The mayor's demeanor changed, he sat up straighter, his smile turned to a grimace. He held the gavel in his hand like it was Zeus' lightning bolt, ready to strike.

"When New Olympus was built, the magic required power—you

cannot make a utopia like this without considerable offering. That power is the Myths of the Pantheon of the Gods. As Vessels, we live our lives as our gods did, because our lives are the offering—they power the gods, they power this *city*. If some gods were rulers, *we* are rulers," anger ground through his voice, "if some gods served, *we will serve.* There are those Vessels who must endure much worse than you but do so *happily* because they believe in the sanctity of New Olympus.

"When you said your Myth doesn't affect others, your ignorance showed. 'Rejecting' your myth brings an entire city into jeopardy. You think you have a choice? When the Fates plucked you out of mediocrity and gave you the gods' magic? You do not question the gods' will—*not when they give your existence meaning!"*

His voice echoed out over the chamber, and Bianca held her breath.

Leila and Blake were still standing, though she didn't know how.

"But—" Leila said softly. The mayor raised his hand.

"Miss Leila, as you're new to our city I can excuse your behavior. Blake, I'm not surprised either—you've never had the honor to uphold your position. Now, you two will uphold your Myth, to its letter. As minors, I can allow you to still go to school—you cannot go wrong with New Olympus Preparatory, though some adjustments will have to be made. Starting from the autumnal equinox, you will be confined to the mountains. As I cannot trust you, I will have a *nomos* watch making sure you, *or any of your friends,* are not disobeying your Myth. You think the Goddess of Spring and the God of Death do not affect other people? You should thank the Fates I didn't send you to the Underworld for a crash course." He turned to the rest of the chamber and banged the gavel, and Bianca could swear Leila had let out a strangled cry at the same time.

Martin carried on as if nothing had happened, moving on to some topic akin to static to Bianca's ears. All she could focus on was Leila's form making her way through the seated crowd, her face crumpled.

Bianca moved to go but was pulled back by a force. She looked down at her hand and saw her fingers entwined with Elliot's own.

Did I grab his hand or did he grab mine? She didn't know and didn't want to think about it.

"Let's go!" she whispered as they unclasped their hands. They sped out of the alcove, through the corridors and across the atrium to see Leila weeping as she walked out of the chamber.

"Leila!" Minnie said as they reached her. She placed her hands on Leila's arms but Leila didn't look up.

"I knew it," a voice behind Leila said. Blake was behind them, raking his hair back, his eyes full of anger. "I knew you wouldn't let your friends get into trouble—even if it meant we had a chance."

Leila turned to him.

"I should never have listened to you," he said. "This was such a waste."

"Stop talking," Bianca put an arm around her friend. "Walk away."

"And now it's so much worse, thank you—*really*."

"She said *walk away*," Elliot said. He stepped in front of the girls. Blake gave a humorless laugh.

"We had to try," Leila muttered. Her voice was thick with tears, but it was steady. "We're not the only ones whose Myth hurts them. But we spoke up about it—that *counts.*"

Blake stepped away, hands in his pockets. "We tried, and I never learn. I was wrong, Leila, you're not here to change anything. You're just here to ruin my life."

He walked away, tendrils of black smoke curling off his suit. *Good riddance.*

Bianca turned to her friends, Leila's quiet sobs echoing around them. The equinox was days away, they were out of options.

MIN-SEO

Saturday in uptown New Olympus was Minnie's favorite. It was cold enough for her to wear her favorite camel coat without overheating, but sunny enough to enjoy the skyscrapers' glitter. She loved the city, loved being in the middle of a busy and bustling metropolis.

One day, she promised. A corner studio big enough for a bed and an espresso maker. Or a loft where she could work on her sculpting without leaving her apartment. She didn't know exactly what her plan was yet, but she was getting there. She stopped at a corner, looking at her directions in one hand and holding her coffee in another. The gallery had to be on the next block.

Minnie had only a couple of assignments to complete for her studio time to keep accountable to New Prep, the rest of the year she could do what she wanted. So far she had been granted a budget big enough to do one big piece, or possibly three smaller pieces.

The marble blocks had to be bought soon but Minnie hesitated to buy something without proper inspiration yet. She wanted to have a plan—Principal Thistlewhait wanted to install one of her pieces permanently.

No pressure or anything.

She didn't want to think about school right now, not when it reminded her of what happened the day before. Today Leila was cooped up at her house with Camille, Bianca running around to head various meetings and committees, and Elliot was out at sea. She missed her friends, wanting to grieve their failure together but real life had pulled them apart—at least for the weekend.

It's also easier to avoid Harvey when we're all separated, she thought of her Zeus friend, the look of betrayal as he learned of what they'd done. *He'll get over it,* once he realizes it won't hurt his chances of being mayor one day.

The gallery was easy to spot: floor-to-ceiling windows with various art on display, from huge oils to small metal designs. Minnie swung the glass door open and entered. No one was inside that she could tell. The assignment was to talk to gallery owners about their requirements for showing. It was a cute idea, but Minnie doubted the intrinsic value a high school report on galleries would have for her career. The large oil painting caught her eye and she stepped closer to it. A girl, with her back turned to the viewer, hugged herself in a bathtub. Her blonde hair trailed in the green water and she could see every ridge of her spine.

"It's such a complex piece, isn't it?" a voice behind Minnie said, startling her.

She turned, grateful she hadn't thrown her coffee at the painting. The tall woman behind her smiled. Minnie saw her name-tag: Claire.

"We don't usually get people this early, especially on a Saturday," she said with a smile. She had pink lips and green eyes that set off her honey hair.

"Sorry," Minnie mumbled, suddenly self-conscious.

"No, I like it! It gives me something to do other than stare out the window, slowly going mad," she said with a laugh. "Are you looking for a piece?"

"No," Minnie said too quickly. Suddenly she didn't want to reveal she was here for school. "No, I'm looking into galleries to showcase my own work." Claire looked like she was in her mid-twenties, with the grace of movement reminding Minnie of a dancer.

Claire gave her a smug smile, her green eyes glittering. "I knew it. You're an artist. Let me guess, watercolor?"

Minnie gave a surprised laugh. "Sculpture, actually."

"Damn, I should be better at this—I'm a Vessel of Calliope," she explained.

"You're a Muse," Minnie said with a tone of awe that made her want to kick herself.

"Yes, and I can see the artist spirit in you, like an aura," she said, squinting around Minnie.

"Good, I need the validation," Minnie said, stilling at her gaze.

"You don't need my, or anyone's, validation. You're the real thing." Claire made her way to the front desk and grabbed a small white card. She walked back and handed it to Minnie. "When you have a piece to show—call me first."

"Thanks," Minnie said. "My name's Min-Seo."

"Claire."

They shook hands briefly, Claire's hand was soft and cool to the touch. Minnie's stomach fluttered at the contact.

"What time does this place close?" Minnie blurted.

"Ages and ages from now," Claire rolled her eyes.

"Take a coffee break." Minnie could barely hear her voice over her own heartbeat. "With me."

Claire laughed until she saw Minnie was serious. She looked back at her desk, eyes torn, before facing her again. Their green eyes met, jade and jasper, and Minnie could tell Claire felt as reckless as she did.

"Only if we go right now."

LEILA

Leila saw Blake only once before the autumnal equinox. Camille had kept Leila close, stalking New Prep's carpool lane like a shark. An early end to the school day gave Leila the freedom she'd craved since the disastrous meeting of the Senators Council. The path to Prep Housing was limned in the afternoon sun, honey gold like Leila's skin. She drank in the sun, her friends carrying the conversation without her.

This was one of the moments she wished she could bottle and take into the mountains. As if her thoughts had called him, she opened her eyes to stare across the parking lot into grey eyes.

"Just ignore them," Bianca muttered. Leila didn't know who she was talking about until she realized Blake wasn't alone: slung on his arm was his girlfriend Kat and some other Vessels she didn't recognize, none of them were in New Prep uniform.

Kat whispered into his ear and laughed cruelly, looking straight at her. He smirked and Leila looked away, shame burning her cheeks. She defended him to Camille, thinking he was different.

Like Bianca said, ignore them.

Leila continued walking the path coming close to Blake's car and his friends.

"Does it bother you how useless you are?" Kat called out to Leila.

"Does it bother you that you're all trespassing?" Bianca shot back.

"Please," Blake called back, spreading his arms out in welcome."Go ahead. Turn us in."

"Let's go," Leila said, desperate to diffuse the sudden tension.

"She really thought she could get out of her own Myth," Kat said to her friends but loud enough to carry across the way. "Spoiled bitch."

Leila's magic was hot, matching her anger, and she moved without thinking. Her hand flicked, the tree nearest Blake and Kat extending down and hitting Kat on the head. As soon as the magic had left her she'd tried to reign it back but it was too late, the tree had bowed to Leila's selfish demand.

Kat looked murderous and kept her eyes on Leila as she extended her palm. Sparks flew out of Kat's open palm and she blew them up into the tree, fire erupting from the branch and quickly spreading to engulf the tree.

"Don't!" Leila cried, the tree only had minutes before it couldn't be saved.

"Not on school grounds," Harvey warned as he gripped her arm, pulling her back. It only made her more angry. Kat didn't have to hold back, why should she? Moving the branch had been a flick of a finger, a drop out of the deep well of power she felt within her.

What am I truly capable of?

"I got this. Don't want to get you in any more trouble." Blake raised a hand then clenched it into a fist, his eyes darkening to black. The tree collapsed in on itself, ash and dust replacing bark and branches. The fire had nothing to burn and the only remnant of the tree was the last of the smoke rising into the sky. Leila heard the rumors, how Blake and his friends had sewn chaos around the city over the summer. She didn't want to believe rumors, not when she hadn't even seen his power. But now she had.

"She's going to cry over a *tree*," Kat squealed with glee, clapping her hands together.

Harvey's grip on her softened and it was the touch she needed to let the emotion drain from her face—a blankness she didn't want to admit she learned from the Vessel of Hades in front of her. She had to let it go now, not because she wanted to but because of what she saw when she looked into her friend's faces: fear. Unlike Kat, they understood it wasn't just a tree Blake had used his powers on, it was a living thing.

Leila walked away, unable to be in Blake's presence any more than she had to—she didn't want to ponder why she wasn't afraid in that moment.

Blake didn't show up to class after that.

She spent the rest of the week watching her newly built life pack itself up around her. The mayor made sure he was heard: sending a letter with the transcript of the Senators Council meeting and ending it with his signature under the inscription: δύναμη στους θεούς - *Power to the gods*. She packed up what little she had: her clothes, her toiletries, and her pomegranate from her Induction. Over the last week it had hardened, its skin crystalizing to ruby. She could see through the skin to the gold seeds inside. It was beautiful but so heavy she considered leaving it, though she couldn't give up her only tangible gift from Persephone.

The packing and preparing meant she didn't see her friends outside of school—Camille picked her up and took her to school, making sure they spent all their time together. The Vessel of Demeter flitted between sweet—packing her extra things she thought Leila would need and soothing her after the disastrous Council meeting—to overbearing, crowding Leila until she couldn't think, crying like she was in mourning, and cursing Hades so thoroughly Leila was sure he could hear her all the way down in the Underworld. Leila's nights were filled with stress dreams of her trapped in the dark, hands pulling at her, soundtracked by Camille's crying. By the end of the week, she was sure she matched Blake's purple under eye bags.

A knock sounded at her door and Leila instinctively clenched her stomach in preparation of what mood Camille would be in on the day of the equinox. The door opened and Leila could feel the relief when she saw Bianca and Minnie walk in.

"What are you still doing in bed?" If Bianca didn't have her hands full of bags, she would have her hands on her hips.

"It's not even 9 a.m.," Leila sat up. "What are you doing here?"

"You didn't think we were going to let you go into this alone right?" Minnie put her stuff down and sat on one of the white ostrich feather puffs dotting her room. Leila's room was decorated in a mishmash of gold and pink—the kind of glamour that made Leila feel like a doll. "We're all going to get ready together—we're your dates!"

"What do you mean?" *What else don't I know?* Leila was resigned to the fact she'd never truly know all of New Olympus' secrets.

"The Equinox is a huge celebration all around the city." Bianca lowered her voice, "if you'd been let out at all this week, you'd know how much the whole city prepares for autumn—it's beautiful."

"So what does that have to do with tonight?"

"Go take a shower and we'll explain everything as we're getting ready. Don't worry, we'll be with you," Minnie thrust an iced coffee into her hand. "It's oat milk. Go."

Leila rolled her eyes but smiled in thanks. *What would I do without you two?*

After her shower she came out in her puffy robe and sipped on her iced coffee. Her damp hair trailed droplets of water on the velvet chais, but she didn't care. While she'd been in the shower, Minnie and Bianca had made her bed and spread all their stuff out—hair tools and makeup laid out in military precision in front of her vanity, heels and jewelry and accessories took up the rest of the flat space. Her room was a princess's fever dream.

"I thought I was going to the mountains tonight?" Leila said as she surveyed what they'd done.

"No, equinoxes are a big deal here—dances, parties, after parties —any reason to let loose and celebrate the shift of the seasons. Since this is the first time Persephone has been represented, people have been getting into the spirit."

Leila nodded, but felt hollow inside. Everyone was celebrating autumn and, indirectly, her own taking. *How am I supposed to feel?* It wouldn't be so bad if she didn't have to be imprisoned with the worst person in New Olympus.

"I didn't think we'd be able to go with you, since your ceremony is at Zeus' temple," Minnie added. "But I think Camille must have some sway with the mayor's office—she got all of us invitations."

A light knock at the door sounded. Camille opened the door, smiling.

"Hello lovelies, something's arrived at the door for you." She held big white boxes. She seemed calm and happy which lifted the last bit of tension off Leila's shoulders. She placed the boxes on Leila's bed and left. "I have some business to get done, but we'll toast some champagne before we set off. A little fun before the festivities." She winked.

"Thanks, Cami," Leila said with a laugh. After Camille left, the girls pounced on the boxes.

"I wondered when these would get here!" Bianca said, handing over the attached card to Leila.

Leila opened the card and saw the note of well wishes from Harvey, Mason, Oscar, and Elliot. They opened the boxes and inside were three beautiful gowns of lace, tulle, and beading.

"Oh *my,*" Leila exclaimed. *Gowns!?* Hers was shimmering gold, like plated armor; Bianca's an iridescent blue that shifted colors with each movement; and Minnie's was a sheer purple fringed with silver.

"Yeah, I guess these boys know what they're doing," Bianca beamed.

"It's long enough to hide my sneakers so I'm happy," Minnie said.

Might as well make the best of it, Leila said, eyeing the gown.

They spent the rest of the day getting ready, curling each other's hair and watching movies. They gossiped as they painted their nails, laughed until they cried, and did everything they could to make the day last longer. If Leila wanted to, she could imagine they were getting ready for a normal dance at the gym of New Prep, and tomorrow they'd spend the rest of the day ignoring their homework and hanging out. But then they were fully ready and they had no choice but to leave the sanctuary of her room.

Downstairs, Camille laughed with her best friend Alicia, a bucket of champagne waiting for them. Leila had only seen Alicia a couple of times, but every time she'd been blown away by how beautiful she was. Tonight she wore a simple pink silk shift, her organza shawl wrapped around her. *She looks like a Hollywood starlet,* with her red hair curled perfectly and—Leila would never say this aloud—her heartbroken eyes. Camille wore a white satin gown with long satin gloves. She was perfection, even her gold lipstick stayed unmarred through each sip of the wine they were drinking.

"Wow, goddesses help the other guests when they see you," Alicia exclaimed as Leila, Bianca, and Minnie came down. "Heartbreakers, all of you."

Sounds like a promise, coming from a Vessel of Aphrodite.

"Well, let's start this party early!" Camille said, grabbing the champagne out of its ice bath. She popped the cork off with a yelp and poured everyone a glass, then raised her own high.

"May the goddesses watch over us tonight, bless us with good food, drink, and handsome dance partners. To the equinox!"

"Hear, hear!" Alicia agreed. They clinked glasses and Leila sipped the champagne, feeling the bubbles all the way down to her stomach. It was still bright out, the sun hadn't started to set yet. They drank their glasses and talked until a honk sounded from outside.

"That's our ride! OK ladies, gather your coats and purses. Oh, Leila I almost forgot!" Camille dashed out of the kitchen and came back in with a rose with gold petals. Leila took it, careful not to prick her fingers on the thorns.

"I know how you like to put these in your hair," she said to Leila with a smile. As her friends grabbed their clutches and finished their champagne, she and Camille moved to the foyer mirror. Bianca had curled Leila's hair loose and put pearls in her hair, and Minnie had applied an eyeshadow that looked like gold leaf on her eyelids—she was the summer sun. The only other color was the red lipstick she'd put on herself, reminding her of Persephone. She took the rose and held it on top of her head, letting all of her anxiety and fear course out of her through her magic. The rose's stem snaked along her head, forming a crown of thorns, then small gold buds formed and flowered. A crown of gold roses to make her feel invincible.

"Wow," Camille said with her hands on Leila's arms.

"Come on, this is one party we don't want to be late to!" Alicia said. And they were out the door, Leila saying a quick goodbye to the only home she'd had for the last couple of weeks.

They rode in a limo together through the city, and her friends were right, the New Olympians were out celebrating the equinox with fervor. Bonfires in the street and fireworks burst in the air as they rode past. There were swaths of crowds in the streets slowing them down but soon they wound up at Zeus' temple. It was even bigger than Leila remembered from her Induction, the columns imposing and the roof taller than the fir trees next to it and a long set of stairs to climb to even get into the temple. Leila tried to breathe but her dress clung to her every curve.

The door to the limo was opened by one of the white-gloved attendants and Minnie and Bianca stepped out, then Leila. She took a couple of steps before realizing Camille and Alicia hadn't followed.

She turned in question and saw Camille smile at her, even though her eyes brimmed with tears.

"This is the end of the road for me, Leila," her surrogate mother said. "Go, have fun."

"No," Leila said, her throat suddenly constricted with emotion. *It's real. It's starting.*

"Yes, my love." Camille reached out of the car and placed a gloved hand on Leila's cheek. "Spring will be here in a blink, I promise. I'll see you then." Then the hand was gone and the limo drove away.

She turned back to friends, they stood on the steps above her. *Might as well make the best of it.*

Leila took their outstretched hands and they walked the rest of the way to the ball.

ALICIA

The door of the limo closed and Alicia signaled the driver to get going, there was no point in lingering at the foot of the equinox party Cami wasn't allowed to go to. She put a hand on her friend's shoulder as Cami watched Zeus' temple get smaller as they wound through the trees. When Cami turned, she'd already pulled a handkerchief to dab the corners of her eyes.

"Tomorrow you grieve, the hardest part isn't done yet," Alicia poured herself two fingers of whatever alcohol she could grab first. They were on their way to the last place she'd ever want to go to—other than Cris's place, obviously. *Why did the Fates smile on me with this messed up love life?*

"You're right. Pour me one, too. You're not the only one with nerves tonight," Cami said.

The sun was going to set soon and even without powers she could feel the buzzing of energy nearing as the night drew closer, like the gods were reaching down to them. They zipped through the streets, bypassing downtown to get to the warehouse where Arnie had opened his garage over a year ago. The street he lived and worked on was quiet —the festivities were ramping up in other parts of the city. There was a bodega with the best cinnamon coffee on one corner and a crowded bookstore on the other. And the whole street was lined with maple trees which carpeted the ground with ruby leaves. For a few months it had been Alicia's home. And then she ruined everything and lost her powers.

How can this work?

"You sure you called?" Alicia's hands trembled suddenly.

"He knows a limo needs servicing. See? The garage is open," Camille pointed to Arnie's garage, a state-of-the-art building of brick and glass where only the city's most expensive cars could be serviced. Arnie was a Vessel of Hephaestus and could build a car with nothing but his bare hands. The limo swung in too quickly and Alicia felt her world turn. There wasn't any time left before she saw Arnie again— before she saw her husband.

It was Cami's turn to hold her friend's shoulder. Alicia thanked her and gripped the door handle, then got out. The air was cool and she pulled her pearl-colored wrap closer to herself.

"Like I said on the phone, with the equinox happening, I let my crew go for the night," the man said from the office. His voice was as deep and kind as she remembered and it sent cracks through her heart. "It won't be for another couple of—" Arnie came from around the corner and stopped. He was wiping his hands on a rag and his coveralls were tied around his waist revealing a heather henley. He'd filled out since she'd last seen him, most likely from the amount of work coming through his garage—he was the best in town—his upper-body straining against the material.

His eyebrows shot up for only a moment and she wished for nothing more than to know what he was thinking. When she had her powers she could feel his love, like a sweet fire that kept her warm. She shivered. In the last year she'd lost weight she didn't know she could lose and rarely left her apartment—without Aphrodite's gifts, she felt like a ghost.

"Hi Arnie," she started.

He placed his rag on the stainless steel countertop.

"Hi. What are you doing here?"

"I knew you'd skip the equinox party; Martin always goes too big, too flashy," she said with a smile. "Have you seen the Vessel of Persephone? I know you must work on Blake's car for—"

"Why are you here?" He cut her off.

The sun was dipping lower and it shaded the whole street,

making the garage feel like an island of light.

"I need a favor," she said slowly. "I need your help, taking in a boy."

"A boy?" Arnie said incredulously.

"He doesn't have anywhere else to go," Alicia pleaded. "I can't keep him at my place any longer, it's not safe for him."

"Why? What has he done? And who has he *pissed off*?"

Alicia only stared back at him. Bartie and her weren't supposed to be a thing. Cris wasn't just any Vessel of Ares, but the leader of one of the more ruthless gangs in the city.

I can't ruin another life.

Arnie searched her face and found the answers there. He sighed and ran a hand through his hair and rubbed his face. His hair ruddy red and Alicia's fingers ached to see if it was still as soft. *Does he feel the same way? I can't be the only one losing my mind over here.*

"How long do I need to keep him?"

Alicia wanted to sink to her knees with relief.

"Until I know my next move. Thank you, Arnie, really."

She motioned to the driver to pop the trunk and out Bartie sprang. His injuries had healed considerably, his face still shaded with the remnants of his last scrape up. It was a tight squeeze for him but it was the only way for them to get him across the city safely.

He walked over and shook hands with Arnie, who appraised him with suspicion.

"Go into the office, we can talk after," he said to the boy. Bartie nodded and gave Alicia a wink before disappearing around the corner.

Arnie turned back to her, his face hard.

"Alicia," he started. Her heart leapt when he said her name, but then fell when he said the next words. "I'll help you with this, I promise. But you can't trick me into seeing you again. You and I have an agreement, it's better if we stay apart. Please don't come back here."

Alicia swallowed what felt like needles and glass, and she smiled.

"Of course, thank you, Arnie," Alicia said. "Bartie is a good guy, he won't let you down." *Not like I did.*

She got back into the car and they pulled out of the garage and went on their way. *That's not my Arnie,* she thought, remembering how soft he'd been when they were together. *That's not the same man I loved because I ruined all the good in him with my betrayal.*

She didn't know she was crying until Cami's arms wrapped around her.

"I know, I know," her friend cooed.

They held each other as their worlds fractured apart, the sun finally dipping below the mountains and bathing the world in gold.

LEILA

Zeus' temple was the most classically Greek in architecture, but the king of the gods had given it over to nature. The main area was sunken and Leila had a good view of the scene from atop the steps. It felt redundant to climb all those steps to descend them, yet the effect was impressive. Autumn was alive in the atrium of Zeus' temple: red and gold birch trees sprouted from between the columns, shedding their fiery leaves and making it seem like the middle of a forest. Pumpkins the size of cars dotted the perimeter stacked with food and beverages. And in the center was the dance floor where guests in suits and gowns of every color twirled as the band played. Vessels dancing with satyrs, their horns decorated like cornucopias; centaurs whose bodies were painted up like jewels; the naiads floated on the dance floor like they'd never left the water; the dryads seemed to be watching Leila, waiting for her to do something—what exactly, she didn't know. Leila *knew* she lived in a city of magic but tonight was the first time her whole body felt electric with magic, her senses overloaded.

"You clean up well," Leila said as the boys met them at the edge of the dance floor, near one of the towering harvest statues. Gourds of all colors and golden wheat braided together around waterfalls of champagne. The sun was beginning to descend and they were in one of the last pools of sunlight, night creeping in from the shadows.

Harvey and his boyfriend Oscar wore matching wine-colored

suits, maize wreaths crowned their heads; Elliot's cream suit reminded Leila of breaking waves, his cheekbones accented with sea glass; and Mason matched Leila the closest with his cape of gold feathers. They crowded around each other, bestowing embraces and kisses on cheeks like long lost friends—even though they'd seen each other in school the day before. Leila was trying hard to push away the rise of emotions when she was surrounded by her friends, especially after losing the closest thing she had to a family.

Stop. She squeezed her nails into her palms to stop herself from breaking down right there. *Be here tonight, with your friends. Be here.*

"Wow, you're blinding me," Mason had his hand raised to his eyes, mocking how the light caught the girls' gowns. They did more than glow, they *sang* with the light.

"Thank you for coming tonight," Leila said, squeezing her friend's hands tight.

"It beats dancing in the gym and watching all the freshmen make out," Mason replied, which earned him an extra hard hand squeeze. "You know we wouldn't miss this."

"Now, which one of you is going to bless me with a dance first?" Elliot swept his eyes over Bianca, Minnie, and Leila. They burst out laughing.

"Is that how you ask a girl to dance?" Oscar winced. He grabbed Leila's hand, bringing it to brush his lips. His head was bowed and he looked up at her mischievously. "May we have this dance?"

Harvey, hold on to this one, he's a keeper.

"*We?*" Elliot scoffed.

Harvey grabbed Leila's other hand and gave Elliot a wink before giving her hand a peck. "Yes, *we.*" Then both boys pulled Leila out to the dance floor, looking back at their friends in challenge. She heard her friends laugh before joining them.

The music wasn't what they usually danced to; the songs never seemed to end, but to blend into a long and dizzying rhythm. There was a woman and a man singing but when Leila tried to concentrate she couldn't quite recall what about, lyrics snatched about lost love or found love didn't make sense, only that it propelled her and her friends to dance. They switched partners often, twirling and dipping, nearly falling on one another. There was little grace in their movements, only the freedom pure folly afforded them. Leila held on to one or more of her friends at all times, trying to soak in their warmth, trying to memorize their faces, their laughter—anything to tide her through the impending fall and winter. More champagne found its way into their hands—more than appropriate at the Mayor's Equinox Ball—yet the little group could not be caught still long enough to be scolded; their arms barricaded everyone out so they could enjoy themselves and themselves alone. If Leila had stopped dancing she would've seen how the trees sprouted golden leaves, how the dryads danced with building fervor, how the music snaked and bloomed like vines around everyone until they too were moved by the playing.

The sunset hit Zeus' temple like a spotlight, the last summer sun giving out in one burst, casting the temple in an orange glow. A spot in the middle glowed brighter than the others. The band's song shifted, the drum beat ringing out with the fervent clapping of the singers. The urge to keep moving died in Leila as soon as she spotted the mayor's broad frame in the middle. She could see his face protruding from the golden mane of a lion. Before he could drink in more attention, a figure appeared at the top of the steps, shadowed by the sunset—though there was no mystery as to who had arrived.

Blake.

Even though she was at the back of the atrium, she could feel his grey stare on her.

The crowd parted a path for them both to the center where the mayor stood.

This is it. Be here.

They both made their way to the center of the platform. As she passed the staring party goers, she focused on keeping her head high. In doing so, she didn't see whose hands squeezed hers, brushed her shoulders, her hair. *Last time I was here a pomegranate tree burst from the floor. Can it swallow me instead?*

The band, to its credit, never stopped its drumming or clapping, the beat kept in time with her jackhammer heart.

Martin greeted them at the center. She couldn't look at either of them, choosing to focus on the sunset.

"Today, we mark the Harvest, the beginning of the end," the mayor's voice boomed out. "The autumnal equinox is the tipping point, the marker between life and death."

Then Leila could feel *her.* Persephone had joined them. It felt like the morning sun. Then a gust of wind blew through the atrium. The crowd gasped, they could feel *him. Hades.*

The queen and king of the Underworld had joined the party. The music faltered only a moment before resuming.

Leila's eyes prickled, how she wished Persephone would give her the guidance she craved. But the goddess was silent, as she'd been since the wildflower field. The mayor put her and Blake's hands together.

She expected Blake's hands to be cold but they weren't, instead they were smooth and warm. A trail of magic wrapped around them, holding them together. Finally she looked at him, catching some emotion clouding his face before he could hide it. Then like water his face was placid as he watched her back, his mouth a determined line. His inky curls were pulled back by a jeweled diadem of black pearl and bismuth, reflecting the purple staining his under eyes. He held onto her tightly, but she didn't think he did it consciously since she held on just as tight.

"New Olympus welcomes the equinox—let us give thanks to those who bless us with life until spring!" And with that the sun winked out and they could feel both Persephone and Hades' magic burst the harvest pillars into flames, candles lighting all around and showering them in sparks before leaving. Persephone's absence left Leila cold.

Martin let go of their hands and the crowd roared, the band kicking off again, singing their incomprehensible ballad once more. The guests started dancing around them, forming concentric circles as Leila and Blake felt their wrists warm with magic. Hematite bracelets circled each of Leila's wrists and one hematite watch circled Blake's. They broke their hands apart to examine the silver stones that had appeared on them. She pulled on a bracelet and found there was no way to take hers off. She looked to Blake and found he was doing the same. Before she could open her mouth, the mayor clapped them both on the shoulders.

"Give us a dance, would you?" he said with a wicked smile, unaware of their newly bejeweled wrists. Martin turned to join the other guests, drinking out of a goblet that hadn't been in his hand before.

Blake took her hands again, softer this time.

"Dance with me?" It felt a little less like a question and more like a life raft.

Be here. Be here. Be here.

"Yes."

BLAKE

It hurt to look away.

He held her tight, trying not to fall over, the guests behind him danced in ever-dizzying circles. The singers of the band didn't help, singing in rounds over each other, belting repeating phrases that circled Blake's mind—yet when he looked into Leila's eyes, it all melted away. Her bright brown eyes were on him, lit by the gold that colored her lids.

Hades, help me.

The fabric of her dress was beaded with sharp glass and metal that dug into his hand but he welcomed the pain, welcomed the distraction from her soft curves underneath the sharp fabric. As they moved every flame refracted off her curves—the sweet light of a lantern in the dark.

Hades, I—

Blake wanted to run, far away from anyone who'd see him. *Tonight is a slow and painful death,* thinking of how the people dancing around him had treated him like shit for his whole life until this evening. He couldn't think of a worse place to be, watched by these elite as he tried not to trip over his feet. But he didn't, they moved like water, the center of an autumnal kaleidoscope, with Leila his pillar.

And if he'd thought about it, he couldn't name anywhere else he'd want to be.

LEILA

Leila felt the prickle of magic tickle her throat and shoulders as they twirled. She looked down. Like a scorching fire, the gold of her dress was being eaten up and left charcoal black.

The gold beading darkened to obsidian, the magic trailed down the length of her dress to her train. She was about to ask if her brooding dance partner had done some sort of Hades magic when a movement caught her eye—the golden leaves of the decorative trees were falling in gilded curtains, leaving them bare as bones. Leila and Blake matched.

The song thankfully ended, the crowd erupting in applause. Leila felt unsteady now that they weren't moving, the champagne was starting to turn on her.

Before she could say anything, Blake let go of her roughly.

"I need a drink," he said before stalking off.

The spot where he'd held her waist was cold.

"Nice costume change, the black is sexy," Oscar said behind her. She whirled around to see her friends making their way to her. She hugged Oscar in a tight embrace, and to his credit, he hugged her back as fiercely.

She reached for her friends when they came near.

"I thought that was it, I thought—" *I thought I wouldn't see any of you until spring.*

"Lucky for you, New Olympus parties go all night." Minnie

chimed.

"Lucky for all of us, Mason just grabbed us a table right next to the biggest cornucopia," Elliot pointed behind him. "Please tell me you're hungry."

"Starving," Leila agreed.

Her friends guided her across the dance floor, the music picking up again. The singers didn't possess the manic fervor as before but it still was enchanting nonetheless.

Mason had already piled their table full of food: steaming rosemary bread, cinnamon baked apples, squash pies, dripping turkey legs, buttered corn cobs—Leila's stomach growled when she smelled the fresh-cooked food.

It was nice to share a meal with her friends; she was still astounded at how light they kept the conversation. Even though she was having fun, she couldn't help but feel they were on borrowed time, at any moment she'd be whisked away to the mountains.

I should've worn a watch, she chided herself. Leila looked around for any indication of the time and her gaze snagged on Blake, the only other person in black, his back to her.

"Oh my goddess," Bianca leaned closer to her, "who let *them* in?"

Minnie was on Leila's other side and leaned in too. "I thought Blake would've thought better about bringing his friends here."

The rest of the table noticed the girls were staring.

"Yeah, especially his girlfriend," Elliot scoffed. Minnie elbowed him. "Ow!"

Leila frowned. The ice-white blonde sitting next to Blake dug her nails into his shoulder possessively. If he was the night, she was the moon.

"At least, they're distracting him," Leila said. Looking at her and Blake may make her stomach turn, but it gave her more time with her friends. *A little freedom.*

They ate and were revived, the group hell-bent on dancing again.

The music soon slowed, the other musicians ceasing their playing to let the front woman start a ballad. Leila's stomach dropped as the crowd around them started coupling up.

A warm hand grabbed hers and she spun to face Mason.

"I'm not as good as Oscar and Harvey about asking people to dance," he said and held his other hand up to her before putting on an awful British accent. "Would you care for a dance?"

Leila couldn't help laughing. "Yes, only if you immediately stop talking like that."

"What? I think I'm nailing it." His smile was bright.

"You're not."

Mason took her farther into the crowd, the gold light of his feathered cape danced on his skin and lit up his freckles.

"I missed when we matched," he said referring to Leila's black dress. "But black is nice too *I guess*."

"I liked the gold," Leila agreed.

They danced for a while, listening to the music. Leila was sure the song was about love but it made her sad.

"Hey, so," Mason cleared his throat. "You know about Harvey, right?"

"Harvey as in our friend Harvey? I think I know him," Leila said, smiling.

"Good one. But do you know what happens to him when he turns eighteen?"

"No," Leila said cautiously. "What happens?"

"He has to get married to a Vessel of Hera."

"What?" Leila stopped dancing, but Mason urged her to sway. "I know, I know. It's bonkers, but Zeus was married to Hera, so he has to. Even the mayor had to."

He's never said anything about it. Leila frowned.

"Wow," Leila breathed. "I feel so stupid. I've been whining and whining and—"

Mason squeezed her hand, bringing her back to him.

"I'm sorry, that's not why I told you. I was trying to let you know you're not alone. We all have a Myth that dictates our life, but we have each other. I mean, I'm in love with—" he stopped and took a deep breath. "It doesn't matter. I'm just trying to tell you you're not alone."

"Oh," Leila said. She felt a lump growing in her throat. She wanted to say more but it hurt, her heart going out to her friends. *It's not fair.*

Mason smiled at her again, but it was like a cloud passing over the sun.

"Did I fuck everything up? I feel like I fucked up."

"No, I promise you didn't. Thank you, Mase."

"You're my friend Leila, I got your back." Mason patted her back in emphasis before wiggling his eyebrows.

Leila rolled her eyes before stepping into his arms to hug him. He smelled like summer and life and Leila wanted to burn that scent into her brain. They stayed like that, holding onto each other as the music played on.

Then her wrists burned, the pain making her gasp. She stepped away, Mason looking alarmed. The pain shot up her arms, dragging a scream out of her. Mason grabbed her before she could fall, her legs buckling.

Leila couldn't speak, couldn't answer as her friend asked her what was wrong.

Then as soon as the pain had started, it stopped. Echoes of pain radiated through her body. She was shaking but Mason helped her stand.

She looked around for her friends, but they were on the other side of the dance floor. Next to them was a table, Blake sitting looking at her curiously. His girlfriend was holding his hand like she was playing with it—not *it*, the *watch*. Kat looked at Leila with a wicked smile.

"What else can this thing do?"

HARVEY

Oscar's head rested on his chest and his hair smelled like clove and cinnamon. Harvey focused on this as they swayed to the slow song. He needed to be present for this moment, absorb everything about it so he could live in this memory forever.

He'd met Oscar at a dress rehearsal for last spring's school musical. Oscar had the spotlight—at least that's how he remembered it —and that was it, Harvey didn't want to see anyone else. Even now, seven months before his eighteenth birthday, he couldn't bear the thought of Oscar dancing with anyone else. There were a lot of attributes about Zeus he admired, even copied—except one: his infidelity.

I'm dancing with him now, he thought and grounded himself in the moment. He rubbed his hands down Oscar's back, memorizing every fold of his jacket. Would this be the last time they danced like this? He wasn't sure.

But he'd hold on until he was forced away.

His eyes were closed when he heard Leila's scream, it was strange and pained and startled him out of his boyfriend's arms. Oscar didn't wait a beat to start pushing his way through the crowd of dancers to where Leila was. Harvey followed, their hands entwined.

No one else on the dance floor seemed to have heard the scream, or didn't care enough to stop what they were doing. They got to Leila and Mason in seconds; Mason held on to Leila like she needed help standing as they faced the table where Blake and his friends sat.

Of course.

"What the fuck did you do?" Leila's voice was low but it was practically a growl. Her crown of gold roses and her red lipstick made her look like a warrior queen.

Kat flicked her pale hair over her shoulder and smirked, unbothered.

"*We* didn't do anything, not on purpose anyway," Kat said.

"So you're saying you're blameless?" Oscar scoffed beside Harvey. "How likely."

"How could we have known that's what would happen?"

What is that thing? Harvey looked at the object they were all focused on. From where he stood, it looked like a regular watch made of black stone. *Weird.*

Leila was clearly still reeling from the pain, tears streaking her face. Oscar threw an arm around her to help her stand. There was no sign of the mayor—not that he'd be any use this late into the party.

He'd seen this group around parties sometimes, usually right before a fight broke out or a crowd suddenly turned on each other. As they grew up, the more Chaotic Vessels got more rowdy, more bold. With Kat and Blake running the group, they were downright dangerous.

He needed to be careful, any wrong word could be the thing that sets off the powder keg.

Blake can be reasoned with...sober and alone. Too bad he's neither of those things. Blake's crown lay crooked on his head, his suit unbuttoned.

"You need to turn that thing into the *nomos*, that can't be legal," Harvey said.

"No can do, Harv," Blake finally spoke. His eyes were glazed over like he was seeing everyone through a fog. He held up his wrist, "no clasp."

"At least apologize," Mason said.

"Why? We didn't do anything wrong," Kat spat back. "It was the watch."

Mason was about to say something else, his form brightening like he was stepping into a spotlight. Leila put a hand on his chest to stop him.

"No need," she said. "I don't want an apology. They've had their fun, let's go." She didn't look at Blake and his friends, didn't wipe the still-wet tears on her cheeks. She turned and left, leading them back to their friends. She held her head high but Harvey could see the way she clung to Mason and Oscar as she walked away.

Harvey's cheeks burned as the conversation replayed in his mind. He didn't stick up for Leila, not in any way that mattered.

What's the worst that could've happened? Oh yeah: I fight back, they fight back, one of my friends gets hurt, I get arrested and never become mayor which sabotages any chance of making any real change. That's the worst that could happen.

Even as he thought that he knew it wasn't entirely true.

But the truth, the fact that he couldn't defy fate for his friends—for the ones he loved—that was a truth he wasn't ready to hear yet.

AUTUMN

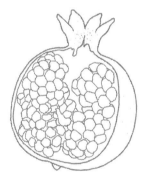

LEILA

They rode into the mountains at sunrise. The limousine was spacious and quiet, save for Blake's soft snoring. He'd lain down and fell asleep promptly after they got in, his jeweled circlet tossed aside.

Leila didn't want to think about the goodbyes she'd just made so she kept her eyes on the window and watched as the city flew by.

The cool morning sun shone on the evergreen trees, giving her a glimpse of the sky. At first she thought Zeus' temple was near the Hades estate as they were both in the mountains, but they descended back into the city to go south to the coastline before ascending the mountains.

They drove on a road that hugged the coast, the waters dashing the rocks below. It made Leila dizzy to watch but she made herself memorize where they were going. As they drove farther up, they strayed from the ocean into a dense forest. They drove for what felt like an hour, winding up the mountain.

Blake sat up, scrubbing his face with his hands. He was a mess— hungover, bleary-eyed, inky hair askew—but to Leila's disappointment it didn't make him look any less good. She couldn't compliment him as looking any better than 'good', she thought that'd be crossing a line.

Thank the gods I don't have to wake him up.

Leila wanted to ask him how much longer it would be, but he didn't look back at her. He bounced his leg as he looked out the window. In the sun's light, the hematite watch on his pale wrist shone like mercury. Leila looked away.

Then the car slowed to a stop.

We're here. Leila got out and shielded her eyes as she looked at the mansion before her. She had been sure it was going to be some decrepit haunted house and lightning would strike at it while bats flew out the window.

Instead it was a modern mansion, black and grey stone wrapped around large glass walls. She was shaken out of her thoughts as Blake swung open the giant slab of slate that apparently was the front door.

Leila wanted to get back into the limo but it had already driven off.

Well, this is it.

She walked the stone path to the door and entered Blake's house, and some feeling she couldn't place prickled the back of her neck.

"Let's get this tour over with," Blake said from the shadows, startling her. *This is the first thing he says to me all day and even now I'm not sure he's actually speaking to me.*

The entryway was dark until Blake flicked a switch and a massive chandelier lit up the space, a spiral of crystal and white stone. Then he started walking and Leila assumed she was supposed to follow.

They whizzed through the house, Blake's long legs carried him faster than Leila in her heels. He didn't bother to stop and explain anything other than the purpose of the room.

"Dining room," he waved a hand. "Living room, kitchen, library, pool."

Everything was grey, black, or glass but Leila sometimes spotted little pops of color: labradorite embedded in the walls, opal lining the pools, malachite on the bookshelves. She wanted to stop and look at everything but couldn't, not without losing her only guide.

Then Blake stopped in front of double doors on the west side of the house.

"This is one of two places you can't go. Ever." Blake looked at her, an undercurrent of worry knitting his brows together.

"OK," Leila answered. *Forbidden room? Not weird at all.* "What's the second place?"

"This way," he said before stalking off again.

They walked past the back of the house, the floor-to-ceiling windows showing the backyard. Leila had to stop for a moment to take it in; the slope of the mountain, the tiered backyard gave her that prickling feeling again. Blake opened a glass door and they stepped outside to the backyard.

As soon as she stepped down the stone path she realized what the prickling feeling meant: she couldn't feel any plant life on the property—the front yard was bare, the backyard only dirt and stone. There were no houseplants inside. *It's all dead.*

Blake guided her down the stone path and she tried not to panic. He held her arm when she stumbled on the stone. Blake stopped them in front of a small pool of water surrounded by tourmaline.

"This is the other place you can't go," Blake said. He squeezed her arm, but she didn't think he was doing it to intimidate her, more like he was holding onto her—like he was afraid.

"Go? How can I *go* anywhere? It's water."

Blake's mouth was a grim line. "It's not water, it's a door. To the Underworld—*to Hades.*"

Leila instinctively took a step back. Now that she really looked at the small pool of water she realized the water was too still and it didn't reflect the clouds or Blake as he stood right above it.

"Is this real?" Leila couldn't believe there would be an unguarded door to Hades in Blake's backyard.

"Yes, it is." Blake didn't elaborate, only turning to take the path back up to the house.

After they got back in, Blake led Leila to the east side of the house. The double doors mirrored the ones Leila was never supposed to go into, except a key hung on a chain from the door knob.

"This is your room. That's the only key so don't lose it." With that Blake turned on his heel and left.

Leila let him leave, not sure where they stood now. She took the key off the knob and unlocked the door, then opened it and took in her new home.

The floor was covered in boxes of her stuff she had to unpack, but the rest of the room was surprisingly nice.

Better than the dungeon I was imagining. Blake had been so adamant that he didn't want to come here but Leila thought it was because it was going to be some hovel. *Why does he hate it here so much?*

She closed the door behind her and locked it, feeling a little bit better at the heavy click of the lock. The suite was similar to the rest of the house: black and grey, but there were natural wood accents and more crystals embedded into the floors and walls.

Exhaustion settled over her like a heavy coat with the last week of stress and sleeplessness weighing her down. She kicked off her heels and tiptoed around all the boxes before she shut the curtains to the french doors of the terrace. Then she changed out of the heavy beaded dress and slipped under the silky covers and fell into a heavy dreamless sleep.

The sound of the doorbell cut through the rush of running water. Leila had woken up disoriented and her mouth tasting like ash.

First, I need to find my toothbrush.

She had eyed the pile of boxes until she found one labeled 'Toiletries' and produced her toothbrush before slipping into the marbled bathroom. It had reminded her of a cavern, her footsteps echoing on the dark stone, the lights covered in glowing opals. A giant rose quartz bathtub took up most of the space, the raw edges catching what little light there was. She'd still felt grimy after brushing her teeth and the bathtub had looked too enticing to pass up.

As she'd waited for the bathtub to fill with water she'd changed into a plush ivory robe and matching slippers.

Then the doorbell rang.

Less than 24 hours and we have a visitor? She didn't question it for long before she shut off the water and ran out of her room. Leila didn't know when she'd see anyone else over the next six months.

As she hurried through the mansion, she met Blake as he came down the stairs, a puzzled expression on his face.

His room must be on the third floor then? Leila's eyes followed him down the stairs while eyeing his outfit: loose joggers and a dark fitted tee. It was almost *inappropriate* seeing him in normal clothes—how the shirtsleeves clung to his biceps, the curls of his dark hair dripping down his neck.

Leila's face reddened and she pulled her long robe closer.

You are ridiculous, Leila. Utterly ridiculous.

Blake unlocked and then opened the front door with a strong pull. A gust of crisp mountain air blew through the house, shooting goosebumps up Leila's legs.

"*Danny?*" Blake said.

The russet-haired boy Leila had seen around New Prep was standing on Blake's front porch, a small dimpled smile on his face. Blake clasped Danny's hand and pulled him into a hug. Danny was gangly and taller than Blake. Leila couldn't grasp Blake being this affectionate to someone she'd barely seen him with. *Curiouser and curiouser.*

"What are you doing here?" Blake stepped back, a smile on his face.

Danny gave a small bow.

"I'm your official messenger. I convinced New Prep to let me bring you your assignments instead of the *nomos.*" He took off the backpack he'd been wearing and took out thick brown envelopes. He handed one to Danny and one to Leila. "Hi, I'm Danny."

"Leila," she replied. "So you just brought homework?"

"Not quite," Danny said, turning back to the road where his car was parked. He opened the back seat and a blur of black fur and fangs rushed at Blake.

It was a large dog with long shaggy hair and it leapt at Blake, scaring a yelp out of Leila. Then as the dog jumped up and down—craning to lick at Blake's face—Leila saw the dog's head split into *three* heads, all of them panting, happy, and licking at Blake.

Leila hadn't been around many dogs, but she didn't know any who had three heads. Danny noticed her bug-eyed look.

"That's Blake's dog, Cerby," Danny explained. "Short for Cerberus."

Cerberus? She had some image of a giant beast guarding the gate of Hades, three snarling sets of fangs.

"Technically, Cerby's a descendant of the *actual* Cerberus. But he is closer to the Groenendaal breed," Blake said to her over his shoulder.

The dog finally calmed down, his heads fusing back into one easily. His tongue lolled as he looked at Leila. Leila looked back, unsure.

"Thank you for holding him for me," Blake crouched to pet his dog. "Hope he wasn't too much trouble."

"No trouble! Cerby's a real hit with the ladies, so it was perfect."

Blake gave a laugh—an actual *laugh*. It was way weirder than the three-headed dog at this point.

"So I'll be by the same time next week to collect your assignments," Danny stuck his hands into his pockets to fish out his keys.

"Wait!" Leila exclaimed. "Can you take messages, too, as well as deliver?"

They'd taken her phone and there wasn't one in the house. She was cut off from any communication.

Danny hesitated to answer. "I don't know—I don't think that's —"

"I want to tell my friends I'm OK," Leila rushed. She didn't think she could have him wait for her to write out a letter, so this would have to do. "Can you tell Bianca? And Minnie?"

"Bianca?" He blinked. "Yeah, I can tell Bianca."

"Oh gods, thank you!" Leila wanted to hug the Vessel of Hermes but then she'd have to cross Cerby and she didn't want to make any sudden movements.

"It's not a problem, really." Danny's face reddened, his copper freckles glowed.

Leila didn't have to be a Vessel of Aphrodite to guess that Danny might have a bit of a crush on Bianca. But if Bianca knew, she'd never mentioned it.

With that, Danny and Blake said goodbye and he left. Blake brought Cerby in and Leila froze, clutching her assignments to her chest like a shield.

"Hi," she squeaked out as the dog kept his dark eyes on her. Cerby tilted his head to one side.

Blake smirked. "Wow."

"Wow what?"

"I didn't think you scared so easily."

"I'm not *scared,*" Leila retorted, very scared.

With that, she crouched down cautiously and extended a hand to the dog. Cerby sniffed her hand, his wet nose tickling Leila's palm.

"Be careful, he doesn't like girls," Blake said.

"What?" Leila wanted to run.

"Well, he's only met Kat—and it didn't go well," he hedged.

Wonder why.

Cerby kept sniffing Leila's hand until he stopped abruptly. His dark eyes went wide and he hopped up and down on his front legs. He wiggled out of Blake's grasp and ran at Leila, running her over with as all three heads barked happily. Then Cerby started licking at Leila's face, hands, hair—she could only try and pet Cerby until he calmed down a bit.

"So is this a good sign?"

Blake finally got a grip on his dog.

"Yes, actually. I was worried I'd have to give him back to Danny."

Leila wiped her face and stood. Blake looked much better than he had at the Equinox Ball, a little color coming back to his cheeks. There was only naked relief in his face.

"I was hoping Danny had brought more than just homework," she said.

"What do you mean?"

Leila looked at Blake incredulously. "Aren't you hungry? What are we going to eat?"

Blake's sharp smirk was at his face again. He seemed to only smile when he was making fun of her. *Yay.*

"Come this way, Princess."

Do I let him cook for me or do I starve? Leila sat on a stool across from Blake as he chopped carrots. Camille had only ever gotten takeout and Leila hadn't expected Blake to show her a fridge full of groceries.

His hair was still damp, and his dark waves swept across his forehead. He cut with precision, his eyebrows knit together as he chopped the carrots into coins. Cerby kept walking back and forth between her and Blake, panting.

"Stop staring at me," he said without slowing.

"I'm not staring at *you*, I'm staring at the watch."

The silver metal watch gleamed on his wrist, little red stones lined the face.

Blake stopped chopping and came around the island to her.

"I don't remember much about last night, after the ceremony." He rubbed his face.

After we danced.

"But that's no excuse. I'm sorry, I never would have done that on purpose—really."

He looked at her then, pleading, his eyes swirling grey. Leila felt uncomfortable under his stare, suddenly feeling bare.

"Thank you," she said looking back into his eyes. She wanted to forget the pain, the awful look on his friends' faces, his own indifference. *I won't forget. To make this work, I'll forgive.*

He looked down at the watch and Leila realized it wasn't a watch at all. There was only one dial, pointing to different jeweled Greek letters.

"What is this thing?"

"I don't know, but this," he pointed to one—the Greek letter Psi, "is what did that to you."

Leila sat back. She knew what Blake was thinking: *what do the other letters do?* A chill ran down Leila's spine. Something was very wrong about this kind of magic—how could this be allowed?

"We need to get these off," Leila said, grasping at the bracelets on her wrists. They didn't stretch, they didn't even budge. Panic was rising in her as she pulled and pulled at the stones.

She felt Blake's hands grab her wrists and gently set them down on the table. Surprisingly, they were warm and soft. Leila didn't realize how hard she was breathing.

"We're going to get these off but we have to do it carefully," he said. "This is magic I haven't seen before."

He was close, smelling of pine and something else she couldn't figure out. Then he let go of her and was back across the island, cutting carrots.

"Go unpack and come back in a couple of hours, dinner will be done by then," he waved his knife in the direction of the hallway.

Leila held her hands up. "Be careful where you wave that thing."

His lips quirked before he went back to cooking.

Leila walked away with her own small smile on her face.

The bathwater was still warm when she got back to her room and Leila let herself soak in bliss for a few minutes before unpacking. There were jars of different salts placed around the rim of the rose quartz tub, and Leila chose to pour in some of the pink one that smelled of gardenia and jasmine.

After she dried off and changed into a silk pajama set—*thank you,*

Camille—she unpacked her things. Camille had packed her extra things like books and nail polish. She even left her a whole box of seeds in little jars. *Does Cami know it's winter?* She could see the barren terraced backyard from her window—the dirt looked like a desert. She didn't like looking at it. With a sigh, Leila closed the box of seeds and pushed it to the back of her closet.

There were more boxes, but she decided she couldn't go on without *something* to eat. The smell of food hit her as she opened the door to leave her suite. The mansion was a maze but she only had to follow her nose back to the kitchen.

Blake was sitting at the kitchen island, eating out of a bowl with a book in his other hand. Cerby trotted over to Leila, eager to be pet. She ran a hand through his soft fur as she walked closer.

Blake turned. "Shepherd's pie—sorry, *vegan* shepherd's pie."

She sat next to him and served herself a large helping of food. Leila didn't realize how hungry she was until she started eating. She didn't bother trying to eat politely, she wasn't trying to impress Blake. He seemed too immersed in his book anyway, some ancient Greek volume she could not decipher.

"How did you learn how to cook?" she asked mid-bite.

Blake set his book down and looked over at her. "So it's good?"

"Better than good—I wish I could cook like this." *Without burning anything down.*

Blake sat up straighter in his seat, the praise seemed to buoy him. "The library has a ton of cookbooks, I took out all the non-vegan parts." Blake nodded in the general direction of the library. "It's just following a recipe."

"Wow, so you had to cook for yourself all these years?" Leila said, scraping her plate. When Blake didn't answer right away, she looked over at him. He was tracing the book cover with his fingers, his thoughts far away.

"That's what happens when no one will deliver this far out," he said, grabbing his book and his bowl. He stacked his dishes in the sink. "I'm gonna head in. Don't worry about the dishes."

With that, he left, Cerby following at his heels. Leila was so taken aback at his hasty departure she didn't know what to say.

What did I do?

LEILA

And then three weeks passed.

Leila rarely saw Blake except for dinner but she could have been sitting next to a statue for all the conversation she got. She'd tried to figure out what was wrong but he rebuffed her enough times she stopped asking.

Leila felt guilty eating the food Blake made every single night so she attempted to cook for herself, which consisted of a steady diet of cereal and vegan yogurt. She kept herself busy by exploring much of the estate until she stopped getting lost, then she picked her way through the library—the only books she wasn't intimidated by were mass-market mysteries so she stocked up on them and a ratty copy of *Cooking for Beginners*. She never ran into Blake in the library and avoided the trail of heavy leather tomes he left open around the room.

Then Leila finally unpacked the last of the boxes she had, though she didn't touch the box of seeds and planting supplies—that seemed like a futile effort. In one of the other boxes was a small record player and records. On top of them was a silver framed photograph of all her friends from the party on her first night: She had her arms around Minnie and Bianca, Harvey and Oscar held onto each other, Elliot raised his drink from the back, and Mason glowed in the front. They were all so happy Leila's heart hurt just looking at everyone's smiles. She put it by her bedside next to her calendar. She played music all throughout the day to fill the silence of the house. There were records from every genre, every era.

Only a small pink box wrapped in gold was the last thing unpacked. In it was a single potted peony, closed up tight. Leila opened the card that came with it and realized it was from Alicia.

Dear Leila,

This is a traditional gift given to many couples of New Olympus when the Myth requires their marriage: it shows you someone's true feelings. Like a mood ring!

Typically, the flower is activated (with a droplet of blood fed to the soil. Gross, I know) and then it's exchanged so your spouse can always know how you're feeling. That's not why I'm giving this to you. I want you to learn what you want, how you feel: there is strength in being in tune with your emotions. Maybe I would've made different choices if I'd known more about myself. I hope you know you always have a way out.

xx Alicia

At first, Leila shoved the card away. *I know how I feel.* She was indignant, wondering how Alicia thought there was a way out for Leila if she only knew her emotions. But the flower called to her in the way only plants called to her, so she took a safety pin and pricked her finger.

The soil drank up the drop of blood, and as Leila sucked on her index finger, she watched the flower fill with color: the stem a deep green and the petals a rich red. Then the petals bloomed outward, fractionally.

Leila expected something else to happen but nothing did. Over the weeks the petals didn't move, neither blooming bigger or closing back into a fist. Leila wasn't surprised, she wasn't exactly happy or sad— she didn't feel anything.

Another box held brushes and acrylic paint but no canvases, leaving Leila to start painting on the one wall that wasn't inlaid with stones or crystals. She'd never painted seriously before but when she had her music on and concentrated she could almost pretend she wasn't trapped in the house.

They got into the habit of avoiding each other, the most Leila saw Blake was when he worked out outside. Leila didn't *watch* him per se, but she was having her coffee at the same time on her terrace and he happened to be running outside with Cerby at his side. He ran shirtless, his skin grey like moonlight. She hadn't been outside since the first day; she didn't feel comfortable going out there alone. Leila couldn't see the dark portal but she knew it was there, remembered the way it looked back at her.

Leila was so desperate for human contact she even started waiting for Danny to come drop off their homework on Sundays. His warm smile and mile-a-minute conversation was like the sun parting, even if only for a brief moment.

Leila wrote a letter to her friends and kept it in her back pocket —writing and rewriting—sometimes spilling her heart out and telling them how much she missed them, sometimes lying and saying how she was having an amazing time and they shouldn't worry about her. What she wanted to say was *please, don't forget about me. I miss you.*

But she never gave Danny the letters. When he came over, Blake and Cerby came out and she was overwhelmed with both the dog and the human interaction. Blake and Danny chatted mostly but for some reason she couldn't find herself able to interrupt. Blake kept the conversation as short as possible and Leila wondered why. *Doesn't he miss his best friend as much as I miss mine?* But she never asked and he never included her in the conversation.

Instead, every week she scratched Cerby's ears and let him lick her face while they talked, and when they were done she told Danny to tell her friends she was OK.

Maybe it was how silly sending a letter felt, like passing a note in class—maybe it was the fact her friends hadn't sent anything to her first. There was an awful part of her that wondered if her friends were better off now without her drama, that leaving them alone was better for them. And every Sunday she listened to it, the letter going unsent.

Then one Sunday in late November, as she paced in the grand foyer trying to gather the courage to finally give Danny her letters, the doorbell rang.

Danny's early—by two hours.

Leila heaved the heavy front door open, the rush of cold air making tears prick her eyes.

It wasn't Danny.

BIANCA

Monday was the start of midterms and Bianca should have felt prepared.

I am, she argued, hoping she could will away the knots in her stomach. She had a whole binder devoted to studying, so there shouldn't be a problem with any of her classes. But she still felt *wrong,* like the world was tilted and out of order. Like she was a step out of beat with everyone, with her friends.

Today was worse—usually the only thing she could rely on was the fact that Danny would find Bianca around campus and let her know Leila was OK. She spent all of Sunday waiting for him to tap her shoulder.

But he never came. And she didn't know him well enough to find his dorm and question him like she wanted to.

It would be better if she could talk to Minnie but...well, she didn't know how to talk to her right now. Minnie was spending long nights in the art studio, coming back to their dorm exhausted and short-tempered.

It was like the art was taking something out of Minnie as she worked. Bianca could feel this rift between herself and her friends she didn't know how to cross.

Bianca stopped walking in the middle of the hallway when she spotted the gangly Vessel of Hermes. Danny's auburn mop peeked above everyone as he walked. Bianca chewed on her lip for a moment before cutting through the crowd to him.

"Hey!" It came out more forcefully than she wanted to but she got Danny's attention."Hey," he said with an easy smile. If she didn't know better, she'd say Danny's resting face was a smile. Which made his friendship with Blake all the weirder to her.

"So, any messages?" Bianca didn't feel like wasting time being polite.

"Oh, uh, no."

What does that mean? Going through a messenger instead of being able to call her best friend was ridiculous and frustrating.

"Leila didn't say hi, or...? What did she say?" Bianca tried to keep her voice level.

Danny rubbed the back of his neck in thought. His face had lost some of the soft edges she'd known most of her life, but his sharp cheekbones and jaw didn't take away any of the kindness held in his eyes. He looked around before leaning closer, close enough for Bianca to smell his aftershave.

"It was weird," Danny said in a low voice. "Usually, Leila, Cerby, and Blake come out but it was just Blake. And we barely talked for a minute before he shut the door again."

"Leila didn't come out?" Bianca breathed.

"No, I didn't see Leila," Danny frowned. "But I swear I thought I could hear other people."

LEILA

They came out of the forest.

At least that's what they said: they cut through the mountains, staying off the road and out of sight of the *nomos*.

When Leila saw Kat's moon-white hair, yellow eyes, and full smirk, she moved to wrench the front door closed. A girl behind Kat stopped the door with a smack of her hand.

"Now, don't be rude," the girl said with a deep laugh. Her head was shaved, the bleached fuzz contrasted with her dark brown skin. "We were invited."

"You know this one doesn't have any manners. I heard they found her in the woods," Kat said with a sneer and walked right past her. There were five of them, each carrying in bags and gear, like they expected to move in.

"Blake!" One of the boys—slim and pale as an eel—bellowed, the sound so loud it made Leila flinch. A room off the second floor landing opened and Blake leaned over the railing, his dark hair flopping into his face so only his smile of disbelief showed.

"How?" He came down the stairs and greeted the group with enthusiasm. Then he and Kat crashed together, kissing with an acrobatic tongue display.

Is this necessary? Leila's fists closed on her letter she still had in her hands. Kat looked at Leila after they were done and Leila gave her a passive smile. Blake's friends recounted how they snuck out and made their way out here. Finally, she could put a name to Blake's friends. Sidonie, tall and lithe; Ivan, sharp and broad; Drake, preening; and Ash with his head of curls and under eye bags that rivaled Blake's.

Chaos had pushed their way into the house of Hades.

"What about school, you don't think anyone's going to figure out you're all gone?"

"Like we go to school enough for them to miss us," Ivan said, slicking his blond hair back.

"And we couldn't leave you alone like this," Ash mumbled drowsily. He reminded Leila of those cherubs who slept on clouds in Renaissance paintings.

"I said my doors were open—I didn't think you'd come." Blake's arm was snaked around his girlfriend possessively.

"You don't trust your friends?" Drake asked, already stretching out on the base of the staircase.

"You know I do," Blake said.

"Good, because we also brought the party." Sidonie unzipped one of the huge duffel bags she'd carried into the entryway with ease. She opened the bag to reveal a trove of amber wine bottles wrapped with gold labels.

Blake let out a breathy laugh. "You trekked all the way out here with *ambrosia*?"

"And we managed not to get mauled by anything in the process. I think that's a cause for celebration!" Kat eyed Leila. "Mind fetching your guests some wine glasses?"

Leila looked at Blake but he seemed to be avoiding her gaze.

She settled her glare on Kat. "I mind. By the way, you're not *guests*, you're trespassers."

Ivan gave a chuckle.

"Don't mind her," Blake said in a way that felt a lot like he was trying to excuse a pet who'd jumped on his guests. And with that they closed their circle back in on themselves. Leila couldn't stand being around them for another second and slipped away to her room.

She closed the door and locked it, and an angry breath rattled out of her.

There has to be a phone here, she thought desperately. *A carrier pigeon, or if I built a big enough bonfire someone would* have *to come, right?* Then another idea crossed her mind. *What if I walked out?*

But that was out of the question. It would take her hours to walk to the barrier the *nomos* had up and the only things waiting for her were a pair of handcuffs and a trip right back here. Leila got into her bed, the covers pulled up around her.

I'm acting like a child. But the covers felt like a comfort in the cold mansion. Having more people in their isolation should have made Leila feel better but they made her feel more alone.

Something scratched at her door, making Leila yelp. The scratching continued and then panting started, and Leila recognized it as Cerby. She rushed off her bed and opened the door to a large shadow of a dog sitting, his tail wagging when he saw her.

"Come in." The dog didn't need to be told twice, he bolted inside and ran around her suite, sniffing all of her belongings. Leila made sure to lock the door behind her.

"Won't Blake come looking for you?" She sat on the bed and watched Cerby inspect every inch of her space.

Why am I talking to a dog? But having Cerby come to her lifted some of the melancholy she felt.

If Leila had been back in New Olympus proper she wouldn't have been at such a loss for words. She should've pushed them out, let Blake know this wasn't right—none of it.

Why didn't I say anything? Leila looked at the peony that sat on her shelf, frozen mid-bloom. If she were to base how she felt on Alicia's peony, she shouldn't be feeling anything at all.

Leila fell back on her pillows, Cerby jumping up on the bed to snuggle with her like an ink blot on her blush colored bed. She tried to hold onto the feelings of anger, to stoke them into a fire, a plan, *anything* to get her out of her prison. But there was nothing.

HARVEY

Harvey knew how busy he needed to be to stop feeling anything.

Between meetings at the Senators Council, running errands for the mayor, jumping between Student Council, clubs, and sports while spending every other minute of free time in the library—Harvey could pretend like nothing was wrong.

Nothing's wrong, Harvey said between urgent kisses with Oscar, stolen in the wings of the theater. That's all he had time for anymore, backstage kisses and empty promises. But it wasn't like Oscar wasn't busy either. Or the rest of their friends.

Harvey couldn't look in Oscar's eyes.

After leaving his boyfriend to his rehearsals, Harvey sped to Prep Housing to change out of his school uniform and leave for the mayor's office downtown. He was already loosening the tie around his neck with one hand while trying to balance his books and his dorm keys with the other. He didn't notice the figure sitting on his bed until he'd closed his door and put his books down on his desk.

"Hi Harvey," she said.

Harvey flinched back, knocking his lamp over. A ripple of lightning circled his fingertips.

"What are—Who are—Um—" Harvey was short-circuiting. Not because he was startled but because this girl was in his room. His *nightmare* was in his room.

The girl was wearing the boys' New Prep uniform, her blazer and slacks oversized in a way that made her look both professional and unreachable. She flicked one brow at him.

"You know who I am."

"Yes," Harvey hedged. "Astrid." *Vessel of Hera.*

Astrid gave him a big smile. "Nice to meet you. Finally."

He looked at her hand and thought about fleeing his own dorm room before putting his hand into hers.

"Nice to meet you."

Astrid wasn't just *any* of Hera's Vessels, she was *his* Vessel.

His manners finally caught up to him. "Do you want something to drink, or—"

She shook her head politely. "No, thank you. This isn't going to be long. I wanted to check in with you since we're officially six months out from your eighteenth birthday."

Harvey gave her a nod.

"I've been working on a motion to move our wedding to summer, maybe even until after college. I'm assuming you've already applied for college—"

"Wait, I—" The room was spinning. Harvey's stomach threatened mutiny. "I'm dating someone and I don't think he'll be OK with, you know..." *Marriage.*

Astrid waited with her hands folded in her lap. When Harvey didn't continue, she let out a breath.

"Look, I'll cut to the chase: we have the same dream. I'm not your enemy—in fact, I've done everything I could to give you space. But I know you can't fight fate." She leveled a look at him. "Not at this time."

Harvey frowned, wondering at what time would be appropriate to rival the Fates.

"You're going to be mayor, you have it in you to go all the way," Astrid continued. "And I'm the lucky one who'll be with you, fighting *for* you at every step. I know you know that's true."

Harvey nodded in agreement. It was natural to be curious about the person he was betrothed to since his Induction. Astrid was a straight-A, type-A tennis star, unblemished in every way. Harvey knew she could easily take on any Student Council seat, yet she'd never run. *Because that was my territory,* he realized.

"And about your boyfriend, I understand. I'm not going to care who you're with, not if we're doing the right thing for New Olympus."

"That's not fair to you. I'm not going to be unfaithful to my wife," he argued.

"Harvey, it's not possible for you to be unfaithful."

"What do you mean?"

"I'm a lesbian."

Harvey's eyes widened. "Oh. *Oh.*"

"Yeah," Astrid said as she gathered her black tote. She flicked her light brown hair behind her shoulders. "See? I'm on your side. Let's talk soon, OK?"

She patted him on the shoulder before opening the door to leave.

"You'd better get to your internship." Then she was gone, the dorm quiet and Harvey alone.

He closed his eyes and rubbed his temples like he could rub all of his responsibilities away. In the silence he thought about the last thing Oscar had said to him in the dark of the theater, something Harvey wasn't sure he was even supposed to hear.

"How much more can you pile on until you break?"

Harvey didn't answer then and he couldn't answer now.

He had an internship to get to.

LEILA

The day started off with a nightmare.

One moment Leila was in her bed, the next sinking through the mattress, her fingers gripping the covers in an effort to hold on. But they slipped through her fingers and she fell down into ice cold water sinking into darkness. It was so cold she couldn't feel her legs as she desperately kicked them, couldn't feel her clumsy hands, couldn't breathe— light winked out leaving her in never ending deep.

With the last of the air in her lungs, Leila screamed.

She screamed, the sound wrenching her up out of sleep and back into her bed. Her heart hammered in her ears and she was shaking. Her throat was raw from screaming, her breathing rasping out of her in shallow, chattering breaths. Cerby was at her side, sticking his faces into hers, making sure she was OK. The blue light of the early morning filtered through the window making it look like she was still underwater.

She was sure now she was awake. But not sure she'd escaped her nightmare.

After the first night, Leila didn't know if she could come out of her room, but Cerby was whimpering and she had to make sure he was taken care of. So she had ventured out as quietly as possible to let the dog outside before making her way around the rest of the mansion. There was evidence of Blake's friends: things strewn about, food and dishes out. But the Vessels themselves weren't around.

They must be sleeping off their celebration, Leila had thought as she looked up to the floors above. She hadn't been up to the other floors as Blake's room was up there, but she was sure there were more bedrooms. Knowing she was the only one awake didn't make her feel better. Dread was hot on her neck and kept her looking over her shoulder. Leila opened the door to the closet holding the dog food, leash, and extra toys, which she had found after her first few weeks of solitude-related nosiness.

Or maybe they left!

"One can hope," Leila had muttered as she dragged the dog food back to her room. After that, she grabbed one of her moving boxes, went back to the kitchen, walked into the pantry, and grabbed every box of cereal she could find.

So much for a balanced diet. She grabbed some granola bars and a bag of chips for good measure. As she was leaving the kitchen, she eyed the electric kettle for only a second before unplugging the machine and grabbing all the tea and instant coffee.

After putting her stuff in her room, she let Cerby back in, his nails tapping happily on the stone floor. She spent that first day with Cerby by her side as she painted her wall.

Blake's friends partied at night and slept through the day, and Leila filled the hours by painting. She didn't see the Vessel of Hades or any other humans for a week, but she heard them. Cerby got more antsy as time went by, either missing Blake or his runs outside—or both. Leila finally took him out for more than just quick bathroom trips after a lot of pleading on Cerby's part.

I can't be stuck inside and scared of a backyard, she resolved, before opening the door and taking the large dog out. Cerby pulled her around the large grounds eagerly, all three heads sniffing every direction. The fresh air felt good and she felt good to be out in nature, even in the bare land of the estate. But something felt wrong, her powers distant. She couldn't feel the thrum of life in the earth, the trees—it all felt dulled.

After a couple of mornings of being pulled by Cerby, she was starting to catch up, even if her lungs and limbs were screaming at her to stop. It's not like there was anything else for her to do, and it helped her feel less restless.

Sometimes, when she let Cerby run freely as she tried to catch her breath, she thought the curtains of one of the rooms rustled. Leila wasn't used to feeling watched and it tripped her up. The dark glass windows of the mansion and the ancient evergreens that surrounded the grounds of the estate gave away nothing, neither comfort nor the identities of her would-be watchers. She hoped she was wrong.

Until a week later, when she had the nightmare.

It was entirely too early to be awake but she got up anyway, making herself coffee and putting on a record to listen to, upbeat pop blowing away the last of the nightmare's hold on her. She took her morning routine slower than usual, finally taking Cerby out for a run when the late fall sun had come out.

As Leila ran she had the slimy feeling of being watched and looked to the house where Kat watched her from one of the balconies.

"Take a picture," Leila mumbled and waved to the girl from the grounds. *What are the consequences of pushing someone into a portal to the Underworld?*

Later that evening, when Leila lost herself in the minutia of painting petals on an ever-expanding mural, she felt it. First it was a whisper. *Come.*

Then it was a tug.

Leila dropped the brush from her hand, unable to fight her body as it got up and left the safety of her room to follow that command all the way to where Blake sat, a ghost of a smile on his face. They were in the living room, lounging on the velvet sectionals in front of a roaring fireplace. Bottles of ambrosia in front of them, the honey-gold drink filled their glasses while music played from one of the speakers softly in a dizzying melody.

"So nice of you to join us," Ivan boomed. "Sleep well?"

Ash gave her a mock bow and something clicked in Leila's mind.

He has to be a Vessel of the god of sleep or nightmares. The handful of weeks of Ancient Greek wasn't doing her any good right now—and didn't help identifying the others.

"We wanted to play a little game," Kat said. "You have to be as bored as us."

"Is there a notch on the dial that makes her dress better?" Drake laughed. Leila shot him a smile and a middle finger. She was in her painting clothes, multi-colored acrylics splattered her sweatpants and cropped sweatshirt.

"Why would you do this?" Leila turned to Blake. He lounged with a drink in one hand and his watch hand in Kat's lap. "Why don't you leave me alone?"

"Didn't you hear Kat? We're bored." His tone was mocking, cruelty brewing in his eyes.

"Find something better to do," she said and turned around, walking out. But her feet brought her right back around.

Blake tsked and the rest of the Vessels' eyes glittered up at her.

"Did I say you were dismissed?" Blake said. She stood in front of all of them, fear blooming cold up her spine.

"We already know this one," Kat pointed at a red jewel on the watch face. "This one is a good one." She twisted the dial. Pain shot through Leila's wrists through the stone bracelets, as awful and searing as it was at the equinox.

It stopped as soon it started but Leila realized she was curled up in a ball, tears threatening to leak.

They don't get to see me cry. Not again.

She pushed herself. None of them were horrified—they were all amused. *Monsters.*

"Let me go." Leila hated how much her voice trembled. "*Now.*"

"Let's try this one!" Kat ignored her.

There was a flash of white and Leila now stood over Blake, her stomach roiling, sure she was going to throw up at any moment. *Not if Kat strangles me first.* By the look the Vessel of Hecate had on her face, she was sure she was going to get hexed. Then she noticed how the rest of them looked at her in disbelief.

She took a step back in confusion, her hands going to her mouth and she noticed her lips were swollen.

"Who knew the princess had *that* in her?" Sidonie said.

"What?" Leila breathed.

"I think we know what that dial does." Drake adjusted his glasses as he stared at her, as if to get a better look. As if she were a zoo animal. "Tell me, do you remember the last twenty minutes?"

Twenty minutes? Leila's face must've been answer enough because they laughed. She looked at Blake, looked at the color that stained his face. Not only that, but the flecks of paint on his face, his shit-eating grin and the unbuttoned collar of his jacket. The urge to throw up was overwhelming as an ugly feeling of disgust and shame bubbled up in her.

"I'm done," Kat said and turned the dial back to pain. Leila dropped to her knees, her wrists feeling like they were being sawed off.

"I've never done anything to you. Leave me alone!" Leila's voice was hoarse with pain. "Fuck all of you and *let me go.*"

"We're not done yet," Kat said. Before she could turn the dial back, Leila turned to Blake.

"This isn't who you are. I know this isn't who you are."

"You think you know him better than his friends?" Ivan scoffed.

"I know he's not a monster without all of you around," Leila ground out. Her wrists throbbed.

Blake's smile slipped from his face and he drained his glass before crossing the room to Leila. He took Leila's chin. She resisted but he had a steel grip on her.

"You don't know what I am," he breathed, his breath sickly sweet and familiar. As she looked into his eyes she tried to see any part of the boy she'd seen at the diner, the one whose smiles were full of warmth. But the only warmth in his eyes was reflected from the fire that blazed behind her. He turned the dial as she screamed out in protest. The scream was cut off, as if someone had pressed mute to her.

"No *way!*" Ivan clapped his hands together in delight.

"Say something," Drake pressed. Sidonie echoed the sentiment. Leila told him to shut up—she tried to at least. She gripped her throat and found no matter what she did, no sound came out.

Black curled off Blake like smoke tendrils.

"I am a monster," he said and turned the dial again. Leila flinched, waiting for pain to come but it didn't. "You're dismissed."

When Leila made it back to her room she sat with the doors at her back and Cerby at her side. He pressed his head into her lap but her arms hurt too much to pet him much. She stayed there, waiting for the sounds of their party to quiet.

Then she let herself cry.

CAMILLE

Camille had been waiting to ask the mayor one question all night. Through the agricultural meeting at City Hall, through dinner in their favorite corner booth, through the car ride to her house. Even now, hours later in her bed, Camille only had one thing on her mind.

She traced her finger down the Vessel of Zeus' broad back.

"Martin?"

"Hmm?"

"Could I, possibly, go see Leila soon? I promise I'll be discreet—"

"No," Martin said flatly.

"Don't you think I could? I mean, I sweetened the farming deal today in your favor." She tried to say it sweetly, but her anxious fingers pulled at the hem of her silk shift.

Martin turned over, blond hair mussed in his face.

"Oh? Do I owe you a favor?" He smiled and leaned in for a kiss and Camille pulled back.

"To see my daughter, yes."

"You're not my wife, I don't owe you anything." He went to roll over but Camille pulled him back.

"You're joking."

"You'll find I'm not."

She got up, throwing a silk robe around her shoulders and opened the french doors to her room.

"I think we're done here." She motioned for him to leave.

"You're acting crazy, you know that right? The calls, the crying, the mood swings. I think I've done enough—I've had enough." When Camille didn't budge, the mayor got up with a sigh. "She's not your real daughter, you do realize that?"

Camille flew across the room, the crack of a slap on Martin's cheek echoing around the room. "You don't get to talk to me like that."

He caught her wrist. "I'm only telling you the truth. Leila isn't your daughter and the quicker you get that through your head, the quicker you'll get over this," he waved his other hand around, "*melancholy* you're stuck in. It's getting tiring."

"Then leave," Camille spat.

"What am I supposed to tell Joanne?"

"Tell your *wife* you were working late." Camille crossed her arms. "Now, *get the bloody hell out of my house!*"

Martin glared at her as he picked up his clothes and left, slamming the front door. Camille watched him stalk to his car from the windows of her bedroom, storm clouds brewing above her house.

How am I going to do this on my own?

MIN-SEO

The gallery was lit up against the lashing rain of late fall. Soft lights illuminated the space and though it was beautiful, it made Minnie feel like she was in a fishbowl. She was in the darkest corner in front of a large canvas, trying to look engaged in the art as Vessels milled around her.

She didn't know the artist, didn't know anyone apart from Claire who'd begged her to come—and who wasn't anywhere to be found.

You're the one who said you were tired of hanging out with me in the studio, Minnie clenched her fist around the flute of champagne she held. This was the first time in a month and a half Minnie had taken a night off from working on her sculptures, and she felt every second away from her work pass by. It was agonizing.

Not as agonizing as these heels. She drained her glass and replaced it as a caterer passed. Claire helped her pick out clothes fit for the gallery crowd, since a lot of her clothes were a little loose after six weeks of sculpting every night and little else. Minnie blushed, thinking of the rest of her free time spent holed up in Claire's apartment.

Then she heard Claire's laugh, high and musical. Turning, she saw the sun in the shape of her girlfriend.

My secret girlfriend. But Minnie couldn't help from smiling as Claire turned her green-eyed gaze on her. It felt good to be on the other end of that look, especially when Claire made her way over to where Minnie stood as soon as she entered the gallery.

Claire gave her a kiss on the cheek and it felt like the summer sun.

"Min-Seo, you're so punctual," she laughed.

"You know me," she replied.

Claire squeezed Minnie's elbows. "Look, I have to do the rounds with all of the patrons, you know, schmooze and sell pieces. I'll be right back."

"I've been waiting for you." Minnie could hear how pleading her voice was.

"And I have a job, don't be so needy. You're so much better than that." Claire tucked Minnie's black hair behind her ear and her eyes softened. "Plus, you're still in high school and I don't think we should try to dodge all those questions while trying to sell art. I'll be back so quickly."

Her girlfriend turned and left and Minnie wanted to protest but it felt like trying to catch sunlight through her fingers.

The evening continued like this: champagne, looking at art, trying not to look at Claire, art, more champagne, staring at Claire.

As Minnie had champagne as her only companion, she watched Claire laugh with and entertain possible buyers. Caterers started to avoid Minnie and she was sure other people steered clear of her too as if they could sense her sour mood. A mood that absolutely plummeted when she saw who came through the gallery's glass double doors.

"Bianca," Minnie said and promptly turned around.

But Bianca had seen her.

"*Minnie?*" Even with the heavy downpour outside Bianca didn't look disheveled in any way.

"What are you doing here?" Minnie forced out, her words hard to pronounce after all of the champagne.

"That's what I was going to ask you, but you haven't answered any of my texts."

"And?" Minnie didn't like Bianca's tone, how it felt like something was Minnie's fault. "Is there a Student Council emergency I should care about?"

Bianca stepped back. "What? No, this is about Leila."

Her mood was in free fall. Minnie tried her hardest not to think about Leila—it hurt too much. Claire had said to channel her negative emotions into her art but she was far from her studio.

"Bianca," Minnie said slowly. "You know she's there until spring. That's it. We can't do anything about it."

Bianca ran her hand through her hair in a way Minnie knew meant she was frustrated. "I understand. But something's wrong. Can we talk, *please?*"

Minnie felt a warm hand around her waist and the smell of fresh hyacinth. Claire's brows were pinched as she looked between Minnie and Bianca.

"Babe, who is this?" Which was Claire's polite way of saying *I didn't say you could invite your high school friends.*

"No one, she's leaving," Minnie said quickly, her words blurring together. Her words were colliding in a way she couldn't stop fast enough.

Now Bianca really was mad, her eyes wide. "*No one?* Great. Well, if you find my best friend, let me know."

"Let's not be childish. Min-Seo doesn't owe you anything." Claire tightened her hand on Minnie's and even in the shitstorm she was in, it felt amazing to have her girlfriend on her side.

"I'm not talking to you," Bianca said and the dim glow of the gallery flared brighter. "I'm trying to help Leila. Remember her?"

"Don't talk to me like I don't care!"

"Do you? Do you care? I wouldn't know since I haven't seen you in weeks! You're a stranger."

Minnie seethed. *This isn't fair.*

"You think I don't have a life other than following you around?" The words were out before she could stop herself, but she was dizzy with fury and the words kept coming out in a rush of pent-up anger. "I'm not like you, I don't need to prove myself a powerful Vessel. *I am one.* You want to feel *needed.* It's pathetic."

Now Claire's hand dug painfully in Minnie's side as she looked at Bianca's hurt face. "I think you should leave."

Bianca was frozen but a lanky boy grabbed her arm and pulled her back. Some distant, coherent part of Minnie's brain registered that the boy was Danny. The image of Bianca and Danny working together was so funny to Minnie for some reason she couldn't stifle a laugh.

Before Bianca left, Minnie saw her face crumple into Danny's arm as they left.

After they left, Minnie breathed a sigh of relief and turned to her not-so-secret girlfriend.

"Sorry about her, I don't know how she found me." Minnie went in for a kiss but landed on Claire's cheek. She looked at her in confusion.

"Min-Seo, I think you should go back to my place and wait for me," Claire unwrapped her arms from Minnie.

"What? *No.*"

Claire ignored her and placed her key in Minnie's palm and a searing kiss on Minnie's pleading lips.

"I'm trying to make sure you don't embarrass yourself in front of future buyers. See you soon." And Claire was off, trying to do damage control while Minnie walked out into the rainy night, her head full of the awful knowledge that she had laughed at her best friend.

MASON

The sun peeked from behind the dark clouds, something Mason tried to make look like a coincidence and not something he was sweating from the effort of.

He wiped his forehead with his arm guard and watched as his archery professor's sleek blonde ponytail swished as she walked. Did she notice? He wasn't sure. Lilly's soft face never lost her determined frown, like all of her students were committing crimes against archery by just existing.

The sun cast a weak beam over New Olympus Prep's stadium, illuminating the track and field course. The archers made sure to keep to one side—Mason wasn't the best aim and maiming the other students wouldn't help his grade any.

"Bows ready!" She shouted. As one, the archers lifted their bows. This was the last shot of the day, a free for all to try whatever trick shot they wanted. Mason looked down the line, where people had multiple arrows notched on their bow, or were pointing their bows up. One naiad had a bandana tied around her eyes. The track class stopped and watched the show. Mason concentrated his power in his empty bow, crafting an arrow of pure sunlight.

"Fire!" Lilly's clear voice rang out.

Mason's arrow was too bright and only too late did Mason realize he'd made a grave mistake. About when the two Vessels next to him winced in pain, shielding their eyes from his bright sun-arrow, one knocking into the next person and the other firing wildly into the air. Mason's sunlight once conjured could not be *un*conjured, and so he let loose the miniature star, students yelling and leaping away as it hit the target dead center and burst into flames. And every target next to it. And all of the grass in a ten foot radius.

"Not again, Mason!" The naiad had ripped her bandana off and conjured rain onto the fire before the flames engulfed the whole field, her seafoam skin glistening with the falling rain. The blast had knocked over the tables of equipment and most of the students.

"My bad?" Mason rubbed the back of his neck. He looked over to Lilly and caught her rolling her eyes, a whisper of a smile on her lips.

Worth it.

He spent the next half hour fielding glares from other students and picking up strewn arrows. He felt a clap on his shoulder before he smelled the salt of the ocean and sweet hair mousse—a combo that only belonged to one best friend.

"Wow, looks like you're having a blast." Elliot had one hand on his hips and waggled his eyebrows.

"Funny."

Elliot still had his fencing outfit on—minus the protectives—the white of his pants and open jacket set off his tanned skin. He didn't seem to notice the girls around him stealing glances. Elliot stuck a finger under his suspenders and popped one while winking at one of the Vessels nearest him.

Never mind, he notices all attention.

Mason looked at his friend, the long hair tied back and the... the…

"What in the name of Zeus is on your lip, El?" Mason couldn't clap a hand over his mouth before a laugh burst out of him.

Elliot glared. "What?"

"Is that supposed to be a mustache?" Mason got closer and his friend stepped back, offended. The 'mustache' was little more than ten straight hairs.

"Put a sock in it, Mase," he swiped at Mason. "You try growing a beard, then!"

"Are you all done, then?" Lilly's voice startled them.

"Almost," Mason stammered.

Even in the late November chill, Mason could feel his cheeks getting hot.

"Make sure to lock up the equipment in the gymnasium please."

"You're not staying?"

Lilly shook her head and stuck a thumb over her shoulder. At the top of the stadium, a man waved a hand. Mason could see the dark brown skin and the black leather jacket and the smile that spurred gossip all over the city.

"Brother needs help with a gala."

"Say hi to Marcus for me," Elliot said.

"OK," Lilly replied then turned to Mason. "Stop with the gimmicks, you don't need them. And I'd like to keep my eyebrows."

Mason smiled and nodded. "Right. Will do."

Lilly walked off, and Mason dragged his eyes away and back to the bundle of arrows in his hands.

"How do you know Marcus?"

Elliot looked at the siblings and blew out a breath. "I don't. But he's my hero. Vessel of Apollo, expensive car, philanthropist, New Olympus's Sexiest Man? I want to be him."

Mason shook his head. "Do they actually have a New Olympus's Sexiest Man?"

"I have no idea, but Marcus is the unofficial holder of that title, don't you think?"

"Right." Mason stuffed the arrows in a quiver and slung it over his shoulder.

"Now I know why you took the class—Lilly is fit."

"Oh?" *Deny, deny, deny.*

"Yeah, too bad she's out of our league. Well, we're not even in her league, you know with her vow and the whole teacher thing."

"Right," Mason ground out. It's not his friend's fault but he was suddenly annoyed. He pushed the quivers he'd gathered into Elliot's arms. "Rake face, if you're going to stand there can you at least hold something?"

"OK," Elliot said slowly. Then he turned and handed his quivers to one of the freshman girls that lingered around him. "Cheers."

Mason tried to concentrate on taking off his arm guard but could feel his friend's eyes boring holes into his back.

"What?"

"Mase."

Everyone thought the Vessel of Poseidon was some sex-crazed prick whose head barely fit into the room. While Mason could attest that was all true, most Vessels didn't know the well of kindness he held locked away.

"I don't want to talk about it," Mason waved his friend off. His whole body felt pinched and bare.

She's a Vessel of Artemis, I know.

But Elliot didn't bother explaining the obvious.

"You're spending a lot of effort on little returns—"

"And so the sun will spend his life chasing the moon," Mason said, looking into Elliot's ocean eyes. His friend threw up his hands in defeat.

"Got it, but you know I think crushes are for losers. Anyway, are you busy after this, Katniss?"

Mason shook his head, glad to have Elliot's cocky exterior back. They gathered the rest of the equipment and started towards the gym.

"Good, because we've been called to duty by our supreme leader Bianca."

LEILA

There was another notch on the watch they hadn't tested.

Though, once Blake eventually figured how to use it to its full potential, it became his favorite.

Obey.

If the dial was turned to that notch, any command uttered by Blake became Leila's only action. Leila wished they used the Forget setting more—she didn't need to remember every awful thing they made her do every night.

Memories of tasks filtered through her mind. Like standing in the rain until her lips turned blue or doing calisthenics to the point where Leila's limbs couldn't hold her. Mostly she became their live-in maid, scrubbing every inch of the mansion until it gleamed. There were other memories that burned through with her more humiliation than the others. The ones of her dancing for them while Blake's friends' lecherous eyes roamed her body. And of course from kissing him that first night, where her lips remembered what Leila had done even when she could not.

Every night she was summoned for more *fun.*

Every night a piece of her fractured.

Every night she got back to her room she spent in a searing bath trying to stop shaking. Trying to stay together, shove everything away.

Leila tore at the bracelets but they wouldn't budge, didn't even stretch.

Why don't my bracelets do anything?

Time stopped to matter, days and nights slipped into a haze. Sleep was fitful and full of nightmares, courtesy of Ash. The winter solstice was nearly upon them, the weather misty and grey at its best and lashing rain at its worst. Leila's only bit of relief was her small time with Cerby, who was glued to her at every other moment of the day she wasn't with the other Vessels.

Ivan snapped his fingers and Leila looked back at him from the floor-to-ceiling windows. It rained so hard streams of water ran down the glass.

"She's real boring tonight," Ivan lamented. Funny coming from Ivan, who seemed to do nothing but drink and break things.

"She wouldn't be if Blakey tested the watch's limits," Kat said in a singsong voice.

Blakey, ugh.

"I don't want her broken before the solstice," Blake said.

"I think he's gone soft," Drake whispered to Ash and the boy gave a lazy laugh.

Blake's eyes blinked black and a slow smile spread across his face. For all of the taunting they did of each other, Leila noticed the shift in the room. *They're scared of him.* For some reason, it felt good.

"What did you have in mind?"

Kat giggled. She twirled her fingers. "Let me do some of my magic on her."

"You have magic?" Leila asked dryly. "I thought you were kind of useless."

The pain hit her quick and hard but she knew it was coming. Leila was so used to it she could bear it, though it still sent her to her knees. Leila coughed out a laugh.

"You've got a happy trigger finger on you, huh?" Ivan asked Kat who seethed. Blake, like always, said nothing—*did nothing*. Leila sat kneeling, any fight draining out of her fast.

"Let's see how much ambrosia she can drink before she pukes," Ash suggested.

"Fuck out of here if you think I'm wasting ambrosia. We're not getting more until the solstice," Drake said.

Something in Drake's words made a question stir inside her but she dismissed it.

Sidonie sat up from Ivan's lap. "Trial by fire."

Leila looked up then, the roaring fire at her back hotter than before. Kat looked thrilled.

Blake turned the dial around. "You heard her: trial by fire."

Leila's mind screamed against the movement but she didn't hold control over her body anymore. She watched herself get up and turn to face the fireplace. Then she stuck her traitorous arm into the flames.

Seconds ticked by as the warmth quickly turned to pain. Her face was hot near the fire. She couldn't cry out, her body a tomb. Inside though, she *roared*.

"*Enough*," Blake growled. As soon as the magic of the watch lifted, she flung herself away.

Leila cradled her right arm, thin wisps of pain tracing her arm like red spiderwebs. Surprisingly, a deluge of curses crept up her throat. She hadn't felt anything but numb, so this heat had woken up some part of her she thought she'd left in the city. Like she'd been underwater and had finally breached the surface, every dulled sense came into roaring clarity.

Leila looked to the Vessel of Hades, his own eyes a mirror of pain and disgust. His jaw worked, like he was trying not to say something.

"Did I push the limits enough?" Small wisps of black floated off of him. He stood suddenly, grabbed a bottle in his fist and stalked off. There was a stunned silence at his exit and Leila took advantage of it by inching away, glad for the distraction.

Stoke your anger, she told herself. When she was dismissed, a plan had hatched in her mind. She skipped her bath and got dressed in rain gear and put a leash on Cerby. Her arm ached in time with her heartbeat, and she held onto it like a drumbeat to propel her forward. Leila didn't know what happened with the group of friends, but from the sounds of blaring music and crashing things, the party hadn't died yet.

It was a couple of hours before it was quiet and then she made her move, slipping quietly through the house. Glass and books were everywhere, furniture upended. A sick feeling stirred in her stomach, and she had to carry Cerby almost all of the way through the mansion to the front door so he didn't cut his paws on the glass. Every shadow felt like it was watching her though no one stopped her.

Leila didn't look back when she closed the front door behind her.

The rain had stopped, the night full of stars that lit the road back to New Olympus. Leila knew there were things in the forest but she wasn't going to stop until she got home. Even if she was stopped by the *nomos* she'd beg them to take her to the mayor, to jail—*anywhere* but here.

The air was cold and made her nose run immediately, but Cerby was panting happily as they walked. Her arm was still hot with pain but she continued on.

A smile threatened to break free and it felt odd to feel so light in the dark of the night.

Then her arms were yanked back, her body tripping in the shock of the motion. After a second Leila realized she was leaning over in the air, her arms behind her. Her bracelets wouldn't go any farther, no matter how much she pushed or pulled on them. Cerby circled her as she tried to breach whatever invisible barrier her bracelets were stuck on. She tried every angle but her bracelets wouldn't move past the spot, her shoulders burning from the effort.

It dawned on Leila that there must be a certain distance the bracelets could be away from the watch. She was lucky the others didn't know this, or they would've surely used this against her.

Leila looked behind her in defeat, where Hades' winter estate wasn't even out of view. The weight of the truth that she'd have to turn back crushed her, all anger doused.

All fight gone.

BIANCA

"This is a shit idea, B," Elliot said. "I'm in."

"Thank you for the confidence as always," Bianca said to the Vessel of Poseidon. His hair was pulled out of his tanned face into a bun, and he looked the picture of easy confidence. Bianca knew better. She could hear the way Elliot's metal prosthesis gently tapped her bed frame, a tic he did when he was stressed.

Mason sat on the bed while Elliot leaned on her bedside table. Harvey and Oscar sat at her desk, and Danny stood a ways back by the sound system. It was a little crowded in her bedroom with all her friends; she didn't know how they were all going to fit into Danny's car with six people and their stuff. She looked at Danny, his tall frame leaning against the wall, the curls of his auburn hair framing his freckled face. He looked like a gangly cherub.

No, he used *to look like that.* It was weird for her to match up the boy she'd grown up with and the man in front of her. In fact, he *wasn't* gangly anymore, not with his muscular arms crossed in front of him.

"We should have spirited her away that night," Oscar said quietly.

"We should have done a lot of things," Harvey agreed.

A scream of laughter sounded in the hallway, startling them. School was officially out for the solstice break and the dorms were emptying out around them. Bianca wished Minnie was here but at the thought her stomach twisted, the words her best friends spat at her still fresh in her mind.

You think I might have a life other than following you around? You just want to feel needed. It's pathetic.

"— if you say we should've stashed her in that death trap you call a boat—" Harvey argued. Bianca had zoned out, her mind replaying her fight with Minnie over and over. That fight was a song that soundtracked Bianca's every move. She hadn't seen Minnie at all since then.

"Yeah, that thing is all rust and prayers." Mason earned a shove for that, causing him to nearly fall off Bianca's bed. *"Hey!"*

Elliot ignored his friend and raised a hand. "I do have one amendment to your brilliant plan—I think we need someone who knows them. Someone who can be a mediator if things get bad."

"What do you mean?" Bianca asked.

"You think he'll help us?" Harvey asked.

"Who are you talking about?" Oscar cut in.

Mason was already grinning. "We know someone who wouldn't mind a free trip to the mountains. Someone who'd be good if things get ugly."

"Are we sure he's on our side?" Harvey sounded concerned but his smile was sharp and excited.

"I mean, how do we know if *this one's* on our side?" Elliot shot a look at Danny, his mouth close to a sneer. "You're Blake's best friend right?"

"Elliot," Bianca warned.

"It's OK," Danny said softly, then cleared his throat. "The Blake I was friends with isn't one I've seen in a long time. I want to know what's happening too; I wouldn't be risking arrest if I wasn't willing to take you all with me."

Elliot looked like he wanted to say something stupid or rude so Bianca clapped her hands together. "Good! We're set then. Let's go pick up your mysterious friend and get going."

"Get going where?" A voice behind Bianca said. The group turned to see Minnie standing in the doorway to the kitchenette. Bianca's stomach turned painfully at the sight of her friend. The boys were silent for a moment upon seeing Minnie. Bianca had been too angry, too ashamed to tell anyone what Minnie said to her at the art gallery. Other than Danny, who'd been there to witness Bianca break down afterwards, none of her friends knew they'd had a falling out.

Maybe they feel as distant to her as I do. The sadness she had felt turned to anger when Minnie didn't immediately come to their dorm to apologize.

"We're going to go see Leila," Bianca said coldly. She grabbed her duffel from the bed and the rest of the group grabbed their things and tittered around, avoiding the girls.

"I'm coming," Minnie said. It wasn't a question.

Bianca nodded to Danny and he got his keys out and headed out of the dorm. Bianca followed.

"Pack a bag," was all Bianca replied over her shoulder.

In the parking lot, the group stood around Danny's car. It was run down, a washed out color that was neither brown nor grey and only sat five.

"How is this gonna work?"

"Trust," Danny smiled and Bianca noticed how sculpted his jaw was. She looked away. *This is not the time.* "Elliot and Mason: grab the back bumper. Harvey, come here with me."

He stood at the front of the car and gripped the front bumper next to Harvey.

"OK, pull!" He called out and the other three boys looked puzzled but pulled at the bumpers.

After a moment, the car creaked and slowly *expanded.*

"Keep pulling!"

The boys groaned. It was like the middle of the car was sheathed in between the rest of it, a third row popping up from the bottom. The car's doors clicked into place and Danny stopped them. Three rows of seats greeted them.

"*How?*" Harvey asked.

Danny smiled ruefully. "Can't talk about it—tricks of the trade."

Elliot made a noise in between a snort and a huff. "Can you take us downtown? That's where our friend is."

"Yeah," Danny said, and they all piled in the car and drove into the city.

A few minutes later, they were parked on a quiet street in front of a sleek garage. Bianca peeked over her sunglasses at the sign reading "Anvil Automations" in big red letters. The boys decided to go in by themselves, leaving Danny, Bianca, and Minnie alone. It was quiet, all of them swimming in awkward silence.

The three boys came back quickly with a fourth. Bianca knew him. Bart, a Vessel of Ares and a friend of Blake's. Danny broke into a smile when he saw him approach the car.

"*Danny boy!*" The boy jumped into the car and shook Danny's seat. His black coveralls were tied around his waist, a black tee contrasted his pale skin. He smelled like smoke and looked like a greyscale photo.

The rest of the boys jumped in and Danny pulled out of the quiet street.

"You guys didn't say you had Danny with you! That sweetens the deal!" Bart's thick Cockney accent rang out through the car. In a heartbeat he pulled a switchblade out of his pocket, the metal gleaming. "So lads, who're we *guttin'?*"

All of them collectively yelled at Bart to put away his blade.

"What exactly did you tell him?" Bianca exclaimed.

"We said we had some trouble we have to take care of up in the mountains," Mason shrugged.

These boys think they're gangsters.

"That's it?"

"And how does *Danny* sweeten the deal?" Elliot interrupted.

"We have the whole drive to figure the rest out," Harvey replied to Bianca. She glared at him through the rearview mirror. Out of all of them, Bianca was counting on Harvey to be at least as much of a Type A about this as her.

Bianca turned on the radio up, drowning out the boys and making Minnie's silence less noticeable. It was a crisp day but the sun was out, shining on them. Bianca could almost pretend they were on a road trip and not a rescue mission.

They made their way out of the city easily, following the coast. The ocean was blue-black and flung itself at the cliffs mercilessly.

"We're going to run into the barricade any time now," Danny warned. Bianca shut off the radio and turned to her friends.

"When we see the *nomos*, stay completely still. This'll only work if you *don't move.*"

When they rose up to the cliffs the barricade came into sight. Two black-and-white cars sat in the middle of the road. Bianca closed her eyes and called her power to her.

I'm not like you, I don't need to prove myself a powerful Vessel. I am one. Minnie's words intruded on her concentration for only a moment before the rush of light caressed her being.

I am one, too.

She opened her eyes, the light around her refracting around her. Without looking, she knew the same was true of her friends—except Danny. Bianca bent the light to reflect an empty car.

Iris, bless me, she prayed.

The car had slowed to a stop and a *nomos* officer walked up to them, a frown on his face. Bianca couldn't turn her head to look at him directly but he came around to Danny's side.

Bianca heard the sound of the window rolling down and the cool breeze hit her face.

"Danny, right?"

"Right."

"Don't you come on Sundays?"

"You're right," Danny gulped. Bianca hoped he didn't look as guilty as he sounded. "I have to pick up their end-of-term homework so they can be graded and if they aren't graded they'll—"

The sound of another car driving up interrupted Danny's rambling.

No way. Bianca looked at the side mirror to see *Camille's* white electric car stopped behind them. The Vessel of Demeter got out, her head wrapped in a silk scarf with big square sunglasses and a bright smile plastered on her face.

She raised her gloved hand. "Hi, boys!"

"Wait here," the officer said and walked away.

As the seconds ticked by, Bianca could feel the pressure of maintaining her powers build up like the ache of holding her breath. Even in the cold, a bead of sweat trickled down her scalp. Another officer walked over to them.

"Hey, you can go through. This might be a while," the other officer said.

"Thanks, man," Danny replied.

The window rolled up and the car moved forward slowly around the *nomos* cars. Then Danny punched the gas and they sped away. Bianca could swear Camille had winked at her over her sunglasses before they'd crested the hill.

The light dissipated in a blink and the whole car exhaled.

But they weren't done yet.

LEILA

Leila hadn't left her bed. There was no point in getting up; her limbs were heavy and useless. Even the silver stone bracelets on her wrists had dulled their shine. If she had a flicker of hope left it was extinguished on the rainy walk back from her failed escape attempt.

She was left in a cold room waiting for the solstice and whatever "big plans" Blake had for her.

Who cares anymore? The thought ran through her mind on a loop. She only had the energy to care for Cerby in the most basic of ways, no energy to walk him—or even feel bad about not walking him. He sat at the edge of her bed, one of his heads watching the door, the other looking out to the grey light of dusk. The third rested on her lap but she ignored him. She was limp in a pile of blankets.

"Leila!"

She puts her hands over her ears.

No, no, no, no.

It can't be the solstice yet.

She wasn't ready.

"Leila!" The voices multiplied, gaining urgency. In horror she recognized Bianca and Harvey, Elliot and Minnie, and other voices ringing out through the mansion. She wondered if this was another one of Ash's sleeping tricks: to make those voices sound like her friends. Every shout was a hot knife in her heart; she curled in on herself.

"Leila? Leila! Where are you!"

"Stop," she moaned. *If they want me, they can make me get up.*

Then they were right outside the door to her suite, nightmares with her friends' voices looking for her, torturing her. Ash must have seen her fantasy of being rescued by her friends while he manipulated her dreams. He took her one escape and twisted it into something awful.

Leila threw off her covers and made her way to the door, her head swimming at the sudden movement.

Who cares, right? They could make it sound like her friends were at her door but she knew the truth: they weren't coming here. *Not to this prison.* Who cares what's on the other side of the door? Nothing matters anymore.

She flung the doors open to find her friends standing in front of her.

LEILA

They stood there for a long moment, Leila staring at her friends and they stared back.

It was overwhelming, all of her friends at her door after three months: Bianca, Minnie, Elliot, Harvey, Mason, Oscar—even Danny.

Is this real? This is too good to be true. Leila wasn't that good at telling nightmare from reality at the moment.

Then Cerby jumped between her and her friends and broke the tension. He was an excited mess of faces, and Leila ushered them inside as Danny corralled the three-headed dog. Then it was a crash of bodies as they tried to all hug Leila. She backed away from them, putting her hands out. This was too much and she didn't trust herself in their arms. She wasn't in control.

"How?" She asked, her voice sore from disuse. Then she narrowed her eyes. *"Why?"*

"We..." Bianca started. "We didn't know if you were OK."

"We had to see for ourselves," Harvey finished. The rest murmured their agreement. Leila felt their eyes on her and she hated their heavy stares. She'd imagined this moment but never thought shame would play such a big part in their reunion.

"I need a shower," she replied brusquely. "Can we catch up after?"

She turned on her heel and made her way to the bathroom, their eyes on her back.

Can I be any more awkward?

She felt restless and hot, her skin uncomfortable. Over her shoulder she said, "Make yourselves at home. And lock the door. I'll be out soon."

The hot water rained over Leila, helping burn her errant thoughts away. She ran some shampoo over her hair and scrubbed her body until she didn't feel so slimy.

Stepping out, she wiped the fog from the large mirror above the sink and looked at herself as she brushed her teeth. The terry cloth robe she wore was loose on her no matter how tight she tied it. Her face was gaunt, her hair limp and stringy—she seemed like she would blow over. Leila looked so different from the girl they'd seen at the equinox. Exhaustion lined her face and drained the color out of her until she was just dull.

Leila didn't just look tired, she looked like she was dying.

And maybe I am. But she couldn't do anything about that standing in the bathroom, and she didn't feel like trying to look any better in front of her friends.

With a sigh, she exited her bathroom.

The hushed tones of her friends stopped when she entered her suite. Leila found she didn't want to know what they'd been talking about.

"OK so. First, we brought you food, so sit and eat."

Bianca's light touch guided Leila to her chair, and Leila could smell the bright floral perfume Bianca always wore—something that smelled so close to home it made Leila dizzy. The styrofoam container was still hot and Leila's mouth watered at the sight of tempeh pad Thai. She didn't want them to know she hadn't had a hot meal in over a month so she ate achingly slow. They all had their own food which distracted them from watching her.

So she watched them. Bianca sat in the chair next to her; Oscar was close to Leila at the foot of her bed, Harvey not far behind; Elliot leaned against the far wall by her abandoned mural; Minnie was sitting in her walk-in closet, as far as possible from her friends for some indiscernible reason. Cerby and Danny were on the floor and it made Leila feel better at the sound of his happy panting. *Maybe Danny can take care of him, better than I could.*

The glint of a blade caught her eye, the face of a boy she didn't know but who seemed to be included with her closest friends.

"So who's the new guy?" She asked after she didn't feel so ravenous. She pointed her chopsticks at the pale boy who'd decided to sit on her dresser. They appraised each other, the afternoon light casting shadows on his angular face, twinkling on his lip ring. A neck tattoo creeped out of the collar of his coveralls. His chin raised slightly, as if coming to some conclusion of whatever he saw in Leila. For some reason, she could only think about how she was going to find his initials carved into the dark wood he sat on.

"Bart," he said finally. "I'm the muscle." He had a heavy Cockney accent and she supposed he was making a joke but she wasn't sure.

"And he's friends with Blake," Elliot supplied.

"'*Friends*' is pretty generous. We ran in the same party crowd," he explained.

"But now he's our friend," Mason said. "Right?"

Bart gave Mason a click with his tongue as an affirmative. "They thought it'd be good to have Chaos on their side."

"How's it been?" Oscar said to Leila, his voice quiet.

"Fine," Leila said before shoving a bite of noodles to try and force down the lump in her throat. Silence spread over them.

"Are you sure——" Harvey started but was interrupted when a knock sounded on the double doors to her suite.

Oh no. Leila's heart dropped. "Don't answer that."

"Your friends made quite an entrance," Sidonie's voice filtered in. "Now open the door before I break it down."

DANNY

Cerby stopped panting in his arms, and a growl rumbled through him. Danny held a slack grip over his collar just in case things got messy.

"I got this," Elliot said quietly and pushed off the wall. The rest of them stood up, Mason flanking Elliot, Bart hopping off the dresser and tucking his knife away in one fluid motion to flank Elliot's other side. He realized they'd all created a wall between whoever was at the door and Leila.

Elliot opened the door slightly and could see the shaved head of Sidonie at the door. She towered over Elliot.

As a Vessel of Kratos, Danny had no doubt she could reduce the door to splinters without breaking a sweat.

"Sidonie," Bart said.

"Bart," she replied. "I thought you were dead."

"Not that easy to kill."

She gave him a wry smile. "I'm assuming you're all here for the solstice. Tell Leila she needs to look her best for the party tomorrow. You all can come too if you play nice."

"I'm sorry, what party exactly?" Elliot said but Sidonie had already left.

They closed and locked the door once again and turned to Leila. And Danny's stomach dropped at her eyes, how dull they looked.

Why didn't I do something? Maybe if he hadn't trusted Blake so much, maybe if he'd been more assertive, more attentive. The faces of the others showed they must feel the same way, the same awful mix of guilt and regret.

"Leila, do you know what they're talking about?" Elliot asked.

"No. They don't tell me their plans."

"Knowing them, it's probably just a party. Something for the solstice," Danny offered.

"Then why do they need Leila?" Elliot countered. "Let's get the fuck out of here."

"I have to agree, we need to bounce before this party gets started," Bianca said.

The others murmured their agreement.

"I can't leave," Leila said quietly.

"What?"

"Yes, you can. Leave your stuff and we can find a place for you," Mason said. "Even if it's on Elliot's boat—"

"Then you'll have to take Blake, too," Leila replied, "because the bracelets can't go far from the watch. I've tried."

"Then we call the cavalry, fuck it, the *nomos* can take Blake away." Mason said.

"*And* Leila," Harvey countered. "The mayor doesn't care if kids sit in jail if it proves him right."

"Did he use the watch on you? Did he hurt you?" Oscar asked Leila.

Leila was quiet, chewing on her lip. "It's not just pain."

"Leila." Oscar was holding onto his boyfriend for strength. "What does that mean?"

She looked down and a tear slid free, but she didn't say more.

"It means that psycho and his psycho friends are doing *gods know what* to her!" Elliot exclaimed.

Minnie ran her hands through her hair in frustration. "Why didn't you tell us this was happening, Leila?"

"What could she have done," Bianca snapped at her, "she had no way to tell us."

Minnie opened her mouth like she wanted to argue but closed it and walked across the room. She didn't look any better than Leila if

Danny was being honest. He hadn't seen the Vessel of Athena since the gallery—he'd helped Bianca in the aftermath of their blowout, had held her in his arms for hours.

Even though Bianca was still the light in the room to him, she still hadn't fully recovered from her best friend's betrayal. He knew too well what it was like to have the person who knew him best turn his back on him.

"Just go," Leila whispered. "Take Cerby and go."

"No," Harvey said. "We're going to figure this out."

"Unless you can figure out a way to get these off." Leila held up her wrists where the delicate silver stone bracelets shone. "Then there's nothing you can do."

"We're not going to go, that's absurd," Harvey said with finality.

"What's *absurd* is you coming here. Why you care so much, I don't know—I mean, I've been here longer than I've known all of you. You don't owe me anything." Leila moved her takeout to the side. "I'm getting dressed." She got up and moved to the walk-in closet, closing the door behind her.

A tense silence followed.

"She doesn't want us to see her like this. I wouldn't," Oscar whispered.

"I don't know what to do," Bianca said and sat down next to Danny on the floor. She gave him a distressed look.

"We're doing all we can do right now." He gave her shoulder a squeeze and even Cerby lifted his head to give her a lick on the face. She scrunched up her face in a smile, making his heart jump.

Rein it in, Blake had said before. *You don't want her to think you're some stalker.* But Blake was wrong in two ways. He wasn't a stalker; he painstakingly went out of his way to never bother her. Bianca was always a shining star at school, she already got bothered enough. And two, Bianca didn't think of him at all—not until his best friend turned into a stranger. Not until he'd finally made himself a future that didn't include her.

I'm going to the Underworld for even thinking about my crush right now. He hoped the flush of his cheeks wasn't so obvious, but he couldn't help it once his cheeks reddened. She was so close, her hair smelled like fresh flowers.

"— the only thing we can do is get the bracelets off and get out of here," Elliot said.

"And hope the *nomos* get the solstice off," Mason agreed.

"I can get you back undetected, the road isn't the only way into the city," Danny chimed in. Bart flashed him a warning look but there was no way they could take that road back. He gave the Vessel of Ares a shrug.

"And how would you know that?" Elliot asked.

Danny was saved from answering by Leila coming back into the main room. She wore a pink pajama set and another fuzzy robe tied around her.

Bianca stood. "How do you feel?"

"Better," she said. "Thank you for—"

Her face went slack and she started to walk through them.

"Leila?"

She didn't answer.

"Leila. Hey!" Harvey held onto her shoulder but she shook out of it and continued walking out the door and into the darkness of the mansion.

"Who else has a really bad feeling about this?" Mason said.

LEILA

It was second nature to obey the watch; Leila's only reservation was that she had an audience. Each of her friends tried to get her to stop walking. One by one they resigned themselves to following the Vessel of Persephone.

Her hair was still wet from her shower, dripping a trail of water behind her.

Through the mansion they went with only the watery light of the moon to guide them. They went to the floor below to the indoor swimming pool. Down there the walls rose and twisted to mimic the shape of caves, expanding into grottos unseen in the dark. As with the rest of the estate, glittering gemstones were inlaid in the walls, floors, and massive columns. The ceiling mimicked the night sky and the constellations twinkled like real stars. The pool water cast phantom ripples on the walls, waves from an unknown current.

"Funny how they always try to weasel their way into everything. I don't exactly remember welcoming you into my home," Blake said, his voice echoing slightly. He emerged from one of the larger grottos across the water. Shadows swirled around him as he walked forward.

"What does Hades do to intruders?" Kat asked from behind him.

"He isn't Hades, you prick," Elliot muttered.

Blake didn't reply, just turned a dial on his watch.

"Come here, Leila. Watch your step," he said with a jovial tone, though his eyes were stony grey. Leila walked around the edge of the pool, feeling everyone's eyes on her.

"What do you want with her?" Bianca said.

"Just leave her alone, we won't stop your stupid solstice party," Mason pleaded.

"I don't doubt that," Blake replied smoothly.

Leila stood in front of the Vessel of Hades. She could smell the syrupy scent of ambrosia on his breath mixed with the salt of his sweat. His eyes flicked over her, twin storms. Then he turned the dial of his watch. Even though Leila knew it was coming, the pain still felt fresh ripping through her arms. A scream scratched its way out of her throat, echoing off the walls. Her body went limp but she didn't hit the ground. Blake caught her with a laugh, his strong arms wrapped around her weak frame.

"Now do you get it?"

Leila scrambled to stand, her legs were shaking. She could see the others emerge from the cave, their eyes bright with bloodlust.

"You're just a freak with an inferiority complex!" Minnie's voice was loud enough to make Leila wince.

"Really?" Blake chuckled humorlessly.

"*You can really go fuck yourself!*"

"For a Vessel of Athena, her strategy is rather lacking," Ivan said. "Don't you think?"

"I do," Blake said with a smirk, his eyes blinked black. "I don't blame her though, she doesn't have the right incentive to *behave.*"

Suddenly, Blake spun Leila so she faced her friends, who stood at the edge of the pool and watched on in concern. He held her waist with one hand, the other lightly grasped her throat. His mouth was at her ear.

"Ask them," he whispered, "ask them *'is this incentive enough for you?'*"

"Is-is this incentive enough for you?" Leila said, her voice trembling. She could feel the press of his body, the vibration of his laugh.

"Now," he tightened his grip on her, shadows wrapping themselves around her like vines. "*Drown yourself,*" he hissed before letting her go.

Every night he brought her closer to the edge, testing the boundaries of how far the magic of the watch could go. It felt like they were always heading here, the final test.

She waded in, her pajamas weighing her down as they got wet.

"What did you tell her to do?"

The water wasn't as cold as she thought it'd be—it was nice, actually.

"Stop, OK, we're sorry."

"Seriously, Blake, stop this."

With each step, Leila waded deeper into the pool.

"I'm sorry! Please, *I'm sorry!*"

"Didn't you hear us? Leila, *stop!*"

"Fuck your apology," Blake exclaimed. "And you know what? Fuck all of you."

Cool water tickled her throat.

"Leila! Stop, you can fight it! *Stop!*"

But that was the thing—Leila was done fighting. The water slipped over her head and the world was quiet. It was a relief to finally have the peace Leila had been craving, surrendering to the command. It was funny, to think of how much she fought—against the Senators Council, against her Myth, against Fate itself—when it hadn't done a single thing. And now all she had left was to sink like a stone and she wouldn't have to fight anymore.

Leila had held onto hope that her friends would save her.

She closed her eyes.

The last of the air escaped from her lips along with a prayer of forgiveness to her friends.

I'm sorry, there's nothing left to save.

LEILA

"Leila," Persephone said. *"Leila, my dear, what are you afraid of?"*

Leila fell, or rose, she didn't know. She couldn't see the goddess, couldn't feel her presence.

"Of life? Of being consumed by darkness? You are darkness and you are life. If you fear yourself, how will you ever bloom?"

It's cold, so cold.

"I can't, I can't," Leila sobbed. "I can't fight any more."

The goddess' voice was honey-drenched steel. *"My dear, you haven't even begun to fight."*

Leila returned to the world coughing up water, chlorine burning her lungs, her throat, her nose.

"--AND YOU NEARLY KILLED HER, ASSHOLE!"

A cacophony of voices greeted her. Leila couldn't tell the voices apart in the shouting match between her friends and Blake's. Someone was crying but she couldn't tell from where—or if it was crying at all. Was someone laughing? Everything was too loud, too cold, pain was everywhere.

Arms held her rag doll body, hands scraped sopping hair from her face. When she opened her eyes, the pool water rippled on the walls in dizzying patterns. She had to shut her eyes tight so she didn't throw up. Someone was talking in her ear and she couldn't tell who it was or what they were saying.

And then she was falling—no, she was being lifted. She gripped whatever she could just to keep from sinking again. Did she cry out? Leila didn't know.

More hands gripped her own, more voices were a chorus around her.

In the silence between the wet and the pain Leila felt the thrum of magic. Not hers—the bracelets'. A current of crooked magic running under her skin; a parasite in gemstone shackles.

And she felt her heartbeat, a roar in her ears louder than anything and strong enough to break her apart if she let it.

Fight, fight, fight, her heartbeat sang.

Fight, fight, fight, she cried back.

ELLIOT

Elliot was too late jumping into that pool. He knew that. He knew too much of people drowning; the ocean was a merciless teacher in the art of saving lives. And he knew he acted too late when he dove in and wrested Leila's limp body from the pool's bottom. But then Leila's body heaved water, clawing her way back to consciousness—he knew he didn't get lucky.

Poseidon, thank you.

Elliot wasn't going to let her go like that again. As he carried her through the house back to her room, he felt the chill of winter chasing at his wet footsteps. Bianca had her arms around him and Leila as they walked, though he didn't know if she was helping to support them or if it was the other way around. Mason held Leila's hands, glowing steady heat to keep her from turning blue. Oscar kept Harvey moving forward—he'd never seen his best friend so ready to kill. Elliot didn't blame him, he wanted to call the sea up to tear this mansion off its foundation stone by stone until there was nothing left. Minnie ran off as soon as Leila coughed up water.

What is happening to us?

He laid Leila down on her bed, Cerby whining and running circles around him in concern. Bianca moved to get Leila's soaking bathrobe off as she mumbled something incoherent. Elliot was a live wire of energy, he could feel the crash of the ocean on the cliffs far beyond the house and the rain pelting the roof outside. He tapped the boys and grabbed his bag before moving into the bathroom.

Elliot peeled his sweater off. Sure, he could use his powers to dry his clothes but he was so worked up he didn't know if he could control his powers. He didn't want to burst every pipe in the bathroom.

"We need to do something," he said while ripping off his tank top. He flung it to the ground and it gave an unsatisfying wet *thunk*.

I feel so fucking powerless.

"What can we do, short of carving that watch off the bastard?" Bart said, sliding out a butterfly knife from his pocket and giving it a few twirls. "Actually, that's not a bad idea."

"I'm not OK with mutilation," Harvey said with a sigh. "Not yet anyway."

"Bartholomew," Oscar began, his Spanish accent rolling over the Ares Vessel's name like a waterfall, "and Danny, perhaps you could help us by telling us more about Blake's friends?"

Danny rubbed his mouth, thinking. Elliot frowned and turned to his clothes so he didn't have to see him.

"Well, I've seen Sidonie wreck a car *by throwing it*."

"Avoid her," Bart interrupted. "Ash, the curly haired one, is a Vessel of Morpheus. As long as we're awake, we're golden."

"Let's sleep in shifts," Elliot added, unbuckling his belt. He was too awake to even think about sleeping.

"The big one with the spiky hair is Ivan, Vessel of Zelus—don't let him in your ear. He can turn brothers against each other," Danny said.

"And Drake is a Vessel of Momus, he's bloody annoying," Bart added.

"Can Kat do anything special, Vessel of Hecate and all?" Harvey asked.

"Nothing more than a flash in the pan, but I wouldn't underestimate the bird."

"She has a bird?" Mason said. "Oh wait, never mind."

Elliot's laugh surprised even him, but he needed it. The door opened to reveal Minnie who strolled in and dumped an armful of books onto the vanity at the far wall.

"I was about to drop trou, darl, do you mind?"

"Please, like I give a shit. I need to find some way to get those bracelets off Leila before she..." Minnie took a breath. "Whip it out, I'm not even looking."

"You think you can find something in these books?" Harvey asked.

Minnie shook her head, her face pinched. "I don't know. The library is one of the most extensive I've seen, but my Ancient Greek is rusty. I grabbed *Metallurgy of Vessels, Charms, Spellwork, and Ethics*, any Greek book with an interesting cover. I even grabbed *Neo: A History of New Olympus* just in case there was something new in there."

"Let me help then," he said and grabbed a book at random and started reading. "I was first in our second level Ancient Greek class if you recall."

"Me too," Danny said. "Blake is the whiz at Greek, so he helped me a lot."

Suck up. Elliot sighed and went to change into his joggers and sweatshirt.

"Please tell me you broke both of the other guy's legs," Bart said next to him. He flicked his knife fluidly but kept his eyes on Elliot's prosthesis. It usually bothered him whenever people stared too long at it but the Vessel of Ares wasn't gawking.

"Didn't get the chance," he squeezed Bart's shoulder with a wry smile. "But I'll let you know next time I go deep-sea fishing—we can find my leg out there."

People were curious about his missing leg so he tried to respond with humor.

It's been four years, it's not like I can get my leg back.

Bart winced. "Can your precious Bernice even take the high seas?"

Elliot gripped his chest. "Ouch, Bartie, you hurt me."

"Bartie is *not* my nickname, bruv," he said with a laugh.

"Really, because I thought I heard your red-headed friend call you that."

"You're mistaken," Bart said. "But I'll let it slide. Hey, are all your friends this intense?"

"I wouldn't want it any other way." He said and pulled on his sweatshirt.

Now as the adrenaline left him, the effort of carrying Leila left his left leg aching. He grabbed a book and limped out of the bathroom, waving off Mason when he looked like he wanted to help. The bedroom was a mess of clothes and the bustle of setting up for the night.

One more long night after another. Some part of him wished he was having a normal solstice at Poseidon's temple. But he always preferred the breakneck waves to calm waters.

Elliot got onto the bed and scooted next to Leila.

"Hi," she said to him. Her voice was raw but strong.

"Hi stranger, how're you feeling?" The scent of chlorine was around her, soaking into the pillows and the new shirt she'd changed into.

She side-eyed him. "Oh, you know, never better." A ghost of a smile played on her lips.

"Bloody great." Relief made him give her a megawatt smile in return.

"It's funny," she said, holding up her wrist, the hematite stones winking up at him. "Dying."

"Is it?"

"Well, *no*, it hurts like the gods. But it puts everything into perspective."

"Like what?"

"Like who I am."

BART

Bart stood in front of the French doors in Leila's room, watching as the crowd spilled onto the Hades estate grounds. The sunset was quick, the watery winter rays winked out into the sea far, far below. He took a drag of his cigarette and pulled his borrowed jean jacket tighter, the shearling collar keeping the evening chill at bay. He tugged on his beanie—also borrowed.

"It looks good on you," Oscar said from behind him.

Bart frowned. "I don't like wearing this much color."

"It's not color, it's denim."

Bart shrugged and offered Oscar a drag of his cigarette which the Vessel of Caerus declined with a hand. Oscar was wearing teal trousers and a multi-colored sweater that on anyone else would scream *I want attention*, though he made it look natural. Bart could never be that loud. Ever since Bart realized he had more power than the other grunts in his gang, he knew what would happen if he stuck out too much. The smoke filtered around him.

"I was told to tell you we're joining the party, are you ready?"

He sucked the rest of the cigarette down then flicked the butt over the railing, watching the orange glow fall down. He'd spent the fall equinox holed up in his boss's loft apartment above Anvil Automations, sure he was going to get found by someone in his gang while Arnold glared at him over training manuals. Three months later and Bart liked the Vessel of Hephaestus—it was better now they had more in common than shagging the same girl. He wasn't sure if he was going to make it out of this party alive to even make it back to work. Anyone in the crowd could be a low-ranking grunt ready to do anything to prove his loyalty.

As if reading his mind, Oscar gripped his shoulder.

"If things go sideways, stick with me. You can say I'm a good luck charm," he said. The boy winked at him, his lashes full and dark. He only gave a nod before joining the others in the main room.

Loud music and sounds of revelers reached every corner of the mansion. Leila was already gone, summoned by Blake. Last he'd seen her, she looked like Underworld walking, all black dress and killer boots and red lipstick. She was doing better than most after nearly dying, a deadly calm confidence he wasn't sure was warranted. They'd all spent last night studying and came up with nothing.

They left Leila's room, the party in full swing. Bart stayed in the middle of the pack watching the crowds. He'd never been to the big fancy solstice celebrations—at least never long enough before getting kicked out—and this was much more than the regular house parties. People were packed in, all dressed like the night. Music blared, a hypnotic beat that drilled down into the ear and took root in the stomach. Moving around was tough but they managed to make it to the great room where floor-to-ceiling glass walls separated them from the grounds.

Waiters in white carried trays of gold ambrosia. They wouldn't leave until the whole group had taken a glass. As soon as the waiters left, Bianca and Harvey ditched their glasses on a nearby end table, the others following suit. Minus Elliot and Bart.

"Seriously?" Bianca crossed her arms. He had a feeling she was one of those girls who had a different planner for every day of the week.

"I always work better with a buzz." Bart took a sip from his glass. Ambrosia had a warm, sunny taste, like freshly picked fruit in summer. This was not summer in a glass; too sweet, too hot, like rotted fruit off the ground mottled with worms. He grimaced and spit the drink out and continued to spit as much as he could. He wiped his mouth with the back of his hand, the awful taste at the back of his throat.

"Don't drink that!" he said, hitting the glass out of Elliot's hand just as he was about to put it to his lips. The glass shattered on the floor.

"Hey!"

"Uh, Bart, mind telling us what's wrong?" Danny said as Bart crouched down and picked up a shard of glass and brought it above him to observe it in the light.

"This isn't ambrosia." The Vessel of Ares turned the shard to examine the small pool of gold liquid and saw a swirl of something darker mixed in. "At least not all of it is—it's cut with something impure, though I'm not sure what. Don't drink this swill. It might as well be poison."

"Selling bootleg ambrosia is illegal," Harvey balked. "Obviously, everything happening here is illegal—but this is another level."

"And what would happen if people were to drink this stuff?" Bianca asked. They all turned to the window overlooking the grounds where bonfires blazed and a sea of people raged.

"Nothing good," Harvey said.

"Like?" Minnie pressed.

"Low end is a wicked hangover," Bart said. "The high end is mania, murderous tendencies, and death."

"Gods," Elliot said.

This place is a bomb ready to go off and every glass is another fuse.

Bootleg ambrosia is a pretty big risk for a party in the woods already surrounded by *nomos*. *What's the big play?* Cris would say in the few times Bart had been in the gang leader's presence. Running card tables for the bankers or doing security for the art district's galas weren't one-offs, they built up to something. Favors and secrets went a long way in New Olympus, although poisoning a bunch of people didn't have a tidy profit at the end of it. Maybe there wasn't more to it—though Bart hadn't risen through the ranks by dismissing small plays like this. Bart dropped the shard of glass onto the floor.

"So we need to stop this right? Before people get all..." Mason made a stabbing motion.

They looked at each other and Bart had the odd sense that he'd traded one gang for another.

"Our end goal doesn't change," Minnie spoke up. "Protect Leila. Poison control is a part of it."

"Agreed," Bianca said. "OK so it's eight people against

hundreds. We have work to do."

"Odds could be worse," Bart replied. His heart was already beating at a war drum's pace, his fingers bristling for a fight.

Night stretched on infinitely before them and Bart saw his muddled reflection in the glass, a knife smile on his face. Elliot was right, he wouldn't want it any other way.

LEILA

Tonight was the last time Leila would let herself be under someone's control. Persephone had given her a second chance and she wasn't going to crawl back to get another. The solstice was her chance and she wasn't one to waste opportunity.

She followed behind the Vessel of Hades, a shadow's shadow, as he walked through the mansion. People didn't shy away from him like they usually did.

Though he deserves it much more now.

He was a god amongst Vessels. Their devotion obvious in their dancing, like a prayer in motion.

Blake wore a deep velvet suit with patterns swirled in the fabric mimicking his own dark power. The obsidian circlet around his head tamed the unruly curls that had grown over the last season. He didn't look fully tangible in the light, like Leila could blink and he'd be gone.

The press of bodies was suffocating, the Vessels unable to control themselves. They made it to the rooftop terrace and Leila was grateful for the cool air that made her shiver. Bianca and Minnie had cut Leila's equinox dress at the thighs. It was already sheer, with only mesh and beading down her arms and torso to shield her from winter—but they weren't trying to bundle her up. With her hair straight down her back, eye makeup dark and smudged, her favorite red lipstick nice and bloody on her lips, and her boots clicking on the stone as she walked, she felt powerful for the first time in months.

The roof gave a view of the terraced grounds, the DJ booth, and the hundreds of Vessels, satyrs, and nymphs in the throes of partying. Lasers cast a kaleidoscope of colors off the far bordering evergreens.

Blake joined his group of friends at the spacious low couches on the terrace, a waiter serving him ambrosia as soon as he sat. She stood to the side, keeping as much space between her and his smarmy friends. There was no sign of her friends, though that wasn't a problem. She sent a prayer to Persephone to keep an eye on them, just in case.

This is going to be a long night.

"—I said not yet. You're boring me," Blake said, his voice all mirth. Leila looked to see him and his girlfriend fighting, both of them spilling glasses of ambrosia in anger. Moon-white hairs spilled out of Kat's meticulous updo. Her wine-red dress matched her red eyes and nails. She was crystal dangerously close to cracking.

"You're supposed to be—" Kat seethed.

"I'm not *supposed* to be anything, *except* a gracious host." His jaw was clenched. "Don't try my patience."

"You're weak for waiting, the party is in full swing—"

"And you're delusional if you think you're calling the shots."

Kat's face was pure malice and Leila could barely turn her laugh into a cough. The Vessel of Hecate didn't buy it, turning her glare on Leila.

"Maybe you don't have the power," she spat before extricating herself from him.

Blake chuckled darkly. Then he flicked his fingers and the couches slid away from each other with enough force to send his friends and other Vessels stumbling for purchase. He was left in his seat, pooling shadows like a fog. One of the shadows snaked around Leila's waist, another holding her hand. She flew to him, landing in his lap. He was surprisingly warm as she grabbed his chest out of instinct to stay upright.

"Like I said, all in good time. There's still a lot of party left," he said to Kat. He turned to Leila then and they looked at each other. The last three months melted away in this moment, and Leila couldn't keep a smile from her lips knowing how close she was to the end, a secret that buoyed her in Blake's arms. His eyes, back to their ever-storming grey,

234

were fixed on her lips. Then he raised his wrist and turned the dial on the watch.

So this is how this feels.

The last time they'd used that notch on the dial was also the first time they'd used Forget—they'd made her kiss him and then she didn't even get to remember. Leila had to admit she was curious how the magic had worked on her to kiss Blake and now she knew. Heat bloomed from her core washing over her in waves. She'd expected Blake to use that notch dial and plunged into the feeling headlong. She wanted to kiss him—her final kiss with death.

Leila brushed his jaw with her fingers, gripping his face. Then she kissed him, his lips soft and syrupy. His mouth was a brand she wanted to burn on. He kissed her deeply and she found herself drinking him in with depthless ferocity. Leila entangled her hands in his hair, pulling his head back to hers. His hands were everywhere, his shadowed power winking out the stars, the Vessels, the world. And she wanted him.

They broke for air and their eyes locked, grey on brown. The magic dislodged all the times she'd ignored how handsome he was, every stolen glance and shameful thought crystalizing into one need. She couldn't deny that ache she'd suppressed, that even without the magic she'd want him. He looked at her strangely, like he'd realized the same thing.

As quick as the warm magic came over her, it was gone, a vacuum that left her reeling. Blake used his powers to push her back. She flew to the edge of the roof, her heels teetering over the edge. She would have fallen if Blake's power didn't grip her, though the hold didn't feel strong enough to keep her from toppling over. Her arms pinwheeled and she looked at the Vessels way down below, still partying without a care.

Leila yelled to Blake to make him stop but no sound came out. She tried again, yelling at him but she'd been silenced. Blake sat on his throne, waving his watch in triumph. Any warmth he possessed leached out in one cold stare. His lips pulled into a stony smirk.

"I'll let you go, all you have to do is ask."

HARVEY

Harvey could feel the strain of magic in his veins, the power waning. The heat of the party crowded him, leaving him breathless. But he pushed on. He'd run through the floors, grabbing each waiter by a pulse point and jolting them with enough electricity to render them unconscious. Then he knocked over every drink he could. He had to dodge swings from incoherent drunk Vessels, who looked crazed enough to lap up the poisoned ambrosia from between broken shards on the floor.

Every few minutes he saw one of his friends running around and doing the same—but there were always more waiters, more bottles of ambrosia, more floors to comb through. And as the Vessels drank more, they became wilder, more frantic.

The mania. He feared what would happen when they all reached their breaking point. Though the Vessel of Zeus didn't have time to imagine what would happen, not until every drop was gone.

Harvey broke out onto the grounds, where he spotted Elliot's broad frame. He was shouting at a satyr who looked like he was fighting to stay upright, his eyes glassy as he stumbled on his hooves. Behind them, a myriad of creatures writhed along to the hypnotic music, even as the party festered into something ugly.

The satyr charged at Elliot but the Vessel of Poseidon only clenched his fist and a rumble of the earth took the satyr down.

"Are you alright?" Harvey gripped his friend when he reached him.

Elliot's mouth was a hard line and he shook his head.

"And I thought I was the arsehole at parties," he breathed. Something caught his attention and he shouted. Harvey looked to the roof and saw a dark silhouette, then realized it was Leila. He couldn't see her face but he saw how she wobbled on the edge.

"Leila!" Harvey yelled but was drowned out by the revelers.

"*Fuck this*," Elliot cried. He grabbed a glass off a tray of a passing waiter and shut his eyes in concentration. Amber liquid rose from his glass, and with a groan, the liquid froze solid, falling to the ground. A ripple of bottles exploding and glass breaking spread through the crowd. Gasps and shouts rose up from the crowd as they realized what happened to their drinks.

"Nice. Now let's see how fast we can get up there," Harvey said. Elliot nodded, looking as spent as he did.

And hope we're not too late.

MIN-SEO

Min-Seo was fucking done. She was done feeling powerless, behind, stupid. Worse, she was tired of dealing with drunks dead sober.

Goosebumps erupted down her arm, something that happened whenever her powers flared.

Not the time, she stuck her foot out as one of the waiters passed her, tripping them and sending the tray of spiked ambrosia flying in an arc of glass and amber liquid.

Oscar whooped behind her—though the victory lasted for only a moment. It made her feel even worse, she didn't deserve it. If Bianca told their friends what had really happened—

"Not. The. Time," Min-Seo ground out.

"What was that?" Bart yelled, taking up the rear of their little squad. He had a scratch on his check that had finally stopped bleeding but his eyes were bright with hope. She could've sworn his eyes had flashed red during a couple of the close calls—especially when he'd spotted Vessels with tattoos that matched the one peeking out of his jacket collar. She shook her head at him.

The heat of bodies around them was becoming too much, the poison taking its effect faster than they could get rid of it. All three of them kept moving against the tide of Vessels until one of the hallways they were in opened up to the large entryway. Wedged between the two boys and nearly half a foot shorter than them, Minnie's view was obstructed to what she could reach. She was helpless to the tide of the party, even as it rose in fevered frenzy.

"Gods," Oscar exclaimed, stopping in front of her.

Minnie peered around him on her tiptoes, getting glimpses of what had made Oscar sound so troubled. In the middle of the great entryway were tables covered in towers of glasses filled with ambrosia, swarmed by partygoers. Illuminating the drinks was the multi-story chandelier above them, glittering in a Fibonacci spiral.

Bart pulled out his knife. "This is the big one, boys." His smile was feral, and the brush of needles under Minnie's skin rose again. She eyed the knife, the carved handle and the serrated edge.

"Can I borrow that?" Minnie asked, stepping in.

For only a split second did Bart hesitate before spinning the blade and pressing it into her palm, like a well-trained soldier would.

"Boost me," she commanded. Both Oscar and Bart put their hands out and she stepped into their palms, steadied her hands on their shoulders.

"Fly, girl," Oscar murmured.

Minnie gave him her best imitation of his lazy grin and then they threw her into the air. The crowd was beneath her as she leapt into the air. Athena had granted Min-Seo more gifts than one—just as Athena's strengths were many. She yanked her arm back, aimed at the cluster of wires up at the ceiling holding the chandelier and let the blade fly. The knife soared, slicing through the thin wires easily. In a cascade of stone and glass, the chandelier fell, crashing onto the tables holding the ambrosia. Minnie's own descent to the ground started and she allowed her powers to flare as she tucked and rolled out of the way. The cacophonous mixtures of screams and shattering glass mixed with the music. A fleeing satyr knocked into her and she remained pressed against the stone wall, observing the mess she'd made. Hands found her arms and her face broke into a genuine smile when she saw who was helping her up.

"We should get to the roof," she said. "Are you guys OK?"

"I got us out of the way, no problem," Oscar chuckled then turned to Bart. "I told you, stay close to me."

"Yeah, no shit," Bart muttered, bewildered. "Damn, we almost got flattened."

"I think I see your knife over there," Oscar said brightly, unfazed by the scene of destruction around him. He trekked on. Bart only blinked for a moment before following him. The entryway was dark now but she could still make out the outline of the spiral staircase to the roof and the fight ahead.

LEILA

The wind lashed at Leila, the toes of her boots scraping at the roof's edge, trying to keep purchase on the thin rail. Only an ever-thinning wisp of power from Blake anchored her to the spot.

"*STOP!*" Harvey shouted from the other side of the terrace. He and Elliot sprinted towards Leila. Blake took a sip of his drink and flicked a finger, knocking the two boys back. Then the others descended on them.

NO, Leila yelled in vain, her voice stolen by the magic.

"I can't hear you," Blake taunted.

Below, the revels continued—the tide of merriment now turning into something more frantic. Laughter was maniacal, dancing turned to fighting, and the search for more and more drink was primal. They were losing.

You haven't even begun to fight.

"Don't worry about your friends," Blake said, standing. "Aren't you tired of being saved? I mean, *I'm* tired of it."

Leila shot him the middle finger with her right hand, her left moving behind her back.

And so darkness I become.

Everything quieted down and in the space of a breath even winter ceased its unrelenting encroachment. It had been so long since Leila had called her power that there was a moment she didn't think it would answer. But her power came readily, warmth blooming in her left hand and finding the seeds taped to the inside of her bracelet. Shoots grew and wrapped around the stones, the waxy leaves caressing her skin. She fed her magic into the small seedlings, a promise of their might in each whisper of her power. As the vines grew into budding English ivy around the bracelet, Leila started to feel the tension of the magic that had a hold on her. The weight of the magic pressed on her—she kept pushing, the magic of spring radiating out of her. Her hand was soon cut off from circulation, her fingers going numb.

Blake had his dark eyes on her now, his brow raised in curiosity. Maybe he felt something, too—the connection between his watch and her being pulled taut. Maybe he could feel the life she breathed, the joy in her being. Maybe his Myth gave him insight into her magic. The vines pulled at the stones and it pinched her skin searching for any weak link. She would find it, she had to. The vines encircled every stone, weaving over itself and dug painfully into her bones. If Blake hadn't had his eye on her, her silent groans of pain would've gone unnoticed.

"What are you up to?" He took a couple of steps forward.

The ivy was running out of room to grow, blood dripped down her wrist in a hot rivulet as the bracelet refused to budge any more. Either she needed to lose a hand or lose the bracelet.

I'm fighting now.

She raised her arm in front of her, showing off the tangled mess of ivy, blood, and hematite stones.

"Don't—" Blake strode towards her. Leila pushed the last of her power out, the heat of her magic a searing pain as it clashed with the bracelet violently, ripping at the roots the treacherous stones had buried into her being. This wasn't just a fight to break the magic of her bracelets, this was a fight for control over her own body, her own voice. And she was going to give everything she had to get control back.

DANNY

Danny and Bianca pushed through the crowds. Bianca refracted light to distract and cloak them while Danny broke bottles and dispatched waiters. He'd always been light on his feet—a power few of Hermes' Vessels could boast—moving through a crowd undetected wasn't new to him.

They were on the second floor landing, darkness enshrouding how far they'd gotten—and how far they had to go. The crash of the chandelier was the tipping point of the party into a headlong fall into chaos. Danny couldn't tell how many manic Vessels stood between them and Leila, he only saw the next target in front of him. A dryad hissed at them, baring thorned teeth as the two of them tipped over another tray of glasses. The tray they'd downed flew at the dryad, hitting her in the face. They turned to find Minnie standing behind them, Bart and Oscar rushing up the staircase not far behind.

"We need to get to the roof, *now.*"

Danny nodded and they ran, outright pushing Vessels out of the way. Panic made a ram out of the group, and they shoved their way up the next floor and the last flight of stairs in seconds.

Danny burst onto the roof first, taking in the chaos of the scene. Furniture was upended, Vessels fought each other, Blake and Leila were having their own standoff.

And in one corner was Harvey, suspended in the air, grappling at his throat. He was being held up by a jet of water as it wrapped around his neck, Elliot standing below him. Poseidon's Vessel stood with a slack face as Ivan stood next to him, whispering into his ear.

Danny grabbed one of the bottles of ambrosia on the floor and brought it down on the Vessel of Zelus. Ivan dropped, showers of glass and ambrosia raining down. With the compulsion broken, Harvey fell to his knees gasping for breath.

Elliot turned, bewildered.

"I told you not to let him in your ear," Danny said.

"Right," Elliot replied, shaken. He went to Harvey to help him up and Danny followed.

They were on their feet for only a moment before they were knocked back by an explosive force.

LEILA

Blake never reached her.

Leila felt the burnout of her power coming and forced the rest of it out of her in one guttural scream. One *loud* scream. The magic broke, sending a blast out onto the terrace. Blake flew back, as did everyone else on the roof.

Leila stepped down from the roof's ledge.

"Loud enough for you?" she asked.

The Vessel of Hades looked shocked for a second, then a lazy smile grew on his face. He clapped his hands together.

"I have to say I didn't expect that," Blake said.

"Neither did I." Which was true—how could she know that'd work?

Leila leaned against the ledge, feigning casualness. Inside she felt feverish and weak, her arms stung and she'd used so much of her power —there was still another bracelet to break.

"Leila!" Bianca shouted, running up. A crowd gathered, Blake's friends were a barrier to her own. She had a painful flashback remembering the pool yesterday.

"That was cute," Blake said. He brushed off debris from his suit and grabbed a downed bottle, taking a swig from it.

"Blake, mate, don't drink that. It's tainted," Bart said. He was being held back by Sidonie, a cut leaking red onto his brow.

"Tainted? Seriously?"

Tainted? Ambrosia was supposed to be the drink of the gods, one of the closest things to divinity—at least that's how it was explained to her. Not that anyone acted divinely drinking the stuff. *Unless they weren't drinking pure ambrosia.*

"I'm not taking the piss out of you, Blake. It's going to kill you."

"Are we sure we want to stop the guy from being poisoned? I'm just wondering," Elliot asked.

Blake scoffed.

Leila recalled all of those horrible nights where Blake and his friends partied, how he smelled sickly sweet, how his glass seemed to always be filled. *But the others' weren't.*

"They're right," Leila said to Blake. "I've never seen Kat drinking the ambrosia. Have you?"

They all turned to the blonde Vessel of Hecate who'd been watching the festivities with a lupine focus. She moved to her boyfriend, snaking her arms around him.

"She's a liar. I mean, we made you forget so many things, how could you even remember correctly? I've been drinking all night."

"You've had the same glass in your hand all night," Leila countered. "You think you can poison hundreds of people, including your boyfriend?"

She went to caress Blake, her long nails like claws. He pulled his face away.

"Have you been poisoning me, darling?" he said in mild disbelief. His smirk was quickly turning into a grimace.

"No," she pleaded. "No—I wouldn't."

"Then prove it," he said quietly. He lifted the bottle of ambrosia to her face. "Drink this."

She took the bottle from Blake."I don't have to prove anything, Blakey, you should believe me."

Blake looked at his girlfriend and then the bottle, his eyebrows knit together.

"These people aren't your friends Blake, they want to use you," Danny yelled. "Why are you siding with them?"

"Because," Blake called back, "because I was tired of being the only freak. They accept me for the monster I am."

"No, they turned you against everyone! Against your best friend.

We were like brothers!" Danny's voice strained with emotion.

"That's not..." Blake shook his head.

Leila's friends burst out all at the same time.

"Don't you see, they want your power for whatever fucked up plan they have——"

"—please Blake, *listen!*"

"You're not like this!"

Blake groaned in frustration, his hands raising to the sides of his head.

"Everyone shut up! Just SHUT. UP!" He wrapped his fingers around the circlet on his head.

"You want to prove us wrong? Ask your girlfriend to drink." Leila arched a brow at Kat whose thin lips were pulled back in a slick smile.

"I don't have to do what you say," the girl spit at Leila and laughed haughtily. "It's too late anyway."

"Why?" Blake said.

"Because you won, you still have her and everyone here at your mercy."

"Wait," Blake muttered, blinking heavily. "Wait. *My* mercy? Kat, what is in this drink?"

"Don't act so innocent." Kat's warmth towards her boyfriend was gone. "I was there every night you wanted to play your *games* with Leila. Those were just the test runs for the real thing."

"What the fuck are you talking about?" He shook his head and Leila could see how dark the circles under his eyes had gotten, how sallow his skin was. He took an uneasy step away from his girlfriend.

Kat grabbed his wrist and pulled him back. "Blakey, you're so stupid. You may have the power but you lack vision, *darling.*"

Kat's eyes went bone white, her mouth a grimace. She'd never used her powers before in front of Leila, not in any noticeable way. They were all reminded that she was a Vessel of Hecate, goddess of magic. She moved her hands around while drawing in a breath, then slapped her left hand over the top of her right wrist. The smell of burning flesh filled the air. She cried out and lifted her hand off the other, a look of triumph shining on her face. The back of her wrist was branded, the skin red and raised. Kat held it up, the charred borders matching those of Blake's watch face.

After the revulsion of her marred flesh subsided, Leila realized what she'd done.

She made herself her own way to control me.

"Let's test this out," she breathed. She clenched her hand and pain lanced through Leila's right wrist. Leila gasped and Kat giggled. "Wow, I should've done this a long time ago."

Blake grabbed for his girlfriend but she pushed him back. The pain washed over Leila, waves and waves of unending pain.

"Ever since you showed up here, you've rotted everything you've touched," Kat growled.

The pain kept running through her body like a fire on kindling. Leila always expected her body to get used to the feeling of the pain, but she never did. It stole her breath and her thoughts.

"And every night I hoped *Blakey* would have the balls to end you. But you know what they say, *if you want something done right...*" Kat's laugh echoed around Leila.

She slid down the railing, the bracelet too heavy with pain. Kat advanced.

"Blakey couldn't, or wouldn't, do what was necessary. You don't belong here; the Fates made a mistake with you. I won't let their mistake live another day, Hecate witness me."

Leila's teeth were clenched together, and when the pain left her body suddenly, she shook in the absence of it.

"Now, *stand.*"

The bracelet's magic might have been halved, but it still held onto her with an iron vise.

"Nothing," Leila panted, "you do to me will *last.*"

"Maybe," Kat said, her eyes bright. "Order never lasts, though." Kat flexed her hand again. "Leila. *Jump.*"

"*No!*" Blake bellowed.

Her freedom wrestled with the magic, her braceleted hand dragging her body up to standing. She had traitorous limbs she fought to gain control over. One foot onto the ledge, then she was back on the edge of the roof, looking out to the crowd far below; an undulating sea that would part for her falling body.

"I said jump!" Kat shrieked.

Leila turned to Hecate's Vessel.

"No."

"You obey me! Jump! *Jump off the roof you stupid bitch!*" Kat screamed.

"Kat," Blake wheezed from behind her. The girl turned to see her boyfriend standing, his wrist raised. The Vessel of Hades was fading, like night yielding to dawn.

"We're done." His powers swirled around him, lifting him off the ground. His wrist was a void of darkness until it imploded, the watch pulling itself apart. Blake's eyes were back to normal, mortal grey, his mouth a watery smirk before he fell to the ground in a heap. The magic of the watch left Leila, disintegrating the stones at her wrist. She felt weightless.

I'm free. A laugh bubbled up in her chest, light and airy.

Danny broke free and ran to check on Blake, lifting his unconscious head. Leila turned her eyes on Kat, who pulled at her hair in disbelief.

"You must not have heard," Leila called to her. "I'm not Order. I'm Chaos."

Screams erupted below them as the sound of barking and commotion upended the crowd. Cerby broke onto the roof, his claws clicking the ground like a funeral march. With every step he grew, his three heads baring their elongated canines. He ran to Leila's side and by the time he got to her, he stood taller than her. His heads snapped at Kat. She stumbled back to get out of the way of the creature's snapping jaws.

"You don't have any power here. Not anymore," Leila declared.

"I'm not scared of you," the Vessel of Hecate said.

"You don't have to be." Leila stepped down from the ledge. "You have to run."

Cerby stopped growing, his canines dripping with slobber, his eyes feral and his hackles a razor down his back. He howled, an infernal harmony that drowned out the music. His howls were joined in by many other sinister things that resided in the surrounding forests. Vessels screamed below, noticing a Cerberus was on the roof. Kat scrambled up and ran, the rest of Blake's "friends" following suit.

Her friends rushed her and it felt like a victory just to have her friends at her side.

And freedom.

"What about the rest of the party guests?" Oscar asked.

"Cerby's on it," Leila put a hand to his massive black shaggy coat. He broke out of the circle into a run, tunneling down the stairs. Screams of panic followed him. Her friends gathered at the roof's railing, all of them bedraggled and limping, to watch the party disperse into the trees and the mountains beyond.

"I'm glad that's over," Leila said.

Then she passed out.

WINTER

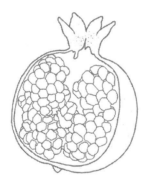

BLAKE

Nausea roiled through him and Blake couldn't seem to keep his eyes closed without the world spinning out. Sleep was out of reach, pain a close companion. It felt like he was being corroded ever so slowly as poison leached from his body. And in the quiet moments, when his limbs were too weak to move, the only thing left to rush in was his memories, a tangled crush of awful things—awful things he'd done.

Sometimes he'd find Danny in his nightmares, then in a chair next to his bed. Sometimes it was Min-Seo. Sometimes they were actually real, wiping the sick from him and putting cool rags on his blistering skin. When he could grip the bed, when he was done vomiting and words could form in his head, he'd plead to them.

"*Just...let...me...die...*"

His voice was a low rasp, but he meant what he said. If his memories were true, he deserved to slip away, a fitting end to the monster in the story.

"Stop saying that," Min-Seo said. Her voice rattled around his head.

"*...let...me...die...*"

"No. We don't get to fade away when we're awful. Hold yourself accountable and make amends."

"*Why...are...you...helping...me...?*"

The world spun again and Blake still had more in his body to expel. He curled up to stop his body from shaking.

"Because," Athena's Vessel said, her jade eyes bright, "you're not the only one who's been a monster."

HARVEY

After the immediate danger of the solstice had passed, Harvey's anxiety kicked in. Too many people had seen him at the party— there wasn't a hope that this wouldn't make its way back to the mayor. He'd kept the panic at bay over the last couple of days but now that they were leaving, he couldn't help but think about the consequences waiting for him back in the city.

He sat on the bench in the foyer waiting for the rest of his friends. They'd stayed at the estate for as long as they could, and today was the day before the new term started. They wanted to make sure everything was fine before they left even if it meant Harvey had a lot of explaining to do for his absence.

And I'm not even sure if everything is OK now.

Harvey had never seen someone go through withdrawals of impure ambrosia—the stories he'd heard didn't get the absolute horror right. The sounds of Blake's agony echoed in his mind, and he hadn't even helped Danny or Minnie with his recovery. A tinge of guilt crept up in him but it'd take a lot to overcome the anger he still had against the Vessel of Hades.

Leila hadn't been spared—the bracelets had taken a toll on both of them, confining her to her bed for nearly two days as she regained the spirit she'd lost over the last three months. Harvey still didn't understand what that magic was and where it had come from.

"Hey," Oscar said, entwining his fingers in Harvey's as he sat down next to him. "You've got that look again."

"What look?"

"The worried look. Or is it the constipated one?"

Harvey bumped his shoulder against his boyfriend.

"Shut *up*," he said with a laugh. "I'm not constipated."

"Don't worry, if the *nomos* haven't busted in here by now, they aren't going to. You know how crazy the winter solstice is, the mayor has more to deal with than us trespassing in the mountains."

"You're right, you're right." He pecked Oscar's lips and gave him what he thought was a convincing smile.

But you don't know the mayor like I do.

Harvey had made sure that he didn't do anything that Martin could use to keep him in his pocket. The last couple of months made that much harder, and Harvey was starting to worry that after all this time, he'd still end up owing Martin in some way or another.

Leila joined the two of them, the rest of their friends at her heels.

"Good thing we have a plan, then," Bianca said to the Vessel of Persephone, answering a question Harvey hadn't heard. "You won't even feel like you're alone for the next season."

"My friends and their plans, it's ridiculous." Elliot had his bag slung over his shoulder. Harvey was surprised he hadn't killed Blake in his sleep and the look Elliot gave Harvey made it clear he felt the same.

"Agreed," Mason said as he carried their stuff to Danny's car.

"I can't believe we're leaving already, mate." Bart's hair had grown and it softened him, making his eyes rounder, his smile a bit sweeter. "There's an infirmary, a wine cellar, and I'm pretty sure we'd never run out of food."

"It's the magic of the house," a raspy voice said above them. Blake wasn't in any shape to be a threat but that didn't stop Harvey's fingers from twitching with lightning. "During the fall and winter, at least."

Standing at the second floor railing, Blake cleared his throat.

"Thank you," Blake said, the words sounding like they didn't want to come out. He looked a bit better with a shower and a fresh set of clothes, though it was disarming to see him in anything more casual than a button down shirt and suit jacket. Minnie followed behind him and gave him a nod.

"I'm sorry," he said with equal pause. Everyone stood silently, in different stages of bewilderment. Harvey didn't trust himself to answer.

Blake turned and went back to his rooms.

Elliot clapped his hands together. "Gods, that was awkward. Let's get going before he comes back out for a group hug."

"I'll miss you." Leila wrapped her arms around Bianca and Minnie. A glow was back in her face, her eyes brightening to their warm, earth brown, and she wasn't as pale anymore. But leaving her again felt like they were leaving her to fall back into whatever abyss she'd just fought her way back out of.

Are we both designed to be trapped, even after all the good we've done?

It was his turn to hug Leila and he wrapped her in his arms. She smelled like fresh roses, and in their brief hug she held him surprisingly tight; a reminder of her strength even after all she'd endured.

There was no point in him worrying now, he realized. Either Martin knew and was biding his time, or he didn't. Either Leila and Blake will be at odds with each other, or they won't. They would have to face these options regardless of Harvey's anxiety.

His friends were here to help him as much as they were here to help Leila.

BART

Bart was on edge the entire drive back. Danny had continued down the winding road instead of turning back the way he'd come. The others were alert with a casual interest in avoiding the *nomos* but Bart kept a steel grip on the grab handles of the passenger seat.

"Are you sure this is the way, Danny boy?" He kept his voice light.

"Plenty of daylight left, *mate.*" Danny gave him a wink, clearly enjoying Bart's discomfort.

Bart knew Danny through overlapping social circles, but not well enough to fully trust his abilities to get them through the mountains in one piece. Though he would never admit it, the endless lush of wild forest was scarier than turning up to the Drachma weaponless. About a year ago, Cris had sent the young Vessel of Ares to run some things up to a shack not far from the city. The gang leader didn't mention what would find Bart in the night—if he would make it through the night.

Danny was right in the end. When he veered onto an unmarked path, he hit the gas and wound them down the mountain like he was calling the path into existence with his tires.

He dropped Bart off in front of Anvil Automations. Bart said his goodbyes then moved around the car to lean against the driver's window.

"Hey, don't forget about me when you go back to prep school.

You know I'm a free man now. Free-*ish*."

Danny threw a glance to the others in the back before lowering his sunglasses and his voice.

"Blake and I aren't on the best terms, *yet*." Danny reached out and shook his hand, the soft slip of a business card passed between them. "Keep an eye out—and light it up if you need me."

Then the car sped off with his friends inside. He turned back to the sprawling mechanic's shop.

He said hi to a couple of the other coverall-wearing mechanics, heading into the familiar bustle of the shop. The smell of oil and rubber greeted him like an old friend. Sure, he hadn't known anything about cars when he started, but he'd always been a quick study when he needed to be.

He spotted the boss by his auburn hair and the consistently knitted brows, like he was sure all the sports cars would roll out of his shop at a moment's notice.

"Arnie, I'm back! Happy solstice!" He boomed. Technically, Arnold did *not* like or even *let* anyone call him any kind of nickname— especially *Arnie*. Arnold turned his tall frame around without even looking at the Vessel of Ares and headed up to his office that overlooked the sleek cars and busy workers.

"Roomie! What'd I miss?" And *technically*, Arnie letting him crash on his couch in the loft upstairs was supposed to be a secret.

"You're fired, Bartholomew," he said without turning.

"Arnie, c'mon, what's wrong? Didn't get a solstice gift?" *This man is wound tighter than an iron belly-bow.* If Bart would prescribe a good shag to anyone it'd be his boss.

Arnold turned, his calm demeanor gone. His eyes were two embers and his jaw jumped.

"I stuck my neck out for you and you ran back to your *friends* to do *gods knows what*," he hissed, raising his eyebrows deliberately when he mentioned Bart's *friends*. "I can't have that in my shop—not if it costs the safety and integrity of my business. Get your stuff and go. I'll pay you a severance for the next couple of weeks but I'm done."

Arnold continued up the stairs to his office. Bart followed at his heels.

"Boss, *wait*." Bart closed the door behind him. The office was a little extension of Arnold's apartment, an industrial build with old English comforts, like the Persian rug and the dark wood table next to the floor-to-ceiling glass windows.

Bart's boss sat in the deep leather chair and put down his clipboard to pick up his telephone.

"I won't have gang members on my payroll. Cris knows that I'm willing to work with her but she can't be planting her own members. That's crossing a line."

Planting? Payroll? Then it clicked.

Bartie clapped his hands together. "Arnie——"

"——stop calling me that——"

"——you think I was——" Bartie couldn't help but laugh. "I was with my friends. You know the posh ones, from prep school?"

"No."

"Yes, you do. Anyway, they needed me to help with..." Then he realized who he was talking to and what he'd just about revealed: breaking the law in front of the squarest man alive.

"Yes?"

"I can't say," Bartie deflated.

"You're going to have to say where you were and what you did that was so important that you would skip out on a week of work with no notice or *I will fire you.* OK?"

Bartie wiped his face with a sigh. "OK," he replied. His friends would have to understand.

It's not like they have room for me in their nice dorms.

Bartie told all he could with only a couple of clarifying questions from his boss. After he was done, Arnold's brows were knitted together.

"Can you tell me more about the watch? What did it look like exactly?"

"I can do you one better," Bartie reached for the pad of paper on the desk and an errant pen and sketched what he'd seen; the little Greek letters notched around the dial. He passed Arnie the pad when he was done.

Arnold studied the page for a few minutes in silence, looking more troubled all the while.

"I may know what this is. This is dark, highly illegal magic. Made by a Vessel of Hephaestus to control his wife." He gave Bart a meaningful look. Arnold didn't have to explain to Bart his own Myth. Vessels of Hephaestus have been trying to stop their wives from straying to Vessels of Ares without luck since the founding of New Olympus.

"Bastard."

Arnold sighed. "Agreed. This is a legend with my fellow Vessels, a beautiful piece of magic and machinery that can grant you freedom from your Myth. But control comes at a price: it runs on the wearer's magic, and powering something like that takes a lot of magic—it deteriorates the wearer, corrupts their soul until they go insane and die."

"Bloody hell." Bartie thought back to the night of the solstice, and the night before that at the pool.

Arnie inspected the drawing again. "The one in control becomes controlled by their own corroded humanity. I feel bad for whoever wears the bracelets, they're at the mercy of someone being eaten by magic. Do you know where they got this?"

"No idea. I heard it appeared at the fall equinox."

"Odd. Don't trouble yourself with this anymore. I'm glad you told me the truth, and consider yourself unfired."

Bartie beamed knowing he could stay.

Arnie inspected the drawing. "This isn't half bad. Have you taken classes for drawing?"

"Classes? You know how the temple is. Lots of stabbin', fightin', that sort of thing." Bart could hit center mass with any weapon while blindfolded on the back of a *hippocampus*—that's what being an acolyte of Ares meant—everything else was a wash. He was lucky he could even write his name, let alone *draw*.

"Hmm," was all he got out of the Vessel of Hephaestus. He kept looking at the drawing and it made Bartie uncomfortable.

Is it that good?

"Other than that it was a good break?"

"Yeah, anything is better than your constant snoring."

Arnold frowned. "I don't snore."

"Sure, boss, whatever you say." Bartie got up. There was work to do.

He spied the drawing he'd made again.

Not half bad.

He could deal with being half bad.

LEILA

The two of us, again.

Leila closed the massive front door and was relieved. Being cared for and attended to by her friends became overwhelming. She had time to breathe, to be in her own skin again—a feeling she hadn't known since the equinox.

She passed the day doing laundry, walking out in the cold, catching up on homework. Enjoying the feeling of each sensation. Then when her stomach growled she felt genuinely excited to try and cook something. She grabbed her beginner's cookbook and headed to the kitchen.

The smell of onions and garlic and hot food made her stomach leap for joy. The dark silhouette at the counter made her stop. She was about to turn around when Cerby spotted her and trotted over to her, making Blake look up. They only made eye contact for a second before he looked back at the counter.

"I'll come back later," Leila said.

"I'm almost done," Blake said at the same time.

Leila hugged the cookbook to her chest, suddenly self-conscious.

No matter what I make it's not going to be as good as whatever's cooking now.

"I just made a vegetable soup; Danny only fed me crackers the last couple of days." Blake's cheeks had a hollow look to them, the circles under his eyes violet. He rested an elbow on the counter, the other stirring the soup like he didn't have the strength to stand alone. "It's vegan."

"Thanks," Leila said. "No poison, right?"

Blake's grey eyes flashed to hers. He chuckled, but his body was still so weak it was barely audible.

"Funny. No poison in this one."

"Good," Leila said, breaking eye contact again. "I'll come back later, I'm not hungry right now."

Leila hated how quickly she turned and walked away, feeling like her heartbeat was in her ears. After locking the door to her rooms, she sat on the floor and waited for her pulse to return to normal.

The Vessel of Persephone groaned. Was she scared of Blake? *No.*

She searched herself for the fear she thought was hidden there but came up empty. If anything, she *should* be scared—right?

Right?

She stared up at the ceiling and waited for the paralyzing fear to come. It didn't. In truth, with the bracelets gone, she didn't have this oppressive feeling of self-doubt weighing over her and crushing her spirit. Persephone was right, she could not fear darkness if it was a part of her. And she felt like Blake had lost some of his own demons the night of the solstice.

What really bothered her was what was waiting for her in his stormy eyes. So much had happened between them, a wide expanse of unsaid things flowed before them. He'd hurt her, made her do so many humiliating things—but *she'd* kissed *him*.

Her cheeks flamed—two blooming peonies on fire.

She'd only kissed one other person since she'd gotten to New Olympus—Minnie—and she had done it on a dare.

Not that I even remember it much, does that even count?

Leila crossed her arms in front of her face. She'd been put through so much and yet she couldn't figure out how to bridge the gap between her and Blake. Did she even want to?

"Ugh," she groaned again. There were more important things to do. So she shoved her clean clothes into her closet and made space for her paint supplies. Then she painted and painted, bright roses, trailing jasmine, crowding dahlias. She painted florals until her arms were sore and her neck was stiff. Then she slept.

Not for long, not with the nightmares chasing her ragged in her sleep. It was like she had to relive every horrible thing Blake and his friends had put her through. And now without Ash to blame on her lack of rest.

She got up with a sigh, her stomach moaning for food, and pulled on a sweatshirt Elliot had left. It smelled good, like the sea in summertime. She made her way through the dark mansion, passing the wall of glass where a winter rain beat on, the moon obscured. The library was open, and Blake sat under a lamp in a leather chair reading. He looked as startled as Leila did when they saw each other. Blake had round, wire-framed glasses on. Something about it was disarming to Leila, as if the Blake at the solstice party was the evil twin to the one in front of her now.

"I can't sleep," Leila said quietly.

He closed his book. "Me too."

Leila didn't want to say why, she didn't want to invite her memories back into focus.

"I didn't mean to make you feel like you couldn't be in the kitchen. I just like to cook." He picked at the leather armchair. "It makes the house feel less lonely."

"It's not a problem."

"I keep thinking, *'this must be the worst thing I've ever done'* and then I go to sleep and I remember more."

Leila didn't reply.

Blake rubbed his eyes under his glasses, his voice rough. "I don't want you to think I'm not sorry, because I am. I will always be sorry. I'm not that Vessel. At least, I thought I wasn't."

Leila got the urge to reassure him the tainted ambrosia had corrupted him, the seductive power of the watch that called forth the darkest parts of him was to blame. But it wasn't up to her to make him feel better.

"I want to say I'm sorry, and I'm going to make these next three months better, I swear. When I was younger, this place was a prison for me. I don't want that for you and I should've done that from the beginning. Pretend I'm not even here, I'm going to try to stay out of your way as much as possible."

"Stop, stop." Leila was overwhelmed. Sleep still clung to her like spider's webs. "I don't want you to be a ghost in your own home."

"I want to do the right thing."

"Ask, then."

Blake nodded. "Right. Sorry, again. What do you want?"

Leila thought for a moment, realizing she hadn't been asked that question since she got to New Olympus. "I think I want to try and have as normal a life as possible. I want to do my homework and learn to cook. I want to take Cerby for a run and paint my room."

"OK." He scrunched his eyebrows. "Did you say *paint*?"

"I want to go back to New Prep without feeling like I missed anything, but I'm not good at teaching myself. How am I supposed to pass my fencing class? I don't know how to fence."

"I can fence."

"Huh?"

"I know how to fence. I haven't in a while—but I can, if you need help." He picked at the armchair again nervously.

"Oh."

There was an offer there, she was sure. She made herself look at him, his eyes nearly silver in the warm light. She lifted her chin up. "Good."

"Good?" He asked.

Leila turned, heading to the kitchen. She didn't have to answer him quite yet.

BLAKE

It took a week for Leila to get back to Blake. In the little interactions they had there was still that stilted politeness between them. Even if Leila had said she didn't mind him around—*he* minded. If he didn't see the Vessel of Persephone, he could stop the guilt flooding him whenever he saw her. And the burn of shame. And the worse feeling: the memory of joy— no, not *joy*, the satisfaction of being obeyed. Of total control.

It was a cowardly move to run, but he saw himself as a better coward than anything else. It's not like he was dodging punishment— he'd punished himself enough going on so many runs even Cerby sat out, or pushing himself in the gym until his hands were raw and he could barely walk. The effects of the poisoned ambrosia still left him weak and reeling but he'd rather pass out than feel anything. He found he could ignore every awful thing he'd done when he was distracted and alone.

Then one morning there she was, standing at the doors waiting for him after his run, clouds of frosted breath surrounding her. It was one of those bright winter mornings where the sun did little to help how cold it was.

"Are you free today to help me with some fencing for an hour?" she asked. The color was coming back to her olive skin like a lamp slowly brightening each day.

Cerby huffed for attention between them, his snouts wetly pushing at Blake's hands.

She raised an eyebrow, reminding him that he hadn't answered her.

"Uh, yeah." He grabbed his hoodie lying on the railing and put it on over his bare chest. She'd watched him run, and for some reason he felt too open without a shirt on. He was still out of breath and concentrated on the zipper of his jacket instead of looking at her face. "Noon? In the gym?"

"That works." And then she was gone.

And so for the next four hours he toiled in misery, trying to figure out how he was supposed to get through one lesson with her.

He wore a pair of dark joggers and a long sleeve shirt to their fencing session. He avoided the mirrors lining one side of the gym, not wanting to see himself—not that the poison had ravaged his body, but he couldn't exactly look himself in the eye yet.

I don't want to recognize that person in me.

She sat on one of the mats, her fencing book open next to her.

Blake cleared his throat, moving past Leila to the wall where rows of fencing swords were stored.

"You've handled a sword before, right? I don't want to teach you what you already know."

"We learned about the anatomy of swords, stance, and basic moves." She got up.

"Great." He pulled a thin sword off the wall and handed it to her, grip forward.

She took it in her left hand, testing the weight of it.

He grabbed his own, rolling his wrist around, the sword whistling in the air with his movements. It'd been a while since he'd trained, his muscle memory was rusty.

"Let's see what we're working with." He tapped the point of his sword against Leila's. "*En garde.*"

She unsteadily stepped forward, crossing her sword against his. He bent his legs and pointed his right foot to her. Blake jabbed and she swung wildly, stepping backwards startled. Blake parried easily. He put his hands up in surrender.

"Stop, stop. You said you went over basic moves and stance?"

Leila grimaced. "Well, yes, the last week we were in school. The rest of it we learned about the uniform, like the mask and the pastry—"

"Plastron," Blake corrected.

"Right." Leila bit her bottom lip. "Oh *gods*. I don't know anything." She sat on one of the plyo boxes, defeated.

"I've had to teach myself all these years, it's not over yet."

Leila looked at him incredulously. Blake sighed.

"I'm going to teach you—seriously. Stand up. Let's start with the stance."

Leila stood, putting her sword back up.

Blake stepped around her. "Bend your knees more but don't slouch. And move your hips back, you don't want to give your opponent so much open area to score. Like this." He mirrored her stance, and moved his hips sideways so his whole body faced her and pointed his sword to his invisible enemy. She twisted around, more off kilter than before.

"Better?" When she didn't like the answer on Blake's face, she frowned. "Can you help me then?"

Blake was thrown off by what she meant, then he moved around her. Her hair was a dark rope guiding his eyes down her back. He snapped his gaze up to the nape of her neck.

"Here," he breathed as he straightened her arm, relaxing her wrist down. Then he moved his hands to her waist, and slowly tilted them so she was a fluid line.

"Is this better?" she said softly.

He could smell her, rosy with a touch of musk. He let her go abruptly.

"Yeah, great. I'm gonna put some music on," he said, turning his back and moving to the speakers at the far end of the gym.

"This place has everything, but no phone?" she called out.

"No service out this far anyway," he said. The speakers blasted out an angry guitar for a moment before he turned it down. He didn't realize how loud he had it during his workouts and switched to a milder Brit rock band.

His fingers fumbled over the controls and tried to take some deep breaths, to no avail. Every slimy, scared part of him screamed to get out of there.

Stop. He faced Leila, who was waiting for him. He leaned into his own discomfort and walked her through some vocab, showing her how to move along the line.

Before long, the hour had passed and Leila thanked him and handed him the sword.

"Tomorrow?"

"Sure," he agreed. Then she was gone again.

Her absence didn't offer him peace anymore.

MIN-SEO

We don't get to fade away when we're awful. Hold yourself accountable and make amends.

It was easier to tell someone else to do the right thing, Minnie knew all too well. One week back and still she hadn't said anything to Bianca—both of them acting like strangers in the moments they were in the same room. Bianca didn't even look at her. It hurt to see Bianca move from committee to club with the same bright joy to sitting at their lunch table with all their friends. Minnie kept to herself, studio to library to late night treks out to Claire's apartment only to restart the exhausting cycle each morning.

Those were supposed to be her places of solace but now she felt trapped.

She stood outside her own dorm room, waiting for the sensation of panic to cease. It didn't.

Open the damn door.

Minnie turned the knob and opened the door before she chickened out.

Bianca wasn't in their kitchenette so she moved to Bianca's room, where she heard her best friend's laugh. There her best friend sat at her desk, her laughter startled at Minnie's entrance. Her periwinkle hair was twisted up with a scarf and she wore a heather grey matching workout set, looking like a model from a catalog.

Danny sat on the bed with a book in his hands, surprising Minnie.

"Can we talk?" she said, not looking at the Vessel of Hermes.

"Now isn't a good time," Bianca started.

"It's not a problem, B," Danny sat up. He gave her a look conveying a conversation and she gave him one back.

I thought we were the only people who had that. Minnie burned with jealousy.

"No, wait—" Bianca turned to Danny.

"I'll be in my room." Danny got up, shouldering his backpack. They stood in silence until he closed the door behind him.

"Yes?" Bianca asked.

"I'm sorry," Minnie said.

The Vessel of Iris nodded and turned back to her laptop. "OK, thanks."

"That's it?"

"Yes, I heard you, thank you," Bianca said tightly. "Now, I have homework to catch up on before student council."

"I'm sorry for what I said, I just want you to know."

"And what exactly did you say that you're sorry for?"

"I—" Minnie recalled the fuzzy, champagne-tinged memories. "Well, all of it."

"You're the most important person in my life and you tore me to shreds, and all you have to say after three weeks is one paltry *I'm sorry?* Minnie, you know what my life has been as a minor Vessel and yet you still called me *pathetic.*"

"No, *I* was being pathetic," Minnie pleaded. "I didn't mean any of it."

This isn't how it was supposed to go.

"You still said it. And before that you lied about the fact you have a girlfriend? Why wouldn't you tell me about her?"

"It's complicated. Claire doesn't want anyone to know because," Minnie took a deep breath, "because she's older."

"How much older?"

"She's twenty-two."

Bianca processed this and Minnie wished she could know what was going through her mind.

"Can I start again? I keep messing this up."

"Go ahead," Bianca sighed.

Minnie took a deep breath. "I shouldn't have lied to you about Claire. She's the first girl who's ever *looked* at me as more than a classmate or a friend. And she's helped me with my art and shown me that maybe I wasn't so unloveable."

"You're *not* unloveable."

Minnie held up her hand, if she didn't get through it all before her throat closed up with tears unshed then she'd never get through it at all. "I know, but everything I said to you was about *me*. I follow you around because you're the only person who's taken a chance on being my friend. Without you I'd have no one, and I am constantly scared you're going to realize I'm not worthy of being your friend. I drank too much and took that out on you. I'm *sorry*. Please, Bianca, you need to believe me." The last words broke on a sob. The Vessel of Athena wiped her tears away with the back of her hand.

Bianca bit her wobbling lip.

"OK, that's much better," she said, making Minnie hiccup with a laugh. "But I'm going to need some time to process, Minnie."

"Anything," Minnie agreed.

"And, you need to let me meet your girlfriend—that's a BFF rule."

"Of course."

"I do have to make it to my student council meeting, Harvey is waiting on me."

Minnie agreed and said goodbye, going to her room. For the first time in months, she could breathe freely.

LEILA

It started with the dog.

It was an overcast Sunday morning, mist spilling out from the trees onto the grounds. Leila finally felt back to a place where she could walk Cerby around the grounds again like she had done briefly during the fall. With her puffy jacket, a glossy white hand-me-down of Camille's that made her feel like a marshmallow, and her New Prep navy beanie on, she was ready. Right as she left the warmth of the mansion, she barely avoided smacking into Blake's bare chest. He pulled on Cerby's lead in surprise, the dog jumping up to greet Leila.

Who runs shirtless in the winter?

She leapt back, avoiding his pale muscles.

"Sorry." She forced her gaze up to Blake's face. "Can I take him on a walk?"

"Oh, don't worry about it, I took him."

"Can I walk him anyway?"

"He just got a run in, you don't have to worry about it." He edged around Leila and pulled Cerby with him. "I got it."

What the Hades?

She watched him retreat down the dark hallway. Not even one of Cerby's black heads looked back.

Traitor.

She set out at a brisk pace, suddenly hot and annoyed, peeling off her puffy jacket. Snow had dusted the ground in the night and she found way too much enjoyment in stomping around.

When Danny and Bianca showed up to drop off their homework, Blake was only there for a moment, showing his face and then shyly leaving.

"Is he still sick?" Danny asked.

"I'm not sure." Leila looked at the grand staircase, where Blake had escaped to.

"Let him be, he's going to be licking his wounds for a while," Bianca said, then pulled Leila into a tight hug before promising to be back next week.

Later she went into the kitchen to make oatmeal and found Blake blending some sort of smoothie, a brackish green thing. She opened her mouth to ask him what he'd put in there when he ran the blender.

"All yours," he said over his shoulder after pouring his smoothie in a cup and practically running away.

He's avoiding me. The last week of interactions clicked into place—a series of excuses to leave her alone. That made her even more mad.

Then it was time for her and Blake to meet for her fencing lesson. Leila enjoyed the hour of practice, actually finding she was a quick study with Blake as a patient teacher.

Today, though, she wasn't here for his patience. Or his placating tone and averted eyes.

Leila hit her sword against his forcibly, making it ring.

"Let's go again," she said. It was the end of the hour and she could see him glancing at the door, itching to escape.

Shouldn't I be the one running away?

"Sure," he said in a friendly monotone that made Leila want to scream. Last week he called himself a monster, but this week he was a shadow.

He lunged, slowly, giving her time to retreat. She stepped back, blocking his sword and hitting it away. He advanced, jabbing at her shoulder, a barely there touch because they weren't wearing the correct protective uniforms. He won even though he hadn't even tried that hard.

It was infuriating.

"You're getting better," he said in her general direction. She glared at his back and strode to the speaker, clicking through until she found a song she recognized and turned the volume way up.

"Again," she said to him.

"Are you sure?" he hedged, standing near the storage wall.

"Yep," she ground out.

Blake ran a hand through his hair and moved back into place to meet her raised sword.

"*En garde,*" she said, then lunged. She took him by surprise but that quickly turned on her, and again she felt clumsy—like a child trying to keep up. She was always trying to keep up. He twisted the sword and it fell out of her hand with a thud.

"Remember your grip." He'd already turned. "We can go over it tomorrow, it's not a big fix."

"Let's fix it now."

"Huh?" he sputtered.

"Do you have anything better to do?" *Because I have all day.* She grabbed at her sword and raised it again.

Confused, he raised his as well. Again she lunged and he parried, though he had to take a step back. He was quick on his feet and she tripped trying to advance. Another slight jab to her shoulder and the bout was done just as quickly as it started.

"Are you OK?"

She pushed off the floor, sweat beading at her forehead. "Great, let's go again."

"Is there something else going on?" Blake asked. "Are you OK, really?"

"Yes, stop *asking* me that. Now *en fucking garde.*"

The Vessel of Hades barely got his sword up before she lunged again, hitting his sword hard enough to make her arm vibrate. Blake jumped out of the way.

"Yield!" he said, his hands up.

She was panting hard. "Why did you do that?"

"Because I've got homework I have to catch up on. It's getting late."

"Seems like you only want to be sorry on your own terms."

"That's not true." He looked at her then and it felt like a small win.

"Stop avoiding me, we're stuck here *together.* I told you I'm not letting you be a ghost in your own house."

"I'm not—" Blake shut his mouth, his jaw working in anger.

Leila narrowed her eyes.

"If you're angry, *talk to me.* I'm sick of you being so condescending and *nice* all the time."

Blake glared at her. "So I can't be miserable by myself and I'm not groveling how you like, is that it, *princess?* Please, tell me how you'd like me to behave?"

Leila's mouth quirked. "Like that. You sound like the real you."

"You don't know the real me," he spat.

"Then stop yielding. *Show up.*" And she raised her sword again, lifting an eyebrow.

He glowered, but raised his sword nonetheless.

"*En garde,*" he breathed.

The swords clicked and they were off, Blake lunging at her.

So he has *been holding back.*

Leila dodged, then retreated, all the while trying to keep up with his blows. Soon there wasn't much space left for her to go. She parried, pushing off one of the plyo boxes and aimed high. He staggered back, his eyes widening in surprise. He recovered quickly when she advanced on him, and he parried and jabbed, touching her in the arm with the point of his sword. That didn't stop her, and she kept jabbing at him, using her other arm to push on his sword. He planted his foot, choosing not to move back, still jabbing at her again and again. Leila wasn't playing to lose and with a groan she swept his foot hard. Blake fell flat on his back with a thud.

The Vessel of Persephone pointed her sword at his chin as soon as he raised his head. Her heartbeat was a kick drum in her ears and rivulets of sweat ran down her back.

His breathing was shallow, matching hers. He tilted his head up, exposing his neck. An invitation.

"See? Don't be so nice. I can handle it."

"Noted," he said, out of breath. "Now you've made your point, can you help me up? I've recently been poisoned, you know."

"Ha," she deadpanned, offering him her arm. He gripped her and nearly pulled her down trying to get back on his feet.

"Thanks," he said, his serious tone catching her off guard, the hint of a smile lifting the side of his mouth. "Seems like I need a reminder when I'm being a jackass."

"You're welcome," she replied. Leila wasn't sure where they stood, but he was suddenly too close, too warm, too real after weeks of absence. She let go of his arm and handed him her sword.

When Leila got back to her room, Cerby was waiting at her door.

"Aw, did you miss me?" she said and his tail wagged furiously. She let him in, unable to stay mad at his sweet, dark eyes.

Tomorrow, it's you and me.

After her long bath, she found Cerby sniffing at the mess that was her walk-in closet. Leila hadn't bothered to organize anything after the solstice, and now it was a mess of clean laundry, boxes from Camille's house, books, and other stuff she'd shoved out of the way so all her friends could fit in her room.

She sifted through her things to find a sweater to pull over her leggings. When she spotted a chunky cream sweater, she found a little pink box rolled up in it.

A tag in Camille's handwriting marked the outside.

Happy Solstice my Leila,

Love,

Cami

A pang of sadness brought tears to her eyes. Bianca had told her about how Camille helped her friends get past the *nomos*.

Only three more months, and then she'd see her surrogate mother again. Leila missed her, even at her most neurotic.

She opened the little blush box and found a thin gold band inside, a heart engraved at the top. She picked up the dainty ring and slid it on her ring finger. It fit perfectly, a reminder of what waited for her in spring.

Even though it was only the afternoon, Leila found herself exhausted from the day. She crawled into bed, vowing to get up and clean her room in the morning. For now, she'd sleep, her hand curled around her gifted ring and her dreams blush pink and stormy grey.

BLAKE

For someone who gave him so much grief about showing up, Blake hadn't seen Leila at all after their fencing lesson. He sat at the kitchen counter with dinner ready to share with her. As the evening wore on and she didn't show, he felt indignant. He may have scrubbed his dishes extra hard. Even Cerby hadn't shown his face.

"Seems like you only want to be sorry on your own terms." Leila's words echoed through his head, scolding him in her absence. And she was right, *maybe* he'd only sat out for so long to prove he could be there.

Blake groaned.

I'm the worst, aren't I?

He dragged himself up to his room, finding no comfort in any of the books by his bedside. Blake fell into restless sleep wondering how he could finally get something right.

The next morning he dressed in his joggers and—spying the slowly growing blanket of snow—pulled on a long sleeve thermal and a beanie. The house was still silent, his dog still sleeping in Leila's room. The poor dog needed his rest since Blake started up running again.

Running the length of the grounds in the blue dawn under the shadow of the towering fir trees, Blake was reminded of the rugged beauty of the estate. There were moments over the years where his Myth felt less like a prison sentence and more like a blessing. As time stretched past his childhood, he thought he might actually love being here. In the depths of winter, the mansion stood as a refuge in a white sea.

When he returned he saw the French doors to Leila's balcony were open. She appeared in a cream sweater that set off her olive skin. He slowed his jog and waved to her, his chest heaving.

"It's finally too cold to go shirtless, huh?" Leila called out from the balcony.

"Yeah," Blake said, too out of breath to say anything else.

"Too bad," she replied and Blake could see she quirked a dark brow.

I didn't think you'd noticed, suddenly aware of how shirtless he'd been.

Blake gave a surprised laugh. "Can't get poisoned and frostbite in the same timeframe. My luck can't be that bad."

"Well, the day is early," she said, turning back to go inside.

He watched the doors close with a smile.

Huh.

After he'd showered and dressed he went down to the kitchen. Leila was there, eating some oatmeal, flipping through a gardening book.

"Do you own anything other than black?"

"Yeah," he replied indignantly. He made his smoothie, throwing in frozen fruits and vegetables. "Like our school uniform."

"That's it?"

He blended his smoothie, thinking.

"I have a grey crew, somewhere." That Danny had left at his dorm once.

Leila giggled, the sound surprising him. She stopped when she saw his face.

"Sorry." She bit her lip to keep from laughing.

Her smile was infectious.

"I guess," he said, pouring his smoothie into a cup, "I'm predictable. Though, I'm not the only one."

He arched an eyebrow at her outfit as he rounded the marble kitchen island. A lightweight pink sweater she had tied up and...his eyes got caught on the strip of exposed midriff.

Blake coughed and met her eyes again.

"Yeah?" she asked.

"You wear a lot of pink and white." He sat on the stool next to her—well, next to the stool next to her. Blake didn't know how she felt about his proximity so he erred on the side of safety.

"Oh," she waved her hand dismissively, the glint of a dainty gold band caught his eye, "that's Camille. She bought all my clothes. I don't even know if I like this color."

His eyebrows knit together. "What do you mean?"

She looked down shyly. "I'm like her doll. I wear what I have because it's there. I haven't picked out my own clothes."

Blake didn't know that.

"I feel bad, because without her I'd have *nothing*—Persephone has no temple, no house—but I feel..."

"Confined?" Blake asked quietly.

Leila nodded, looking down at her food. She pushed back her chair and put her bowl in the sink. "Though I do have to give her credit, I look good in all the clothes she bought me."

Blake didn't know how to agree without sounding like an ass. Leila leaned her elbows on the counter.

"Do you think we can postpone our fencing lesson today?" she asked.

"Sure," he said, trying not to sound too crestfallen. After yesterday's lesson he was eager to fence against her.

"I need to focus on my Ancient Greek reading. It takes so long for me to decipher everything, I'm never going to get all of it done in time."

"What level are you in?"

"One," Leila rolled her eyes. "You know, the level all the New Olympus newbies are in."

"Like, for toddlers?"

"Yes, for toddlers. It's hard!" She bemoaned.

"I can help," he offered.

"I can't have you helping me in fencing *and* Greek, too," she argued, getting up.

"Like you said yesterday, I have nothing better to do." Leila had offered him an out—and the Blake from yesterday would have gladly taken it to wallow alone. But he didn't want to do that anymore.

"OK!" She beamed. "I'll get my stuff and meet you in the library?"

The Vessel of Persephone put her hand on his arm, warmth radiating. He nodded and she was off, walking to her room.

Oh gods.

Leila wasn't joking, she was bad at Ancient Greek. Vessels learned Ancient Greek across all schools and temples, on top of whatever other languages they wanted. Blake had an edge being inducted so early.

He winced at her stilted pronunciation. She had to read *Aesop's Fables*, and was struggling to get past the first page of "The Honest Woodcutter".

"You look like you're being tortured," Leila said.

"I'm not." He was. "Why don't we focus on tenses. And writing the alphabet."

"So, only the silent activities then?" Her eyes sparkled.

"I——" he laughed. "Yeah, sorry, you sound awful."

"No," she moaned, hiding her face with the book. He reached out, pushing the book down gently with his hand. Underneath, her cheeks bloomed pink.

"Are you *embarrassed*?" he chuckled.

"Yes? Is that a crime?"

"No! I'm just surprised. You don't *get* embarrassed," Blake said.

"You're making fun of me."

"I'm not! It's a compliment." It was cute, actually. Her bottom lip was in a pout and she played with her hair when she was nervous.

"I guess I only get embarrassed around you."

He was taken aback. "Why?"

She sighed, moving her hair behind her ear. "You trip me up. Even before all of this." She waved at the mansion.

"When you say I 'trip you up' you really mean I'm an *asshole*, right?" he grimaced. "Because I've been nothing but an asshole this whole time."

Leila gave him a grin. "We should focus on the reading, don't you think?"

Blake snatched the volume from Leila's hands.

"Hey!"

"Tell me I'm an asshole, I know you want to!"

Leila grabbed at the book but Blake was too fast, pulling the book back behind him. She overreached, tipping her chair into his. Suddenly they were face to face, frozen between breaths.

"You weren't an asshole in the diner," she said softly, bringing her fingers to his overgrown curls. In the lamplight her eyes were molten brown.

"Oh, really," he murmured.

"We almost made a pretty good team," she breathed into him, bridging the gap between them with her lips.

It was a rush kissing Leila completely sober, in untainted clarity. Not that the last time was bad—he thoroughly enjoyed the last time, too. But compared to this, he'd been numb underwater. She let the kiss linger in agonizing slowness. Her lips were so soft on his, so, *so* soft. Leila broke away, sliding back into her chair. She waved the book in her hand, swiped from his.

"The reading?" she reminded him.

He scoffed, taking off his glasses.

"Fuck that."

Blake leaned over her chair and cupped her face with his hands and kissed her proper. Her hair was silky, he twined his fingers around her dark brown locks like an anchor. He stroked her jaw, her neck, her collarbone. She felt like the sun shone through her skin. He broke their kiss to trail his mouth down her neck to her pulse point, listening to her breathing hitch and break.

Blake slid one hand to Leila's waist, the other under her leg, lifting her to him so she sat on his lap. He teased her hip bone through her leggings and she groaned, pulling his chin up to hers and kissing him deeply.

Sometimes, his power flared outside of his control. As she wrapped her arms around him, he could feel how his own powers snaked around them.

The memory of their last kiss, the mania had a hold of him then, the way he'd made her kiss him—

"Wait, wait—" He pulled back. "Stop. Wait. No." Leila sat back, her eyebrows rising with alarm. Her hair was messy, her lips swollen—

Panic rose in him and he blinked away his power. He felt sick, poisoned all over again.

Oh gods.

"What's wrong?" Leila reached up to touch his face but he stood up, sliding her off him ungracefully.

"I need some air," his words came out in a rush. He strode out the door, the world lurching around him.

Monster, monster, monster.

"Where are you going?" she called after him. He burst out of the double doors, stumbling out onto the snow. "Why are you running away?"

"Why did you kiss me?" He spun around. "You should hate me, you have to, have to, to..."

"I don't hate you," she muttered, barely audible over the freezing wind. She wrapped her arms around her stomach. "And I don't *have* to do anything."

The cold stung Blake's eyes, burning all the places she'd touched. "I don't deserve this, why don't you leave me alone? Let me rot here like I should. Cast me away, I don't deserve your kindness."

"Ouch," she said, a tear sliding quickly down her face. "You *are* an asshole."

He let out a humorless chuckle, spreading his arms out. "That's all I'll ever be!"

"Do you believe you deserved to be poisoned?" When he didn't answer she took a step towards him. "*Do you?*"

"You know what I did to you, *I almost killed you!*"

"Even at your worst, you broke the watch; you were being controlled by it as much as you controlled me."

"You don't know that," his voice was raw. Blake couldn't look at Leila anymore, it hurt too much. But there she was, in front of him, looking up at him.

"Would you hurt me now?" She moved her face to catch his eye.

"No," he croaked, a lump forming in his throat.

"Would you burn me?"

"No."

"Silence me?"

"No."

"Drown me?"

"*NO.*" He locked eyes with her again. "I wouldn't—*I won't.*"

Tears fell down his cheeks and he felt even more stupid for crying.

Leila reached up and wiped at the wetness of his cheeks.

"Don't you know how beautiful you are?" she asked, her own eyes brimming with tears.

Blake had nothing to say but to hold onto Leila as tight as he could, her words breaking his world down. And she was the only thing left standing.

BLAKE

Blake woke up with Leila sleeping soundly on his chest, her room smelling faintly like paint, and the snow falling in thick puffs. He lay there, his hands trailing through her hair, replaying their conversation. Even in the deep cold he felt warm.

There was still more he had to say. Leila may have been there for the last three months, but he and Kat had been dating since last year. How long had she been dosing him? How long had he not been himself? And why did he believe he'd changed for the better? In that heady summer with Kat he felt like the more he hurt others the closer he came to achieving some sort of sick justice.

Who am I now?

With a long sigh, he moved gently and tried to lift Leila's sleeping form off of him. They'd ended up going back to suffering through *Aesop's Fables*, eventually falling asleep in Leila's bed. He couldn't help but feel like he had to take things deliberately slow, he wanted to make sure he did things right. Blake still felt dizzy from the whiplash of emotions the day before.

"No," Leila mumbled, snaking her arms around him.

He breathed a laugh.

"I need to let Cerby outside," he whispered. At his name being mentioned, Blake's dog raised an ear and whined.

Leila gave a groan. "Fine." She rolled onto her back, her eyes closed. He pulled the covers over her and went out to give his dog some exercise.

He came back an hour later, showered, with a coffee in hand for Leila. He put the coffee down on the side table next to a sad-looking potted peony then he leaned on the bed, planting a light kiss on her mouth.

"What's with the flower?" he said when she'd sat up.

"Something Alicia sent along," she said with a yawn. "It's supposed to tell me how I feel. It didn't work until the bracelets came off, but it must be broken again."

Something about the way the peony was closed tight like a fist made him uneasy. He soon forgot when Leila's hands snaked around his shoulders.

"Good morning," she said from behind him.

The cool kiss of metal caught on his skin and he took her left hand in his, observing the thin ring she had on her finger.

"Leila, were you going to tell me you were spoken for?" He turned his face towards her.

Leila's laugh was in his ear. "I got this from Camille as a solstice gift. I wouldn't put it past her to betroth me to someone, though." She looked at him with a smile and it was like the sun had peeked out from behind the winter clouds.

They spent the rest of the snow day inseparable, and Blake saw for the first time how the cold, dark mansion could feel with the warmth of a home. While he was cooking, Leila watched from the counter as she practiced her Ancient Greek with him. After they ate, Blake was on DJ duty, flipping the records while she painted her mural.

The day went by too quickly for Blake, he wondered if he could stretch it out. Even on the happiest of days, Blake couldn't remember ever wanting to relive any of them. He had lived most of his life counting down the hours, the days, the years. But today he was present and it was disorienting, for the first time he felt still.

While Leila was in the shower, he went to his room to get his things. He could navigate this place in the dark but today he felt like he was seeing everything for the first time. Every stone inlay in the walls wasn't random anymore but looked like crystal bouquets, the sconces took on a pomegranate shape. He hadn't seen any of it before.

This isn't my house anymore.

"Blake!" Leila's scream pierced through his thoughts and he sprinted down the rest of the staircase in Leila's direction.

"Leila!" His heart pounded, his thoughts running through a thousand awful images. He saw her silhouette in front of the glass walls. The night was still but Persephone's Vessel was shaking.

He reached her, searching for injuries. Her face was crumpled, violent sobs racking through her.

"I came out of the shower and you were gone," she said through tears. "I couldn't find you."

Leila held on to his sweater and cried. Blake kissed her forehead, glad she couldn't see how perplexed he looked. He rubbed circles on her back and that uneasy feeling came back.

BLAKE

Blake spent a good part of the night consoling Leila, repeating his apologies and promising he wouldn't leave her again. Her sorrow at his minutes-long absence troubled him—how he could have hurt her again made him feel like garbage.

She held onto him hard, even in her sleep, her hands fisted around his shirt. Though Leila seemed she was over everything he'd put her through in the last year, he could see the cracks now. She shouldn't be fine after almost dying, and her healing wasn't going to be linear. He slept badly, frequently waking to check to make sure Leila was still in his arms.

The next morning he woke up to her coming back into the room, Cerby's tail whipping her legs.

She put a coffee on the side table and leaned toward his frowning face.

"Thank you for calming me down last night, I'm sorry I got so upset." She touched her forehead to his before getting up.

Her smile was unbothered and she didn't seem to harbor the obsessive need to hold him close.

"So you're feeling better?"

"Totally," she replied. "I feel great, I even walked Cerby. It doesn't even matter how much snow there is, he wants to play."

"Yeah," he said, taking a sip of the hot coffee. He watched her cross the room, and rolled over as she shed that awful puffy jacket. She dropped it on the floor, along with her scarf and beanie.

"I'm glad you're feeling better, you think you're up for some fencing practice today?"

She shot him a grin. "Only if you're ready to lose. Again."

She moved to the bed onto his lap, wrapping her fingers around his face still chilled from being outside, and kissed him, tasting like coffee. He gripped her waist, his fingers playing with the hem of her shirt.

"Hey," she chided with a laugh.

"I was helping you out," he replied, grinning. She kissed him a final time then got up and moved into the walk-in closet as she took the shirt off, out of his view.

"*Sure,*" she called out from inside the closet.

Blake saw the trail of stuff she had on the floor, stacks of paperbacks and clothes. Her messiness should've bothered him, but he thought it was cute how she focused on something so entirely everything else dropped away. He spotted a blush pink ring box open on its side hiding under a sweater.

Blake stretched out from the bed to grab it, intending to put it on the side table out of the way. A tag attached to it had Leila's name written in looping cursive. Blake turned the card over and nearly dropped the box again, his whole body tensed with cold dread at what he saw.

A drawing of a cat's face. Blake knew someone who loved to sign their name with a smiling feline—someone who'd spent the last three months plotting Leila's demise.

He scrambled away from the box, nearly falling off the bed. The sudden, overwhelming need to get away, to get out of the room and get air, seized him.

He *knew* that drawing, had seen his girlfriend—ex-girlfriend—tag it on walls, pass him notes labeled with it, even drew it on his chest in permanent marker. How could it have gotten on the card?

Blake only noticed the ring three days ago, which meant whatever magic Kat had worked had been active for at least three days. He scraped his hair back going over every moment of the last seventy-two hours and if there'd been any change in Leila.

One change, a small, sick part of his brain hissed.

No.

It couldn't be, this had to be some twisted coincidence.

"Are you OK?" Leila walked back, her clothes changed.

"Take off the ring," he whispered.

"What?"

He didn't want to look at the girl in front of him. "Take off the ring, please, Leila."

"No, I don't want to."

His stomach dropped, the unnamed fear crowding too close to the surface of his mind. He took a deep breath.

"Please, I need to know. *Please take off the ring.*"

She shook her head and clutched her hand close to her. "What do you need to know? You're freaking me out."

I need to know if this is real.

Blake moved closer to Leila, his knees at the edge of the bed.

"You like me, right?" he asked.

"Yes?" She blushed again. "I think I've made that clear."

"When," he pleaded, "when did you start liking me? Please, I need to know."

"That's a weird question." Leila tilted her head in thought. "I can't pinpoint the 'start', not really."

Blake sighed in relief.

"But," Leila continued, "a couple of days ago I woke up and it was like I *knew.* This is so embarrassing, is that what you wanted to know?"

He nodded and gave her a weak smile.

"Thanks. I'm going to go get changed for my run." He turned and left, not waiting for her reply.

If Kat had something to do with her ring, he couldn't let that magic fester while Leila was still wearing it.

When he got to his room he locked the door and went to his closet.

I need to know if it's real.

Blake dug through his suitcase, looking for his wallet. He and Danny had figured out a messaging system for when Blake left for the winter: rudimentary and single-use—this was for when shit hit the fan.

The wallet had Danny's card tucked inside, along with matches.

His fingers shook when he struck the match but the paper caught with bright red flame. On the other side of the city, Danny should notice his own card burst into red flame. The Vessel of Hades watched the card burn, hoping Danny forgave him enough to answer his call. He'd have to wait and see.

Trying to act normal for the day was a challenge. He'd been able to dodge Leila by going for an extended run and shower, but he couldn't avoid her forever. When he was making a smoothie she tried to hug him from behind. He was so wrapped up in his thoughts he didn't know she was there until her arms were around him.

He bristled and moved away, playing it off with a laugh. Inside he was a turmoil of self-loathing.

Of course she'd never like you. You're pathetic and you fell for a love spell. You don't deserve love and—

"Is everything all right?" she asked.

"Hmm? Yes, sorry," he replied. He could only put so much space between them. If she was being compelled to like him, he wasn't going to reciprocate anything—not unless he knew she truly wanted him.

Leila looked like she wanted to say something but a knock sounded on the door.

Thank the gods. He raced to the door to greet Danny and Bianca. They stood looking alarmed and out of breath, like they'd run all the way from New Prep.

"Hey," Danny said apprehensively.

"Hi!" Leila exclaimed. She flung her arms around Bianca, who looked even more alarmed.

"Leila," Blake said hastily, "Danny needs to talk to you about...school. Right?"

He looked at his friend.

"Yeah," Danny said slowly, "Principal Thistlewhait said it was urgent." He led Leila inside and down the hall. She looked back at Blake and he gave her a reassuring wave.

After he closed the door, his calm facade slipped. He turned to Bianca.

"Did Camille give you a gift for Leila? For the solstice?"

"No, I haven't spoken to her since the equinox." Bianca brushed the snow off her blue hair. "What's the emergency?"

Blake cringed. He didn't think he would have to explain what he suspected. "I think Kat has compelled Leila..."

Bianca waited.

"...into liking me."

"Uh-huh. Danny said you were a good friend—I know, I was surprised, too. Give yourself a little more credit." She cocked her head. "Wait. Are we talking about *friendship* here, Blake?"

Blake rubbed his face. "No."

Bianca's eyebrows rose. "Oh," was all she said. She was polite enough not to say anything else.

"I need to figure this out. And I need Danny with me."

"Yes, *go*, I'll look after Leila." Bianca took off her mittens and winter coat. "Whatever it is, Kat needs to be stopped. She's gotten away with too much."

Blake nodded, pocketing his car keys. He couldn't synthesize his rage into proper thought but Bianca was right.

"I'm sorry," he said. Bianca caught his shoulder.

"I know."

Apologize all you want, the traitorous part of him said, *the damage has already been done.*

BLAKE

Blake was going to get answers. He didn't care how.

Danny drove, silent as he concentrated on the needle-sharp turns of the forest path. He was always a better driver than Blake, and they sped through the mountains quickly. They spoke in necessities, only responding in need-to-know. The Vessel of Hades didn't want to think about how deteriorated his friendship with Danny was—he could only solve one problem at a time.

They parked outside of Anvil Automations and Blake couldn't help but think of the last time he'd been there with his best friend, the summer full of promise as they picked up his McLaren GT.

Now, in the blue of winter, Blake looked at the Vessel of Hermes, the wave of his hair meeting the collar of his olive wool coat so only his brow was exposed. But Blake knew Danny like the back of his own hand, and he could tell by the pinched set of his shoulders his thoughts had to have wandered back to last summer too.

The glass garage doors were closed and foggy with humidity, the sound of mechanical work and jovial shouting hitting him as they entered. Blake wasn't worried about being ratted out here, Arnold didn't care for upholding the Myth's laws. They strode in to his office without obstruction, finding the Vessel of Hephaestus at his desk, a pencil stuck behind his ear.

"Blake," he said, surprised. "Didn't think I'd see you for another couple of months."

"I need your help." Blake cut through the invitation for small talk. He didn't have time. "I need to speak with your wife."

Arnold gave a reflexive frown, putting his papers down. Blake had never known his wife so he had no clue what their relationship was like. Whatever happened between them had changed Arnold, made him harder, colder.

"Why?"

This was the problem, the shame of explanation. Even though Arnold wasn't interested in any gossip, Blake still wanted the man's respect. Falling for a love spell was laughable in every sense and only fueled Blake's self-loathing even more.

"I need advice," Blake sighed. "To help break—*undo*...love magic."

Arnold's eyebrows lifted, then he took a sheet from a legal pad and scribbled something down. He tore the piece of paper and handed it to Blake.

"The first line is her address and her doorman," he said, placing the pencil back behind his ear. "The next is her favorite Chinese order. That's your ticket in the door."

"OK." Blake scanned the sheet before sticking it into his overcoat. "Thanks, Arnold."

"Don't mention it." He paused. "Don't mention me to her, please. And I'm hoping we can talk after the spring equinox?"

Blake nodded and with that he was off, Danny calling the order in.

"Need a hand?"

Blake turned to see Bart behind him, wiping grease from his hands. The young Vessel of Ares had to have some knack for turning up at the wrong place at the right time.

"I think we're good, thanks," Blake dismissed. Bart had been there at the solstice, yet there wasn't that anger he'd seen on Leila's other friends.

"If the Prince of Death is trying to get a certain reclusive redhead to speak to him, don't you think you would want to bring her boyfriend along?"

Of course, he pinched the bridge of his nose. *Ares, Aphrodite,*

Hephaestus all tangled up in each other.

"And what do you want?" Blake asked.

Bart shrugged, his smile a knife's edge. "I heard you were ordering Chinese. I'm hungry."

"Done," Danny said hastily. Blake wasn't going to question Danny on his decision so he shrugged.

Thirty minutes later, Blake sat on Alicia's plush sofa while the other boys moved around the kitchen. The smell of noodles and moo shu pork permeated the beautiful space. Alicia sat across from him looking like a Hollywood starlet out of time. Her red curls offset her pink skin and the robin egg blue cashmere sweater she wore.

"You know Camille will kill me if I talk to you?" This was the first thing she'd said since Blake finished explaining his problem.

"I'm here because I'm trying to help Leila," Blake replied.

Alicia narrowed her eyes at him. "If I'm going to tell you what you want to know, I get to ask about Arnold."

"I—" Blake sputtered but Alicia put up a hand.

"That's the deal."

"Fine," Blake said. He would have agreed to practically anything at this point.

"Love spells are the worst power we have," Alicia sighed. "To manufacture love isn't just tasteless and illegal—but morally wrong. I can't imagine any of Aphrodite's Vessels stooping to spell a ring like that."

"So if it's not a love spell then what is it?"

"I didn't say it *wasn't* a love spell. I said I doubt any of my Vessels would do that. A Vessel of Hecate like your girlfriend, well..."

Alicia accepted the plate of food from Bart. "Thank you, Bartie," she cooed. It was a genuinely sweet moment he had to look away from before he sunk deeper into despair.

"You need to break it, *soon*," Alicia warned.

"Why?"

Alicia popped a piece of orange chicken in her mouth and chewed daintily. "Love spells are delicate, they can deteriorate easily into something uglier. Because true love can never be recreated—not sustainably. Once can mask the spell's weakness by disguising it as infatuation or admiration or even obsession. Poor Leila."

"How do you break it then?" Blake asked desperately.

Alicia looked at him now, really looked at him. There was something heavy pulling at her features, an ugly sorrow holding on to her.

"You only have to take off the ring," she started. "But Blake, it might break her heart. Truly, *truly* break it. That'll ruin your relationship —whatever it may be. Love spells are a curse."

BLAKE

The three boys entered the estate, not bothering to kick off the snow packed on their shoes.

"Blake," Leila ran out from the entryway and Blake could see tear streaks on her face. Bianca followed behind her, concern etched on her face. "Where did you go? You were gone for so long."

She held on to him, her tears soaking his shirt. He couldn't embrace her back knowing that this wasn't how she felt—not truly.

You're just like her mom, treating her like a doll.

"I missed you," her voice broke.

"Don't cry," he soothed. He nodded at Danny who led the others to the kitchen, giving them space.

"You left me." Her voice was muffled, her face buried in his chest.

He sighed, knowing there was only more pain to come.

Once, when he was younger, he dislocated his finger. There wasn't any help for him at the estate and he couldn't drive yet. The pain in his hand had made it almost impossible for him to read the first aid book, the wrongness of his limp index dangling out of its socket made his stomach turn.

Nothing prepared him for the pain of setting it back into place.

Danny came behind him and handed him a glass of water, then retreated back to the kitchen. Blake was thankful he had at least a little privacy for what he was about to do.

"Here," he stepped back to hand her the glass. "Drink this.

You're dehydrated."

She sniffled but took the drink dutifully.

While she drank, Blake took a deep breath and braced himself for what he had to do.

"I'm sorry, Leila," he began. "I know I have too many things to be sorry for but I want you to know I'm sorry all the same."

"What do you mean?" she said after she finished the glass. He took it and put it down.

"Kat spelled the ring you're wearing to make you...love me. Nothing you feel for me is real."

Leila frowned. "I don't believe that."

Blake tried to reassure her. "I'm going to break the spell and you won't have to cry over me anymore."

"No," Leila stepped closer to him, laying her delicate fingers on his neck. "That's *bullshit*. I know how I feel. *I love*—"

"Leila, don't say it," Blake interrupted, his calm slipping. "It's the ring speaking."

Leila held onto him harder, making him look at her in her soft brown eyes. "No, you're wrong, *you're wrong*. I love you because I just do. *Why don't you believe me?*"

"It's not real, Leila. Take off the ring and tell me and then I'll believe you."

"No. I don't even care if you don't love me back. You're not going to leave me again!"

I can't do this again. All I do is hurt you.

He didn't want to hear any more of the conversation, every word felt like a taunt. He grabbed Leila's face, gently pushing the hair behind her ears. Her lips trembled and she held her hands around her ringed finger protectively.

"I'm sorry," was all he said before he blinked black, his powers wrapping around the ring and pulling it free from her finger.

"No!" she yelled, strangled around a sob. Her eyes rolled back and the combination of the spell breaking around her and the sedative Danny had put in her water knocked her out. Blake caught her as she fell. He carried her to her bed, pulling the covers over her shoulders and brushing the hair out of her face one last time. The peony at her bedside had opened up slightly and Blake didn't feel any better about being proved right.

He came back out, the other Vessels sitting around the marble counter in the kitchen.

"She should be out for a couple of hours," he told Bianca. "We'll be back long before then."

He straightened his coat, his eyes still black from corner to corner, the rage he'd kept in check was slowly boiling over. Bart and Danny followed as he passed.

"Wait," the Vessel of Iris turned. "You're leaving again?"

"I have a ring to return."

BLAKE

The ring burned in his pocket. For the second time in a day, Danny drove down the mountain at breakneck pace on the thieve's road. His car was made to look invisible, run-down, but underneath was a hand-built engine that could rival most sports cars.

It was tense in the car, Bart's jovial mood gone. Blake turned to the boy in the backseat who was grey as a ghost.

"We're gonna drop you off at Arnold's before we go to Kat's," he said.

"No way, I'm coming," he argued. "This may not be my fight, but I'm gonna help you finish it."

"I'm not going to fight her, I need to know why she's doing all of this. Kat's not exactly..." He struggled with a way to describe Kat.

"Smart?" Danny answered.

"I was going to say *ambitious*. She's not one to plan things. I want to know why she poisoned me and all those other Vessels."

"Then you need an interrogator." Blake could see the flash of steel as Bart pulled out a knife.

"Can you please keep the weapons away while I'm driving?" Danny said, exasperated.

Bart pocketed the butterfly knife easily. "I missed almost a whole day of work, at least let me come along so the whole day isn't wasted."

They drove to the small apartment complex Blake had basically lived in over the summer. Most of the tenants were students from North

New Olympus High with some college students overlapping. The red lights in Kat's windows were on, the curtains drawn. Sounds of parties raging reminded him painfully of all the nights he'd thrown away being blacked out, doing anything he could to numb himself.

"We don't have to do this," Danny said as he locked the car.

"I do." He stopped and turned. The day felt so long already yet it was barely sunset, the sky an icy gold. He looked up to the Vessel of Hermes. "Danny, I—"

"Blake, stop, you don't have to say anything. Really." Danny gave him an easy sly grin, reminding him of when they were kids.

"You didn't know what I was going to say," he scoffed.

"I do, believe me. If you want to prove you're sorry then buy me breakfast at Barry's Diner come springtime."

Blake nodded, relief washing over him.

They made it to Kat's door. Music blared from different apartments, Vessels hung out in hallways, and plastic cups passed around them.

"I told you, you need me." Bart grinned, stepping between them. He was shorter than both of them but they got out of his way. Most locks were warded against Vessel magic—but not brute strength.

His eyes flashed red before he kicked the door down, the thick wood falling with a heavy thud. He gave a mock curtsy and Blake stepped inside.

The crowd in Kat's apartment was all familiar faces, the Vessels who frequented the same parties as him. He never knew them, they were a gallery of blurry memories he'd mistaken for friendship.

"Leave." His eyes were black. In his recovery, he'd realized any emotion he had when he was poisoned paled in comparison to the true feeling. The anger simmering in him was overwhelming, lashing against him to break out.

The crowd thinned, Kat was left on the couch, her eyes wide. The neon lights continued to whirl, the music hypnotic and grating against the other apartments' own party music.

"Blake," she said. She'd lost that luminous quality he'd always seen in her; she looked dulled, faded yellow like an old photograph. Kat didn't seem surprised he'd shown up.

"Why?" Blake asked.

"Why what?" She lifted her glass to her lips.

Blake had no patience, he flicked his hand and the drink went flying across the room, crashing into the wall.

"Rude," she said with a sigh. "So you found my little present? You moved on quick, but then again, the Myth makes fools of all of us."

"The note was clever," Blake replied. "The cat face? Not so much."

"This way!" someone shouted from the hallway.

"Apparently some people are looking for you, Bart," Kat said. "I thought it was a good idea to make sure they knew who your new friends were."

Heavy footsteps approached. Danny gave Blake a look and he understood. His shadows grabbed Kat's wrists and the four of them strode to her room. He pushed her to the opposite wall while Danny and Bart barricaded the door with a dresser.

Kat's room stunk of her candy perfume and was heavy with memories. She moved far away from him, laughing at the chaos around her. Blake stepped closer.

"Was this a game, Kat? Was this all a big, fucked-up game?"

"I thought you'd like it, you had fun, right? Tell me, when did you figure it out? Before or after you slept together?"

Blake powers, rising with his anger, cuffed her hand to the wall.

"You think you can kill me?" Kat sneered. "I know Hades' Vessels don't control death and those little tentacles don't scare me."

He cuffed her other hand so her arms were splayed. Shouts came from the other side, Bart's former associates making a meal out of the door. He didn't dare turn to see if they were OK, instead he stoked his fury like a bonfire.

"You're right, I'm not *Thanatos*—I'm not death personified. But that doesn't mean I have no dominion over the dead."

Kat's smile slipped a fraction as he raised his hand to her, the charmed ring in his fingers. His eyes fluttered closed and he felt the ring turn to ash in his hand. He wasn't destroying the ring exactly, only calling it back to the Underworld.

It's all the same in the end.

"Tell me what your motives are, not the *bullshit* you've been peddling since we got together."

Kat raised her chin and spit at his feet. "The only bullshit I've peddled is that I liked you. Good luck finding anyone to love you without my ring."

He was on her in a flash, her long, white hair in his fist. The clash behind him fell away, the Vessel of Hecate watched as he turned her hair to ash in front of her.

"Next will be your fingers," Blake ground out. It was hard to keep a hold of his power, like trying to keep a flame from consuming paper too quickly. Leila's face flashed in his mind—not the soft one who'd been spelled but the one in Athena's temple who'd looked at him with true revulsion. "*Speak.*"

Kat kept her eyes on her hair. "You can't have her, you know that, right? So you had to destroy her. The bracelets, the ambrosia, the ring. I needed you to destroy any chance with Leila, now let me *go!*"

"*Why?*" Distantly, he heard Danny and Bart shouting.

"*I don't know why, I just did what Dom said!*" she pleaded.

The name was a cold streak through him and his power retreated. She slipped to the ground, her hair a tattered mess, but her smirk remained.

"Your brother says hi, *Blakey,*" she laughed and the sound was high and cruel.

No, no, no, no, no.

"We need to go. *NOW!*" Danny grabbed Blake's shoulder and wrenched him across the room, Bart following behind. Danny opened the window and kicked out the screen.

"Are you mental, we're four *bloody* floors up!" Bart said.

"If you want to live, *hold on to me,*" Danny said. The window was big enough to fit all of them on the ledge. The makeshift barricade was cracking, fists and leather-clad arms reaching out of the disintegrating door. Kat still laughed, her jeers lost in the noise.

"Gods save me," Bart muttered.

Blake couldn't speak, he could only hold onto Danny's jacket. Distantly, he entertained the image of Danny's abilities failing and him plummeting into the distant bushes. Danny was a Vessel of Hermes, one of the only to actually be gifted with the *talaria*—the winged sandals. The strain of the extra weight on Danny made his flight more of a slowed fall. They sailed above the street, landing hard against the car's side, their shoes slipping in the snow.

They scrambled inside, the tires screeching as they peeled out, turning back to the mountains. Their dissolved brotherhood wasn't as dead as Blake thought; Danny was always a better friend than Blake thought he deserved.

"Your brother says hi, Blakey."

There were other memories that surfaced when he went through the ambrosia withdrawals, memories he thought he'd forgotten. Of a Vessel walking through his nightmares like a spectre, who dogged his steps. Of a terror he thought was out of his life.

"What the *fuck* was that?" Bart panted, looking back as the city faded behind them.

"I don't know," Danny replied. "Blake, what did she say?"

Blake shook his head. Repeating what she'd said would be like a summoning and he didn't want to corporealize his growing suspicions. Not yet.

"Blake?" Danny repeated.

"Drive," Blake said. "It's not over yet."

Danny nodded, turning back to the road. The car sped up, crossing into the dark pines of the mountains. The night was upon them and the thieve's road offered no protection from what loomed in the dark. Blake concentrated on enveloping the car in darkness and hoping nothing was too hungry for them. Even Bart kept quiet. Even the most powerful Vessels knew they had nothing over the ancient creatures who called this forest home.

They parked in front of the estate and Blake ran in with the others close behind. The wrongness gnawing at Blake would only be dispelled when he could see Leila was OK.

"Hello?" Bianca yelled from somewhere in the darkened mansion. *"Danny? Blake? Over here!"*

They sprinted through the house, finding Bianca in a chair in the library, her wrists bound by a trailing plant.

Danny knelt next to her with Bart on the other side with a knife and got to work on the thick vine ensnaring her arms.

Bianca looked at Blake, panicked. "The sedative didn't work—I don't know why—and she trapped me. She kept saying she needed to go, she said it hurt too much and there was only one way to get there?

Blake, I'm sorry, I don't know where she is! *Find her!*"

Blake ran through the house, her words echoing through him. Cerby whined at the door to the grounds. The Vessel of Hades' stomach dropped, Leila's intention clear. He hoped he wasn't right, again and again as he trudged through the snow, he hoped he wasn't right.

He made it to the dark pond, the portal to the Underworld, the surface still rippling.

Blake had just missed her.

BIANCA

Bianca was back across from Anvil Automations dropping Bart off like they had done only two weeks ago. She felt awful leaving but she couldn't follow Blake into the Underworld, into a place mortals couldn't trespass. Though it killed her to admit it, she was in over her head.

They'd stayed at the mansion until dawn, the morning a blue storm.

"Well, let's pray I've still got a job after this, Ares help me," Bart said as he got out of the backseat.

"Tell Arnold we kidnapped you," Danny said.

"Will do, mate. See you later, B." He waved at Bianca.

"Bye, Bartie," she called and saw him stick out his tongue. As soon as he entered the dim mechanic's shop, her nerves shot through the roof.

"She's going to be fine. I know you might not believe it but Blake is going to bring her back," Danny said gently.

"How do you know?" She looked at the Vessel of Hermes. For so long all she'd known about him was that he was this jittery, lanky boy. His eyes were the same shade of red-brown as his hair and they glittered with a whole life hidden away.

Tell me your secrets, she wanted to ask.

"He and Hades have a different relationship than a lot of other Vessels. He's been to the Underworld before—"

"What?" How could a mortal come back from the Underworld unscathed? How could a Vessel be so close to their god?

"I don't know much, but I have to trust him."

They sat in the parked car and Bianca felt like this was one of the only places she could be so vulnerable, so open. Everywhere else she had to be perfect.

"If Blake doesn't let me know he's OK within twenty-four hours then we'll have a problem."

Bianca pursed her lips, she didn't like it at all. It was all out of her control, too much could go wrong.

Too much has gone wrong.

Danny grabbed her hand. "I promise, I'll tell you as soon as I know anything."

He gave her a small smile and her heart fluttered. Bianca was taken aback at how Danny could make her feel like the sun; it was something that didn't fit into any of her schedules or plans.

"Wow," he exclaimed. The car's interior was bathed in rainbows, a kaleidoscope of colors. She reined in her powers and let go of his hand, her cheeks on fire.

"Let's go," she said hastily. Usually she didn't let her powers slip out like this; everyone used to make fun of her when she was happy and rainbows danced from the ceiling in class or at parties.

Danny didn't say anything else, and Bianca was glad he was driving, at least to keep his eyes off her face. The city was beautiful this time of year, even in the early morning. The snow on the ground, the glow of solstice lights on the trees.

He kept on the road parallel to the Styx, the rough waters reminding her where her friend was.

Iris keep her safe, she prayed.

There was a difference between sending a prayer and getting an answer back. Bianca couldn't help but wonder how Blake had managed to keep a conversation with a god.

They parked in the student parking lot in front of the upperclassmen dormitory.

"I know I need to sleep, but I can't," Danny said, shutting the car off. "I might get in line for brunch, I might actually have a shot at getting some French toast this time. The only time I got French toast it had pumpkin in it and I'm not a fan. You know there's—"

"Wait," Bianca interrupted.

"Sorry," Danny blushed. "I still have this bad habit of rambling. Honestly, I think I'm growing out of it."

"No, it's not that. Danny, you're not freaked out at all?"

"About Blake? Of course I am, I just know he's going to be

OK."

"How?"

Danny didn't answer right away. "I told you I trust him."

"You told me you *had* to trust him. There's a lot that's not adding up about you—I mean, how did you learn to drive like this? Why do you have a car like this?" Bianca could feel herself getting more emotional, maybe it was better to focus on this instead of the horror of losing Leila. "I'm not stupid, Danny."

Danny pocketed his keys and shook his head. "No, you're not." He took a deep breath. "Look, I can't tell you everything for a lot of reasons, one of them being this isn't my story to tell. All I can say is Blake and I have been through *way* worse than this. If we can make it this far, we can make it through anything."

Bianca took this in. "That's not exactly an answer."

"I know, I'm sorry. I'll tell you the rest someday."

That felt like a promise she wanted to keep.

"But first, brunch?" she asked, ready to stave off the feeling of losing control—at least for one meal.

BLAKE

Stepping through the portal felt a lot like coming home—a part of Blake's soul always felt the tug of the Underworld and being here was like he could finally catch his breath. There wasn't much to bring with him, including Cerby. He would feel too left out at home.

The Underworld was the same as he left it, the world in purples and oranges like an inverted photograph. Expansive plains rose into hills and eventually mountains. The portal didn't drop him right in front of the palace where the God of the Underworld resided—time and space bubbled and broke around him and he was never deposited in the same place. The Hades part of him could find his way fairly easy but he didn't know where he had to go to find Leila.

Stay away from me.

He said that to her the same night Leila had come to New Olympus. At least in that state he had some sense to try and push her away. Everything he touched was stained.

Blake stood in waves of wheat, looking for some sign of life. Cerby bounded ahead, overwhelmed at being back, his tongues lolling out of his mouths.

Where are you, Leila?

He sighed, the only thing he knew was how much he wanted to sink down in the soft fields and make a meal for the carrion harpies passing shadows overhead. He'd rather take Sisyphus' place than face his own god but he could not avoid Hades any longer. They were more than overdue to catch up.

Blake tore at the wheat and blew his powers over the falling kernels, magic twisting and turning them into metal and wood, stretching into the spun gold of a chariot. The ground shook as Cerby padded over, taking his true monstrous form, his eyes smoking red and his hackles raised. Each of his mouths dripping saliva over elongated fangs, lips curled back in a growl. Blake's magic attached the chariot to his collar and Cerby was off, racing over the plains, pulling Blake at a breakneck speed.

He wasn't scared of falling off and dying, not here. Not in his own home.

LEILA

The Underworld wasn't like she'd thought: a miasmic damp cave full of the screams of tortured souls. But she couldn't take in any of her surroundings, not when her heart *hurt*. Everything could've been ash for all she cared.

The portal dropped her at the top of a rolling hill shadowed by a range of umber mountains. The numbing cold of winter was gone and the air was mild and smelled like autumn. Her heart was an open wound and she went to her knees, the last of her strength gone.

Persephone, let me sleep, she said, her body heavy and her mind sluggish. The sedative Blake gave her must finally be kicking in.

Leila woke in a bed, red silk sheets curled in her fists. Her mind took a second to recall everything that happened but when it hit her, she curled in on herself, tears flowing freely. A logical part of her knew the sorrow she felt was manufactured, a side effect of breaking whatever spell she'd been under. But every other part of her grieved the love taken from her.

"*Shh,*" a voice said above her, gentle hands stroking her hair. Leila couldn't raise her head as the sobs racked through her. "*Let it out, Leila-joon.*"

Leila dear, an endearing term from a life before and one she didn't realize she'd been longing to hear.

"Drink this," the voice said, bringing her up to a sitting position. She raised her eyes to see the goddess Persephone sitting on the bed next to her. She had a young face, beautiful rosy cheeks and full pink lips, but her eyes were like the sun of spring eternal. Her hair flowed down her back and onto the floor, braided with flowers of all kinds. A gold circlet rested on her brow, gold vines with ruby pomegranates.

The actual goddess was in front of her, not a voice in her head or the caress of a warm breeze, but *Persephone* was here.

The goddess held a delicate gold bowl up to Leila's lips and distantly Leila worried if this counted as food and if it was a trap to keep her down here.

"It's medicine," Persephone said with a sad smile, "for your heart."

Leila drank the dark liquid, the minty concoction soothing its way down her throat. When she was finished, Persephone put the bowl on the elegant side table and folded her arms over her flowing robes. The tension Leila felt in her chest eased a bit.

"Why did you come down here, *Leila-joon?*"

"I didn't know where else to go," Leila said. *I panicked.*

"The Underworld is not safe for mortals to travel alone. Why didn't you ask Blake to bring you?"

Leila fell silent.

"Well, he followed you anyway and he's going to bring you back —"

"No!" Leila shot forward, grasping at Persephone's sleeves. "Please, can't I stay here?"

Persephone tilted her head in confusion.

"I can't go back, not yet," Leila pleaded. The medicine soothed her pain but she knew it would come back, the feeling of being ripped apart. She couldn't live with this wound, she didn't want to feel so hurt ever again.

Blake's lips, his hands, his love. Hours before, he was the center of her universe, the only thing she cared about. It was scary, the obsession ravaging through her gone. She was hollow and out of orbit.

Lost.

"The feeling will pass, Leila, I promise. Remember you're a fighter."

You keep telling me. Leila didn't have the courage to say that to the goddess's face so she just nodded.

"I chose *you* as my Vessel. My husband knows I don't make

decisions lightly or without reason."

It was odd to hear her speak of her husband like he wasn't the ruler of the Underworld. The goddess tipped Leila's chin up to hers. She could feel the magic thrumming in her fingertips, a twin to her own. "The Fates will test you, but heroes are always tested. A broken heart will mend—and beat stronger."

Leila took a deep, shuddering breath. "You're right." The goddess was always right. The fear and shame and embarrassment churning in her stomach at the thought of having to see Blake again quieted down as she held Persephone's hand.

"We have to wait a while before you can leave, so I thought you might like to bathe and change." The goddess got up and Leila realized her form was larger than that of a normal mortal.

"Why do we have to wait?" she said. Maybe the portal only functioned at night. The stained glass windows of the chambers didn't help indicate if it was morning or night.

"Blake and Hades are not going to be done screaming at each other for a while."

BLAKE

Blake's voice was hoarse from yelling. Hades was in his element and could keep arguing for eternity. The god of the dead stalked closer to Blake, his fur cape trailing. Blake didn't retreat, standing his ground.

"You think I *misunderstood* what happened? *I ALMOST KILLED HER. HADES, I ALMOST DIED.*" His bellows echoed off the throne room's vaulted ceilings.

Persephone always said they were cut from the same cloth and Blake could see that. Not in looks, though they both shared the same pallor and dark hair. Hades' hair was an inky curtain and he was bedecked in so many jewels he'd have to have superhuman strength to keep himself standing. His long fingers itched at the sword at his side—a sword taller than Blake himself.

"*DO NOT BE INSOLENT WITH ME, BOY,*" Hades shouted back.

They both had the same stubborn set of their chin, their quick temper, and were pessimistic verging on self-loathing. Of course whenever they saw each other it devolved into a shouting match.

It's like screaming at a mirror and a brick wall at the same time.

Blake felt the exhaustion of being awake for almost two days straight. A tightness in his back and a dull ache behind his eyes made it hard to focus. As soon as Persephone had told him Leila was sleeping off the sedative and was safe, he'd been waiting to leave and return to the mortal realm.

Persephone had left them to catch up—she knew better than to intervene. The air crackled with their respective powers. The throne room had seen many of these fights, and Blake noticed Hades had never fixed the crack in the marble spanning the left wall from the last time he visited. He didn't know if it was supposed to make Blake feel guilty or was a point of pride like a father showing off his kid's artwork. Not that Hades was his father in any way.

"My Vessels aren't barbaric enough to plot against each other," Hades said in a steely voice. This was the crux of the issue, the thing they danced around for hours as Blake caught his god up on what happened since Leila came to New Olympus. Since he'd met Kat.

My Vessels are better than that, was the excuse Hades gave every time. He refused to believe anything Blake said against Dominic. It used to make Blake feel crazy, now it made him tired.

"I'm done trying to convince you," Blake said quietly. He looked down at his shoes on the black marble. He could see an outline of his reflection, the deep purple under his eyes, the tips of his curly hair. "You asked me what happened and I told you what I know."

Hades looked away, obviously trying not to start shouting again. "I'm disappointed you could think of your brother this way, when he comes back I'll make sure to ask him of his involvement—and you'll regret doubting him."

He's not my brother, Blake thought insolently. Vessels from the same god weren't related but for some reason this relationship was forced on him—maybe it was the closeness in age. Maybe it was a strategy to instigate friendship. It didn't work.

"Of course," he said, deflated. He was alone, even his god didn't believe him, leaving him for the wolves camouflaged as sheep.

"You must know he has to be jealous, you *are* my most powerful Vessel. I would like to think you're the most powerful in the city."

Power-less, Blake bitterly corrected in his mind. What was power without result?

"And the Fates brought Leila to you," Hades continued, turning back to his obsidian throne. "An auspicious gift, if you were to accept it."

Blake blinked, scoffing at Hades' words.

What?

Before Blake could begin to gather his thoughts, the gargantuan throne doors rumbled open behind him and the goddess Persephone glided in with unnatural grace. Trailing behind her was Leila, dressed like a mortal queen and glowing under all her gold.

Fates, he rubbed his face, a weight lifting off of him at the sight of her, safe. What he would give to know what else the Fates had in store for him.

LEILA

Leila held the skirts of her dress as she stood at the base of the palace, saying goodbye to her goddess. Tears stung her eyes when she was wrapped in Persephone's embrace. She was a child again in her arms.

"I'll always be with you. You're never alone, remember," Persephone whispered in her ear.

They stood on one of the large terraces looking out to the palace gardens. Leila wanted nothing more than to explore the nearly endless mazes and greenhouses. It was so long since she'd been around plants, even in the realm of the dead she could feel the vibrancy of *life*. The terrace's floor featured an intricate mosaic of a pomegranate and Leila guessed it was the portal back to New Olympus.

Blake and Hades still stalked each other like angry cats, giving each other the same glare and brusque hug. Hades was a study of terrible beauty, all diamond-sharp cheekbones and upturned mouth. He commanded the Underworld with a word and yet Blake turned his back on him.

Then Persephone wrapped him up, showering the Vessel of Hades with kisses. Hades turned to Leila, taking her hand.

"Leila," his voice was deep and his focus was solely on her. It was unnerving. "I do hope the remainder of your winter is more enjoyable than the beginning."

Leila stared back, unsure how he meant *enjoyable*. "Thank you."

"When the time comes, it will become your favorite season."

OK...Leila gave a polite smile and let his cool lips graze the back of her hand.

Blake, Leila, and a normal-sized Cerby stepped through the portal, and Leila wondered if she'd ever see the Underworld again in her lifetime.

They were hit with the harsh reality of being deposited back into a snowstorm. Even Leila's gifted layers of skirts and embroidered robes didn't do much to help against the oncoming storm. After hurrying inside, they faced each other, suddenly aware they were alone again.

"I—" she said as he opened his mouth to speak.

"Go ahead," he said.

"You first," Leila replied. What was she going to say anyway?

Blake rubbed his eyes. "Can I show you something?"

Leila nodded and followed Blake as he walked through the mansion to the east side of the house, to the double doors that had been locked since she'd arrived. Blake grabbed a key ring from his pocket and unlocked the door. He didn't step inside but motioned her to look. She peered around the door, and saw the twin layout to her rooms. Except this room was completely trashed: the bed gutted, sheets shredded, furniture broken to splinters, glass strewn on the floor, holes in the walls.

As she looked at the room Blake spoke softly, "this was my room. This was Dominic's present to me when he found out he was studying abroad."

"Who's Dominic?" A chill ran down her back looking at the destruction. Everything was meticulously broken beyond recognition. This was more than a fit of rage, this was calm and precise and so much worse.

"My brother." Blake put his hands up when he saw her face. "Not really, but he is the other Vessel of Hades. He...did stuff like this for fun. That's why I think he was responsible for the bracelets and the ambrosia."

"Why?"

Blake looked down. "I don't know."

There was a silence and Leila turned away from the mess, the image of a younger Blake crystallizing in her mind. "I can help clean this up."

He was tired and gave a small shake of his head. "I want to keep it, for now at least. I know it's weird but this is the only proof I have Dominic actually...did something. He's careful not to leave scars."

Leila couldn't breathe, her fists clenched at her sides. Fury and sorrow raged for the little boy left unprotected.

"Leila, it's not that bad," Blake backtracked, his cheeks coloring. "See, I have a power in the Underworld, where if I die there, I come back—he wouldn't do anything that could get himself in trouble—"

"How do you know? What did he do to you?"

Blake exhaled a long breath. "The first time was an accident."

How many more times?

Leila was pacing, Blake following behind her. Hot, angry tears ran down her face. There was a whole ocean of pain swirling in his grey eyes, memories of whatever torture he'd experienced shared in those few words. Blake's power over death could only be taken advantage of by a complete sociopath.

How many invisible scars do you carry?

Blake cringed. "Wait! I'm sorry, I know this is a lot—"

Leila scraped her tears away with the sleeve of her robe. "Don't apologize, please. You don't have to say sorry—I can't believe someone would be that cruel."

Blake's face shadowed as he ducked his head. "No one does."

"I do. I believe you." *And if I ever see Dominic I'm going to kill him.* "I'm sorry."

"It's not a big deal." Blake coughed. "I guess I learned from the best." He gave a sad smile. He meant the torture, he meant the way he'd tormented her when the watch deteriorated his sanity. How much of what he'd done to her did he go through with Dominic? Leila fought the urge to march back into the Underworld and make Hades beg for an apology. To start.

"Please don't cry over me," Blake said.

"It's not right," Leila said, looking up. She could still feel the sting of heartbreak though it was easier to dismiss now.

"I know," he said. He sighed, wiping his nose. "Can I show you something else? It won't make you cry, I promise." He stood up taller, shaking away the memories.

Leila gave a shaky laugh. "Sure. If you promise."

"You need to change then. Bundle up."

LEILA

Leila muttered to herself as she changed out of Persephone's dress and robes. She only got to wear it for a couple of hours and felt like it deserved to be worn in a ballroom, not hanging in her closet. She pulled on a pair of leggings, then another, and then layered shirts and a sweatshirt before zipping up a long winter coat worthy of an Arctic expedition. She threw on a scarf and her New Prep beanie, laced up her winter boots, and went out onto the grounds.

She found the Vessel of Hades on the third level of the terraced garden. He had a shovel and was making quick work of clearing the snow from a patch of ground. The snow had stopped but the sky was still threatening and dark.

"Oh my gods," she said when she reached him, "this is where you bury me."

He side-eyed her. "Not a chance. I have a feeling this is where it's going to come up." His breath came out in a heavy cloud.

Leila kept her hands stuffed in her pockets, angry she forgot out of everything. "Where *what* is going to come up?"

All she got was a mischievous grin as Blake picked at the earth. Cerby yelped, excited at the commotion.

"One," Blake panted, "*quirky* thing Hades' Vessels can do is...well, I don't know how to describe it...I guess we're stone magnets?"

"What?"

The shovel broke through the frozen ground and Blake dropped to his knees and started digging with his bare hands. Leila crouched too, the snow soaking through the layers of her leggings.

"Jewels, stones, precious metals—I don't know why but they come through the ground and I can find them," Blake said.

"That's so weird. What's coming now?"

"No idea." He had the hint of a smile on his face and even in the cold, sweat beaded on his brow from the effort of digging. Leila joined in, the feeling of soil almost foreign to her after so long. It was painfully cold, her fingers numb in seconds.

"So you just find diamonds in the ground?" She was warming as she worked.

"I've yet to find a diamond. Got a hunk of amethyst as big as Cerby once— well a mini Cerby. Dominic found a chunk of gold the size of a golf ball."

Leila's hands stilled in the earth at the mention of his name. Blake's fingers found hers.

"Sorry," he said. "I didn't mean—"

He stopped talking as they both felt their magic respond to the touch. His eyes went black and waves of his power rolled over him. She suddenly felt the heat of spring rush through her body, shooting down her fingers into the ground. Their powers reacted without their control. The ground rumbled, making Cerby whine.

They both looked at each other with the same *what just happened* expression. Leila felt the change, the ground below becoming *alive.*

"The soil," Leila gasped. "It's different."

"Different how?" Blake blinked his eyes back and they were the same snowy grey as the sky.

"I don't know how to explain it, but I think things can grow now." She looked out to the expanse of the grounds. Right now there was nothing, but soon the season would change. A million possibilities bloomed in her mind.

Potential.

"Look," Blake breathed. She looked down at the ground and in the shallow hole they'd dug, something was sticking up.

They both lunged for it, scrambling their hands around the clear stone sticking out of the ground. After a couple of minutes of more digging and pulling, they unearthed the mineral structure. It was almost as big as Cerby, a jagged formation of clear obelisks sticking out like a crystal crown.

"Is it a diamond?" Leila asked.

"Clear quartz."

Oh. Leila blushed, feeling stupid.

They hauled it up the slope to the house.

They were both out of breath carrying the heavy crystal, and Leila plopped down, exhausted. She huffed a laugh looking out over the grounds and the white-tipped evergreens beyond.

Blake sat on the other side of Leila, dirt on his face but his eyes bright. "What's so funny?"

"It's just," Leila struggled to describe the lightness she felt, "I keep thinking I'm going to get used to this and I don't. I hope I don't."

Magic is real, she thought. It thrummed through her, around her. Even in the bleakest winter, magic took root.

BART

Bart, by some miracle from Ares himself, still had a job. It was hard work, a steep learning curve, and long hours, but Bart loved it.

As he walked out of the shop, he felt a friendly clap on his shoulder from one of his coworkers.

"Hey, bundle up, baldie!"

"Yeah, yeah," he said to the older man. Bart was the youngest and newest, and the other mechanics never let him forget it, griping at him about everything like grandmothers. He grabbed his beanie from the rack of coats and put it on. He was on his morning break and didn't have much to do but walk down to the quiet corner store to buy gum or smokes.

The above the door dinged and he appreciated the stuffy warmth. His cheeks and nose were probably flushed pink from the cold. He worked his way down the crammed aisles, stopping in front of the snack display. Arnold had no imagination in terms of snacks and Bart was craving something cheesy and processed.

"Hi Bartie," a voice called from the end of the aisle.

Fear, cold and slick, slithered down his back. He knew that voice. He looked to see Cris, the leader of the SFNX gang, his former boss.

"I miss you," she said with a feline smile. She flicked her black hair behind her like she wasn't the most ruthless gang leader in the city.

He turned to spot her right-hand men standing at the other end of the aisle, cornering him.

"Hi, Cristina," he said, forcing as much politeness into his words even as adrenaline pumped through his body, screaming at him to *run*.

"In your *cowardice* you actually did me a favor, you know. You can grant me access where I need it most. How's Arnold?"

His stomach turned to stone, all hunger gone.

"Good," he mumbled.

Cris smiled sweetly. She hated Arnold; they both knew it. "Good. I want you to tell me everything he's doing. His business is *your* business now."

Bart couldn't breathe.

"You want to earn your wings back, don't you?"

The back of his neck burned where the sphinx tattoo sat. A creature with the head of a woman, the body of a lion, and a great span of wings. Every ranking member got the tattoo after proving themselves, after *earning their wings*.

If they survived.

He said nothing, his heart ringing an alarm in his ears.

"No," he said finally. "I won't do it."

She *tsked*, muttering a swear in Mandarin. He'd heard it enough to know what the gist of it meant: *idiot*.

"Do you know how easy it is to get up to Alicia's apartment? I mean, I know *you know*. But to bypass security, the doorman, and knock on her door. Do you know how easy that is?" Cris straightened out the collar of her trench as she spoke, as if she wasn't casually threatening her ex-girlfriend.

"Don't," Bart whispered. "Please, *don't*."

Cris looked at him, one Vessel of Ares to another. All the pretense was gone, only the naked strategy left on her angular face. She always had all the cards, he'd never truly escaped—she'd only let him go as far as it benefitted her.

"Get the intel. We'll be in contact."

She walked past him, and the rest of her men left, the store bell ringing and ringing. He stood there until he could convince his legs to work again.

He walked back to the mechanic's shop hastily, hands in his pockets. He entered, the whine of machinery making him jumpy, and he went to the side stairs, taking them two at a time. The roof's door sounded like a gunshot as it slammed behind him. His hands shook as he emptied his pockets, keys and receipts discarded for the lighter and a tattered box of smokes. He took a long drag of his cigarette, trying to figure out how completely *fucked* he was. He smoked the cigarette down to the filter and smashed it under his heel.

"Fuck, fuck, *FUCK!*"

There was no choice: betray Arnold for Cris or let Alicia get hurt. Why couldn't they have stuck him in the corner store? At least he could've chosen to bleed out like a hero instead of the rat they wanted him to be.

Bart tore the beanie off his head, crumpled it up in his hands and screamed into it. Within ten minutes his future was gone, he was back to being a grunt. He could feel angry tears sting his eyes. Then he threw the stupid beanie on the ground, sending the business card Danny had given him fluttering up.

"Light it up if you need me." Danny's words echoed through him like a lifeline. He bent down and grabbed the card stock, his fingers trembling as he flicked the lighter open. Hope drifted up in his chest. It was the kind of stupid, blind hope that that he thought had been beaten out of him in the SFNX's.

He watched the card burn to ash.

I went to war for you, he thought, *now you can go to war for me.*

LEILA

It was like a triple exposure, looking at Blake. There was the power-drunk, poisoned version of him, with the cruel twist of his mouth. Then there was the one she'd seen while love-spelled and sickly sweet version, soft-touched and tousled. Underneath both was a boy with grey eyes, a stranger to her still. She didn't trust herself to know him, but she wanted to.

The nightmares still cropped up; flashes of the watch's pain lacing through the phantom bracelet. And when she woke she reached for his form, though he wasn't there—a lingering muscle memory from the love spell. They'd only slept in each other's arms but for some reason that innocence felt more intimate than if they'd gone any farther.

Every week, Bianca asked her how she was doing.

"Good," she'd said. And every week she meant it more. Leila leaned into the monotony of routine. Walking Cerby in the morning, then homework, lunch, gardening until dinner, then painting. She even got through *Aesop's Fables* all by herself.

And Blake was there, showing up like she'd asked him after the solstice. There wasn't friendship yet, but a comfortable acquaintanceship.

Are we friends? She didn't know. They both stayed in the small boundaries they'd made for themselves.

But she didn't mind putting him to work in the garden—winter was losing its grip on the Hades estate. It was still cold but the snow had melted. And they had a lot of work to do. Blake stepped in line with all of Leila's plans as she took the reins. Many grueling afternoons of gardening were spent together. Every time Blake sensed some gemstone making its way up to them, he'd stop what he was doing and he would put it in her hand. Bubbly malachite and prickly silver and rainbow opal.

"Hold this," he'd say, plopping the gemstone in her palm, still covered in dirt. He said it every time he found one, and every time it made her laugh.

The grounds were too big to do all at once, so Leila put all her effort into what she could and used her magic not only to germinate but to last. Blake, had been right; there were no real monuments to what he'd gone through, other than a room ruined beyond recognition.

Even in between packing and getting ready for the spring equinox she tried to feed the rest of her magic into the small oasis she'd built. Leila wanted a different memory, something solid to show she'd *survived.*

Here is my mark, Leila declared. *Here I am.*

BLAKE

Of all the times over the years Blake had pleaded and prayed for spring to come quickly, this would be the year he'd get his wish granted. The little garden they'd planted was growing ever so slowly and Blake knew he'd be back at New Prep before he could see all their hard work in full bloom.

No matter his feelings, they'd both have to leave the mansion and go back to New Olympus and go back to their lives.

If he'd learned anything in the last six months, Leila didn't deserve to be held here. She was meant to flourish with her friends and live a full life.

Even the most irrational, selfish parts of him agreed, even if it left him a ghost again.

The car came for her the day of the spring equinox; her things were to be taken later. Blake would drive down tomorrow back to his dorm and return to school shortly after. He didn't want to think of school because he didn't want to think of the people they were outside of these walls.

I have a lot of rebuilding to do.

He was good at destroying things, he knew that. After years of being chipped at by his brother, he took over the task and got to work on himself. Blake was ready to turn his life to ash.

He didn't want to now.

A little too late.
Leila was already gone.

LEILA

They were back in Bianca and Min-Seo's dorm room. In some ways Leila felt like the last eight months weren't real, like she'd wake up in the field of wildflowers at any moment.

"Are you dying to come back to school?" Bianca asked as all three of them hurried around the room putting on earrings and strapping on their heels. They had way less time to get ready than the last equinox but Leila didn't care.

"Yeah, I'm sure she can't wait to be back in class to do homework," Minnie deadpanned.

Leila laughed. "I'm pretty sure I have at least a dozen tests I have to make up for. *Yay*."

A knock sounded on their door and suddenly the room was crowded with more friends. Leila was pulled into many, many hugs and she was so happy to see everyone she wanted to burst.

"Hey, can we try not to step on the lady's dress please?" Minnie scolded. For the shortest person in the room, she had the most commanding voice.

"How can we not? You're all dressed like cotton candy," Mason defended.

It did feel that way. Minnie was in an emerald tulle tea-length dress, with emerald sequined high-tops. The neckline was off the shoulder, her delicate collarbones and shoulders on display. Bianca's dress was the shortest—showing off her long brown legs—the purple-and-blue tulle puffed out like a cloud, and a jeweled headpiece sat on her coily hair. Leila was not surprised by the color of hers: a shimmering pink tulle gown. Regardless, she loved the beaded bodice that shifted between pink, gold, and green like a fractured kaleidoscope. The bodice was tight on top then flared out to a full skirt.

"I do feel like cotton candy," Leila agreed. She grabbed her matching wrap and draped it around her arms.

The boys were all in their own jewel tone suits, with assorted floral collars and boutonnières. Elliot hooked one arm in Leila's and the other in Bianca's. They made their way to the limo to take them to Zeus' temple.

I guess the mayor didn't find out about all our trespassing after all.

"I'm so glad you shaved that thing off your face," Leila pointed to Elliot's upper lip.

"Wow, you too?" Elliot glared. "My friends don't get me."

"We want the best for you, El," Harvey piped up. "That was *the worst.*"

"Was it even a mustache? It was five long hairs and sad," Oscar piled on.

Elliot's ocean eyes swirled angrily and he grumbled under his breath while the rest of them cackled. Leila bumped the Vessel of Poseidon's shoulder. The car ride was just as boisterous and crammed as the dorm but Leila wouldn't trade it for the world.

The temple was made into a verdant paradise: pillars lush with greenery and blooms everywhere. A sweet breeze lifted billowing silk banners that matched the sherbet sunset. They entered a crowd of people dancing to a full orchestra. Leila realized how little she'd been around people in so long and felt the familiar flutter of panic grip her.

Then Camille strode towards her and all her fear fell away. Camille wore head to toe gold: a gilded sheath dress and long gloves. She looked like the sun and gripped Leila fiercely, murmuring into her hair and rocking her from side to side. The Vessel of Persephone was reunited with her mother at last, and Leila could've kept hugging her for a long time. Camille broke away to hold Leila's face, her gold eyes searching.

"How was it? Are you OK?"

"Yes, I'm OK. It was boring," Leila said. "Really."

Elliot snorted into his drink and Mason gave him a shove. How they got drinks so quickly, Leila didn't know.

"I don't want to ever let you go." Camille squeezed her. "Oh look, it's Simon— from the senators council. I'll be back."

And off she went to socialize, and Leila was pulled to the dance floor by her friends. Last equinox, she was possessed by the need to have the time of her life before being whisked away to the mountains—like she *had* to have fun for the last time in six months. This equinox, she could breathe, knowing she had made it through, knowing in the end her friends were there for her and she was happy.

As the night wore on, the beauty of the ethereal temple started to feel stale. As she danced, she felt like someone was in her peripheral vision, or she turned to say something but she'd forgotten what it was— or who it was for. She declined champagne after champagne, instead drinking sparkling pomegranate juice. The magic of spring thrummed through her, making her feel more buoyed than any alcohol could.

Leila sat in one of the delicate gold chairs around the table her friends had grabbed for themselves, watching Mason and Oscar have a dance-off. Danny had snuck in a while ago and hadn't left Bianca's side since. He even wore a suit the same shade of periwinkle as her hair, though they danced far enough apart it made Leila wonder if he'd even done it on purpose.

She kicked her feet up on Minnie's lap; Athena's Vessel was catching her up on the school gossip—a subject she didn't realize Minnie had so much investment in. It was nice to sit back and *be*. To be around the Vessels she loved, the charged, living air of spring setting her alight.

Even if a piece of me is missing. She didn't want to admit it but it was true; there was a Blake-shaped part of her life missing at that moment. As soon as the thought crystallized, she couldn't dismiss it.

"You don't have to tie me up again, I can take a hint." Bianca sat next to Leila.

"What do you mean?" Leila mused.

"I can see it on your face. You know, Danny's parked not too far from here, right?" She looked to the Vessel of Hermes who twirled his keys conspiratorially. It hit her what they were insinuating and she sat up straight in her chair, suddenly electric with energy.

"Did I ever tell you how sorry I was?" Leila grinned.

"Tell me at school."

Leila flung her arms around her friend, planting a kiss on her cheek. "Thank you, *for everything*," she murmured. Leila would never be done owing Bianca back for all she'd done. She vowed to make up for it —after a quick trip to the mountains.

"Go."

She ran.

LEILA

Leila ran through the dark mansion, her heels echoing off the stone walls, her heart hammering in her ears. She didn't know how but she knew he'd be there, in the garden they'd built together.

It must have been the magic of the equinox because there were little buds of flowers ready to bloom, the terrace in all shades of greens and pinks and reds. And in the middle was Blake. His back was to her as a pile of fairy lights lay at his feet, the only light on the mountain.

He turned, his grey eyes finding hers immediately. Blake's smile was a mixture of confusion and unguarded happiness, making her almost trip walking down to him. She was out of breath, her chest heaving against the tight corset.

"Hi," she said, suddenly shy.

"Hi," he replied. Blake looked her up and down, dark eyebrows knitting together. "I think you might be in the wrong place, the party's that way." He pointed in the direction of the city.

"Yeah," she exhaled. "I just—what are you doing with the lights?"

He looked down. "I found these and thought it would be cool to string them up. It's a lot harder than it looks."

"Ah." She looked around. The air up in the mountains was much colder, and goosebumps rippled up her arms. She forgot her wrap on her chair back at the temple.

"Is something wrong?" Blake said softly, hands gripped around the fairy lights.

"Yes." Leila couldn't hold it back any longer. "Ever since I got here, I've been told what to do: how to dress, where to go, even my friends—*who I love*—were there from the start. I didn't have a choice in any of this."

She was breathing hard. "I want—I want to live my life deliberately. *I want a choice.* So, well, I want you to be there for me while I try to find myself. I'm choosing you. That's what I wanted to say—*ask*. I wanted to ask if I could choose you."

Can I choose you? Tears brimmed and fear fluttered in her heart. She wanted to take all the words back and run. The seconds of his silence made her feel like her heart was being dragged over hot coals.

"Yes," he said, his voice thick. He pulled her close, resting his forehead on hers. Their magic mixed together, dark and light, their garden growing and unfurling all around them.

The Vessels of Hades and Persephone held onto each other as hundreds of flowers bloomed. Spring's arrival could not tear them apart.

EPILOGUE

There are a multitude of threads that make up the fabric of the Universe. Some are gilded, some are frayed, and some are dipped in kerosene.

Down in the Underworld, Persephone embraced her husband for the last time. She wouldn't see him again until the autumnal equinox; the queen gave up her crown to bring spring to the world.

On her way to Mount Olympus to see her mother, she stopped to watch over her Vessel in Zeus' temple, smiling to herself when she found her missing from her own party.

Out at sea, a storm raged. Winds and water tossed a boat around like flotsam. There were places where the magic was worn thin, places where one could slip through from New Olympus to the mortal realm—right under the noses of the gods. The single passenger was soaked to the bone trying to keep boat steady, his eyes black as obsidian. Tendrils of powers curled off of him, a sign he was nearing home. Nearing his little brother.

Power to the gods.

Leila and Blake's story will continue...

Power to the Gods
New Olympus Book 2

Coming Spring 2022

Vessels

Leila, Vessel of Persephone
Blake, Vessel of Hades
Bianca, Vessel of Iris
Min-Seo, Vessel of Athena
Elliot, Vessel of Poseidon
Mason, Vessel of Helios
Oscar, Vessel of Caerus
Harvey, Vessel of Zeus
Camille, Vessel of Demeter
Alicia, Vessel of Aphrodite
Bart, Vessel of Ares
Danny, Vessel of Hermes
Kat, Vessel of Hecate
Claire, Vessel of Calliope
Ash, Vessel ofMorpheus
Martin, Vessel of Zeus
Astrid, Vessel of Hera
Arnie, Vessel of Hephaestus
Sidonie, Vessel of Kratos
Marcus, Vessel of Apollo
Lilly, Vessel of Artemis
Ivan, Vessel of Zelus
Cris, Vessel of Ares

Acknowledgements

For as long as I remember, I've been a huge fan of Greek mythology— a huge fan of stories in general. Though I'd never set out to write a story based on my favorite myths, I couldn't get rid of Leila and Blake from my mind. I started writing their story in 2014 and through the years I was able to expand the world slowly and surely until I had a series on my hands.

I want to thank all of the people who supported me through this journey, long and arduous as it was. From my humble beginning on my Tumblr to the wonderful community I found on Wattpad I had amazing support. I had a lot of irl support as well, my family and friends who lent an ear and loved my writing before anyone else saw it.

To my cover designer— I am honored to have your art gracing my book.

To my editor— thank you for the work you put in to make this manuscript shine!

Don't give up on your dreams, even if the road is long and the path out of sight, you never know what blessings will find you on the way! (:

For updates, extras, and and behind the scenes, make sure to follow @DeviantOrDivine on instagram and @HunterKayAuthor on twitter.

Made in the USA
Monee, IL
19 January 2022

89115306R20199